Second Chance

Second Chance

Elizabeth Wrenn

W F HOWES LTD

This large print edition published in 2007 by
W F Howes Ltd
Unit 4, Rearsby Business Park, Gaddesby Lane,
Rearsby, Leicester LE7 4YH

1 3 5 7 9 10 8 6 4 2

First published in the United Kingdom in 2007
by HarperCollins*Publishers*

A CIP catalogue record for this book is available
from the British Library

ISBN 978 1 40741 209 2

Typeset by Palimpsest Book Production Limited,
Grangemouth, Stirlingshire
Printed and bound in Great Britain
by Antony Rowe Ltd, Chippenham, Wilts.

For Stuart

You must have been a dog in a past life because never in the world has there been a better best friend.

Tteote

ACKNOWLEDGEMENTS

It takes a village to raise a writer . . .

I give thanks:

To the women in my writing group (current and retired) who've nurtured me for nearly fifteen years, both as a writer and a woman: Ina Robbins, Phyllis Perry, Leslie O'Kane, Ann Nagda, Claudia Mills, Claire Martin and Marie DesJardins. To my agent, Marcy Posner: I think it was kismet that we were each where we weren't supposed to be on that snowy day in April. Thank you for your many thoughtful readings and insights, your belief in my work, and your friendship. To my editor, Tracy Bernstein, who also came to me in an unexpected way, and that too seemed fated. Thanks for your great wit and keen eye for story and detail, all of which helped me make a better book. To my writing gurus over the years, named and unnamed, but especially my beloved parents, John H. Wrenn and Catherine B. Wrenn (who always led us around the next corner, and will be waiting there). To my other parents, in-law and in-choice, for their wisdom and love: Bernita Franzel, David and Beverley Grogan, and Claire Woodward Wrenn. To my sisters, for a lifetime of love and support: Ali Yarnell, Peggy Wrenn and Jenny Wrenn. To the CUCC family, my spiritual well, especially to Pete Terpenning, and the Women's Group. To Wendy Davis Crocker, for a friendship born in the redwoods and as long and strong. To Claire McCrea, who stuck with me for weeks on my first journalism assignment and for years now as my friend, and to Peter Moore, friend, mentor and chocolate champ. To Sharon and Michael Doucet: Thanks for laughing at my letters and asking for more. May there be many more haircuts and Mexican dinners in our future. To Karen Leve Braverman, for nearly thirty years of cheering me on and up. I treasure our May-December friendship. To Sue Nazarenus, whose face lights up a room, and did so even when the candle flickered. You inspire me in so many ways. To Landis Parsons, for friendship, and a portrait of love.

Special thanks also to the GDB Puppy Raisers Club of Boulder, each and all, for being a wealth of information, anecdotes and support. Special pats to Heidi and Lauren Grimditch, Cathy Greenwald, Susan Sterling, Angela Schwab, Bonnie Gallagher, David and Sara Pahl, and Jill Nieglos (for both canine and airline advice). And while this story and K-9 Eyes are both wholly fictional, the good folks at Guide Dogs for the Blind in California and Oregon, with raisers across the Western states, are real and genuine and doing heartfelt work every day, as are service dog raisers everywhere. I salute you all.

And to Lucca, for . . . everything.

Finally, and most important, my deep, deep gratitude to Stuart and Ella: Your ongoing support and encouragement mean the world to me. I love you both more than these or any other words could say.

A dog can never tell you what she knows from the smells of the world, but you know, watching her, that you know almost nothing.

—from 'Her Grave'
MARY OLIVER

CHAPTER 1

Hairy took some sort of perverse feline pleasure in shedding his voluminous white fur into my cookware. I'd been cleaning behind the kitchen sink when I'd seen him paw the door open and slip into the spinner cabinet. In my simmering anger I didn't think it through and I'd gone in after him. Now my hips were stuck in the door opening, my torso wedged between the two tiers of the giant lazy Susan that held my pots and pans.

My derriere was blocking most of the light, but just enough found its way in for me to see Hairy's smug Persian face staring at me from the depths. I probed with my toothbrush. He retreated farther into the dark recesses, his tail swishing with satisfaction.

Hairy loved all cabinets, but especially the spinner. He often clambered over and around the small towers of pots and pans, heaving his girth over hill and dale, sending the circle spinning as he jumped into the empty back corner. He'd then watch the pans fly by, looking like a kid at an amusement park debating whether to hand over

1

his ticket and actually go on the ride. But the spinner was motionless now, held in place by my shoulders. Hairy lifted a paw, gave it a single neat lick, and stared at me from the back of the cabinet.

'Hairy, get out of there!' I growled. He was just beyond my reach and he knew it. It made me crazy to find him in a cabinet, especially the spinner, since white cat hairs had a way of turning up in my stir-fry.

How did I end up here? I wondered. Not here in the cupboard, but here as the owner of a cat, much less a fat, white Persian cat. I'm a dog person.

I'd always had dogs, growing up. My family lived on a cantaloupe farm in southeastern Colorado. We grew Rocky Ford cantaloupes, among other things, and over the decades we'd had a succession of black Labradors. Always two, always named Rocky and Fordy. My farm family did not routinely demonstrate the height of creativity.

My parents got Rocky number one before they had us. When I was three, they got Fordy. When Rocky one passed on, we got a new puppy, named him Rocky, and off we went. When Fordy died, enter Fordy two. My aging parents still have Rocky four and Fordy five. My brother Roger absconded with Fordy four. Which means there are two Fordys running around at every family reunion. Then Roger went and named his son Rocky. Don't get me started.

When Neil and I married, I got not only in-laws

2

in the deal, but cats. Three of them, all gone now. Hairy was 'Lainey's cat.' Lainey's cat for whom I cleaned the litter box, and who I fed and watered, took clawing and yowling to the vet, and, every so often, to the groomer for a first-class cut and poof that cost three times as much as my own economy-class haircuts.

It wasn't that Neil disliked dogs; he loved Rocky and Fordy. When we went to the farm, he was often out throwing a stick or taking them for walks down to the lake. He explained that he didn't want to *own* a dog because 'dogs tie you down.' Like a wife, two teenagers at home, a son at college, and a thriving medical practice didn't. He was also fond of saying, 'The only good dog is someone else's dog.'

The phone rang. I pushed back, trying to wriggle out, but the only part of me moving was the flab on my upper arms. The phone rang a second time.

'Damn!' It might be one of the kids calling from school. Or even Sam. Although Matt and Lainey rarely called these days – very uncool in high school – and Sam had called only once since he'd left for college last year. For money. But old instincts die hard. A third ring. I pushed myself backward but my hips were stuck. Painfully stuck.

'Ow! *Goddamn it, Hairy!*' I had to blame someone for my big butt, and Hairy was as good a candidate as existed. I twisted sideways, pushed off the center pole of the spinner, and finally shimmied out, lunging for the phone.

'Hello!' I said, somewhat angrily.

'Deena? I was getting ready to leave you a message.'

'Hi, Elaine.' I breathed deeply, trying to catch both my breath and my temper.

'Are you okay?'

'Yeah. I got stuck in my cabinet.'

A pause. 'Come again?'

'That damn Hairy got into the lazy Susan cabinet again and he won't come out for Pounce or punishment and I can't reach him and he gets cat hair all over *everything*!'

'Oh, God! No!' she shrieked in mock horror. 'Has the press arrived?'

Elaine had a way of trivializing my problems, which were, admittedly, mostly trivial. I leaned back on the desk and pulled a paper clip from the drawer and began pulling it apart.

'Very funny. I'll have you know we had another Szechuan Persian Hair incident the other night. It grossed out the whole family. Even Matt.' If my sixteen-year-old eating machine wouldn't eat something, it *was* newsworthy.

'But especially you, I bet. A little cat hair's not gonna kill you.' A pause, and then just the slightest change of tone. 'Y'know, you didn't used to be such a neat freak.' True. Elaine and I had lived together for almost two years at the University of Wisconsin, and we would not have won any awards for the cleanest apartment. But it was Elaine's boyfriend at the time, with the unusual first name

4

of Meyer, who was the real culprit, a world-class slob. He drove Neil crazy. Thank God Elaine hadn't married Meyer.

'Hey, have you seen Peter lately?' I asked, changing the subject. It was Peter Ham she'd married. Before she'd reckoned with the fact that she was a lesbian. I'd always suspected it. Peter had too, it turned out, but loved her so much he'd married her anyway. Now Elaine and Peter both delighted in telling people that they'd been married just long enough for Elaine to become a Jewish Ham.

'He's great! Just saw him and Bethany at the grocery store yesterday, actually. They're making all sorts of plans for next year. You know Seth's graduating from high school this year?'

'No!' Seth was their youngest. Well, it made sense. Peter had married Bethany about a year after his divorce from Elaine was final.

'Yeah. I think they're kind of looking forward to the empty nest. They're talking about going on a cruise next fall.'

'A cruise! Where?' Neil and I used to say we'd do that after our kids were all gone. But it hadn't come up in years.

'Alaska. Not my idea of a cruise, but they're all excited about it.'

'Let me guess, your idea of a cruise is something more tropical?' That's what Neil and I had fantasized about.

'Exactly. Give me that sun, sand, and margarita

any day!' A little sigh from both of us as we contemplated life in a lounge chair.

'So,' we both said in unison.

'Your turn,' she said, laughing. 'I've been yakking away, as usual.'

I missed her. Over the decades she'd come out to visit every few years, and we talked on the phone often. But I was amazed our friendship had stayed so strong. Our paths couldn't have been more different.

'Okay. I was just going to ask about Wendy, and your art.' I loved and hated asking about both. Elaine was always so passionate about those subjects that it tended to draw a sprawled sidewalk chalk line around the lack of passion in my own life.

'Wendy's fantastic! New accounts all over the place. I'm so proud of her. As for me, well, suffice to say I'm having a ball. Doing some new things. We'll see where it goes.' She was unusually circum-spect. Probably swamped at work. She was the art director for *Art of the Matter* magazine. Unlike me, Elaine had not only gotten her bachelor's in art, but had gone on for a master's, then built an impressive résumé. Plus, she'd been doing art on her own all this time for her own pleasure, even had an occasional small show in Madison.

'So, what were you doing before you got into the cat-extrication business?' she asked. I loved Elaine. She could always make me smile.

'Scrubbing grout.' The words clunked to the floor like bricks.

'Oy-vey, *girlfriend*!' she cried across the miles, sounding both Jewish, which she was, and black, which she was not. 'What is it with you and cleaning the past few years? You gotta get out.' She said it like 'owwww-t!'

'But I'm a full-time mom, it's my job. And my kids still need me, even if they don't think so.'

'Well, of course they do, Deena-leh, but not every waking minute. It's not like they're babies, hon.'

Babies. Now there was unconditional love. These days it felt like all my kids needed me for was as a wall to push off of. 'No, they're not babies.' Another little sigh slipped out.

'Whoa, Nelly! Don't tell me you're thinking about another baby again!'

In my early forties, my ovary must have burped or something and I'd approached Neil about having another baby. After we'd poked the vein back into his forehead, we'd agreed we were way too old. Besides, babies grow up into teenagers. I'd eventually be right back where I was now. Which, ironically, was wanting to be something other than a wife and mother. More and more I found myself fantasizing about leaving. Just up and leaving. *Fantasizing.* I wouldn't actually do it. Probably not, anyway. No. Of course not.

But I could fantasize, right? Every day.

'No. No more babies. Probably couldn't even if I wanted to. Haven't had a period in months.' Not to mention the part about having to have sex in order to become pregnant.

7

I put the straightened paper clip down, slid off the desk, walked to the sink, and gazed out the window at the leaden sky. 'But you know, E, only a baby has the power to make the world a better place simply by existing.' But then again, they also had a way of sucking up your own existence when you weren't looking.

'I feel like opting out of my life right now, E.' There. I just blurted it out.

'You just need to get away, Deena. Come see us! For once.' Elaine had stopped lobbying me to come out there since I'd refused for decades, hating to fly and unable to stretch the maternal ties, but usually claiming timing or money or both.

But now I *wanted* to go. Sort of. The mere thought of flying sent my blood pressure soaring, and going by car or bus didn't appeal to me either. If I could only be there without having to *get* there. That was how I felt about losing weight. And fitness. And menopause.

Transitions. I guess they named the hardest part of giving birth that for a reason.

But then there was also the terrifying thought that even if I got to Madison, what if I didn't want to come back? I picked up the toothbrush and started scrubbing grout again and told Elaine, 'I don't think so. It's really tight now with Sam's tuition.' I pressed the toothbrush under the base of the sprayer, going after a bit of grime.

'Deena, is it really that tight? Or are you just addicted to sacrificing for your family?'

What was that supposed to mean?

'Look, come out, we'll have a girls' weekend. I'll pay for it, your trip, some pampering. My treat. It'll be your birthday slash Christmas present. Let me and Wendy take care of you for a change.'

'I— can't. Besides, my birthday and Christmas, as you well know, were both last month, and you already sent gifts for each.' I knelt on the floor, holding the phone with one hand and the toothbrush in the other. I scrubbed forcefully at the grout between the floor tiles.

'What are you doing? Are you scrubbing the grout again?'

'The floor grout. Not the tile grout.'

'Who cares?! Put down the damn toothbrush! You're using a toothbrush, aren't you?'

'Well, yeah.' I stood and obediently put the toothbrush in the sink. Still with the phone to my ear, I bent down and glared into the spinner cabinet at Hairy, who was now sitting demurely in the wok.

'Dammit, Deena-leh! Anyone who cleans with a toothbrush anything other than her teeth has completely lost perspective. I'm worried about you.'

There was another long silence. What could I say? I was worried about me, too.

Elaine finally spoke. 'So, will you come?'

I couldn't tell her the real reasons. It was nigh unto impossible for me to justify something like a trip alone. As in, by myself. For myself. Plus,

9

I was scared to fly, scared to travel alone. I didn't even like walking alone on the lovely mountain trails above my house. Sometimes I wondered if I hadn't become a little agoraphobic.

'Deena?' Elaine's voice was now tentative, a cupped hand around my vulnerability.

I looked out the kitchen window at the snow beginning to fall. Big, fat flakes. I massaged my temple. 'I'm sorry, E. I just can't.'

After we hung up, I stood with the phone in my hand, just staring at it. Finally, I dialed Sam's cell phone, struggling a bit. I knew the number by heart, but my damn hand was trembling. Ridiculous. He never answered anyway. I imagined him, in the shade of a tree somewhere on campus, stopping to look at his phone, seeing the number of the caller, shoving the phone back into his pocket, striding on. His voice mail clicked on. 'Hey. It's Sam. Leave a message.' I hung up. I was not going to leave another message. I put the phone back into its base.

I really had been trying to give him space, as he'd requested in a lone e-mail. But Colorado to California is a damn lot of space.

The vacuum's roar was not enough to drown out the voice in my head. *Just up and leave. Go spend a weekend with Elaine. Go now!* But I was truly afraid. Afraid to fly. Afraid to ask Neil for the money when he was working so many long hours lately. Afraid to leave. Afraid I'd arrive and curl up on a bed in Elaine's house and not come back. I pushed the vacuum over the plush emerald depths of the carpet, back and forth, back and forth. My thoughts still raced, but I could always count on that huge hum to drown out most everything else: phones, cats, kids, husbands. Lawn mowers worked well, too. And both left those satisfying clean, dark tracks. Like dozens of little fresh starts.

I slowly sank to the floor, the vacuum still roaring. At first the sobs were silent and choking. Then I began to roar right along with the Hoover, my hands clinging to its plastic neck. I didn't know where it was coming from, this deep animal cry.

I loved my family. *Loved* them. But, God! What if it was now simply out of habit? An 'on paper' love?

I don't know how long I cried. Exhausted, I flipped off the vacuum and pulled a box of tissue off the end table. I was as swollen and snotty as a post-tantrum two-year-old. If only I'd get a period, maybe these moods would end. But maybe I wouldn't ever get another one. Although, just when I thought I'd seen the last, a crimson flood would show up at the worst possible time – for instance, the very day I'd tried my first master's swim workout, and I'd left little pink puddles all the way into the locker room. That had put the kibosh on exercise of all sorts.

I blew my nose and clicked on the TV for something other than my own thoughts. The painting instructor Bob Ross was on PBS. He was even more soothing than the vacuum. Neil used to tease me that I would leave him for either of two men: Mister Rogers or Bob Ross. Both represented the parts of my life at opposite ends of the spectrum of how I defined myself, or didn't any longer. The former was the equanimous host of the children's television show 'Mister Rogers Neighborhood,' and was known for being encouraging, kind, gentle and an advocate for children. Bob Ross was a soft-spoken TV painting teacher, known for being encouraging, kind, gentle and an advocate for squirrels. Both were gone now. I wondered if I'd reached the age when I knew more celebrities who were dead than alive.

The show was almost over. He had mostly finished his painting of snowy mountains behind a glistening alpine lake. A single pine tree stood sentry in the foreground. The lake looked clear and crisp and . . . liquid. I could never get water to look like water. At least thirty years ago, when I took that painting class, I couldn't. Elaine had always said I was good at figures, though. *Was* good at figures. My artwork of the past few decades had been limited to things like glue-and-glitter pinecones, doily valentines and gingerbread houses. Which, to be honest, I loved every minute of. But now . . . Where had it gotten me?

As the credits rolled I grew suddenly ravenous. And decisive. The kids would be home in an hour, and until then it was going to be me, a big – no, huge! – bowl of Corn Pops, and Oprah.

12

It was one of my favorite pastimes, eating cereal and watching Oprah. I sometimes squirmed a bit when she was doing a program on weight loss or exercise, which, of course, she often did. I didn't care anymore, though.

My Tupperware bowl filled with the golden nuggets of carbohydrate bliss, I settled onto the couch just as Oprah was striding into the studio, gently touching the hands of a few of her many-hued disciples. I wondered if I were ever to go see a taping of the Oprah show whether I'd scream and get all teary-eyed and reach for her holy touch. I hoped not. Well, I'd definitely get teary-eyed. Lately I tear up at everything, and nothing.

'Today we're talking about using your life.' I clicked up the volume on the TV. '*You*-zing your life! You-*zing* your life!' I smiled. Oprah loved to emphasize syllables. After the introduction came commercials, during which I channel surfed and ate Corn Pops. I lingered too long on the Weather Channel and was a little late back to Oprah. But I got the gist of it. A ten-year-old girl had started collecting donated suitcases from friends and neighbors for foster kids to use as they went from home to home. A ragtag group of about a dozen kids, every color and size, bore their suitcases proudly as they left the house. It was hard to eat the Corn Pops through my tears. Next was a piece on a flight attendant who was building a school for orphans in Vietnam. Then there was a man who helped inner-city kids learn new skills and

13

teamwork by building low-income housing. Then a husband and wife who'd adopted eleven siblings so they wouldn't have to go to different homes. *Eleven!* Lord.

I could collect backpacks and suitcases maybe.

During the next commercial break I scurried to the kitchen and refilled my Corn Pops. This was just what I needed. Fill up the void. I was pouring on the soymilk as the Oprah theme music started in the den. The soymilk was supposed to help with the menopause symptoms, although I hadn't seen any evidence of that yet. But it was tasty on Corn Pops. I hurried back down into the den as Oprah began speaking.

'My next guest, Annie Forhooth, falls in love repeatedly, for approximately a year each time, only to bid a fond farewell to her loves, again and again. Why does she do this? To help provide loving eyes for the blind. Take a look.'

The piece opened with an eight-week-old black Lab puppy gamboling over Annie's lawn. I set my cereal bowl on the coffee table as Annie's taped voice-over talked about how exciting it is to get a new puppy, to know you're going to raise it with love and care for a special purpose, a special gift. I sat up, gripping my knees in my hands as I watched.

The last shot of the piece was of Annie, with a blind woman, during some sort of graduation cere-mony. Her voice-over said, 'You do fall in love with the dogs, but you know from the beginning

14

that you're raising them so they can help someone; these dogs love to work. They love to be a part of the world. I just help them get started.'

In the video, Annie, crying but smiling broadly, handed over the leash of a full-grown, sleek, and boxy black Lab to a blind woman, her unseeing eyes also teary, her face uplifted. Annie put the leash into her hands, their four hands clenching around it in a tight ball. The two women then hugged, laughing, crying. The dog was sandwiched between their legs, tail wagging, eyes bright.

Sitting there wiping my own wet cheeks and eyes, I had only one thought: That's what love looks like.

CHAPTER 2

I was having another Art Instructor dream. I'd been having them off and on for several months now. They weren't really erotic dreams, not in the usual sense of the word anyway. Although my definition of erotic was quickly becoming 'any time spent alone.' What was especially erotic, by my definition, was that Art Instructor never wanted anything from me; he only offered me things, beautiful things, to look at, to linger over. Then he'd politely disappear.

This time, we were strolling through an orange grove. Art Instructor was tall and handsome, though far from dark – he was actually stone white. He was always naked, at least the part I saw, which was typically just his chiseled upper back. A *David* back, deeply muscled and perfectly symmetrical. In this dream, he reached up with his also deeply muscled arm and picked a fat, absurdly brilliant orange, the color pulsating from it. Without turning around, he handed it back to me. This is when I realized he had no hand. The orange was just kind of stuck on the end of his wrist, and its color contrasted deeply with his whiteness. Then he turned, and for the first time ever, I looked down. Between his legs. His yoohoo was broken off, too. Dream-me smiled.

Suddenly all his detail began to fade and Art Instructor disappeared, as did as the grove. But the orange remained, and I could see each individual pockmark on it. I could even see the shadows in the tiny craters.

That was when I felt Neil slip back into bed, his hair still wet, his body smelling of soap.

I remembered with some dread that it was Saturday.

It wasn't a given, exactly, sex attempts on Saturday. But over the years it was the one day we could pretty much count on all three kids being either happily mesmerized by cartoons down in the den, at a sleepover, or, as they grew into teens, dead asleep, sometimes till noon or better. And over the years, in the mood or not, mostly not, I'd obliged. But not for weeks now.

I knew he was going to work on the clinic – a low-cost health clinic, his dream for years, but finally in its genesis – again this weekend; that's why he'd showered. So he was clean. Teeth brushed. Shaved. But still, inside I cringed, a shriveled part of me shriveling further. I didn't want to have sex. I wanted to paint an orange. Probably from watching Bob Ross the other day. I hadn't painted in years. But lately, I'd rather have a root canal than have sex.

Neil lay quietly for a moment, then gently began

17

stroking the backs of his knuckles against my upper arm. *Sex knocking*. And, once again, nobody home.

Was it my fault? Neil's? Why was I turned on by a damn orange and not by my husband of over two decades? How and when had sex become one more duty? Part of my job description? *Full-Time Homemaker: Be available at all hours to do all things for just about everyone. Must respond attentively to all demands for attention, physical and otherwise. Immediate supervisors include, but not limited to: husband, kids, cat.* The pillow still over my head, I pulled the quilt up under my chin and rolled to the other side of the bed, trying to also pull back the cover of sleep.

'Dee? Deena? Dee-deelicious . . . .' A pause, then a whispered, resigned, *'Shit.'* I waited, breathing silently. What was I supposed to say? I'd already said no in every way possible. I could write a book, like a cookbook, but with different recipes for how to deliver the news to your husband that it ain't happening.

But I knew I wasn't supposed to *say* anything. I was supposed to roll over. Make Love. Or at least Be Compliant. But I just couldn't. Not anymore. The hasty retreat of estrogen from my body was making my breasts tender, my joints and muscles ache, and I was getting headaches at the drop of a hat. Or the raise of a penis. And I was irritated a lot. Really irritated. In a way I'd never been before in my life. A don't-touch-me-or-I'll-yank-it-off-you kind of irritated. Although I never

18

let those feelings out. Never. Just kept the lid on. Tight. Part of my job.

Neil exhaled sharply, muttering, 'I wish you'd take some hormones. This isn't good for us.'

He climbed out of bed and noisily dressed, banging drawers and cabinets. Then it sounded like he was putting every clinking, jingly thing from the dresser in and out of his pockets several times. Finally he left the room, his heavy footfalls down the stairs further conveying his feelings. I didn't blame him. But I did. Neil was one of the good guys. Or was when we'd married. I supposed he still was, but we'd drifted apart the past few years, sailing merrily along in our life sailboats, our courses charted by the gale force winds of responsibilities, rarely by the gentle breezes of love. And as for me personally, as a woman, I felt like I'd recently looked up and realized I was in the doldrums.

I heard Neil downstairs, kitchen noises for several minutes, complete with slamming fridge door and cabinet, a few minutes' pause, then going through his medical bag, opening the hall closet for his coat, then, *Bang!*

The doors and cabinets in the house were paying a price for our lack of sex.

Sex. It had once been so great. But now . . . If one person's legitimate need is to have sex, and the other person's legitimate need is to *not* have sex, whose need trumps? Why were women supposed to take hormones in order to be horny?

19

Why weren't men pressured to take hormones to make them able to have three thoughts and not have two of them be about sex? That way they might be able to think over the myriad facets of 'good for us,' like the fact that working seventy-hour weeks, even for a good cause, was a kind of infidelity.

The garage door went up, his car started, then backed out. The garage door went down, and, even though it was a remote, I swear it too landed with more of a thud than usual. I exhaled, my eyes still closed.

But I was solidly awake, and still wanting to paint an orange. And yes, when I pictured myself holding a paintbrush, there was that feeling again. Arousal. What is it about nearing fifty that one's life becomes steeped in irony?

I climbed out of bed and raised the blind. It was another spring day in January. Colorado was famous for its quickly changing weather and seasonal confusion. It was forecast to hit the upper fifties today. From our second-story bedroom I looked over my quiet suburban street. A few withered designs of snow held stubbornly to the shadows of trees and houses. But those too would meet their evaporative demise today in the warm chinook winds that were already whistling down the canyon. Across the street and two doors down I saw the Kellermans' shepherd-mix, Melba, tied up to a tree in their front yard, her fur blowing in the wind. I watched her for a long minute. Since the divorce, Melba spent too much time tied to a tree.

I briefly thought about going out for a walk. Maybe I could take Melba. I could head up the mesa trails, get some exercise. It'd been years since I'd done that. Not exercise, the trails. Well, the exercise in the past few years had been pretty sketchy, too. I felt the tips of my breasts touching my ever-protruding stomach. It was like a race – breasts down, stomach out. Hard to tell who was winning. They were both doing pathetically well. But I wanted to paint. For the first time in years.

I pulled on my ancient gray zip sweatshirt and matching pants, both patterned with the set-in stains of motherhood, and headed down to the basement. I paused in the kitchen, a note on the counter catching my eye.

D – out of tea bags. Call Sondra O'Keefe about dinner Friday. – N.

Damn. I'd completely forgotten about the O'Keefes' dinner party. A benefit for seed money for the clinic. The dinner was going to be a fancy, dressed-to-the-nines affair, and my total wardrobe added up to maybe five and a half. But it was yet another duty. The O'Keefes were nice people, it's just that I didn't even feel like being with my family, much less with a bunch of people all decked out and hobnobbing for a cause, even a good cause. I just didn't have the energy. I looked down at the note, noticing the absence of an x and o where Neil signed off, a usual given in notes from him. When had he stopped? Maybe this morning. I pushed the note into the pocket of my sweat jacket and went down to the basement.

First, the laundry. I shoved in a load of whites, scooped out the detergent, then tipped in the perfect amount of bleach, watching as the agitator sucked the socks, underwear, and T-shirts into its spiral abyss. But I was smiling when I finally walked into the storage room. I had seen the large Art Department shopping bag when I'd put away the Christmas things last week. I started moving the precisely labeled boxes. *Glass Ornaments & Lainey's Ornaments* I gently set on the floor. *Garland for Bannister* I set atop another stack. We hadn't opened some of these boxes in a couple of years. Teenagers neither require nor admire festive stairways.

It was behind *Fireplace Wreath and Red Candles* that I found the bag, stuffed into a crevasse between the Christmas boxes and the spring holiday boxes (Valentine's through Easter). I gathered the paper hoop handles and lifted. The handles broke free of the paper, no doubt rotted over the years. I was holding the two loops when Lainey's cannonball bellow shot through the house.

'Maa-ahh-ammm! Where *are* you?!'

Loops still in hand, I climbed the stairs. The paints were almost certainly dried out anyway.

22

Lainey was just coming around the corner into the kitchen, yelling again when she ran into me.

'MA—oof! There you are. Where *were* you?' She said it as though I'd been deliberately hiding from her. Hairy was yowling on the desk chair, wanting some canned food in addition to his overflowing bowl of dry kibble.

'Lainey, it's Saturday. What do I always do on Saturday? And on Wednesday?' Her puzzled face stared back at me. 'Here's a hint: We all magically have clean clothes every Sunday and Thursday.'

She rolled her eyes. 'Fine. Whatever. You need to drive us to the mall at eleven. Sara can't now.'

Lainey and the neighbor girls, Nan and Sara Kellerman, had planned to spend the day at the mall, shopping and ogling boys. Matt was going to hitch a ride with them, to meet his friends, maybe catch a movie. I was going to have the house to myself on a Saturday. But apparently not.

'What happened?' I asked, walking past her to the kitchen table. I began gathering up her breakfast dishes.

She leaned dejectedly against the doorframe, arms folded over her ever-growing chest. 'Kurt,' she said rather dreamily, seeming to think this would explain everything.

I stared at her while still holding her cereal bowl, juice glass, and toast plate in a stack in my arms. I shrugged and began loading the dishes into the dishwasher. 'Am I supposed to know who Kurt is?' My slipper stuck to a tacky spot on the floor.

What was that? I'd just mopped yesterday afternoon.

'Oh, Mom! *Kurt!*' The juice glass still in my hand, I looked at my daughter. I felt my own mother's clueless expression on my face, and hated it. Lainey drummed her fingers on her arms, giving me that fifteen-year-old's look of, 'Are you naturally this stupid or does it take effort?' I remembered that, too. I mentally apologized to my mother. Lainey pushed off the doorframe with her shoulder, flipped her long brown hair over her other shoulder, and took a step toward me, her hands now on her hips. 'Sara's *boyfriend*?!'

'Oh,' I said. I put the juice glass in and closed the dishwasher. Ah, yes. The fabulous Kurt. I vaguely recalled that last month sixteen-year-old Sara had also canceled on a ski trip with the girls because Kurt 'doesn't like to ski.' I grabbed the cleanser from under the sink and shook some into one side of the aged white porcelain sink. When we'd redecorated the kitchen several years ago, I'd wanted one of those high-tech composite sinks, but couldn't justify the expense. The porcelain was still perfectly good, albeit chipped and dulled. I stopped scrubbing. One of my good dish towels lay in the other side of the sink, a wet orange wad.

'Did you use the dish towel to wipe up orange juice?' I asked, barely keeping my voice calm in my rising tension. So that was the tacky spot.

'No, it was there. Dad must've.'

'Goddamn him!'

24

'*Mom!* You owe me a dollar!' Lainey said, looking first stunned, then gleeful. Shit. Shoot. She was right. I was trying to curb their use of expletives and so charged them a dollar each time. I never swore. Until recently. And although I usually didn't actually collect from the kids, just warned them that next time I would, I felt compelled to pay up.

As I walked to my purse and handed her the dollar, I got back to the subject at hand. 'And this Kurt said Sara can't go shopping with you and Nan? Does Sara *want* to go?' I asked, scrubbing at a stain left by Neil's tea bag.

'Oh, jeeze, Mom! 'Course she does. But guys don't like shopping. And, you have, like, certain responsibilities when you're boyfriend and girl-friend. So you need to take us now, okay?'

I knew I should make her rephrase that, put in a 'please' somewhere. Instead, I scrubbed harder at the stain, partially regretting that Neil and I had revoked Matt's driving privileges when, backing out of our one-car garage, he'd smashed the side-view mirrors on my old Camry wagon. Both of them. First he'd scraped the driver's side nearly off, leaving it hanging by just the wires. But then, in his panic, he'd pulled forward into the garage, then backed out *again*, overcorrecting, and cracked both the plastic casing and the glass of the other side mirror. Poor guy. I think he was almost relieved to be absolved of the responsibility of driving. It wasn't a complete surprise. When he

25

was three he'd practiced riding his new tricycle in the garage for a week before he would head out onto the wilds of the sidewalk. I guess he was doing the same thing with my car.

With Sam's tuition at Stanford, I was, more than ever, pinching every penny. So the mirrors of my car were decoratively held on with half a roll of duct tape. And Lainey was already agitating to get her learner's permit. Oh, Lord.

'Mom! Will you drive us or not?'

I rinsed out my sponge, pleased with the clean spot where the tea-bag stain had been. 'I guess. Okay. Maybe I'll do the walking course. Get a little exercise.'

'Yeah. You should.' She must have heard how that sounded because she came over and hugged me briefly before she turned and headed back upstairs to gather her things.

I was stopped at a red light with Matt, Lainey, and Nan all sitting in the backseat. I remembered when my kids used to fight over the front seat and who would get to sit next to me. It wasn't that long ago. But it was.

All three were now engaged in a lively game of rock, paper, scissors. As I watched the light, listening to their repetitive counting to three then bursts of laughter, the hot flash began. Streams of perspiration started from my underarms and slid down my sides. I didn't have to check the rearview mirror to know that my face was flushed to nearly purple. I could feel my scalp moisten. Then the rivulets started down my face.

'Whew!' I said, unlatching my seat belt, pressing the window button down. 'Warm in here.' Now I couldn't help glancing in the rearview mirror. Matt and Lainey exchanged knowing looks with each other, rolled their eyes and turned toward Nan.

'She does this a lot lately,' Lainey said. 'You might want to put your coat on.' Matt, his long sandy bangs shaking back and forth with his head, blushed.

I was struggling to unzip first my fleece vest, then my sweat jacket, having worn a thin tank top beneath. I'd learned to dress in layers. The vest was easy, but I wrestled with the jacket zipper, which was stuck at the bottom. The light turned green and the car behind me immediately honked. A kid about Matt's age in a red Mazda Miata.

'Mah-ahm! Go!' Lainey cried. In the rearview mirror I saw Matt looking out the window, suddenly very interested in the look-alike condominiums springing up like a bad rash on what used to be rolling farmland. I had one arm in a sleeve and one arm out. I grabbed the wheel with my free hand and pulled into the intersection, slowly, because I had not yet rebuckled my seat belt. I stuck my sleeved arm out the window and leaned my head out too, the delightfully cool air rushing over my face, blowing my ponytail out behind me as I picked up speed.

'Mah-ahm!' Lainey said. 'You look like a dog!'

The backseat erupted in a different kind of laughter.

Miata kid honked again, then sped around me, cutting off a woman in a yellow bug in the other lane, then pulling back in front of me. Yellow bug honked and Miata kid gave me the finger out his window.

I quickly redid my seat belt, still half in and half out of my jacket, my heart pounding from being assaulted by a sixteen-year-old's middle digit. And the laughter from the backseat.

As I pulled into the main drive of the mall, the kids started gathering their things for a quick getaway. Matt was meeting friends and knew he'd be safe from me at Scourge of the Underworld, or whatever the arcade was called. But as I pulled into a parking space, Lainey felt the need to lay down the law about my proximity to her.

'Mom, just so you know, we want to hang out *alone*.' I pictured the girls floating deliriously in and out of various teeny-bop clothing shops, and those olfactory overload candle and body-liquid emporiums; I assured them it would not be a problem. I'd go for a good walk, then buy myself a skinny latte and go sit on the leather couch in Pottery Barn and stare into space. A middle-aged woman's nirvana.

As the girls clamored out, I yelled, 'Shall we meet back at the food court at twelve thirty?' Lainey waved without looking back as they ran off.

'See ya,' said Matt. He ambled off, careful to

affect the loose-kneed, slumped-shouldered australopithecine walk of teen boys.

'Twelve thirty! Food court!' I said to his back.

I found the beginning of the mall walking course, strategically located next to Godiva chocolates. What *were* they thinking? Well, selling chocolates to fat people is obviously what they were thinking. But I was motivated and strode right past. I successfully made it past the Orange Julius, too. But it did remind me of the dish towel, and that nameless anger surged through me again. Still striding along, and getting increasingly breathless, I pulled my cell phone out of my purse and punched in the direct dial to Neil's cell phone, which I was pretty sure would be off. As I'd hoped, I got his voice mail's brief greeting, then the beep.

'Neil. For the hundredth time (puff, pant) in our marriage, please do not use the dish towels (gasp) as floor mops. We have paper towels, or *an actual floor mop* (wheeze), for just that purpose!' I hung up and kept walking, stuffing the phone back in my purse.

My stride slowed somewhat at the Popcorn Palace, but I kept moving. Three assaults and still standing. Maybe starting my new exercise program in the mall wasn't the best choice given all the temptations, but my anger was like a fuel, propelling me forward.

Ten minutes later, however, I was again panting with fatigue, but the anger had somehow morphed into desire for the almost visible waves of

29

cinnamon, sugar, and butter wafting over me from CinnaMania. And right across the corridor was the Coffee Cauldron. I was being mugged in the mall by three out of the four American food groups: fat, sugar, and caffeine. And there was undoubtedly the ubiquitous salt in the bread dough, rounding out the Fab Four. I pulled up, holding on to a nearby brass railing to catch my breath. It might be misinterpreted if I breathlessly ordered a cinnamon roll. Or worse, it might be correctly interpreted.

Ten minutes later I was near Victoria's Secret, licking the last of the hugely and delightfully excessive cinnamon roll frosting from one hand, my coffee in the other. I had my index finger entirely in my mouth when I looked up and saw my reflection in front of a tiny, seemingly magically suspended floral bikini bra and panties in the display window. I had frosting on my cheek *and* nose.

My ears burned with embarrassment. Even though this new mall was not in Fairview, its sprawling largesse drew the masses from there, Denver, and beyond. I could only hope that no one had seen me, or rather 'Dr Munger's wife.' Neil was much loved in our little community, being one of the older and last remaining independent family-practice docs in town. He was starting to deliver the babies of the now-grown babies he'd delivered. I didn't want my lack of willpower to strike a blow to either his practice or my pride – the former being quite healthy, the latter in tatters.

My fingers were still sticky so I tossed my empty cup in a trash can and fished out my little packet of hand wipes from my purse. Despite my embarrassment, or maybe to assuage it, I felt a smack of satisfaction: If you needed it, this purse contained it. Early in our marriage Neil used to affectionately tease me about my purse, saying I carried a diaper bag long before we had babies, prepared for anything from a medical emergency to an auto breakdown. But, to his credit, he never balked about holding it for me if I needed to try something on, or just tie my shoe. I couldn't help but smile, remembering Neil holding my purse at a carnival. It was before we had the kids, back when we still took just ourselves to fun places. We'd gone to the county fair and I'd wanted to ride the Ferris wheel. Neil had trouble with vertigo and would rather do boot camp than an amusement park ride, even a Ferris wheel, so he'd offered to hold my purse, a big red straw bag that I adored. It had rolled leather straps, a large gold fastener, and, the pièce de résistance, half a dozen multi-colored daisies embroidered on each side. The ride had been fun, but what had made me laugh riotously as I sat by myself in my gently swaying, ever-rising chair was watching Neil holding my big red purse, walking back and forth below me, hips swaying, blowing me kisses and waving like

31

a beauty queen. He'd then insisted on carrying it the rest of the day, laughing good-naturedly at the people trying to hide their smirks behind their cotton candy.

Neil no longer carried my purse. It embarrassed the kids. Holding your water glass wrong could embarrass teenagers. But, as in most things, we accommodated their tender sensibilities. Then again, it wasn't really even an issue any longer. Neil and I rarely went anywhere together these days. As our kids outgrew their jeans at record pace, so too did Neil and I seem to be outgrowing each other. But like those jeans, I wasn't aware of any particular seams of our marriage giving way, just that they had rather suddenly begun to feel terribly binding.

I tossed the used wipe in the trash can and put the packet back in my purse, carefully tucking it in its spot between the travel pack of Kleenex and the tin of mints. I grabbed an open pack of Doublemint and pulled a stick out with my teeth, then returned the pack to my purse and wrestled with the broken zipper. I looked up, once again self-conscious.

With the tip of the foil-wrapped gum still between my teeth, I turned to the left, then slowly to the right, the silver stick pointing at the myriad passersby.

No one noticed.

No one saw me.

Good.

That was good. Wasn't it?

I sat heavily on a nearby bench and took the stick from my teeth. When had I . . . disappeared? Somewhere along the line, a cloak of invisibility had dropped down and covered me from head to toe. It wasn't just here in the mall, I realized. I was invisible in the grocery store, in my neighborhood, to my family. When had this happened? My forties? My *thirties*?

Maybe I wasn't just invisible. Did I, Deena, even *exist* anymore? Not Deena mother or Deena wife but Deena, formerly Hathaway, formerly a person with thoughts, feelings, dreams and a life ahead of her. That Deena?

I looked around again. The crowd bustled by; no one met my eye. I looked back toward the storefront again. It was probably because I'd moved a few feet, so the light was different here, but I could no longer even see my reflection in the window.

CHAPTER 3

I wandered toward Victoria's Secret, feeling physically struck by my newly acknowledged lack of existence. But if you want to challenge the notion of invisibility, try heading into a Victoria's Secret in the body of an overweight, middle-aged woman in dingy sweats.

I tried to appear as bored as if I'd been in here just yesterday. In fact, I wasn't absolutely certain I'd *ever* been in a Victoria's Secret. I'm more the Sears type. Highly convenient to get your Cross Your Heart and Crock-Pot in the same trip. I stepped over the threshold feeling like I was slipping into a brothel.

'Can I help you find something?' the teenaged wraith asked, her dark eyes looking me up and down. Was she wearing *black* contact lenses? She continued to once-over me in a way that used to alternately flatter and infuriate me (sometimes in the same moment) when young men did this to me a lifetime ago. Now, I just felt blood pulsing into my ears.

I almost turned and skulked out right then, but a sign at the back of the store caught my eye. A single word, in passionate red. The most seductive word in the dictionary: 'Clearance.' It made me swallow my pride and embarrassment long enough to quietly respond, 'Just looking, thanks.'

I strolled past the bins of confetti-colored underpants, most looking roughly large enough to tie a tomato plant to its stake. I couldn't help but think my tomatoes would get a kick out of that. I could sell them at the farmer's market this summer. Thong Beefsteak. Scanty Panty Early Girl. It would give vegetable cultivation a whole new image.

I continued on through the middle of the store, past rack and bin islands of lacy, shiny, slinky things. I stopped to finger a gorgeous jade-green negligee and cover-up combo. That's what I needed: a negligee *with* cover-up. Talk about an oxymoron. I lingered to see if they had it in a large, not that I was seriously interested, but I felt the eyes of Phantom Girl on me so felt compelled to look like I was looking. I tried to back far enough away from the tag sewn in at the neck while still holding it, but my arms were not long enough for me to make out the small letters. It occurred to me that if you need magnifying glasses to read a lingerie tag, it's probably God's way of delicately informing you that you're too old for this. But I did it anyway. I dug through my purse again.

With my brown half frames perched on my nose, I finally found an 'L.' Would that be big enough? I pulled it out and held it up, also at arm's length, too self-conscious to hold it against me. Close. Probably it would fit, but maybe not. The pounds had been creeping on with the years, each tiptoeing on as if I wasn't looking.

It wasn't that I was obese. At five eight and weighing about the same as my five eleven husband, I was probably the American average, but larger than I'd ever been in my life, almost as heavy as I'd been for each of my three pregnancies. But the currents of middle age had carried me past caring. That and various Oprah shows about loving your body. I'd gotten as far as not hating my body. I'd reached the dubiously successful stage of ignoring my body.

But maybe I could love my body in a green negligee. I put the large back on the rack, and, glasses still perched on the end of my nose, found that there was indeed an XL lurking in the back. A forgotten, adolescent kind of thrill ran up my spine. Wouldn't this be fun! Neil would be beside himself, delirious with shocked joy!

A pause in the thrill. If I bought this, it would probably lead to sex. Well, of course it would. That's what this store was all about. Women bedecking themselves as sexual beings. For someone else. But I just wanted this for me. I wanted to take a long, hot soak in the tub, dry myself off with a fat new bath blanket, those obscenely huge towels that are practically a load of laundry in and of themselves. Then I wanted to put on this little Green Goddess number and lounge on satin sheets, sipping a nice merlot and then, well, then I'd slip under the covers, very slowly, very gracefully. When the heat of my body had taken the chill off the sheets, I'd reach toward it, my hand sliding across the satin. Then, and only then, would I pull toward me the object of my desire: that Barbara Kingsolver novel I'd been wanting to read for ever so long. I think it's about a woman who lives by herself in the woods.

I let out a slow, resigned breath. Fiction had replaced foreplay in my life. Solitude was way more seductive than sex.

So, maybe I could wear this some weekday – an unsuspecting Wednesday, perhaps – when everyone was at school and work. I reached for the dangling price tag, peering through my half frames: $89.00. I gasped, lodging my Doublemint way too near my esophagus. I began a coughing and gagging fit of extra-large proportions.

Phantom Girl glided over. 'Are you okay, ma'am?' She seemed not so much concerned as alarmed that I might keel over, leaving her with a big pile of frump in the middle of her store to clean up. Flushed and panicky, I nodded, grinning like a fool. I wheezed, 'Fine! Fine, thanks!'

I hustled over to the clearance area and buried my crimson face in the terry robes that hung there. They were thick and deliciously plush, and I kept my face between the sleeves till my gum had come up and my color down.

It was nice in there. True, it was sort of ostrich-like, hiding my head like that, with the vast majority of me taking up most of the aisle. But I felt safe with my head in those robes. And almost alone.

What was I thinking over there, anyway? This was much more my speed. I was a terry-cloth-and-flannel kind of gal. I'd momentarily been lost in the dark and seductive Satin Forest but had stumbled home finally to Menopause Meadow.

After a long minute, I pulled my head out and looked the robes over. This time, I *started* with the price tag. At the very bottom was a crossed-out $110.00. Above that was a crossed-out $89.00. Above that, a crossed-out $59.00. Finally, written in red pen, $24.99. Clearly their final offer, otherwise why the 99¢? Talk about sexy! I found final markdowns *very* attractive.

They were down to just a few odd colors in only large and extra large (evidently my kind didn't venture in here all that often), but they were like no other robe I'd ever owned. It seemed like the kind of robe they'd have hanging in your closet at a fancy resort, waiting to wrap its sleeve arms around you and take care of you for a change.

I decided I deserved this little indulgence. Even at a clearance price I still felt that way: I was indulging myself. Between growing up on a farm, us getting Neil through med school, then using his one income to support us, save for both our retirements *and* three college tuitions, and add in trying to make sure the kids got most if not all the things they 'really, really, reeeeally needed' – well, it meant that I lived pretty low on the hog.

I was trying to decide between the soft but odd pink called Little Girl Dawn (how absurd to have a robe in a plus size with a name like that!) and a pale, and also slightly odd, dusty purple called Violet Haze, when Lainey and Nan suddenly appeared beside me. I dropped the robe sleeve I'd been holding as if I'd been caught masturbating.

'Lainey! Hi, girls! What're you doing here?!' I asked, trying to sound delighted and loving and motherly, but fearing my tone was more accusing and guilty at the same time.

'More like what are *you* doing here?' Her smile was both intrigued and horrified, as though I'd just lifted my shirt and said, *Oh, hi, honey, want to see my third nipple I've never shown you?*

Suddenly indignant, I shot back: 'What do you mean, what am I doing here? I come here a lot. Sometimes. I come here, I *shop* here, from time to time.' God! Complete role reversal. I was behaving like an adolescent male caught with a *Playboy*. What was wrong with me? I'm a forty-nine-year-old woman and I can damn well shop at Victoria's Secret! I'm looking at terry-cloth robes, for God's sake! I pushed a piece of my over-grown bangs back behind my burning ear and returned my attention to the robes.

'Are you getting one of these?' Lainey's tone was soft and genuine now, as she rubbed the sleeve of the pink robe against her cheek in an endearing way. 'They're really soft.' She smiled and picked up the sleeve of the purple one, touching it to Nan's cheek. 'Feel.'

'Yeah,' said Nan, relief flooding her face that the

mother-daughter standoff was over as quickly as it had begun. I perpetually wanted to put my arm around Nan. When her father had run off with a younger woman last year, Nan, Sara, and their mother, Amy, had had their lives blown up into puzzle pieces. Melba's too, now that I thought about it.

'They're so soft, Mommy,' Lainey said, temporarily losing her armor and gazing at me with loving, childlike eyes.

I smiled. Little Lainey. My love.

'I know,' I said, nodding conspiratorially to both girls. 'I'm thinking about it. Which color do you like for me?' I lifted the pink one off the rack and held it under my chin, then grabbed the purple one with my other hand and switched. As I did so, my purse strap fell off my shoulder and onto my elbow, its weight yanking my arm down, both robes spilling off their hangers and onto the floor.

'Mah-ahmm!' Lainey hissed. An eerie *'she's baaa-ack'* sounded in my head.

'Oops, sorry. Here, help me get them.' We reassembled the robes on their hangers, and I put my purse on the floor between my feet and held each one up again. I was going to buy myself one of these damn robes.

'Which do you think is best for me? I'm kind of leaning toward the pink. I'm thinking the purple's kind of dark – too plummy and . . . frumpy.'

'Well, they're both nice,' she said, again sweetly. A person could get whiplash from teenage tone-of-voice changes. 'The pink might be a little young for you, though. I think the plummy suits you.'

Bam! A brick upside my head. I looked up, seeing myself in her eyes. Not the adored mommy of her girlhood, not the cool mom of her preadolescent years, but the alternate-reality mom who was best neither heard nor seen. Certainly not in pink anyway. She was voting for the cloak of invisibility.

I looked at my watch. Twelve fifteen. I sent the girls to go meet Matt and took the purple one up to the counter, not because I thought plummy 'suited me,' but because I was afraid I'd look like a very large wad of bubble gum in the pink. I handed the girl my Discover card, trying to think only of the savings and 1 percent cash back we'd get, not the 100 percent bill we'd get.

Neil used to proudly say I could pinch a penny till it screamed, and it was true. I knew women who spent forty to a hundred dollars on their hair every couple of months. I waited for a coupon for my local Quickie Clips and went about twice a year. My lack of extravagance in all things personal was why my staying at home as a full-time mom was financially lucrative for us. Where another woman would need nice outfits for work, or treat herself to a necklace, or makeup, my old sweats had lasted decades and I treated myself by only very occasionally buying the house something new, and then only on deep discount. A table runner. A colored glass vase. I bought virtually nothing outside of meeting our basic needs for nearly a year so we could buy a new dining table. Our minimalist kitchen remodel meant years of extra saving, since we prioritized college and retirement, living much closer to the bone than Neil's income might indicate. But it would have *cost* us money for me to work whatever odd job my un-degreed self could have landed. Just under two years at the University of Wisconsin – one year as a Humanities major (why not just stand on the roof of the chancellor's office and shout, 'I have *no idea* what I want to do with my life!'?) and part of another taking a few art classes – didn't get a person far. Call it housewife, homemaker, or domestic engineer, there's still no paycheck, so I always felt like I was spending someone else's money. My value to my family was my time, like beach sand: warm, inviting, fun to grab big handfuls, squeeze it and let it slip through their fingers before they ran off over it.

Phantom Girl handed me the credit slip. I signed my name and handed it back to her. She stared at the credit card and then at the slip. 'Ma'am?' she said, sliding both back toward me again.

I stared at my signature. I had a feeling of shrinking downward and backward through a tunnel, a roaring in my ears. I hurriedly scratched out Deena Hathaway and signed my married name of twenty-three years, Deena Munger.

'Sorry. Spaced out there for a minute.' I could feel the damn blood rising in my cheeks again. Lately, if I wasn't flushed for one thing I was flushed for another. Or welling up in tears. It was a nearly perpetual emotional bath of one sort or another.

'Can I see an ID, please?' she asked, her voice tinged with suspicion.

I handed her my driver's license, the worst picture of me ever taken, just last month when I'd had it renewed on my birthday. I stared at my license after she handed it back, wondering if she would call security. I didn't even recognize *myself* in this photo. But she smiled, completely satisfied that the haggard woman with the dazed expression in the photo was me. She handed me my plummy robe in the pink striped bag and with a practiced smile said, 'Have a nice day.'

At the food court, Matt's friend Josh offered to bring everyone home later. Prior to my arrival, they'd all decided that after lunch they'd go to a movie, then after that head over to Josh's for Ping-Pong and pizza. Having suffered the boys' blatant confused, then amused, stares at my pink striped bag, I escaped without further questioning, or joining them for lunch.

At home, I hung the robe in the back of my closet and stuffed the bag into the trash in the garage. That way Neil would not find it and start asking questions, either about the cost or why buy *that* at Victoria's Secret.

I was heading up to the bedrooms with an armful of the kids' textbooks and papers, which had been

43

strewn about the living room, when I noticed the bouquet on the dining room table. An unusual bouquet, to say the least. Smiling, I set the schoolwork on one of the stairs, a little ray of warmth shining deep within me as I headed back down. There were four colorful new dish towels rolled up and stuck into one of my glass vases, tied up in a bow with one of Lainey's hair ribbons. Neil must have taken a nearly unheard-of hour off – even on a Saturday – to bring them home to me. A piece of junk mail, pulled from the recycling basket, no doubt, a note scrawled on the back, was taped to the vase.

> *Sorry about the dish towel, D. I got these at the dollar store, two for a dollar, a good deal, I think. Thought maybe we could have lunch but you weren't home, and nothing was prepared, so I left. Meet me for dinner – we'll splurge, go get some pasta at Guiseppe's. It'll have to be late, I'm meeting a guy from the Washington Square Health Foundation at 6:00 for drinks. I'll meet you at 7:30 at G's. xo N.*

I suddenly had a cacophonous orchestra of emotions playing in me. A trumpet of delight to be asked out on a date by my husband; a sweet flute trill that he'd shown and expressed remorse, especially in such a creative way. But there was also an entire off-tune strings section that he'd called attention to the price, and didn't ask so much as inform me of

44

dinner plans tonight. A certainty that I'd have no plans. I shrugged off the strings. I *didn't* have plans, and Neil hadn't made a gesture like this in a long time. I smiled again, picturing him picking out the dish towels, debating whether to spend the extra dollar on ribbons or bows and deciding he could use one of Lainey's. Ah. I remembered now that Dollar Mania was right next to Guiseppe's. That was probably why the evening plan had occurred to him.

I started getting ready at six p.m., showering, styling my hair as best I could, given that the cut was about four months overgrown. I even tried to put on a bit of mascara, but the tube was mostly dried out and came out in clumps, which I had to pull off with a tissue, pulling out several eyelashes in the process. I slid a pair of tan slacks from their hanger in the closet and was stepping into them when I saw my blue dress, probably the only dress I owned that would still fit me. Neil was always complaining that I never wore a dress anymore. I rarely had call to, plus, pants were more comfortable. Especially elastic-waist pants. I fingered the dress, navy blue with big white flowers, a little tie in the back. Hopelessly out of fashion. But he'd made a big gesture; I wanted to make one back.

I wondered if it was still warm enough out to wear it without hose. I hated hose. I looked at my stubbly white legs. It didn't matter if it was eighty degrees out; I shouldn't inflict these legs on the gentle patrons of Guiseppe's, not that the restaurant was at all fancy, but still. I dug around in my drawer and found an old pair of stretchy blue tights. They'd do. I hung the slacks back up and took the dress off its hanger, laid it carefully on the bed. I pulled on the tights, the elastic waist loose to the point of being scalloped. Not exactly reliable-feeling, but way more comfortable than hose. I slipped the dress over my head. It was even tighter on my stomach than I'd thought it would be, and it made me look older than my not-quite-fifty years. Sighing, I spritzed on some ancient White Shoulders, wrote the kids a note in the kitchen, and headed out.

I got to Guiseppe's at 7:15. I sat listening to the radio, debating whether to go in or wait in the car. Despite my recent craving for solitude, I hated to be at a restaurant alone, conspicuous and uncomfortable. But as I watched a couple go in, I thought I'd better put our names on the list.

At the door, though, I stopped, my hand on the wooden door handle, greeted by a large hand-written sign in bright red marker, misspelled and apparently randomly capitalized.

SpeciaL: Tonight onLy! ALL ouR Terriffic spaGhetti You can Eat: $3.95 aduLts, $1.95 kids Under 12.

Another little sigh escaped, and I immediately chastised myself – it didn't matter that the bargain was what had made Neil choose this restaurant. It was the thought that counted.

Unfortunately, Guiseppe's was not terribly crowded and the hostess seated me straightaway at a table for two. I ordered a glass of Chianti, and while I waited for it, I sat trying not to look as uncomfortable as I felt, sitting all alone. I wished I'd brought a book. I studied the menu, just to look like I was doing something besides waiting, although I wouldn't dare suffer Neil's silent recriminations by ordering anything other than the 'Terriffic' Saturday special.

My wine arrived and I sipped it, looking out the window. There was really nothing to look at. A bleak little strip mall with a bleak little parking lot, yellowed weeds growing up through cracks in the asphalt along the edges. Then a girl about ten, walking a dog, crossed the street. They came into the parking lot. It was a funny-looking curly black mutt – maybe cocker spaniel and poodle. Suddenly it was sniffing the ground almost maniacally, hot on the trail of something, pulling the girl this way and that; she willingly let it, laughing. I smiled, watching them zigzag their way across the parking lot, my head twisting till I had to turn in my seat to watch them disappear down the sidewalk.

I looked at my watch: 7:40. I reminded myself that my wait was long only because I'd been early. Plus, my watch might be fast.

At 8:03 I called his cell phone. I hated when people talked on their cell phones at restaurants, so I turned toward the window and murmured to his voice mail, 'Neil. I'm at Guiseppe's. It's after eight. I hope everything's okay. Please call me on my cell.' The waitress stopped by as I hung up, and, more out of embarrassment than want, I ordered a second Chianti.

If Neil's meeting was running late, surely he could break away long enough to call me. He probably figured he was on his way anyway, why pull over to make a call? I did admire that about Neil: he would not talk on his cell phone while he drove. Being a doctor, he saw and heard about plenty of tragic consequences from that practice.

At 8:30, after I'd left two more messages on his cell phone and was feeling too tipsy to drive after two Chiantis on an empty stomach, it was now clear to the waitstaff, to the few patrons scattered around the restaurant, and most of all to me, that I'd been stood up. But I had to eat something before I drove home. When the overly sympathetic young waitress returned yet again to check on the poor old woman in that ugly blue dress with the crotch of her blue tights nearly at her knees, the old woman ordered the spaghetti special, and more than got her money's worth from the three platefuls she packed away.

Neil met me at the door. His excitement ran head-long into my anger. And my dyspepsia.

'Did you stay for dinner?!' he asked, surprised, but not waiting for an answer. 'That's good. I'm sorry I didn't make it, Dee, but it looks like we're going to get the last of our funding from these guys!

I stayed to celebrate the partnership with them!' He was almost jumping up and down. Neil had so fully thrown himself into this cause, he was truly clueless that he'd thrown over his family. Or me, at least.

'Neil, why didn't you call me?' I said, staving off tears. I wanted to stay angry, but my stomach hurt and I felt miserable, inside and out. But more than anything, I didn't want to cry again.

'I did try, but I couldn't get a signal. I didn't want to leave the meeting to go traipsing all over looking for a pay phone. Look, Deena, you're a big girl. I figured you'd realize what was going on. I was at a *business* meeting, after all.' He held out his arms. 'Sorry, but I figured you'd understand.'

I bolted into the bathroom, slamming the door behind me, thinking I was going to throw up, but didn't. I flipped on the loud bathroom fan, sat on the closed toilet and cried. I did understand that Neil was working, not just to support us, his family, but also for a very good cause. I was hurt more than angry, and what hurt me the most, what really got to me, was not being stood up. It wasn't even the lack of the simple courtesy of a phone call. Nor was it Neil's inability to apologize without a 'but' to excuse it all. What really hurt, especially after three plates of spaghetti, was his calling me 'a big girl.'

CHAPTER 4

'You got that at Victoria's Secret?' Neil had an almost sick look on his face. *'That?'*

I'd just pulled off my new bathrobe, having worn it for the first time and gotten exactly the reaction I'd feared. We were dressing for the O'Keefes' party, and, as much as I didn't want to go, a sense of duty drove me. And, I believed in the clinic – there were too many people for whom health insurance was an impossibility. Besides, I wasn't 'You-zing' my life; the least I could do was support my husband in using his.

I hung the robe on the closet hook. It now looked more prune-colored than purple to me. I sighed. 'Yes. It was on clearance.'

'But, Dee, *you*, in Victoria's Secret?' He chortled. 'The one time you go and that's what you get. Of all things.'

Neil, in worn but clean undershirt and briefs, looked at the robe, and he too sighed. 'You could have gotten something for *me*, if you know what I mean.' I knew exactly what he meant, and I didn't even come close to having enough energy to explain to him that I was tired of always doing and buying and *being* for someone other than me. I said nothing, and Neil went into the bathroom to shave.

I sat on the bed and slipped my thumbs down into one leg of a pair of suntan panty hose, gathering it up as I went. I placed my toes inside. Sitting there on my bed I couldn't even remember the last time I'd worn panty hose. It could well be that the pair in my hand were more than fifteen years old. Ten minutes earlier I'd excavated them from the back of my underwear drawer and taken them out of the sealed package. When I'd gotten out of the shower that evening, Neil, predictably, had begged me to wear a dress to the O'Keefes', rather than one of my ubiquitous pantsuits. 'You used to look so good in a dress and you never wear them anymore,' he'd said. 'This may be our only opportunity to really dress up till one of the kids gets married.'

'I had it on the other night, you know,' I muttered, too low for him to hear in the bathroom, as I spread the dress out on the bed. It was somehow even less stylish than it had been six nights ago.

I sighed. I didn't want to go to this soiree at all; it wouldn't matter if I was unhappily there in a pants outfit or unhappily there in a dress. 'I tried to call Sam again today,' I said, staring at my foot. I was sitting with my ankle on my knee, still with only my toe in the hose, waiting for the motivation to pull them up.

'Diddah you yust caw heh a cuppa day ago?' he said, sounding like an old man who'd removed his false teeth as he contorted his face to shave under his nose.

'Yes, but I didn't *talk* to him. I never talk to him, I just leave messages.'

A little laugh from the bathroom, accompanied by his razor swishing in a sink full of water.

'Aw, Dee. He's just busy, having fun. You remember college, don't you? It's a whole new life for him. We're not his life anymore. We've got to accept that.' Meaning *I* had to accept that. Neil seemed to be fine with the fact that we'd gone from three kids to two, and that the two would also soon disappear from our lives.

Slowly, morosely, I pulled the leg of the hose up over my ankle, then calf. I stopped, just above the knee, wondering if there was an expiration date on panty hose. The nylon felt more granular and restrictive than I remembered. I gazed down at the box on the bed. No 'use by' date. It should at least give a use by *weight*. Which, come to think of it, it did on the chart on the back. I flipped the box over to the height and weight chart; I was precariously close to the outer limit. Darn near expired.

I pulled the hose up over my knee. I wondered if the fabric got unstretchable with age. There just simply did not seem to be enough material here, considering how far I had yet to go. I gathered up the other leg, slipped my foot into the suntan donut, then slowly pulled that side thigh-high. I put my stockinged feet on the carpet and stood. I tugged on the right, then the left, then the right, all while swinging my butt hither and yon trying to stretch a couple feet of fabric up on to an acre of hips. I took a breather and caught my hunched-over reflection in my dresser mirror, my pale flesh bulging out in more than the usual spots. There was the familiar boobies-in-the-back bra bulge, the see-I-have-two-waists! panty bulge, and now I had added the glorious bisected-saddlebag thigh bulge. Worse, it was not only me staring at my bulginess. There in the mirror, staring at my reflection, was Neil's reflection. He was leaning on the doorframe of the walk-in closet, mostly dressed now, a twinkle in his eye.

'What d'ya say we show up fashionably late to this thing, Dee?' he said suggestively.

Oh. My. God. If he could get turned on by this, a bent-over, middle-aged manatee-shaped woman wrestling her way into a garden hose, it was indeed Neil who needed some hormone therapy.

'Give me a break,' I said, irritably. I stood upright, yanked on the hose, and promptly poked a finger-nail through the fabric. As I watched the run cascade down the side of my leg, the tears slid down my cheeks. 'Goddamnit! Goddamn them! *Goddamn them to hell!*' I started to sob.

'What's wrong? Calm *down*, Deena. Who are you mad at?'

'Everyone! Men. The men who made the first panty hose!' I glared at him. 'You know it was a man, don't you?!' *I* actually didn't know it was a man, but I'd have bet good money on it.

Defensively, Neil held up both palms toward me.

'Well, it *was* a man! Goddamned men. They invented high heels, too. And girdles. And makeup.' Again, I had no idea if this was all true, but at the moment, it felt it could be no other way. 'All the things that tell women we're not good enough the way we are. We need to be tanner, smoother, taller, prettier.' Neil looked at me as if my face was familiar but he couldn't recall my name. 'And especially *younger and thinner!*' I screamed. Whew. When the lid blows off a pressure cooker, it blows hard.

Suddenly Neil was sitting on the bed next to me, patting my knee and talking as if I was a four-year-old. 'Now, now, Deedle.'

'Don't patronize me.'

'Who said I'm patronizing you?'

I just stared at him. I half expected him to pull out a roll of stickers from his breast pocket and hand me one, the way he placated his youngest patients. But suddenly his expression changed, softened. Quietly, he said, 'Do you just want to stay home?'

Tears of relief slipped down my cheeks. 'Oh, Neil, can we? Yes. Thank you.' Instead of forced chitchat in tight shoes, I saw us walking around our neighborhood lake, in comfortable sneakers, and hand in hand. Like old times. Maybe I could even broach the idea of the dog thing I'd seen on TV.

He looked sheepish, then impatient. 'Not *we*, you. *I* have to go. I *want* to go. I've put my life into this clinic. It's important.'

I just looked at him. Part of me wanted to say, *And your family isn't?* Yes, the past couple of years you've put your life into the clinic. Not your kids. Not your marriage. No wonder he seemed so unaffected by Sam's departure, and Lainey's and Matt's growing independence and absences. He was able to throw himself into his work with impunity.

Neil stood, walked to the door, put a hand on the knob, then turned toward me. He looked as handsome in his dark gray suit as I'd seen him in years. 'What's it going to be, Deena?'

I stared at the blue dress, the blue tights with the shot elastic waist now my only option. We wouldn't even look like we belonged together.

'I'll stay home with the kids.'

'For God's sake, they're teen— They don't need a— Oh, never mind.' He closed his eyes, shook his head, and left.

I sat on the bed, peeling the panty hose from my legs. I looked up to see myriad fat Deenas looking at me. The closet door mirror was angled just right to catch my reflection in the dresser mirror, making multiple mes, each disappearing into the next. I wadded my panty hose up in a ball and threw them at the mirror. But they had no substance or weight and merely arced limply for a few feet, and dropped silently to the carpet.

When the house was still again after Neil had driven away, I came downstairs in my pruney bathrobe, walked into the kitchen, and was greeted

55

by three unpacked lunch bags on the counter and Hairy sitting on the desk meowing for food again.

'No,' I told him. 'You have your dry food. You only get wet food in the morning.' His meowing ratcheted up a notch. I couldn't stand the noise, so I gave him several Pounce treats in his bowl. As he devoured them, I began unpacking the lunch bags, pulling out dirty Tupperware containers, chip bags and largely unused napkins. As I was throwing the trash away, Matt came into the kitchen.

'Hey, Mom,' he said laconically, not looking at me, walking straight for the pantry. 'How come you didn't go with Dad tonight?' He'd pulled open both pantry doors and was hanging on the handles, which I'd asked him approximately three hundred times not to do. He stared with a bored expression at the choices in front of him.

'I— I'm not feeling well.' I was struggling to open a small Tupperware container in which I'd packed Matt's favorite homemade chocolate pudding. Lainey preferred the store-bought variety, feeling that anything else would make some sort of horrific social statement to her friends. But Matt said he preferred mine, which made me happy, although I'd evidently packed too much because he hadn't finished it. I pulled again at the stubborn top, unable to leverage it. Just once I'd like to see a commercial not about how well a lid holds, but how the hell to get these small ones off their containers.

Matt grabbed an opened bag of popcorn from

the pantry. 'What's for dinner?' he said, shoving a handful in his mouth.

'Yeah, I'm hungry.' Lainey had suddenly appeared behind me. I was sure the only reason they were home on a Friday night was because they'd expected their parents, both of them, to be out.

'I thought you guys were going to order pizza. Didn't Dad leave money on the desk?'

'No, he said since you were home, you'd cook.' Lainey was fingering the tie of my robe. 'You know, Mom, I don't like this color as well out of the store. You should have gotten the pink. Don't take this the wrong way, but this purple kind of makes you look a little fat.' She stood a step back from me, a sympathetic expression on her face.

And just what was the right way to take that comment? I wanted to ask her. But I didn't. I didn't want to start crying again. What was it about adolescent girls that they thought some sort of verbal disclaimer made plunging a knife into your gut okay? It didn't really help that I knew she wasn't trying to be deliberately hurtful.

I looked at Matt, who was crunching another mouthful of popcorn, his hand already back in the bag, gathering the next handful. 'So, like, are we going to eat soon?' he said, rather messily.

My hands tightened into a chokehold on the Tupperware. Then, to punctuate the tenor of my evening, I felt the perspiration begin to ooze out the pores of my forehead and upper lip, the familiar temperature surge building in me like an over-heating engine.

I pulled off my bathrobe, grabbing the top of my worn pj's, pulling it in and out rapidly, trying to cool myself. I looked at my kids. I didn't know what to say. I hadn't planned anything. I knew I could always make a tuna casserole. But I hadn't *planned* on cooking tonight. I didn't *want* to cook tonight. The anger I'd felt upstairs surged again. I wondered if other women going through the change had anger flashes, in addition to hot flashes. I put the Tupperware bowl on my hip and ripped the lid off, losing my grip and inadvertently flinging the lid across the kitchen. It Frisbeed its way right into Hairy, who, his white fur spattered with chocolate pudding, stood, yowling and hissing at me.

'Dammit!' I yelled.

'Maw-ahm!' yelled Lainey, rushing toward Hairy, but stopping just short. 'Poor kitty!' She glanced back at me, eyebrows up. 'And you owe me another dollar.'

Matt bent forward, laughing and spewing little globs of half-chewed popcorn across the tile floor. 'Now he's a Dalmatian cat!' He convulsed in laughter again.

'Poor kitty,' repeated Lainey, still not touching him, trying in vain not to smile.

I handed her a wet paper towel. 'Wipe him off, please, Lainey.' I dabbed at the chocolate on my robe with a wet sponge.

She took the paper towel from me but merely held

it, as she was overcome finally with laughter. 'I'm not the one who threw pudding all over him,' she said, leaning on the desk and covering her mouth, then turning away, as if she didn't want Hairy to see her laughing at him. He had a blob of pudding on one side of his forehead, a Groucho Marx eyebrow. I was worried it would go into his eye.

'Okay, fine, I'll clean him up.' I snatched the paper towel from her, and she grabbed her stomach with both hands and bumped into Matt, who was also still convulsed with laughter. I wiped Hairy's eye, then, with a grunt from both of us, lifted the enormous chocolate-spattered cat from the desk and took him to the sink. 'Sorry, Hairy. It was an accident.' He glared back at me, the angry-looking face that is every Persian's lot in life now looking downright murderous.

'I'll be downstairs,' said Matt breathlessly.

'Me too,' said Lainey. 'Call us when dinner's ready.' Holding Hairy firmly in the sink, I watched, my mouth open but nothing coming out, as she reached over Matt's shoulder into the bag of popcorn as they descended.

In the next couple of hours I bathed the cat, put a bandage on the scratch on my arm, swept the kitchen floor, made and served a tuna casserole, and folded and put away some laundry while the kids ate. I wasn't hungry after Lainey's comment. While the kids watched a movie, I did the dishes, mopped the floor and dusted, all in the name of therapy.

At nine o'clock I headed up to bed, wanting to be asleep before Neil got home. I wasn't, but I again faked it. It was a mystery to me how I could perpetually be so tired and yet have so much trouble sleeping. But I was getting very skilled at playing possum. I lay still, on my side of the bed, the edge really, my back to the center. Neil came into the room, undressed, was in the bathroom for quite a while, then finally slipped in on his side. Thankfully, he didn't reach for me.

But pure guilt made me reach for him. I fulfilled my wifely duties then returned to my edge.

I lay for close to an hour, frozen in my assumed position, till I was sure he was asleep. Then I silently slid out of bed, wrapped myself in my new prune-colored, fat-emphasizing robe, and went downstairs to the kitchen. I pulled out the tuna casserole, grabbed a fork, and shoveled in a big mouthful. Then another. Still chewing, I loaded up the fork again, gazing at the pictures and memos on the door of the fridge. An upcoming birthday party invitation from one of Lainey's friends. A shopping list. Matt and Lainey's wallet-sized school photos. A picture of Sam with his friends at a graduation party. Another mother had given it to me. And under a magnet from a car mechanic was an old snapshot of Rocky and Fordy, both going after a stick in the lake. I stared at it, holding in one hand the ancient white CorningWare we'd gotten so many years ago as a wedding gift, and in the other my laden fork. I swallowed what was in my mouth, looked at my forkful, and let it drop back into the casserole. I put the lid on and pushed the dish back into the fridge. I put my fork in the dishwasher and quietly closed the door. Tightening the tie on my robe, I walked down the second flight of stairs to the den. I sat, turned on the computer, nervously pulled at the cuticle of my index finger, waiting. As it hummed into being, the monitor's dim blue screen softened the too-clean room. I clicked, typed, and clicked again, until the Google box appeared. I took a deep breath, then carefully typed in the letters, one by one:

RAISING GUIDE DOG PUPPY

CHAPTER 5

I had just set the last, and biggest, bouquet on the coffee table of the sunroom. I'd been extravagant, buying two different bunches at Costco, mixing and arranging them anew into four bouquets, adding some of my daffodils that had bravely emerged in the early spring warmth. In the morning I'd put the finishing touches on some of the most furious cleaning I'd ever done. And for me, that was saying something. I'd even pulled out the toothbrush again, despite Elaine's admonishments. I hadn't told anyone about my 'project,' not even Elaine.

At a little after two in the afternoon, I emerged from the shower, blew-dry and styled my hair, and put on a crisp white oxford shirt and my just-pressed khakis and stared at the mirror. God. Was this the best I could do? The fat, preppy look? I touched the gray hairs at my temple, the lines at my eyes. I wondered if I'd be judged too old to take on raising a puppy.

By three o'clock I was ready for my first job interview in a very long time. I was glad it was in my home. If I'd had a résumé, my home and my kids would be the only things on it.

'Wow,' said Bill as we finished the tour and sat down to tea in the sunroom. 'Your house is so pristine, inside and out.'

'Thank you,' I said, beaming. It felt so good to beam. And Bill, the local leader for the K-9 Eyes group, turned out to be someone who elicited beaming. He was tall, with thick dark hair and bright blue eyes, an irresistible combination. The sprinklings of gray in his hair looked sexy, not old.

He looked down at his teacup, his brow furrowed, and said nothing else. My beam retracted.

'Is everything all right?' I asked. 'Would you like some sugar for your tea? Or a brownie?' I picked up the plate of my famous Death *and* Resurrection chocolate brownies and offered him one. 'They have *four* different kinds of chocolate in them!'

Bill averted his eyes. 'No, thank you, Deena.' He gazed around the room. When he finally looked at me he was smiling, but a cosmetic smile. A smile that is the Band-Aid in advance of the cut.

'Deena, I'm not sure you're really the best candidate to be a puppy raiser.'

The words echoed in the silence. I felt my throat constrict. I hadn't won the inspection. I hadn't even passed. My hand went to my open collar, clutching it closed.

'Why?' I whispered. My faults and shortcomings lined up in my mind like obedient soldiers.

Bill reached out and put his fingers on my other hand, trembling on the table. His touch surprised me, making me look up into his kind, blue eyes.

'You obviously put a great deal of love and care into your house, and you have some gorgeous things.' He pointed to the colored glass on the windowsills, then to the largest bouquet, which I'd strategically placed for greatest effect on the glass coffee table. 'Everything is so tidy and clean. I'm worried that a dog will not fit into this picture. Especially a K-9 Eyes dog. They're not like pet dogs and can't be treated that way. You have to be with them nearly all the time, morning, noon, and night. And there are lots of restrictions. For example, they can never go off-leash in an open area. And they have to learn to go to the bathroom only when you say. They can't be working guides and have a strong retrieval instinct, so they can never chase a stick or ball or Frisbee.' He looked at me, compassionate but concerned. 'And Deena, dogs, puppies especially, chew and dig and knock things over and get into all kinds of mischief. Your house and yard just aren't set up for that. Is a clean house very important to you?'

Oh, God. How was I supposed to answer that one?!

My house was . . . it was my . . . what? My life? Oh, God.

How had I, a farm girl, come to this? Well, probably because my mom, a farm wife, worked her whole life to prevent the farm from coming inside.

Rocky and Fordy were never allowed in the house, even on subzero winter nights. They did get to sleep in a heated barn, so they were comfortable, but they and their muddy paws and constant shedding were not welcome inside. I knew that K-9 Eyes required that the puppies sleep in the house, so I'd set up a little bed in the laundry room on the vinyl floor. Easy to clean up little accidents down there. When I'd shown him around the house, Bill had clarified that the requirement was not only that the dogs sleep indoors, but that they sleep near the bed in the room with you, since that's how it would necessarily be once they were assigned to a blind person.

Here I'd gone to greater lengths than usual to clean my house and prepare for this inspection, and now I was about to be denied because of it. My life was becoming too damn ironic.

I put both my hands up to my face. *Do not cry. Do not cry.* I took a deep breath, removed my hands, and looked directly at Bill.

'Yes. It has been very important to me. But not as important as doing this. I'll do whatever it takes. Tell me what to do. I'll bring a wheelbarrow full of dirt in here and spread it around, I swear to God.' I took a breath, calmed myself. 'I really, really want to raise a puppy for K-9 Eyes.'

Bill was silent, staring at me, but to my relief he looked intrigued rather than alarmed by my outburst.

Finally, he spoke a single word. 'Why?' His

gentle, sincere voice pulled a lump up into my throat.

Why indeed? Now I was on guard. I'd missed all the cues about the house. It seemed like everything was riding on my answer to this one-word question.

The silence stretched across the room like a taut rubber band.

I forced a smile so I wouldn't cry. 'Because I'm a dog person, and I'm, well, trapped in—' I realized I was nervously twisting my wedding ring. I stopped, put my hands flat on the table, but then to my horror realized I'd begun the sentence without knowing how to finish it.

I looked around the sunroom, my breathing shallow and rapid. Hairy was snoozing in a warm pool of March sun on the couch. A single cat hair was floating with the dust motes in the yellow shaft above him. Without looking at Bill, I told him: 'Because I'm a dog person trapped in a cat existence.' Now I turned. He was smiling.

I'd never really thought about how much meaning different kinds of smiles conveyed. Bill's eyes crinkled, his face softened.

'Okay, then. Let's get started,' he said, and reached into his briefcase and handed me my thick training manual.

At first no one spoke. Matt, Lainey, and Neil each stared at me, sitting artificially all together on the couch in the den. You'd think goldfish, not words, had just spewed from my mouth. In fact, they themselves looked like three gap-mouthed carp sitting in their green plaid bowl as I stood before them.

Finally, Matt spoke. 'A *dog*, Mom? You're gonna let a dog come into the house?' The three of them looked at each other as if to confirm they'd heard right.

'Yes.'

'Unbelievable,' said Matt. One of his eyebrows lifted, the other dropped, as did his jaw.

Lainey had only one concern: 'What about Hairy?'

'Hairy can hold his own against a wolf. I'm more worried about the puppy,' I said.

'But Hairy will feel jealous,' she whined.

'Well, maybe you could spend more time with him.'

She folded her arms across her chest and glared at me.

'Deena,' said Neil quietly, 'don't you have enough to do around here without having to look after a puppy? Besides, I thought we'd agreed on this. No dogs. They tie—'

'I know,' I cut in, raising my palm, ' "they tie you down." But it won't! Not at all! I'll take him everywhere with me. It's required. And the local puppy group has lots of volunteer sitters. If we go away for the weekend we can just call and they'll take care of it.' Why I felt compelled to mention this, I wasn't sure. We never went away for a weekend.

Our last family vacation was a road trip to Disneyland when Sam was twelve. Neil and I hadn't been away, just the two of us, in . . . well, we'd had that honeymoon trip to Vail after our wedding.

Before he could mull over another argument, I added, 'And besides, *we* didn't agree. I've always wanted a dog. And this is exactly the kind of dog you've said is a good one: someone else's. This dog will really always sort of belong to someone else. And, if everything goes well, the dog we raise—'

Neil's eyes widened.

'I mean, *I* raise, will be a huge gift to a blind person.' I waited. No one spoke. 'It's something I can do for someone. I can do this.'

'DeeDee,' Neil said in that pediatrician voice. My skin crawled at 'DeeDee.' Years ago it had been affectionate. Now most of his nicknames for me just irked me. 'You know you're going to fall in love with this dog, and then what? You'll be *devastated* having to give it up.' He said the word with uncharacteristic drama.

'You say that as though you think I'm a basket case perched on the edge right now.' Maybe I was, I thought, but I'm fighting to hang on. This was my fight. 'I'm going into this with my eyes wide open, Neil. I *will* fall in love with the dog. It's part of the assignment. But I love Sam and Matt and Lainey, also part of the assignment, and Sam's off at college, and soon, Matt and Lainey will be. Do you think my world will fall apart then?'

68

He looked up at the ceiling, pulling at his chin with his hand. His thoughts were all too visible. Yes. He did think I would somehow cease to exist without the kids. I had told him that it felt like a little part of me had died when Sam left for college. Neil had evidently surmised that it was one-third of me, and when the two-thirds sitting on the couch right now left home, that would be it for Deena Munger. No kids, no life.

But the prospect of this dog, this worthy work, had put a tiny spark of life back in me. I wasn't sure why, exactly. Was it simply the idea of having a dog again? Was it going up against Neil? Or was it that I needed to nurture another dependent being so I could feel useful? Whatever was driving me, I didn't care. The point was, I was driven for the first time in a long time.

I took a deep breath. 'Look, I really think it'll make a difference that I know I'm sending this dog on to a really important job and a good life. The blind people who ultimately get these dogs get all kinds of training and support and probably provide some of the best homes a dog could ever want.' I knew I was persuading myself as much as Neil, but something was making me bullheaded about this.

'Well—' said Matt. 'Uh, if we're going to get a dog, can't we get a real dog? I mean, one we can keep?'

My son! A dog person! Who knew?

Neil sat back on the couch, eyes closed.

'Let's see how this goes, okay, Matt?' I said, restraining myself from rushing over and gathering him into my arms. He shrugged, rose, and headed for the kitchen, undoubtedly to fill his hollow leg. Lainey left right behind him, calling plaintively, 'Hair-eeee? Hair-eeee!'

Neil sat staring at me. I waited for him to speak. He didn't. He often did this when we disagreed, knowing I'd feel compelled to fill in the silence with my own jabbering and backpedaling, usually giving in all on my own. This time I stood there, leaving the silence hanging in the air. Finally, I headed to the basement to fold laundry, catching my breath as I went down the stairs.

CHAPTER 6

The parking lot was covered in a wet, late March snow and most of us were shivering; the temperature had begun dropping again just after noon. But the crowd was waiting patiently, as were the various dogs. Well, most of the crowd was patient. Lainey and Matt kept jumping up and down, swinging their arms, whining, 'When is it going to *get* here?' 'We're freeeee-zing to death!'

'I'm sure it won't be long now,' I kept saying.

'I'm going over to the 7-Eleven to get something to eat,' said Matt, already walking away.

'Here, Lainey,' I said. I fished in my purse for my wallet, handed her a ten. 'This is for both of you. But just hot chocolate and a snack, okay? Nothing else. And I'd like the—' She snatched the ten from my hand and ran after Matt. '—change back.' I smiled sheepishly at Bill.

He reached out and patted my shoulder. 'Excited to be getting your pup?' Once again I was surprised by his touch. Surprised, but pleased.

I nodded. 'And nervous.' *There* was an under-statement. I scanned the crowd again.

Bill had explained on the drive down that there would be people here from several different puppy-raising clubs from all over the greater Denver metro area. As we stood in the three or four inches of snow, he filled me in on the who's who of folks from the Fairview group, names that largely went in one ear and out the other. Only one or two sounded familiar from the couple of puppy meetings I'd sat in on last month.

The kids, thankfully, had been uninterested in going to the puppy meetings, or studying the manual. I was feeling like it really was my own special work. But two weeks earlier I'd received 'the call' from Bill, and that had piqued some interest from the kids. Bill told me the breed, the gender, and the first letter of the name of the pup – H. He explained that every pup in the litter received a name beginning with that letter, and that K-9 Eyes tells the puppy raisers only the first letter, in case something comes up requiring a last-minute sibling substitution. The kids and I thought of dozens of name possibilities for my dog, a spayed female yellow Lab, just as I'd requested. We'd put a long list of H names on the refrigerator, each circling our favorite. Lainey liked Harmony. Matt was rooting for Hooter. I had circled, in bright blue marker, my own choice on the list: Hope. Neil refused to join in, but then one day a new name was mysteriously scrawled at the bottom of the list. It was Helen, his mother's name. In the past weeks Neil and I had fallen into a relationship not unlike graduate students sharing a house: careful, quiet, usually speaking only to discuss some household logistic. My conversation with Bill now was much easier.

'Are all these people getting dogs today?' I asked as Bill waved a greeting to someone across the parking lot.

'Well, most of them,' he said. He blew warm air into his cupped hands. 'Lots of families here though, so of course that can be five or six people for one pup. Basically this crowd falls into one of three categories. First-timers, like you.' He smiled. 'Then there are some folks who are getting another puppy after a sabbatical from raising. Like Jeannie Marris, although I'm actually picking up her pup for her today. This will be her sixth or seventh dog she's raised.' His voice lowered just a fraction. 'Then the last group is here to return the dog they've raised for the last year or so.'

They were easy to spot; they were the ones with full-grown – and remarkably well-behaved – green-jacketed dogs. These people stood on the edges of the group and in almost constant physical contact with their dogs.

'A few of these,' Bill said, 'will get another puppy right away. Today, even. Most will wait a while, though. They need to grieve the loss before starting again.' He pointed to a snow-covered picnic table under a big cottonwood. There, a boy, maybe sixteen, his face covered in acne, sat on the bench, bending over a large black Lab. His hands stroked either side of the dog's big, square face. I could see the tears on the boy's rough cheeks. He lowered his head, burying his face in his dog's scruff, his arms wrapped around its rib cage. The boy's shoulders began heaving. I had to look away.

I wasn't sure if it was the cold or emotion making me shake. This was an uncomfortably mixed group. Half were in mourning, spending the last few precious moments with their dogs, the other half waiting expectantly, joy mixed with a bit of trepidation, as they were about to be presented with a new and darling baby. It was as if the hospital had placed the morgue in the same room as the maternity ward.

Though I was part of the latter group, I was compelled to watch the former, knowing that that would be me in a year. The teen boy was now kneeling on the ground, in the snow, his Lab eagerly licking the tears off his scarred cheeks. A smile slipped over the boy's face, his chin up, head turning left then right, tanning evenly in the rays of canine love.

The roar of an engine gearing down suddenly turned the group's attention, en masse, to the street. A white motor home with a green K-9 Eyes logo was rumbling toward us. I glanced at the 7-Eleven – still no sign of Lainey and Matt.

Expectant silence fell over the group as we watched the truck slow, then turn in to the lot. A little girl in the crowd began to clap her mittened hands, jumping with excitement. My stomach was doing a similar move. As the vehicle parked, I stole a glance at the boy. He had his arms possessively around the Lab's neck, his head on the other side of the dog, shielding himself from the view of the motor home.

The door opened, a cheery woman of about sixty emerged, standing on the high step of the motor home. 'Hey, ya'll!' She waved her arm over her head, her apple cheeks pushing up into her sparkling eyes. She was small, but strong and sturdy-looking, her short, curly blonde hair liberally sprinkled with gray. 'Come on, everyone, scooch in! We'll keep each other warm! And that way I won't have to shout,' she yelled in a voice that could carry halfway to Nebraska. As most of the crowd compressed toward her obediently, I got the feeling even the biggest male German shepherd wouldn't mess with this woman. I also got the feeling that same dog would adore her.

'I'm Josie!' She nodded around to the group. 'I know you folks are anxious to get going, so here's how we're gonna do this. We'll start with the pups, then collect the big guys. When I call your name, step right up, take your pup and papers, then clear right out, please.' She grinned, and disappeared into the truck.

I scanned again for Matt and Lainey. They were probably looking at magazines.

'I think I should go get my kids,' I said, turning.

Bill put a hand lightly on my sleeve. 'No, you need to stay here, in case you're called. They're

75

big kids. They'll keep an eye out.' But I doubted they would. They would expect me to let them know that the truck had arrived.

Josie emerged again, this time carrying a sleepy-looking yellow Lab puppy. My heart raced. Matt and Lainey were on their own. This might be my dog!

Bill had assured me that many people requested a specific breed or gender for all kinds of reasons. K-9 Eyes tried to meet the requests, although it was never guaranteed. I suspected he knew my request was based on housekeeping; the yellow hair wouldn't show as much on my tan tile and oak floors. I hoped he hadn't guessed that I'd requested a spayed female because I figured she and I would have something in common right from the start.

'Covington!' Josie called out. Okay. Not me. I let out a shaky breath, unaware that I'd had it trapped in my lungs. A couple about my age stepped forward, the man receiving the puppy. 'This is Amaranth,' said Josie. 'Here's your packet.' The man and woman burst out laughing, but immediately headed back through the crowd, the woman linking arms with her husband and stroking the puppy's head.

Amaranth? What a name for a little pup. Or even a dog. I knew the puppies arrived with names and the names must be honored, but . . . *Amaranth?*

'Marris?' This time she stood on the step holding a German shepherd puppy that appeared to be two-thirds ears. 'He looks like a little donkey,'

76

I whispered to Bill, and we both laughed quietly. The pup gazed at the crowd, more than a little fear evident in his sweet, brown eyes. No one was stepping up to claim him, and I felt myself leaning forward, wanting to gather him up in my arms and reassure him.

'*Marris?*' Josie repeated, even louder.

'Oh! Golly! That's me!' said Bill, lightly touching his forehead and striding to the front. He called to Josie, 'I'm picking up the pup for Jeannie Marris. She's at her niece's wedding this weekend.'

'Hey, Bill! How are ya?' said Josie. 'Say hey to Jeannie for me. This is Donald.'

I lifted my purse in front of my face and giggled into the leather wall. Donald. Donnie. It just sounded too much like donkey. But once that shepherd grew, I figured no one would laugh at his name. Or his ears.

I looked over my shoulder. Still no sign of Matt and Lainey.

'Munger?'

My heart banged into my sternum. I spun back around. Bill was working his way through the crowd, grinning at me. Josie was standing on the step, searching the crowd. In her arms was a perfect, petite yellow Lab pup, her soft eyes barely open in the bright sun, the tip of her tiny perfect tail poking out from under Josie's elbow.

'*Munger!* Listen up, people!'

'Me! Here!' I called, raising my huge purse above my head. I quickly pulled it back down, feeling the red fill my face. *This is not an auction, Deena!* I slung my purse back over my shoulder and worked my way through the smiling, parting crowd.

I stood in front of her, my heart still pounding, but at the same time some sort of rigor mortis setting up in me. Josie slipped the warm ball into my stiff but cradling arms. 'This is Heloise. Here's your packet.' She tucked it firmly under my arm, and I struggled to hold puppy, purse, and packet.

Time stopped as I gazed into the puppy's shining brown eyes. Her tan eyebrows lifted, her small forehead wrinkling skin that was at least a size too big for her face. Her perfect triangular ears lifted too as she gazed up at me. Her eyes were rimmed in thick black – like puppy eyeliner. I put my cheek against her head, so soft and warm. She licked my chin eagerly, her sweet puppy breath filling my senses. If this were a movie, I thought, this is where everything would go into slow motion and a symphony would swell and crescendo. Then the camera would pull in tight on my face, then tight on—

Werrrrittt! The needle pulled across the record in my mind.

Did she say Heloise? I looked at the writing on the top of my packet protruding from under my arm. Munger/Heloise.

That was a name for a Holstein, not a dog. *I'm goin' out to milk Heloise, Pa!*

'Step back, please,' said Josie firmly, but not unkindly. She smiled at what must have been a slightly stupefied expression on my face. I turned and merged back into the crowd. I searched for Bill, and found him leaning against his car. And hurrying across the street were Matt and Lainey, each with a cup of cocoa in one hand and a magazine in the other. The packet was slipping out from under my arm. Despite the temperature, sweat was running into my eyes.

I started walking across the large parking lot to meet the kids halfway, but turned, instead walking in Bill's direction. I glanced back; the kids looked momentarily stunned, then they too veered toward Bill's car.

He was smiling at me. I could feel an absurdly large grin on my own face. Bill was holding Donald in the crook of one arm, rubbing a knuckle behind one of his huge ears. I deeply inhaled and exhaled, again not realizing I'd been holding my breath. If I was going to succeed at this, or even survive it, I'd better learn to breathe. I looked at my furry baby, held securely in my down coat arms, lowered my face to hers, and again breathed in her sweet puppy scent. *Heloise.* Now that I thought about it, it was a lovely name.

'Mom! Why didn't you come get us?' Lainey demanded, breaking into my puppy reverie.

I saw Bill study her, then glance at me.

'Well, honey, they called my name. Look, this is Heloise.' I pronounced the name carefully, Hell-oh-wheeze.

'*Heloise?* That's a weird name for a dog!' said

Lainey, sticking her comic book under her arm and scratching Heloise behind the ear. Heloise immediately mouthed her finger, and she laughed. 'She's cute! Can we call her Harmony?'

'Don't let her mouth your finger like that, okay, sweetheart?' Bill said pleasantly.

Lainey looked taken aback but didn't move her finger. 'It doesn't hurt.'

'That's not the point,' said Bill, gently pulling her arm away from me and Heloise. 'These pups need to learn right from the start not to be mouthy with people.'

Lainey looked sideways at Matt, but said nothing more.

Bill turned to me. 'Do you want to head home or stay? They've started the recalls.' He nodded toward the truck.

I watched, transfixed, as the acned teen again knelt by his dog, now next to the truck. Josie waited quietly nearby, no longer in a hurry, giving them time. The boy grasped his dog's head and shoulders in a last tremulous embrace.

'Let's go,' I said, the tears welling in my eyes.

We gave the puppies a chance to pee, which they both took advantage of. Bill opened the back of his ancient station wagon, revealing two small crates for the dogs. The crates were on top of a platform box, built onto the floor of the back of his wagon. He lifted a thin, hinged door and stowed the leashes and paperwork inside. Matt and Lainey climbed into the backseat and traded magazines.

Bill tucked Donald expertly into one small crate, looked at me expectantly, then to the other crate.

'Do I have to put her in there?' I asked, clutching her to my breast. Bill nodded. I somewhat clumsily set the squirming Heloise into the crate. Bill quickly latched it before she could get her gangly feet under her and sprint out. She immediately started whining. I looked at Bill, my lower lip out. This time Bill shook his head, smiling.

'Nope. She's safer back here.' He turned both crates around, so we'd be able to see the dogs through the silver bars of their little prisons on the trip home. 'Okey-doke, troopers,' he said, closing the wagon door on Heloise's whimpering.

We pulled out onto the street, and when Bill shifted into second, Heloise geared right up, too, adding sorrowful little yips to her whines. I'd read in a women's magazine about results from a study that showed that a baby crying in a public place would raise the blood pressure of nearly all women within earshot, but if the woman was a mother, her pressure soared. Evidently my maternal instincts covered even young canines. The need to rescue surged in my bloodstream. I thought of the teen boy, wondering if he'd finished his good-bye to his dog yet. Wondering what he'd do the rest of today. Tomorrow. The next day.

My two teens in the backseat had already said good-bye, as in checked out. They both wore their headphones, the volume high enough to drown Heloise out and for me to hear the bass pulsing

81

through on their different choices of music. I wondered if they'd have any hearing at all by the time they were my age.

I looked out my window, watching the strip malls whiz by. When we stopped at a red light, my eyes landed on a young mother walking along the sidewalk, a baby on her chest in a carrier. Then the light changed and they flew behind us, along with the donut shops and dry cleaners. I had to blink back sudden tears. Heloise switched to moaning. My eyes became unseeing, as colors, shapes, and years flew by.

The thing I remember most is clenching newborn Sam, still waxy and bloody from birth, to my chest. And I acutely remember them taking him away from me. Repeatedly. First they'd taken him from me to clean him up, weigh him, and who knows what. I felt like they'd pulled some vital body part out of me and disappeared with it. Which, of course, they had. Then they took him again 'to let me sleep.' But even with drugs, sleep eluded me. I pressed the buzzer and pleaded for my baby, till finally they'd wheeled him in in a Plexiglas bassinette, like my disembodied heart beating in a petri dish beside me. I longed to hold him, but I was too exhausted and in pain, and the nurse would not lift him out for me.

'You need your sleep, doll,' she'd said. 'He's fine in there.' I was more assertive with Matt and then Lainey, often sleeping with them in my arms.

I'll never know if I would have slept if I had been able to hold Sam, but as it was, I spent all the dark hours of that newborn night with my neck bent toward him, watching him watching me. I never closed my eyes, much less slept. Nor did he. I lay in the dual company of my wakeful but quiet baby and the unshakable thought that I was doing something wrong before he was even a day old.

'Yowww, yip, yip!' Heloise's mournful cries filled the car.

'She's a noisy girl, that one,' said Bill, his eyebrows raised above his crinkling eyes and warm smile. But it was his hands, lightly gripping the steering wheel, where my gaze lingered. Long, rectangular backs, not too hairy; slender, strong fingers with clean square nails. I'd always been fascinated with hands. I'd fallen in love with Neil's hands, when we'd first met. And Neil had loved my hands, too. 'Strong but feminine,' he'd said, on our third date, holding both of mine in both of his between two mugs of coffee at a Denny's after a movie. 'If I could have looked only at your hands to decide if I wanted to date you, the answer would have been yes,' he'd said, then added softly, 'and I would have been ecstatic when I saw all of you.' Then he'd blushed apple red. I'd laughed, but my internal romance-o-meter just about blew off the dial.

I shook my head, suddenly embarrassed that I'd

even made a mental comparison between Bill and Neil. 'She's scared, I bet,' I said, quickly responding to his comment about Heloise. I looked over my shoulder at the crates, self-consciously tucking my hair behind my ear. 'It's okay, girl,' I cooed across the backseat. 'It's okay. There, there.'

Both Lainey and Matt pulled up one earpiece of their headphones.

'*What?*' they both asked.

'I'm talking to Heloise.' I pointed over their shoulders. They both slid their pulsing headphones back over their ears.

Heloise was looking right at me. 'It's okay, girl,' I repeated, turning back around.

Who was I kidding? It wasn't okay. She'd been taken from her mother and now was in my care, and surely even her young, unrefined dog sense told her of my lack of experience, that my need for escape from my own existence had landed me in this canine terra incognita.

I looked back again, careful to avoid eye contact with Matt and Lainey, and through the door of the other crate I could see little Donald, lying quietly on his side, gazing toward me, his expression for all the world looking the dog equivalent of embarrassed exasperation. He seemed to be thinking, *Girls!* Or maybe it was *Labs!*

I was starting to feel carsick from looking backward. Twisting forward once again, I told Bill, '*Donald* seems to be doing fine.'

'You know, Deena,' Bill said, 'Heloise might be

picking up on your anxiety. They're like kids that way. They instinctively tune in to whatever you're feeling.' He shot an encouraging smile my way.

It was like he'd read my thoughts a moment ago. I'd often wondered if it was I who had kept Sam awake that night, and for many nights after, bathing him in my anxiety. It was an indisputable fact to me that I instilled fear more often than courage in my kids. They were always fine after they'd fallen if Neil was on the scene. But the moment I dashed over to their crumpled bodies on the sidewalk, the tears began. Too often, theirs and mine.

'So what should I do?'

'Just talk to me. Try to forget they're back there.'

Easier said than done with Heloise playing every part of *The Backseat Opera*. Plus, I didn't know how to talk to men. I didn't even talk to my husband anymore.

'So, too bad about the Nuggets, eh?' *Oh, that was bright, Deena!* I hated sports. I had just stated my sum total knowledge about Denver's basketball team. Last night while chopping green pepper for the salad, I had overheard the television Matt was watching in the living room. The Nuggets had lost every road game and all but one at home this season. Even I knew that was bad.

'Uh, I don't really follow sports too much, Deena.'

I smiled with relief. 'Me either, actually.' I bit my lip, thinking, as Bill merged onto the interstate. Kids! 'Tell me about your kids, Bill.' Parenting was a subject I could converse in. Or at least commiserate in. On the drive down, he'd obliquely mentioned having kids, so I knew we had that in common. Heloise had switched to barking now. I couldn't help but smile, thinking that this little puppy was using ambulance logic, switching from siren wails to horn blasts to get people's attention.

'Oldest is twenty-eight and working for a high-tech firm in Denver.' He spoke calmly, but just over Heloise's volume. 'Next is twenty-six and in grad school. Next is twenty-four and in seminary. Youngest is fourteen and getting an advanced degree in hormones.' Bill chuckled, darting driver's glances at me. He must have read my face, revealing active calculation occurring in my brain. Numbers are not my strong suit, so it pretty much always looks like I'm chewing on a lemon rind when I do mental math.

'Yeah, there's a big jump there,' he said, nodding and smiling. 'My wife, now ex, went through a kind of withdrawal and, to be honest, it was kind of a last-ditch attempt to save our marriage. Glad we had Macie though. She's a pistol, but a lot of fun. She has strong opinions on everything and lets you know 'em. But she's been the most hands-on with the pups.'

I stared at this charming, handsome man next to me. This charming, handsome *divorced* man. Clearly after many years of marriage. I suddenly jerked upright, realizing I was twisting my wedding ring again, a nervous habit I'd had for the over two decades I'd worn it. But now a rush of guilt made me clasp my hands tightly in my lap for the remainder of the drive home.

CHAPTER 7

olding the surprisingly heavy and wobbling crate, I smiled weakly as Bill backed out of my driveway.

'Okay, Heloise, we're on our own,' I told her. Matt and Lainey had already dashed inside, the door slamming behind them.

I hauled the crate into the kitchen, trying hard not to bump against the doorframe or swing her around too much. But she was standing, or trying to, inside the crate, which made her boat rock even more. Finally, I set the crate down on the tile floor.

'Let's let her out!' said Matt, his workout bag over his shoulder.

'Are you going to the rec center?' I asked.

'Yeah,' he said. 'Are you going to let her out?'

Lainey arrived, saw Matt's bag, and said, 'Wait for me, Matt. I want to go too.' She ran upstairs.

'Mom?' said Matt. I looked at him. 'The dog?'

'Uhh, I think I'll wait,' I said, as Lainey came thunking down the stairs and into the kitchen. 'Let her get used to the place a bit first from in there.' I glanced around for Hairy.

Lainey pulled on her brother's sleeve, her gym bag in her other hand. 'Let's go, Matt. We wasted the whole day getting the stupid dog and now she's just going to sit in the stupid box.' They left together, leaving the wooden door open, the storm door closing behind them.

'Be home for dinner,' I shouted behind them, closing the door and returning to the kitchen. I squatted in front of the crate. 'Hello, little girl. Welcome home.' Inside, Heloise cocked her head. We both were motionless for a minute, the silence washing over us like a tonic. Heloise wasn't barking or yipping or even whining.

I sat at the desk and looked at her packet of information. Forms for vet visits, and monthly reports, heartworm tablets, and a dozen or more information sheets that I shuffled through without really reading. Finally I found something inter-esting, Personal Information Sheet for ____. *Heloise* was handwritten in the blank.

Her parents' names were Kaylor and Raspberry, also handwritten in blanks. I scanned down the page till I found what I was interested in. Heloise's birthday was January 19, a little over a month after mine. I looked at the calendar on the wall and counted. She was ten weeks old.

Heloise whimpered. Still seeing nothing of Hairy, I figured he was snoozing in the sun somewhere. Heloise barked. 'Hush now, girl.' I squatted in front of the crate again and this time her whole body started wagging. 'Way-aait. Way-aait.' As I pinched open the metal grid door, Heloise shot out like a pea from a shooter, straight for me. I realized, too late, that if I'd been kneeling she wouldn't have knocked me over so easily. I looked like a ready-to-be-roped calf, my legs in the air, Heloise standing on my chest, licking me under the chin. I giggled like a schoolgirl as she covered my face with her sweet puppy breath and wet kisses.

'Okay, girl, that's enough,' I gasped. I remembered Bill mentioning at one of the meetings that these dogs were bred to be very bold and confident and we weren't supposed to let them jump up on us or be out of control. So much for that one. But she was so cute!

'C'mon, girl.' I sat up and lifted her above me, kissing her round belly. I guessed she weighed about the same as two small bags of flour, roughly ten pounds. I set her on the floor and heaved myself onto my feet. This would have been easier twenty years and thirty pounds ago. Heloise abruptly sat and chewed an itch on her haunches. Then she was still, legs splayed in a decidedly unladylike posture. She looked up at me, her liquid-chocolate eyes shouting, 'That was fun! What's next?'

'Here, girl.' I walked across the kitchen, calling. 'Here, Heloise! Come!' She sat for a moment, looking like she was expecting another roll on the floor and would wait, thank you, for that.

'Here, girl, c'mon!' I cajoled, slapping my jeans.

She cocked her head briefly, then bounded over to me, her tail a waving flag of anticipation and delight.

'Good girl!' I said, patting her side.

'Hey, girl, look here.' I showed her the water bowl. I'd set it on a flowered plastic tray to try to contain some of the splatter I knew was inevitable. She lapped some water with gusto, her whole body participating in looping her tongue under the water then flipping it up into her mouth. Finally she stepped back, dripping like a moose, dribbling water in a neat line outside the tray. I grabbed a paper towel and started to wipe it up, but Heloise immediately began biting at the paper. Still squatting, I scooped her up under my arm and wiped the water with the other hand as she squirmed. Suddenly a very bizarre sound filled the kitchen. Heloise and I both froze, my hand still on the paper towel, motionless on the floor. A low, guttural yowl, like a tremulous violin note in a suspense thriller, emanated from behind us. From her trapped position under my arm, Heloise twisted her head around my elbow to look behind us. Still squatting, I turned and looked, too. Hairy stood in the doorway of the kitchen, his excessive fur looking more excessive than ever.

His eyes were locked on the now-writhing yellow mass under my arm. I wouldn't have thought it possible, but the hair around the cat's neck swelled, making him look even more of a puffball than ever. Another low, meowing growl issued from deep within him. I understood him perfectly: *What–the–hell–is–that?*

Heloise, for her part, was anxious to meet her new playmate. Either she wasn't naturally aware of what raised hackles meant, or she was too dumb to care, or she was certain her charm and exuberance would win him over. I suspected the latter. How could she know that Hairy was not only unimpressed by charm and exuberance, but that he actually held those qualities in contempt? But Heloise was more than willing to have a go. If I hadn't dropped the paper towel and grabbed her with both hands, she would have squirmed out and made a dash for Hairy, who had now upped his warning to hissing and his sirenlike intruder alert, usually reserved for moths and crickets in the house.

'Okay, guys,' I said, my voice some weird mix of amusement and dread. 'Hairy, meet Heloise. Heloise, Hairy.' I got a firm grip on the puppy and put her in Hairy's direct line of sight, but held her tightly. He hissed again. Heloise squirmed wildly in an effort to get to him. Bill had said to proceed slowly with the introduction and trust my instincts. My instincts made me fear for Heloise's safety. I didn't want her to get a claw in the eye, although I had taken Hairy to the groomer for a nail trim just two days earlier in preparation for our new arrival. But I also wanted Hairy to learn where his escape routes and safe hiding places were. And I wanted him to know he might have to run. I didn't know if he even knew *how* to run.

I put Heloise back into my one-armed football hold and carried her across the kitchen. Hairy's fine white fur was now perpendicular to his body, and he arched menacingly. The arching surprised me. I'd thought his stomach too big to lift. But he was actually kind of graceful in this modern dance of warning. Still fully arched, he pivoted slowly in place as we passed into the living room, a radar tracking the enemy. I slowly lowered Heloise toward the wood floor, still clutching her vibrating torso.

'Get ready, Hairy!' I called. Hairy had moved to the middle of the kitchen. His hair was beginning to relax and his back was no longer arched. Oh, dear. I could tell from his superior expression that he assumed I had fulfilled my duty and removed the offensive material from his kitchen. Little did he know that offensive material would be residing with us for over a year.

'Okay, calmly, dear,' I told Heloise, for all the good that would do as I let her paws touch the floor. My hands still on her sides, her little legs immediately began churning under her. I held tight. Heloise squirmed and flailed, desperate to be released. Hairy's fur immediately engorged again. He looked like a furry blowfish. I let go of Heloise very slowly. For a few seconds, her slipping paws against the polished wood floor took her nowhere. Hairy watched her, a look of confused amazement on his face as he viewed her spastic ballet. Then he discerned that Heloise was, in fact, making slow but sure progress toward him. As she hit the tile floor of the kitchen, and traction, Hairy flicked his tail, and in three decidedly graceful moves for a fellow of his girth, jumped from floor to chair, chair to desk, desk to counter. Heloise was still a churning ball of slobber, headed in his general direction, so he continued his upward ascent, now in a not so easy jump and clamber, nails clawing on metal, to the top of the refrigerator.

His sides heaving with the exertion, he assumed a vulture pose, staring down at the yipping and leaping Heloise. Because he's a Persian, and because Persians have no nose to speak of, Hairy always had a sort of angry, disdainful look, but this was indignation of the highest order. As far as I knew, Hairy had never been on top of the refrigerator in his life. He'd never had to be. He ruled the roost just fine from the floor and furniture.

I did feel kind of sorry for him. There didn't seem to be anything for it but to let them do their thing. But Hairy hadn't had that much exercise since . . . well, ever. He was the most sedentary of cats. Jabba the Hutt comes to mind. But my lack of affection for Hairy didn't rule out a modicum of compassion for the poor, wheezing cat. His life was now unalterably changed. He and Heloise would have to work it out. Or Hairy would be spending the year atop Mt. Kenmore.

I grabbed Heloise, clipped on her leash, and

94

headed for the backyard, leaving Hairy to recover his pulse and dignity. I slipped on the boots that I'd shed in the mudroom, opened the door, and Heloise immediately forgot about Hairy as she pulled me, lurching down our two back steps, into the backyard.

'*Oh, how fabulous!*' she screamed in body language, her ten pounds pulling with the strength of a small tractor. '*We have a backyard!!*' The sun was now shining and much of the snow was melting. From what remained, I cleared an area with my boot, and, nose to the ground, Heloise spent a minute sniffing the wet grass. Finally she squatted, and, as instructed by the manual, at that very moment I began exuberantly giving the command to eliminate. 'Do your business! Do your business, Heloise! Do your business! Yay! Good girl!' As she peed, she stared dubiously over her shoulder at the lady cheering her urinary success. When she finished, I began what Bill said was the most effective training device: praising.

'*Good girl!!* What a good girl!! Good girl, Heloise!' I went on and on as she wagged happily into my arms.

Well! Look at that. She was already on her way to being housebroken. Maybe this wasn't going to be so hard after all.

CHAPTER 8

It was a short honeymoon. Heloise slept for about an hour, allowing me to make dinner, but then it declined from there. I'd pulled out the old baby gate, so she was confined to the kitchen, but she'd peed on the tile floor not once, not twice, but four times before bedtime. She'd also demonstrated an endless appetite for chewing: fingers, clothing, Lainey's and my hair, shoelaces, her crate, the desk chair legs, the cat – although he was learning to stay just out of her reach. Neil and the kids had played with Heloise a bit right after dinner, but between my anxiety about how we should play with her, and her propensity to relieve herself at inopportune moments, all three decided she was too much trouble and were downstairs watching TV before her second pee. Finally, at about nine, she collapsed in fatigue, and I'd carried her up to her crate in our bedroom. Then I, too, collapsed into bed.

Now it seemed I'd slept mere moments and she was whining. Again. I hadn't even gotten back to sleep from the last time she'd woken me. Us. I couldn't help but wonder if the person who'd made the requirement that the puppies sleep in the bedroom of the raiser was in fact a puppy raiser himself. I fumbled for the small alarm clock by my bed: 1:49. A.M. She hadn't even made it an hour. She'd woken twice already, once around eleven thirty, and again shortly after one a.m.. I'd taken her out to the front lawn, into the cold night, both times. The first time she'd peed; the second she'd just chewed on a stick.

Neil groaned angrily, wrapped the pillow over his head and rolled over. Heloise started barking. I stumbled out of bed, felt my way across our dark bedroom to her crate, making shushing noises. Before I could open the door, Neil sat up in bed. 'Deena! Shut the damn dog up! I've got patients in the morning!'

All I could think was, *You sure don't have patience at night.* But I said nothing.

'Put it in the basement.'

'I can't. She's supposed to be with me.'

'Then put it in Sam's room and sleep in there.'

'Fine,' I said, kneeling by the crate.

'Fine,' he said, then grunted, pulling the covers over his head.

When I opened the door to her crate, Heloise was in my arms in a single leap, all wags and licks, delighted at my touch. But I was aching with fatigue, and her charming ways were losing their appeal as the night wore on.

'It's okay, girl,' I whispered. After my interview, Bill had brought over an extra crate for Heloise to sleep in so I wouldn't have to carry one up and down my stairs each night and morning. He'd also told me that the puppies could usually make it through the night by the time they were twelve weeks old or so. I had a minimum of two more weeks of this. I wearily rubbed the back of my neck with one hand. But, weary or not, I had to take her out again, just in case. As I rose, Heloise in my arms, my knee banged into the corner of the metal door, slamming it with a clang. Still gripping Heloise in one arm, I grabbed my knee with my other hand, holding my breath in a silent scream of pain, trying to balance on one foot with a puppy in my arms. My balance wasn't up to the task, and I took several hopping steps, banging my shoulder into the wall. 'Shit!' I whispered loudly. Neil groaned again under the covers.

With Heloise chewing on the sleeve of my pajamas, I leaned against the wall till I could breathe. I looked at Neil in our bed, in a cocoon of covers, already using the whole bed, his legs forming a long L across my side. I tucked Heloise back into the crate, closing the door. I quickly lifted it by its carrying handle and walked out of the bedroom.

I paused in the hall at Lainey's room, her door open to let Hairy come and go. Her old fairy nightlight that she still loved, but hid when she had a friend over, cast just enough glow to see that she was on her side, face resting peacefully on just the lower corner of her pillow. Hairy was contentedly sprawled across the rest of it. I tiptoed on. Matt's door was shut.

At the end of the hall, I stopped at Sam's door. I'd kept it pretty much closed since he'd left, entering only to dust and sigh. I held Heloise tight with my arm and turned the knob with my free hand. The door opened with a small creak. The single wedge of light from the hall made the trophies, team pictures, and memorabilia on the shelves look somehow historic.

Heloise started squirming, so I stepped in and set her crate under Sam's desk, next to the twin bed. Before she could start up again, I grabbed her leash and we headed downstairs, and out into the night. Again.

It was colder than even an hour ago, but this sky seemed to be yielding up a second layer of stars. I snapped on her leash, set her on the lawn, shivering in just my flannel pj's and Matt's boots, praying for her to quickly do her business. I'd only read chapter one in the manual, overwhelmed by the many rules, not the least of which was that the puppies were always supposed to be on their leash when eliminating. Heloise looked up at me, wagged her tail, and began sniffing the grass. Good girl. But she soon found a small stick and plopped down with it, the ends protruding from either side of her mouth. It pushed her lips up in the back, giving her a toothy grin. I sighed. She didn't have to pee. She needed a puppy cigarette break. I was in no mood to enable her habit. I pulled the stick from her mouth and carried her back upstairs. At the top, I started to turn right, to the master bedroom, remembered, turned again, and carried her into Sam's room. I tucked her into her crate and closed the door. Immediately she began to whine.

'Shhh, Heloise!' I whispered. I stuck my finger through the silver squares and she mouthed it. I withdrew. Sitting, she pointed her little snout up toward the ceiling of her crate, barked twice, then twice more.

'Shh!' I whispered with more urgency. Heloise stood, wagged her tail and barked again.

'*Mah-amm!* Shut the dang dog up!' Lainey yelled from her bedroom, her voice cracking with sleep and anger. I opened the crate again and took Heloise out, just as the door to Sam's room opened. I turned, startled. Matt stood in the doorway, wearing only his pajama bottoms, his broadening chest incongruous with the little-boy knuckle rub he was giving his eyes.

'What's wrong with her?'

'I don't know, honey. I guess she misses her mom.'

He nodded sleepily.

'Everything's okay, honey. Go back to bed.' Matt shuffled back into his room. I waited, breathing only when I heard his bed creak.

'Are you too young to have left your mother?' I whispered, kissing Heloise's soft ear. I left her on the floor and moved to Sam's desk, did a little

100

figuring with a pencil, but couldn't get the seven-years-to-one ratio to work out in weeks. But it seemed like she was comparable, developmentally, to a human one-year-old, mobile, exploring the world with her mouth.

A one-year-old taken from her mother?

That didn't seem right! I turned in my chair and reached for her. There was no Heloise. Panicked, I peered under the desk, in her crate, calling her name in an urgent whisper, 'Heloise! *Hell-oh-wheeze!*' I scanned the room and realized Matt had left the door open. The stairs! I stepped into the hall, terrified I'd see her crumpled little body at the bottom. But there she was, safe and sound, not at the bottom, but at the top, just finishing up a nice little pee.

Heloise woke me again at six forty. I'd finally drifted off in Sam's bed sometime around three, after locating the carpet foam and working on her pee spot. Still, I managed to spring out of bed when she started whining, not wanting her to wake the household again. Holding her in my arms, I stepped around the spot, which I'd marked with three of Sam's old summer league swimming trophies as stanchions, positioned equidistantly around the circle. The gold figurines, each bent at the waist, hands behind them, looked ready to dive into the pee spot.

Downstairs, I clicked on Heloise's leash, quickly slipping my feet into Matt's boots again. We stepped outside. It was no warmer out, despite the rosy eastern horizon. Finally she lowered her haunches, and I sleepily told her to do her business, praising her as she did. When she finished, I lifted her under her front armpits, her little body hanging below so any little drips could air-dry as I carried her into the house.

In the kitchen, I scooped two cups of puppy chow into her stainless steel bowl on the counter, as she manic-ally jumped at my legs and against the cabinets. 'No, Heloise. Down.' Damn. Chapter one said not to say 'No' or 'Down.' Down was solely for lying down. I couldn't remember what I was supposed to say instead of 'No,' and frankly, 'No!' pretty much covered my feelings on the matter.

I'd gotten her too soon. I hadn't studied enough. I was in over my head. There was a puppy meeting that night, but the day stretched out miserably between then and now. Already my body ached with lack of sleep.

I grabbed Heloise under one arm and put her bowl on the floor. She was flailing wildly, so I positioned her about two feet away. 'Easy now, girl. Wait. Wait.' I slowly let go and she shot toward her food, her mouth gulping before it even touched the mound of nuggets.

I stepped to the refrigerator, grabbed the egg carton, thinking my family deserved pancakes this morning, given all of Heloise's noise last night. But by the time I put the eggs on the counter, Heloise had already finished her breakfast. I looked at the microwave clock. Almost seven. I was behind

schedule. The kids would be down for their breakfast any minute.

Think and they shall yell. Right at that moment,
Lainey hollered from upstairs, '*Mom!* Why are
Sam's swim trophies on— Ewww! Never mind! I
think I know. The dog wee-weed here, didn't she?!'

'Just step around it, honey,' I yelled. It was then
I heard the preliminary retching. I spun around.
Heloise looked like she was studying one particular
square of tile intently, her little rib cage squeezing
in and out. Then, in one enormous spasm, up came
her breakfast, just as Lainey was walking into the
kitchen.

'*Oh, God!* Oh, how gross! *Oh–my–God!*' She
pivoted, her pink puffy slippers scuffing back up
the stairs, her complaints continuing to drift down.
'Oh, gag me, why don't you! First this, then that.
Why did we get a stupid—' Her bedroom door
slammed.

I looked down at Heloise again; she was enthusiastically reconsuming her breakfast. I turned away.
I figured she couldn't be too sick if she was so eagerly
eating it again, but I thought *I* might be sick. I stood
at the sink, my hands gripping the counter. I looked
out the window at the new day starting as I listened
to the happy smacks behind me.

I couldn't face food. I pulled out several boxes of
cereal from the pantry and left them on the counter.
The kids would have to fend for themselves this
morning. I took Heloise upstairs with me.

Neil was in our bathroom, shower on, door closed.

I pulled our bedroom door shut and let Heloise roam. I'd put safety plugs in all the empty sockets and otherwise baby-proofed the bedroom, so I knew she was safe. Plus, she'd peed less than twenty minutes ago. I pulled on my jeans and a sweatshirt. I found my sneakers and was sitting on the edge of the bed tying the second one when Neil emerged from the bathroom in his robe, a towel around his neck.

'Hey. Where'd you sleep?'

I stared at him, then said, 'I took Heloise into Sam's room so she wouldn't bother you all night. Remember?'

He ran the towel over his ear and wet hair. 'Not really. Where's the dog now?' He said 'the dog' like the words were large cotton balls rolling out of his mouth. But he was smiling.

I pointed. 'She's right there.' Heloise was emerging from our small walk-in closet where she'd been exploring. She looked up, saw Neil, and I swear to God *she* smiled as she ran to him, her wagging rump making her course across the bedroom floor zigzag slightly. She jumped at his ankles, begging for his touch.

'Hello,' he said, tentatively reaching down to her. She happily wrapped her teeth around his finger in greeting.

'Ow!' He jerked his finger back, straightening.

I dashed over and picked her up. 'Sorry. She must be teething. I'll take her into the bathroom with me so you can dress.'

Neil glared, massaging his finger.

Safely in the bathroom, I closed the door. I set her on the damp bath rug, which I immediately had to pull from her mouth. I put it in the tub, and she turned her attention to sniffing the floor. I had just started brushing my teeth when Neil yelled.

'Jesus H. Christ!'

I opened the door, toothbrush still in my mouth, and saw Neil, white-faced in the closet. His right hand gripped the hanger bar. His robe had come undone; his temper was not far behind. His right ankle was propped against his opposite knee in a kind of sideways flamingo pose. A small, smashed brown pile was on the floor under him. The rest was between his toes. A foul odor filled the room.

'Oh, Neil! I'm so sorry. I took her out just a few minutes ago. She— I—'

'Could you get me something to wipe this mess on, please?' he said evenly, his face now filling with color.

'Oh! Yes! Sorry.' Careful to keep Heloise confined, I darted back into the bathroom and emerged with a roll of toilet paper. I unwound a wad and began to pull the mess off his foot. He grabbed it from me, doing the job himself. He dropped the tissue onto the pile and hopped, an angry pogo stick, into the bathroom. I followed him, grabbed Heloise, and retreated. The door slammed behind us and I listened as the tub faucets came on.

I looked at the poop and sighed. This was not turning out to be what I had pictured. I was beginning to wonder what I *had* pictured. Me and puppy rolling around in a flower-filled meadow. Me and puppy out in the world. Me and puppy creating a whole new life for me. Basically, a TV commercial.

It occurred to me, as I stood holding the contented Heloise in my arms, that any commercial that uses an adorable little puppy to sell their product should be required to also show dog poop oozing through the toes of an angry spouse. And if we're going for truth in advertising, then ads with cute little babies should also show complicated, remote teenagers. Or the empty bed of a son who left for college and has barely been heard from since.

Everyone should have to tell the ending, if they're going to lure you with a beginning.

CHAPTER 9

Neil left for work without another word to me. The kids had also made a hasty departure, walking the six blocks to school. They usually begged me to drive them. I usually did. But this morning, they'd dashed out without a word.

Now it was just me and Heloise. She was sniffing around the kitchen. I was sitting at the desk, staring sightlessly ahead, my hands wrapped gratefully around a mug of coffee. Heloise made her way over to the baby gate I'd put across the entrance to the living room. The other entrance to the kitchen, the front hallway, had a door, which was now securely closed. I'd found out the hard way that Heloise could push open doors if they weren't fully latched. She'd nosed her way out of our bedroom, and I'd had a few panicked moments looking for her, again worried she might fall down the stairs. I'd found her in the kids' bathroom, enthusiastically snacking from Hairy's litter box. If I was to last with this puppy, I was going to have to work on my gag reflex.

I'd put three chew toys on the kitchen floor for her to choose from, but she was too busy exploring.

I smiled at her concentration, her whole body involved in reconnaissance. I turned back to my coffee, sipping slowly, needing the gestalt of the coffee – the smell, the warm ceramic in my hands, looking into its quiet blackness – as well as the drug. I raised the mug to my lips, just about to take a sip, when I heard a horrible scraping sound. I spun back around.

'*No*, Heloise!' I pulled her off a cabinet, wincing at the tooth gouges in the wood. I set her in the center of the floor and put the little blue rubber bone in her mouth. She placed one of her big paws over it and began chewing, her teeth squeaking against the rubber. I sank with a thud into the desk chair and took a sip of coffee. I pulled the note pad toward me and began a list of chores for the day: *#1 – Vacuum upstairs spots.* I'd gotten more trophies, and now little gold swimmers guarded both of Heloise's spots, each covered with carpet foam.

I'd just put pencil to pad to write another chore, when I heard it again. Gnawing on wood. I spun around. This time she was working on the sink cupboard.

'*Heloise! No* – er, *stop!*' I tucked her under my arm and dug out the bottle of bitter spray that had come in my starter kit. I sprayed all the cabinets at her level, using almost half the small bottle.

'Okay. That ought to do it,' I told her, setting her back down in the middle of the kitchen with her bone.

I added some hot coffee from the pot to my mug, took a sip, then finished my list of chores. When I looked up, Heloise had fallen asleep, on her side, in the middle of the kitchen floor. Her little ear flopped over backward and her toes were twitching. She looked completely innocent and darling. I looked at her and sighed.

I suddenly realized there was no time to waste. Nap time is a mom's most productive time. I couldn't vacuum, that would wake her, so I quietly grabbed the dust mop from the closet and stepped over the baby gate. Heloise immediately woke up and rushed to the gate.

'Oh, baby,' I said, stepping like a large wading bird over the gate, picking her up and stepping back over again. 'Why couldn't you stay asleep?' She licked my chin. I smiled. 'Okay, you stay here with me, where I can keep an eye on you.'

I set to dust-mopping, Heloise set to sniffing. I watched her make her way over to the bookcase, trying to wedge herself in the space between it and the wall, but I knew it was too narrow, even for her sinewy little body. I slid the dust mop under my grandmother's antique desk and pulled out a small wad of fur and dust. I had to admit, however, it appeared to be mostly Hairy's fur. I got down on my hands and knees for a second pass.

My excavations were interrupted by a screeching meow, followed by Hairy streaking through the living room, hair on end and hotly pursued by a euphoric Heloise. Hairy's ears were flattened against the back of his head, his tail straight out behind him. Heloise's ears couldn't have been any more forward, her tail high.

'Stop!' I yelled, crawling bravely into their path, dust mop extended. Hairy, maintaining impressive speed, turned at the dust mop and dashed under the love seat. Heloise had to make a last-minute adjustment and came up short, her paws again slipping out from under her on the wood floor. She slid on her side, with enough momentum to upend the standing lamp. I lunged for it but was too late. The resulting crash sent Heloise scrambling in the other direction, but once she hit the throw rug, she made no progress whatsoever, as it merely bunched up under her. Finally, she jumped off the mound of rug and resumed her tear after the cat, who stupidly shot out from the relative safety under the love seat. The white and tan blurs then careened into the sunroom, with me bringing up the rear, yelling and shaking my dust mop.

'Heloise! Stop!' Hairy jumped up on the couch arm, his sides heaving. Heloise was trying to climb up after him, but her little legs were neither long enough nor strong enough. She did manage to get her nose within Hairy's reach, and he promptly boxed it with a tight paw. I was impressed with his restraint. I doubted that Heloise would get more than one warning shot before the claws came out.

'Heloise! *No!* Or cut it out! Or whatever the hell I'm supposed to say! *Stop chasing the goddamned cat!*' I pulled her away from the couch with one hand, still brandishing my dust mop in the other. No one could say I wasn't prepared, should a dust bunny join the fracas.

I thought maybe a little supervised face-to-face time was called for. I set down the dust mop and scooped Heloise up, holding her close and cooing to Hairy. But Hairy still boxed at Heloise in my arms, apparently interpreting my interference as a vote for his side. Heloise snapped at each reach of Hairy's paw, but about two seconds delayed each time. I put the dust mop between them. 'Hairy! Stop swatting at her! Heloise, stop biting. Look, you two, you're going to have to learn to get along.' Heloise barked gleefully. Hairy backed himself up against a couch pillow, hissing. Heloise was beside herself with joy, yapping in appreciation at the delightful variety of sounds she was discovering that this great new toy could make.

Surrendering, I carried Heloise into the kitchen, stepping over the gate again. I stood in the middle of my kitchen, eyes closed, hands on knees, catching my breath. For just a moment, I had an image of myself, having just fallen out of a huge frying pan, into a robust fire.

I thought I'd better go check on Hairy, make sure he wasn't having a heart attack there on the couch. I was just stepping back over the gate when Heloise jumped under my leg, front paws on the

111

white mesh of the gate, making me leap more than I could to avoid her. I caught the toe of my slipper on the top of the gate, slammed my wrist against the door frame, and fell forward into the living room onto my knee, the same one I'd banged on the kennel door the night before.

Lying facedown in the crumpled throw rug, I uttered a couple of expletives while gripping my knee. When I sat up, Heloise was still standing on her back feet, front paws on the gate. Her whole body was shaking from her exuberant tail wagging, but her little ears were alternately lifting, then dropping. I'm sure she was trying to figure out if I'd intended that fantastic maneuver over the gate.

At that moment, Hairy, very much not in cardiac arrest, came around the corner, a piercing gaze on Heloise with his every tentative step. When Heloise saw him, she began a barking fit worthy of a rottweiler, hurling herself against the gate. Hairy froze, one paw poised in front of the other on the wood floor, tail flicking warily behind him. He waited, watching her frenzy behind the gate.

'Quiet, Heloise,' I said with a sigh, still sitting on the living room floor. It was an admittedly weak attempt to calm her, but my knee and wrist were throbbing.

When Hairy realized Heloise couldn't get to him, he continued his one-cat processional, his cautious steps now back to his look-at-me sashay. When he was directly in front of her, he stopped. He stared at her, increasing her hysteria, then he turned a regal half circle and sat, his back to her, front paws perfectly together, his tail swishing provocatively across the floor behind him, and, I daresay, directly at Heloise. He looked over his shoulder at her, then turned his smug stare toward me.

'You little provocateur!' I stood, scooping him up under his belly. With Hairy in my arms, I limped around the corner to the stairs. I set him on the second step, gently scooting his bottom upward with my slippered foot. 'Go on!'

A sudden loud crash got both our attention. We were frozen for the split second it took Heloise to come racing toward us. Either I must have loosened the gate with my foot or her repeated body slamming had done the job.

Hairy shot up the stairs. Heloise tried to clamber up after him, but the polished oak stairs were too slippery, the steps too high for her. I took her back to the kitchen and resecured the baby gate. Heloise dashed across the kitchen and pounced on her blue bone, thrilled to her core. She brought her treasure over to show me. 'Good girl, Heloise. That's a good thing to chew. Chew the bone. Not the cat.' I heaved another sigh, then very carefully stepped over the gate and headed upstairs to check on Hairy.

I found him in Lainey's room. The poor guy had sought refuge in her trundle bed. This would not have been so pathetic if the trundle bed had been pulled out. But Hairy had somehow wedged himself in; only two glaring points of green stared out at me from between the two mattresses. Even though Heloise was now securely locked in the kitchen, I saw no reason to haul the poor cat out. At least he wouldn't torment Heloise from there. Although, regardless of Hairy's intent, at no time did Heloise seem tormented. Her life seemed to be all about fun. Ecstasy, even. I bent and looked at Hairy's radioactive eyes. I could hear his nasally breathing, so I decided he was okay in there. I just had to remember to pry him out tonight if he didn't emerge on his own. Being as remembering wasn't my strong suit lately, I wrote myself a note on Lainey's scratch pad. *Get Hairy.* I pushed the note into the breast pocket of my pajamas.

When I got down to the kitchen, my intention was to tape the note to the microwave, so either I or Lainey would notice it in the afternoon. But I forgot all about it when I saw that Heloise, although still secure in the kitchen, had abandoned her blue bone and was again happily chewing on a cabinet door. She evidently considered the bitter spray a condiment of sorts.

'Heloise! *No!*' I stepped over the gate, directly into a still-warm puddle. 'Oh, *crap!*' I said, not entirely inaccurately. I pulled my wet slipper off, gimped across the kitchen and pulled Heloise off the cabinet. I realized, obviously too late, that I should have taken her outside after her little escapade with Hairy. I remembered all three of my kids, when they were little, needing to pee immediately after arriving at carnivals, zoos or amusement parks, their little bladders over-whelmed by excitement. Hairy was Heloise's personal entertainment venue.

In the front yard, I told her to do her business. 'Don't have to anymore,' her big brown eyes said. She began chewing a stick.

Back in the kitchen I showed her the gnawing marks she'd made in my cabinet doors. 'No!' Her little ears went back; I could tell she knew I was unhappy with her; it was equally clear that she didn't have a clue as to why. My heart broke for her and my own ineptitude. 'I'm sorry, girl,' I said, giving her a kiss on top of her head.

'I'm sorry again,' I told her, leaning down, putting her in the crate. I quickly closed and locked the door. She immediately started crying, making me wince. I tucked the small white bone through the slats, but she ignored it, putting her little paws on the metal bars and whining, with a peppering of little yips. She looked like a prisoner. All she needed was a little metal cup to rake across the bars. I took a deep breath and left.

I quickly straightened the living room rugs, then pulled out the vacuum. When I clicked it on, Heloise barked loudly, audible even over the Hoover. I ran upstairs and grabbed Matt's old Walkman. Between the roar of the Hoover and the histrionic caterwauling of Matt's favorite band, DeBased, I could no longer hear the complaints of little Heloise.

I vacuumed the living room to 'You Leave Me

Heaving,' the dining room to 'Get Down, Get Dead,' and the sunroom to 'Loser From Leavenworth.' When I turned both appliances off, my head was pounding and my ears were ringing in the silence. Silence! But it was short-lived; the lack of vacuum noise was enough to restart Heloise barking. I looked at the time. Twelve thirty. It felt like it had taken three long days just to make it to lunchtime. I ran some water into a glass and swallowed down two ibuprofen.

I let Heloise out of her crate, picked up her food bowl, then set about fixing her lunch, scooping out two cups of kibble. As I did this, she leapt and barked around my knees. 'No! Er, Wrong! Naughty! Heloise. Please don't, honey. Easy, girl!' My reprimands were worthless. She looked like a dog version of a Masai dancer, repeatedly springing up, trying to see the counter.

I set her bowl on the floor and she lunged for it, again consuming it in record time. I braced for it to come back up, which it did. I turned my back again, and when she'd finished the second consumption, I took her back outside. After a while, she actually did her business in the grass. 'There is a God,' I murmured, and began praising both Him and Heloise profusely.

When I put her back in the kitchen, she climbed into her crate of her own accord, and, thankfully, fell fast asleep. I stepped over the gate and sat on the couch, staring into space. My head and vision blurred from lack of sleep, all I could think about was resting my head on the couch pillow. Just for a minute. My eyelids labored under their weight. I listened for any sound from the kitchen. There was only the ticking of the clock in the sunroom, a metronome for 'An Ode to Sleep.'

I awoke to the unmistakable sound of small teeth on wood. I lurched into the kitchen, still drunk on midday sleep. There she was, by the door. She wasn't chewing on the cabinets. The door trim, however, looked like a bear had mauled it, long grooves cutting through the paint and splintering the wood below. I castigated myself for not locking the crate before falling asleep myself. She'd gone in there on her own, after all. Bill had told me that the pups generally like their crate; it's their own little house. Why, then, did I have such a problem with locking her in there?

While I was examining the damage, Heloise began sniffing around the kitchen floor. 'You won't find any crumbs down— Heloise!'

I grabbed her, midpee, and carried her under the armpits, belly forward – dripping position again – out to the backyard. To hell with the leash. I set her down and told her to do her business. But she just sat in her usual splayed position, head cocked, big eyes blinking at me.

I fell to my knees, my hands grabbing on to fistfuls of grass, as though the earth's spin might hurl me off at any moment. Canine vertigo. Could anybody fail more miserably at this than I was?

Heloise, delighted that my face was now nearly on a par with hers, jumped up and playfully bit my chin.

'*No!*' I yelled. I stood, touching my chin and checking my fingers for blood. There was none. It was all pounding in my temples.

'You stay here!' I told her. The puddle in the kitchen was not going to wipe itself up. I left Heloise in the backyard, hoping she would finish in the grass what she'd started on the tile.

I took care of the puddle with a paper towel, then went at it with antiseptic wipes. I briefly considered mopping the entire floor, but knew I shouldn't leave Heloise on her own too long.

Stepping back out onto the patio, the warm spring sun on my face, I realized how lovely the day was. I inhaled a deep, calming breath, the scent of wet earth and new growth a salve to my senses. The daffodils near the back fence bobbed their yellow heads in the slight breeze. Spears of tulip fronds dotted the border near the house, only a hint of a hidden bud visible on a few. But a large, lacy dandelion was spreading out menacingly nearby. I stepped toward it, then stopped, reining in my desire, nay *need*, to pull something up by the roots.

'Heloise!' I called. I was out there to take the pup back inside, not to garden, I reminded myself.

'Heloise?' It was not that big a yard.

'Heloise!' I stepped quickly toward the side of the house, a seizing feeling creeping through me.

There were probably plenty of things toxic or dangerous to a little pup out here. What was I thinking? Would I have ever left my children outside alone at her age? Even her developmental age?

We met on the corner, Heloise greeting me with perked-up ears, paws caked with mud, delight in her eyes and a single bedraggled daffodil hanging from her mouth. I picked her up, slid the flower from her teeth and tucked her under my arm, muddy paws and all. I stepped around the corner. It could've been worse. She could have used a bulldozer to excavate the side flower bed.

Little trenches veined across the bed, mounds of soft spring soil lay mixed with the cedar mulch, a small botanic battlefield. She'd sampled a couple of grape hyacinths, but evidently they were more inviting than tasty; their purple heads lay in the dark soil near the feet of the plants. Several fronds of tulips looked like a fringed ribbon on a birthday present.

Across from the flower bed I noticed that she'd also dug under my lilac bushes. Fortunately, the plant matter was high enough that she could do no real damage to either the heart-shaped leaves or the dozens of hard, dark clusters, hanging like little triangles of miniature grapes, waiting for something more trustworthy than March sun to open up. March. And I was to have this dog for fourteen months? There was no way.

I checked the date on my watch. No, I was wrong.

Standing in my shredded garden, the shredder happily whapping her little tail against my back and arm, I saw that it was no longer March. It was April. April first.

'Hi. It's me, April Fool.'

Elaine was laughing, despite my morose tone. 'So? Are congratulations in order? Did you get your new baby?' She was almost breathless with pleasure. Elaine had been more excited about my puppy-raising project than anyone in my family. I'd even shared with her how handsome and wonderful Bill was, although she'd been less receptive to that news.

Bill. He'd taken a gamble on me. Already I was imagining the weight of his disappointment in me, and it was crushing. But nothing compared to my own disappointment.

'I can't do this, E.' She stopped smiling. Funny, how I could hear that.

'Sure you can, Deena-leh. What's wrong?'

I stared at Heloise, sleeping peacefully in the middle of the kitchen floor, her paws and round belly still wet from her bath in the sink. 'What isn't? There are spots all over the house where she's gone to the bathroom, she chews constantly, anything she can get her teeth into. Especially our new cabinets. *And* the door trim. She dug up one of my flower beds. She whines most of the night, and I have to get up and take her out at all hours.' I gazed sullenly around the kitchen, stopping on Hairy's food dish on the desk. Hairy. The note! I'd forgotten

120

about the note I'd written so I wouldn't forget. Memory must be heavily supported by estrogen. And I didn't have any of either, apparently. I dug the note out of my pajama pocket. Oh, God. It was late afternoon and I was still in my pj's. As I taped the note to the microwave, I told Elaine, 'And she chases the cat.' I pressed my finger more firmly than necessary to the tape. 'Hairy's hiding in Lainey's closed trundle bed.'

'And you think that's a bad thing?' I could hear her smiling again, teasing me about my something less than love for Hairy. But it just made me more despondent.

'I'm just not cut out for this. I don't know what made me think I was. I feel like I can't do anything.'

'Oh, sweetie, sure you can. You've had her, what? A day or two?' My point exactly. I nodded, my throat too stinging and constricted to talk.

'D? You okay?'

I shook my head side to side, hoping she could hear it.

CHAPTER 10

'Mah-amm!' Lainey's shriek from upstairs was one part shock, one part anger, eight parts drama queen. When she and Matt had walked in the door from school, I'd pointed to the note on the microwave and explained. Lainey had immediately dropped her backpack and run upstairs, calling Hairy's name. Matt had followed, only pretending to try to stifle his laughter.

Lainey yelled again. Even though I knew her propensity for drama, I ran to the bottom of the stairs with pinpricks of alarm. What if the poor cat *had* expired in the trundle bed?

Lainey, in her tight and well-filled tank top, came down the stairs as if she were Miss America carrying a bouquet of roses across her arms, except the roses looked very much like a flattened and angry Persian cat.

'Look!' she whined. 'Look at him! He's all . . . smushed.' She stuck out her lower lip, making the two of them an interesting couple, Lainey all – protruding – and Hairy, well, not. Now, in addition to his pushed-in face dictated by his breed, he had to suffer the indignity of his fine fur being flattened all along the top of his head and down his back. His ears, too, had either been pressed down by the mattress too long, or he was still royally pissed off. I was pretty sure it was the latter. Spending the afternoon in a trundle bed wouldn't press ears that flat.

Before Lainey had gotten all the way down, Matt emerged from his room and stood at the top of the stairs, still looking highly amused, and holding something. 'Check this out, Mom!' He held up one of his enormous black sneakers, a hole chewed into the toe.

'Lord! When did she do *that*?! I'm so sorry, Matt. We'll get you a new pair.'

'It's cool, Mom. They're too small anyway.' He turned and disappeared into his room, closing the door behind him. Lainey turned too, climbing back up the stairs, presumably to comfort Hairy on, rather than inside, her bed. She closed her door with an editorial slam. I returned to the kitchen to start on dinner, serenaded by the ever-vocal Heloise.

When Neil came through the front door, I froze at the cutting board. Of all nights for him to come home at a reasonable hour. To survey the wreckage and gloat, no doubt. I could almost feel on my skin all the damage Heloise had done today, especially the cabinet beside my right knee. I decided no reaction was the best reaction.

I was fixing a salad to go with the lasagna bubbling in the oven. I'd made and frozen the lasagna last month. One of my many culinary preparations in advance of getting a puppy. I had six or eight meals in the freezer, thinking, in my naiveté, that that would make puppy raising easier. I wasn't sure what preparations I should have made, but a lasagna didn't seem like it was going to help curb Heloise's night-time crying, cabinet consumption, potty accidents or anything else.

Hanging his coat in the hall closet, Neil called to me. 'So how was your day? With the *dog*?'

I stopped, my knife halfway through a tomato. I stared at the cutting board. 'Disaster' was probably exactly what he wanted to hear. A wave of heat passed through me. Oh, sure. Let's add a hot flash to the moment. 'Not great,' I said. I grabbed a paper towel and dabbed at my forehead.

I looked up, still dabbing as Neil stepped into the kitchen. I watched his eyes as they scanned the room, taking in each and every tooth mark. Drips ran down my sides.

'Jesus, Deena! This kitchen took years to save for, two months to redecorate, and it's not even a year old and your dog takes one day to maul it.'

'She's not my—' Neil's stern look stopped me. 'I know. I'm sorry. I put the bitter spray on it, but . . .'

'Look, Deena, this is not going to work. What is it you're trying to prove here anyway?' He was standing in the middle of the kitchen, his arms folded over his chest.

Good question. I looked down at the cutting board again, the hot flash over, just like that. Now I felt chilled. I set my knife blade back on top of the tomato. 'Don't worry,' I said quietly. I stared at several tomato seeds lying on the cutting board, each enveloped by its own little protective membrane. All that planning nature puts into seeds – protection, transportation, food. All for naught, when I would soon wash the cutting board, sending them all sliding down the drain.

I stared at the doomed seeds. 'I've thrown in the towel, Neil. I'm going to give her back at the puppy meeting tonight.' I pushed the knife through the tomato, a clean slice falling away from the blade.

Heloise was whining from the back of my wagon, locked securely in her crate, even though it was only a short drive to the puppy meeting. We'd crash for sure if she was leaping around inside the car. Wouldn't that be just like me, a puppy causing me to have a car accident on my way to give up the puppy?

When I'd left the house, my family eating dinner, Neil's forehead vein was still bulging, and he was stabbing the lettuce in his bowl as though *it* had chewed the cabinets. Standing in the kitchen, holding Heloise in her crate, I'd offered the kids a chance to say good-bye to her. Neil looked up, gave me a false smile, then continued to jab at his greens. Lainey uttered a monotone 'Bye' from the dinner table. Matt got up, came into the kitchen, stuck his finger through her crate and let her gently mouth it. I said nothing. 'Good luck, girl,' he offered softly, then returned to the table without so much as a glance at me.

I'd wanted some separation from my family, but what I had now was alienation. And I didn't blame them at all. I'd vastly underestimated what I was getting into.

As I pulled up to a red light, Heloise still whining behind me, I rehearsed aloud what I was going to say to Bill. 'I'm sorry, Bill. You were right. I'm just not the right person for this. I barely survived a night and a day with her.' At the sound of my voice, Heloise quieted. Our eyes met in the rearview mirror, her little head framed in the crate door, just visible over the seat.

Blinking tears away, I lifted the turn indicator as we approached the building. The meetings were held in a warehouse building in an industrial zone, donated by a local businessman. I'd been to several meetings here before I'd gotten Heloise, listened as they'd discussed problems they were having, watched as they negotiated obstacle courses. But they'd all had mostly grown dogs. They'd somehow all survived the puppy stage. But it was more than I could do. Now my first meeting with my puppy would also be my last. As I parked the car, Heloise began to bark again.

I snapped on her leash and set her on the ground.

She immediately started pulling toward the building. For her size, she was strong. I barely got the wagon door slammed shut before she dragged me off. As she pulled me through the door of the building, her little toenails scrabbling on the concrete floor, I saw that we were among the first to arrive. A circle of folding chairs was in the center of the otherwise empty room. An attractive silver-haired woman, a bit older than me, holding the leash of a sleek red golden retriever, stood in the middle of the circle talking to a young couple with a huge black Lab. I took a seat near the door, Heloise in my lap, waiting for Bill.

As people and dogs filed in, I marveled at what a mixed group this was. There were two sets of parents and teens, close in age to my own. There were several men and women even older than I, and two young couples. There were two other new pups around Heloise's age, several fully grown dogs, and several others somewhere in between. Most were yellow and black Labs, with just two golden retrievers and one German shepherd pup. Judging from the ears, it had to be Donald.

Bill still hadn't arrived. I checked my watch. Seven ten. In order to avoid a scene, I realized I'd have to go through the meeting, then wait, in order to catch a moment alone with Bill, to – resign. I hated even thinking the word. This wasn't even a real job, and I didn't last two days.

Bill walked in finally, apologizing for being late. All eyes, canine and human, were on him as he smiled and nodded to every person, shaking a hand here, giving a hug there. Oddly, he seemed to be ignoring the dogs.

The man got more handsome every time I saw him. He was wearing a crisp salmon-colored shirt, new jeans, and, the pièce de résistance, cowboy boots. When he ran his fingers through his salt-and-pepper hair, I nearly swooned. When he hugged the woman with the golden retriever, I wondered what a Bill hug would feel like. Stronger than a Neil hug, no doubt. Suddenly he was looking at me. He was walking toward me! I was pretty sure my shirt was flapping from my banging heart.

I didn't get a hug. I was too new, of course. He didn't shake my hand either. But as he passed, he gave me a nod, a killer smile, and a wink as he strode to an empty chair. Just before he sat down he reached over and hugged the woman with the German shepherd pup. But I felt his arms around me.

'How's it going?' A woman taking the chair next to me broke my reverie. My absurd reverie. What was going on with me? I was here to resign, leave this man with a huge burden of where to place this puppy, disappoint him in every way, and I was swooning over him like a teenager. And, I was married. Married.

'Uh, well, not great, actually,' I said. It was the silver-haired woman with the golden retriever. My head down, I stared at Heloise. Suddenly the woman was patting my knee.

'No, it's never great the first few days of your first one,' she said. She had kindly soft blue eyes. 'Too much to learn, too fast. But it gets better. I promise.' She extended her hand toward me. I reached my hand to her and she firmly shook it. 'I'm Marilyn Grigsby,' she said. 'This is Salsa.' She tipped her head toward the golden lying quietly at her feet. I was pretty sure Marilyn was older than me, maybe by as much as a decade, but it was hard to tell because she looked so happy, relaxed, and healthy. She wore a teal-and-yellow plaid button-down flannel shirt with the sleeves rolled up to the elbows. Her tanned wrists were small, but her forearms looked remarkably strong. 'Are you using the kennel?' she asked, smiling.

I assumed that meant the crate, and my deer-in-the-headlights look gave her the answer. I was saved from having to explain by Bill. He clapped his hands twice and the room immediately quieted, and he again had everyone's full attention.

'Okay, sorry I'm late, gang. Let's get started. We've got two people here tonight with their first puppies, so I'm going to start with the Golden Rule of puppy raising.' The young couple across from me, with the black Lab puppy, a little smaller than Heloise, wore the same uneasy smile I did.

Bill held up his index finger. 'Number one: To succeed at this, you've got to stop thinking like a person and start thinking like a dog. Specifically, a pack leader.' He went on to talk about setting

129

boundaries, expecting and enforcing good behavior, and being a confident leader. '*Expect* the behavior you want. You have to know what you want, and you have to communicate it clearly and consistently. If they sense you're weak, unconfident, indecisive, you'll have a tough time. Always be gentle and loving, but at the same time strong and consistent, and they'll understand what's expected. That's what makes them feel secure. Then they trust you and listen to you.' He paused rather dramatically. 'Usually.' Everyone laughed. Bill also went into great detail about how important it was to use the crate – kennel – in all this. Never as punishment, but as a way to shrink their environment to limit choices, and therefore lower their stress. That had never occurred to me, that it would lower *her* stress.

'Okay. Wake the pups up,' said Bill, clapping his hands again. 'We're going to pass 'em.' While I'd been giving Bill my rapt attention, Heloise had fallen asleep over my foot. One of the other puppies was also snoozing away. I gently slid my hands under Heloise and brought her to my face, hugging and kissing her awake. She stared at me with sleepy eyes.

Puppy passing turned out to be just that. Everyone stood up, and at Bill's command we passed our pups carefully to the person on our left. Some of the bigger dogs simply walked from one person to the next; the younger ones were gathered up in loving arms. Each dog seemed to regard me with careful interest. I was sure they knew I was new. Untested. But I did as the others did, and confidently greeted each dog, patting their sides firmly, speaking with energy in my voice. But with each pass, I kept my eye on Heloise traveling around the circle, limp and staring warily into the eyes of each new person. When she finally came back into my arms, her little tail thumped against me and she eagerly licked my chin.

She knew me! After a mere two days, she knew I was her mom!

'Deena, why don't you take Heloise out,' said Bill. 'Corrine, too. I think they might have to pee.'

What, did he have a direct connection to their bladders?! How did he know that? But I obediently stood, fastening on her leash again. The other couple headed out ahead of me, little Corrine in their arms. 'Go ahead and carry her, Deena. She won't pee in your arms, but she probably will pee on the floor, and we want her to wait till she's outside. A hundred times more effective to praise the behavior we want than correcting the behavior we don't want.'

I carried her outside. She sniffed the cold grass briefly, then lowered her belly, happily relieving herself.

'Do your business! Do your business!' I chirped. Then, 'Good girl! Good girl, Heloise! Good girl!' I laughed when I heard Corrine's people giving her the same chants in another part of the dark yard. Amazing. How did Bill know?

When we came back inside, he was talking to the group, so I picked Heloise up again and we quietly took our seat.

'I want you all to say good-bye and good luck to Redondo sometime tonight,' said Bill, his voice suddenly somber, pointing to the young couple with the huge black Lab. 'He's been recalled and leaves for guide school before our next meeting.' A gasp went up from part of the group. Bill held up his hand, nodding his head. 'I know. It's sudden. As most of you know, the recalled dogs usually go back on the puppy trucks when a new batch arrives, and we typically will get a couple of months' notice for that. But sometimes national has a slot open up unexpectedly, or they need extra time to evaluate a dog with special circumstances. This time it's a slot open. Josie's flying in to Denver with a BSD next week. She needs to take back the oldest and/or the best trained to fill the slot at guide school. Of course, our star right now is Redondo.' He looked straight at the couple, his eyes soft, his smile genuine. 'Kent and Isabelle have done a fantastic job with the big guy. They're to be congratulated.' They looked more like they needed to be consoled. Like they wished they hadn't done such a good job. They clutched each other's hand and kept their eyes and other hands on their big dog. Several people walked over to pet Redondo and say a few words to Kent and Isabelle.

I leaned toward Marilyn. 'What's a BSD?'

'That's our group's tongue-in-cheek name for dogs that aren't going to become working guides. Officially, they're TIPs, for Transitioning Into Pet, but we affectionately call them Beauty School Dropouts, or BSDs.' I laughed as Bill clapped his hands again.

The meeting then turned into a question-and-answer period, with every single question providing an answer I needed.

With commands, less is more. Get their attention by calling their name, then tell them once *what you want. Let them have a chance to get it right the first time. Expect obedience and you usually get it. With the little ones, use the crate, which most people called a kennel; let her know it's her safe place. When she's out of the kennel, have her out for a reason: a meal, a potty break, supervised play time or, most important, Bill said, a walk. Give them lots of exercise, get them used to walking on a leash right away.*

Walks. I hadn't taken Heloise on a single walk yet. Bill even suggested using a baby carrier with the small puppies, for breaks on longer walks. I still had my Snugli! I looked at Corrine's people – also new – curious if they were as enthralled by this information as I was. The young woman was furiously scribbling notes in a spiral notebook. I quickly dug through my purse and found a pack of sticky notes, bright pink, heart-shaped stickies that Lainey had wanted but then never used. I too began furiously writing as Bill talked.

Housebreaking, I wrote. Then underneath:

- *Out after every meal, again 15 minutes later.*
- always *after waking*. So that's why he'd sent us outside earlier.
- *watch their water intake*

Suddenly I felt flushed again. But this was no hot flash. I was giddy with excitement as my pen ran across heart after heart. I felt like a college student taking notes on the first day of class, in the course she most wanted to take. Bill continued itemizing reminders on his fingers and I kept jotting. Signs they need to go out, like sniffing the floor, or suddenly stopping what they're doing. Of course! Heloise had done all these things. I just didn't know her language.

After Bill was done with his lesson for the evening, some people left, but several of us lingered, chatting. Included in the remaining group were Marilyn and Bill, an older man named Hank who was raising his tenth puppy, and the new couple, whose names were Heidi and Alan. Hank had us all laughing, telling us about one of his pups that, unbeknownst to him, had slipped out of its collar at the movie theater and had licked its way four rows down the tacky-sweet aisle before Hank realized she was gone. Marilyn told how Salsa had an affinity for a certain pair of Marilyn's shoes; she didn't chew them, just hid them. A guy named Jeff told us about trying to quiet his squirmy

134

black Lab at a restaurant one day by yawning suggestively at it, and that – amazingly! – it had worked. The pup 'caught' the yawn and soon settled down. Emboldened, I described the chase between Hairy and Heloise, an event that mere hours ago had nearly had me in tears. Now we were all teary from laughing. Everyone shared a story or two. It was like war stories between parents about their kids. There was a camaraderie here that I hadn't felt in a long time. Sharing it somehow transformed it from things going wrong to just part of the process, the journey. Most of the dogs slept through the entire conversation.

When I checked my watch and saw it was after nine, I reluctantly excused myself, thanking everyone for their support. I didn't even want to think about Neil's reaction when I came back with Heloise. Because, I was. Coming back with Heloise. I realized I'd decided it way back at the puppy passing, when she'd clearly recognized me. But now I also felt empowered by solid, practical information.

Marilyn was scribbling something on a slip of paper as I put on my coat and gathered Heloise up in my arms. She tucked it in my coat pocket. 'Here's my number. Call if you need anything, have any questions, just want to cry . . . .' She grinned. 'We're all here to help each other. And use that kennel, Deena!' I nodded sheepishly.

Driving away from the meeting, Heloise sleeping soundly in her kennel in the back, I was inspired, full of resolve. Hopeful, even. Here was the support I needed. I could do this!

When I walked in the kitchen door, the bold, euphoric 'I can do this!' had changed to a timid little-engine-that-could chant. *You can do this, you can do this* . . . I set the kennel on the kitchen floor, careful not to wake Heloise. I could hear the TV in the den. Den. The rest of the pack was in the den. I headed down.

'Hi,' I said from the doorway. Neil and Lainey sat on opposite ends of the couch; Matt was sprawled on the floor. Lainey neither looked up nor spoke. Matt raised his arm from the floor but kept his eyes on the television. Neil actually stood up, arms extended. 'Come here, baby. You did the right thing. I know it must be hard for you, but you did the right thing. Come here.' He took a step toward me, arms still extended.

I squared my shoulders, staying where I was. 'Yes, Neil. I think I did do the right thing. I brought Heloise back home with me.' I almost went on, but literally bit my tongue to stop there. If I said more, I'd start making excuses, or worse, backpedaling.

Neil looked like he'd been punched in the stomach, his arms suddenly caving at the elbows, his mouth opening.

I couldn't help myself then. 'The meeting was so helpful!' I blurted out. 'I was doing so many things wrong, Neil. But now I know what to do! I—' He ran his fingers through his thinning hair, exhaling sharply. He cocked his head to one side. That particular pose looked much cuter when Heloise did it.

I sucked in a quick breath. 'So, this is what I'm going to do. Uh, what I'm going to do tonight. Since Heloise is already tired, I'm going to take her outside, and then we're going to bed, because we're tired, and we didn't get much sleep last night because—' *Babbling! I don't think pack leaders babble.* 'Anyway, I want to get her out for a walk first thing tomorrow morning. So.' *So what?* 'Good night,' I chirped. I looked past Neil for the first time and saw both kids staring gape-mouthed at us, looking to Neil then to me, back again to Neil.

Less is more. Short and sweet. 'Good night, kids.' I blew them a kiss and turned. Forced my feet forward, with each step hyperconscious that I was walking away from my family, and toward my Heloise.

The next morning I awoke to Heloise's soft crying from her kennel under Sam's desk. I grabbed the clock. Six ten! She'd only cried twice last night. Each time I'd confidently told her she was okay, forced myself to relax on the bed, wait at least thirty seconds. The first time she'd kept crying, so I'd taken her outside, in my arms, all the way till we hit grass, and she'd promptly done her business. The second time, she went back to sleep before the thirty seconds was over. And she'd made it all the way to six a.m.! And in Sam's small twin bed, I'd actually slept pretty well.

I pulled her from the kennel and carried her down the stairs in my arms, a warm, happy ball. I whispered to her what a great girl she was, as she worked her little tongue over my neck. I couldn't get enough of her breath. I didn't know what it was, but I knew it had a real, physiological effect on me. It filled me with a sense of newness and possibility. I laughed quietly, thinking what might happen if old married couples could wake up to the sweet smell of puppy breath from each other. There might be a little more interest as the years wore on.

We stepped out into the spring morning and I set Heloise in the grass, still wet with dew, the sun creating tiny rainbow worlds clinging to nearly every blade. She did the deed and I bent, praising her.

I stood with her in one arm and rubbed my swollen eyes with the other. I had stayed awake till after midnight reading the manual. I was especially intrigued by a section on the propensity of puppies, Labs especially, to eat so fast that they throw up. One suggestion to solve this problem had made me laugh out loud. I couldn't wait to try it.

Inside, I put Heloise in her kennel, and poured myself a cup of coffee. I then prepared her breakfast. In my bundt cake pan. I couldn't help chuckling as I added warm water to the kibble in the heavy, cast-iron bundt that my grandmother and mother had both used, for a variety of cakes and even Jell-O molds. But I was pretty sure this was its first foray into dog dining.

I drank restorative sips of coffee while Heloise whined from her kennel. 'You're okay, girl!' I told her in a confident voice. She quieted. When the kibble was soft, I let her out. She began leaping and barking, driven by the primal scent of kibble. But between the manual and the puppy meeting the night before, I was armed with knowledge. *Make sure you have their attention before you give a command.* 'Heloise. Sit.' I said firmly. I had to help her at first, but she quickly got it. Then I went through the steps Bill had shown us, lowering the bowl to the floor, but raising it quickly each time she came out of her sit. After just five or six tries she understood that she had to sit calmly and wait for my command before she got to eat. It was like magic! And because she had to eat around the center column in the bundt pan, she was slowed considerably from her usual NASCAR style of eating.

Watching her eat, I remembered more of the manual. *Many dogs are stimulated to defecate after eating a meal.* She'd pooped in our closet right after breakfast! I felt like a detective! When she was finished eating, I scooped her up and headed outside. I stood in one spot, letting her sniff around me on the leash. *Keep your pup in a tight perimeter around you. Once he's smelled a complete circle, he'll usually do his business.* Sure enough, as soon as Heloise had sniffed all the way around me once or twice, she pooped. You'd think she'd just laid the golden egg. In various ways I told her that I thought she was a veritable poop artist, lavishing praise on her. I cleaned her deposit from the yard and we headed inside. I was shaking my head, marveling at how a little information and technique made all the difference.

I put her back in her kennel, telling her, 'We'll walk soon, girl. I just have to make the breakfasts and lunches.' She sat in her kennel, whining. In a firm voice I said, 'Heloise. You're fine. Wait.' I then set about my sandwich assembly line, singing softly. When I stole a quick glance, she was sitting, listening, her little head twisting side to side, irresistibly cute. I could hardly wait to take her out into the world.

Today the kids and Neil would get peanut butter and jelly sandwiches. Nice and quick. I slapped those together in record time, added chips, fruit, and a cookie to their bags, then set upon breakfast. I pulled the carton of eggs from their compartment in the door of the refrigerator, grabbed the bacon from the meat drawer, then stopped, door open, package in hand. No. No time for bacon today. Or eggs. I shoved them both back in the refrigerator.

I set out cereal, bowls and spoons, arranging them on the counter, and scrawled a quick note on the desk pad:

H. and I gone for walk. xo Mom.

I let Heloise out of the kennel and hooked on her leash, but then remembered something and carried her in my arms down to the basement. I pulled on the string in the storage room, both our eyes blinking as the bright bare bulb clicked on. I scanned the walls, stroking Heloise's soft head. There was the Snugli, in the back, in the shadow of the furnace. A little faded after all these years, the yellow not quite so sunny, the small blue flowers now faded, the padded shoulder straps compressed from the weight of three babies. But as I lifted it down from the hook and into the light, it seemed to brighten at the prospect of carrying just one more.

CHAPTER 11

'Come on, girl! Come!'
Heloise was backing her way up the
driveway, not at all keen on the idea of
the leash. We'd been at this for a good five minutes
already. I again tugged gently on the black nylon
leash. She would eventually graduate to a handsome leather leash, but it was too heavy for her
now. But Heloise didn't like being told which way
to go, regardless of the leash type. She planted
her bottom firmly on the driveway, front legs stiff.

I was wearing the Snugli on my chest and knew
I could just plop her into it and carry her on our
walk. But it seemed to me that, in order to count
as exercise, she really ought to take more than five
steps, in reverse, up the driveway.

I squatted at the end of the leash and called her
again, patting my knee. She ran to me, jumping
up as I stood. 'Good girl! Let's go!' I stepped
forward, the slightest pull on the leash, and she
again stiff-legged me, trying to pull her little head
out of her collar.

Okay. Time to act like a pack leader. A mother
wolf would pick up her pup by the scruff of the

neck, in her teeth. I was committed to this, but not that committed.

'Okay, Heloise. We're leaving now.' I picked her up, carrying her on my hip with my arm under her belly. She drooped like a small bag of potatoes, but I was not going to reward her behavior with proximity to my heart or face. I would carry her across the street, but she would have to walk at least a little bit before she rode in the Snugli.

I set her on the sidewalk, and tried again. She spotted a stick and charged, pouncing on it as if it were live prey. I pulled the stick from her mouth and encouraged her on. She looked at me, took a couple of steps, then spotted a cigarette butt and got to it before I could stop her. I fished that from her mouth, too. 'Gross, Heloise!' I pulled on the leash again, but she stubbornly sat, stiff and resolute. I waited a few seconds, then urged her on again. 'Heloise! Let's go!' I put one foot in front of me, pumping up and down on it. She stared at me, her bottom still planted on the sidewalk. I made a mental note to look in the manual for a chapter called How to Walk a Dog Who Doesn't Want to Be Walked.

Frustrated, I blew the bangs off my forehead. Heloise looked up at me, her brown eyes sparkling. I stepped behind her again, to the full extent of the leash. I made a running start, exaggerating my movements but making my steps miniscule. 'Heloise! Let's go!' I sang to her. As I came up beside her, she grabbed the leash in her mouth

143

and began running with it. It was forward progress, anyway. She ran excitedly for about a dozen steps, then dropped the leash to bite a dandelion. I pulled it from her mouth, a yellow smudge remaining on her lip and nose. She dashed forward and pounced again, this time on a pebble, gobbling that up, too. I reached in her mouth, moving my finger all around her sharp teeth, but couldn't find it. Was there anything this dog wouldn't eat? I removed my finger and picked her up, holding her eye to eye, her little body hanging in front of me.

'Listen, little girl. You shouldn't eat rocks. Didn't your mother tell you that?' She pricked her ears, then lurched forward and nipped at my nose, her tail wagging playfully.

'Ow! Okay, that's it! *I* need a walk, even if you don't.' I eased her into the Snugli, threading her tail out one of the leg holes. In this way, 'we' walked around the block.

Heloise enjoyed the ride. I enjoyed the walk in the early morning quiet, broken only by the outbursts from birds, happy to be back from their winter sojourns. I was thrilled to have them back, to have spring really on the way. I loved seeing what was poking up in people's gardens, bursting forth on the trees. I deeply inhaled all the subtle scents, cool and subdued at the beginning of our walk, still just whispered promises, not fully released from the night's chill. As the sun climbed into the china-blue sky, the blossoms warmed, releasing their varied fragrances, a celebration of their short existences. The neighborhood became a perfumery.

I knew that in Colorado, Mother Nature usually had her fingers crossed behind her back even into early summer, ready to hurl a snowstorm or two at any time. But for today, the sun was warm, the air soft, the world new. I felt like unzipping my skin and stepping out.

As we came back around to our street, I saw Amy Kellerman in her driveway, bent over, picking up her newspaper with one hand, holding her red-and-gold satin robe closed with the other. Melba was tied to the tree.

'Good morning,' I said.

Still bent over, she looked up. Her face was start-lingly pale, her eyes still puffy. I didn't know if I'd *ever* seen Amy without a significant amount of makeup – full foundation, huge spidery eyelashes, big red, outlined lips. Amy was a flight attendant, her husband, now ex, a pilot. Neighborhood scuttle was that it was the tawdry worst: he'd left her for a much younger flight attendant.

'Uh, good morning,' she said, pulling her robe tie tight, furtively smoothing a hand over her tousled hair. I didn't know what color her hair might have been originally. It had certainly changed many times over the years. Currently, it was an overprocessed blonde.

Amy and I weren't close. In fact, I think she held me in a kind of contempt for staying home full-time. And I often resented her, mostly for her

145

frequent, sometimes last-minute phone calls, often from Chicago or New York or L.A., asking me to 'carpool with the girls,' which meant 'drive my daughters with your kids' to and from school, soccer practices, games, and so on, which I always did, for Sara's and Nan's sakes. I only rarely admitted to myself that I also envied her, traveling as she did, seeing the world, having an income, some independence. But there was that airplane thing that she did that I could never do. Plus, I acknowledged that just by having an outside job she, along with all the other women out there, was helping ensure choices for my daughter and all daughters. She'd made her choice, I'd made mine.

But I knew Amy didn't think my choice involved doing much of value, even though what I did, she and Marty had hired someone else to do. Actually several someones. Housecleaning, grocery shopping, meal preparation, lawn care, landscaping were all done by others. Not to mention the nannies. Over the years Amy had mentioned more than once that she'd go 'stir crazy' if she had to stay home full-time with her girls, 'like you, Deena.' She always said it in a pseudo-admiring way, but I could hear the disdain and even pity in her voice. Worse, nearly every time I saw her she'd work in some mention of what she thought I 'should be.'

'You should be an interior designer,' she'd said when she saw our new couch being delivered. 'You should go into catering,' she'd told me when I brought homemade chicken soup over when they'd all been laid low by the flu. 'You should be a nurse,' she'd offered when I'd cleaned up Sara's knee when she was seven and crashed her bike in front of our house. Amy was always pleasant, but it was clear with all these 'you should bes' that she didn't think I *was* anything now.

But it had never been an option for me to delegate care of my kids to someone else. And virtually all the things she suggested for me, I already was doing. For my family, and often for others', especially hers. I just didn't get paid for it. And both Neil and I had always seen value in what I did, felt that what we both wanted was a strong connection to each other, our family, and our community. And having one person at home full-time was the best way to foster that, to give us the quality of life we both wanted. And it had been good. Very good. Till recently. Until I'd seen my forced retirement on the horizon and had no clue how to transition. Or what to transition to.

Neil had always tried to acknowledge my work, but I'd often wondered if he really *knew*. He'd sometimes make a rather belabored point to tell me that my job was the most important job in the world, but I think he was parroting what he'd read in my women's magazines. More than once I'd found my O, *Women's Day*, *LHJ*, or others, in our bathroom, not where I'd left them. The fact that he pilfered my magazines, like so many things

147

about Neil that used to charm or amuse me, now just annoyed me.

As I continued to walk up the sidewalk toward Amy, she turned to go inside, but stopped suddenly, doing a quick double-take. I couldn't help but smile at the fleeting – *another baby at her age?!* – look that flew across her face as she stared at the Snugli. She momentarily forgot about her appearance, furrowing her thin eyebrows at the bulging mound on my chest. Heloise had fallen asleep, a little slumped ball inside, only her tail protruding from a leg hole.

I was sorely tempted to pretend it was another baby, but I saw Amy's eyes focusing on the tail.

'What in the world do you have in there, Deena?' she said, a tiny smile trying to force its way onto her pursed lips.

'A baby. With a tail,' I said, smiling at her. 'This is Heloise. I'm a volunteer puppy raiser for K-9 Eyes for the Blind.' That felt so good to say! My dog-filled Snugli puffed out a bit more with my pride.

'*You're* raising *a seeing eye dog*?' The incredulity in her voice rankled me. She'd put equal emphasis on both parts of her question, so it was hard to tell if she thought it more incredible that *I* was doing something – anything – or this particular thing, raising a guide dog puppy.

'Yes,' I said simply. I was beginning to find a whole new appreciation for brevity.

'Can I see it?' She was holding her newspaper to her chest, arms crossed over it.

148

'Sure. But she's asleep at the moment. You know what they say about letting sleeping dogs lie.'

She looked up at me with a half smile, then took two careful steps, leaned far forward, and peered into the Snugli. Heloise had her head tucked over her shoulder, sleeping like a bird, only minus the wing over her nose. In fact, she was snoring noisily, not unlike I remembered Big Bird doing on *Sesame Street*.

Amy's face softened, and I was fascinated watching her watch this pup. She seemed almost transformed, as if her troubles lifted, a dark mass still hovering nearby, but for the moment, some great weight was off her shoulders.

Then she looked at me again, her unbreakable face back on. 'You sure you know what you're getting into?'

A rush of hurt, anger. Then Heloise repositioned herself in the Snugli, snorting lightly. I looked at Amy and shrugged, smiling. 'Do we ever?'

Over the next several weeks, Heloise and I practiced everything from meal preparation behavior, to waiting for an 'okay' before going either through a doorway or jumping in or out of the car, to going into her kennel on command. She was also getting pretty good at 'Sit,' 'Stay,' and 'Come.' But the training broke down dismally in my driveway. Heloise nearly always refused to walk down it, as if she didn't want to go for a walk. But once I carried her across the street, she was euphoric about setting off, often pulling at the leash, eager for any new adventure. When I'd brought her driveway behavior up at a puppy meeting, Bill said every dog has his or her own quirks and odd behaviors, I just had to keep working at it, check the manual for suggestions, and 'get creative.' From the way he smiled at me I knew he wanted me to solve this one on my own. But I didn't, exactly. It was the middle of May when we had our major breakthrough, with help from unexpected sources.

On a lovely spring afternoon, Heloise and I were inside, preparing for our second walk of the day. Well, Heloise was chewing on her blue bone. I was reading the manual, trying to find solutions to the driveway dilemma. I was sitting at the kitchen desk chair, the open manual on my lap. The chapter on 'Walking On Leash' was only marginally helpful. *At first,* it said, *let the puppy lead you, but don't let him pull.* That was followed by eight bulleted suggestions about how to keep your puppy from pulling. But Heloise had shown no interest in leading, much less pulling. At least not in the driveway. There, all she was interested in was sitting. I scanned down to the next section. It built on the first section, discussing only how to get the puppy who now likes to lead to begin to follow. I looked in the index for 'Sitting' but found only instructions on how to teach your puppy to sit. There was no listing for 'Stubborn.'

I looked at Heloise, standing by her kennel, having a staring contest with her blue bone on the tile floor prior to pouncing on it. She was getting bigger, but not much less silly.

'Heloise?' She looked at me, as though she'd forgotten I was in the room. 'Have you even *read* this, girl?' I asked her, my index finger tapping the manual. She wagged her tail. 'According to the manual, when we go for walks, you're supposed to want to *lead*. You're not supposed to want to stay in the driveway and sit.' She sat, making me laugh. 'Good girl!' I told her.

I kept reading and finally found some possibly helpful advice, but I was dubious. *To encourage your puppy to follow you, get low, so your face is near his face, and use it to draw his attention toward you. Be verbally encouraging at the same time.* 'So, I'm supposed to use my face as *bait*?' I asked out loud. Heloise had pounced on her bone and had it in her mouth as she heard my voice. She turned to look at me again. I read on, now aloud to Heloise, just so she'd know that what I was about to try was officially sanctioned behavior. *'The following actions may also serve to encourage your puppy to follow you: happy clapping, body movements such as crawling, wiggling, jumping, skipping, patting the ground in front of the puppy, et cetera. Always keep the exercise fun for the puppy.'* Right. I was to keep all that crawling, wiggling, and skipping around on my driveway fun for Heloise. Gamely, I grabbed Heloise and her leash, and headed outside.

I could only hope that, midafternoon on a weekday, no one in the neighborhood was home, or at least not looking out their windows. She leapt off the front step, walked slowly to the top of the driveway, and sat. I urged in a high, squeaky voice, 'Come, Heloise! Let's go!' I half bent, half squatted in front of her, patting the concrete. It was pleasantly warm from the sunny day, not hot, so she didn't have that excuse. I patted the driveway again, giving the slightest little tug on the leash. She stood, pulling backward. I sighed, stepped toward her and carefully lowered myself to my knees. I put my face near hers. She stopped backing and her ears went up. 'Hi, baby! Let's go!' I pulled my smiling face slightly away from her. She cocked her head, but her ears went down. I brought my face close again. Her ears perked up again. I pulled away. Suddenly she lunged, snapping playfully at my face, one small sharp tooth catching my cheek.

'Ouch!' I sat back on my heels, rubbing my cheek with my free hand. Heloise was still standing, ears up, wagging her tail a mile a minute. Well, I was succeeding marvelously at one part of the instructions: clearly I was keeping this exercise fun for my puppy.

I got on my hands and knees again, put the end of the leash in my mouth and began crawling down the driveway. 'Ere, Eh-oh-wee!' I called back to her through a mouthful of leash, trying to maintain eye contact with her by looking back over my shoulder. She was following! I crawled faster. 'Ere, Eh-oh-wee!' I called, looking at her excitedly.

'Uh, *Mom?*'

I froze. Slowly I brought my head forward, already feeling the heat in my face. There, at the end of the driveway, were Lainey and Matt, each with their backpack over one shoulder. Was it three thirty already? My cheeks prickled with embarrassment.

'What in the world are you doing?' Lainey asked, her hands on her hips. But both kids were smiling.

'I'm using my face as bait.'

Matt cracked up. Lainey smiled, then asked, *'What?!'*

They walked up the driveway, toward us, as I explained. 'For some reason, she refuses to walk down the driveway.'

I sat back on my heels as Heloise jumped up to greet the kids. She was usually in her kennel when they deigned to come home right after school, so they typically ignored her. Now, both kids reached down to greet her.

'Wait a minute, kids. Let me have her sit before you pet her. And if she pops up, stop petting her right away, okay?' They nodded. To my surprise, both looked pleased to be a part of her official training.

I stood, faced her. 'Heloise?' I said. She looked at me, pure focus. 'Sit.' She obeyed immediately.

'Wow!' said Lainey, and both kids bent to pet her. My breath quickened with pride. But Heloise popped up. Immediately Matt and Lainey stood upright, like soldiers, smiling, pulling their hands out of her reach.

'Uh-uh,' I told Heloise, giving a little upward tug on her leash. I had her sit again, then told my kids: 'That was perfect, you guys! Let's try it again.' Now the pride was theirs. It was catching! We repeated the exercise, and after just three more tries, Heloise understood that she was only going to get attention from them if she stayed seated.

'Wow,' said Matt. 'She's a smart little thing.'

'Good girl, Heloise,' said Lainey, scratching her behind one ear.

'Thanks, guys. That was great! Would you help me with something else?' They both looked at me suspiciously. I laughed. 'I'm determined to get her to walk down the driveway.'

'Do we have to use our face as bait?' asked Lainey, her expression pained.

'No.' I laughed. 'But she really liked that attention from you guys, so why don't you both go to the end of the driveway and call her.'

'Sure.' They both flung their backpacks on the lawn and jogged down the driveway. When I nodded, they enthusiastically called her, patting their legs. Heloise put her ears up, took a step forward, then started backing up, pulling so hard I thought she was going to pull her little head right out of her collar.

'Why don't we use some food,' said Matt. 'I could go get those turkey pepperoni slices we have in the fridge. Or some cheese! We have popcorn in the pantry! Oh! How 'bout some beef jerky?' Leave it to Matt to have full inventory of our family foodstuffs.

'Nope. Not allowed. We can't use food to train her. It makes her do things for the food, instead of learning to trust and obey us.'

Matt shrugged. 'Whatta we do then?'

'Well, I'm not sure,' I said, looking at Heloise. 'I've really tried everything.' *Think like a dog.* I looked at Matt and Lainey, waiting at the end of the driveway. They were both looking at me with the same focus as Heloise. *Pack.* 'Okay!' I told them. 'Here's what we'll do. I think she was about to follow me when you guys walked up. So maybe if we all crawl down the driveway, she'll follow. We'll be like her pack, and she'll want to be part of the pack.' I got down on my hands and knees again, put the leash back in my mouth, gave a little tug on it by jutting my jaw, and called her.

'Ere, Eh-oh-wheeze!' She sat. Matt laughed, but walked up the driveway and got down on his hands and knees next to me.

'Oh, what the heck,' said Lainey, joining us.

We all looked at Heloise, then began crawling down the driveway, calling excitedly.

She cocked her head, then, with ears up, tail wagging, she took a tentative step. Then another. It was working! 'Guh girrr!' I said through the now-slobbery leash. Hand, knee, hand, knee, we all crawled, calling, the kids getting more and more excited as Heloise slowly followed. I could feel pebbles digging into my palms, and I knew I was getting the knees of my jeans dirty. But Heloise was walking down the driveway! 'Fhahstah!' I said, and we all crawled faster. Sensing we were nearing the end of the driveway, I turned my head forward, and stopped. Directly in front of me, on the ground, was a large pair of sensible black walking shoes. Slowly I tracked upward: navy blue ankle socks, hairy white legs, followed by those distinctive chambray shorts with the black stripes down the sides, big bag on hip. Walter. Our mailman.

''Lo there, Ms Munger, kids,' he said jovially, staring down at me. I could feel my face going four shades of red. Lainey stood up suddenly, looking like she was about to start crying, and bolted into the house, leaving her backpack on the lawn. Matt looked from me to Walter, then at his own backpack. Heloise immediately headed for Walter, jumping up on his bare legs.

'Uh-uh, Heloise!' I told her, pulling her back with the leash, now in my hand. I pushed myself up off the ground. Standing, I brushed the hair out of my red face with my fingers. Walter held out our bundle of mail. I took it from him with as much grace as I could muster.

'Thanks, Walter. I, uh—' I gestured to Heloise. 'She doesn't like to go down the driveway, so we, uh—'

'No need to explain, Ms Munger,' said Walter, laughing and scratching Heloise behind the ear. 'I've raised several dogs myself. They call it dog

156

training, but that's just short for dog is training its person!'

I nodded, laughing in agreement, as perspiration began streaming down under my shirt. It was happening again. With my sleeve, I wiped the little rivers running down my face, hoping Walter wouldn't think I was having a heart attack or something. 'I was desperate,' I said energetically, to demonstrate my good health. Relatively speaking. 'I don't know what it is about walking down the driveway. Anyway, I'm raising her for K-9 Eyes for the Blind. She's a guide dog in training.' I fanned myself with the mail in my hand.

'You don't say?! That'll be tough to give her up, I bet.' I nodded. 'Well, that's fantastic that you're doing this, Ms M! Good for you!' Matt smiled, still sitting in the driveway, now idly scratching Heloise, who'd decided someone at her level was her best bet. Both of them were looking back and forth between me and Walter. 'Say, I have an idea,' said Walter. 'Why don't we see if she'll follow *me*?' He playfully raised and lowered his eyebrows. 'You know how dogs love mailmen!'

I shrugged, laughing. 'Sure. Lord knows I don't want to have to crawl down the driveway with her every time. We'll try anything, right, Matt?' I said, wanting to include him.

Matt rose. 'Sure. Except food. Because that makes her trust food, and not us,' he told Walter with authority. He didn't quite get it right, but

I wanted to hug him just the same. Instead, I handed him her leash and we walked Heloise back up the driveway. Walter followed. I was a little worried about Lainey. I wondered if she had recovered from her embarrassment, or if she was buried, crying, under the comforter on her bed. I glanced toward the house. To my surprise, she was at the window, drinking a soda, watching. She waved. I waved back.

At the top of the driveway, Walter lifted his mail bag off his shoulder and set it gently on the ground. 'Oooh! Lookie heeere, pup!' he said, as if he was revealing a pound of sirloin to her. 'Here's the delicious *mail*! Come on—' He looked at me. 'What's her name?'

'Heloise,' I replied. His eyes widened.

'She came with the name,' I said, smiling and shrugging.

Walter gave a little laugh, turning toward Heloise. 'Heloise it is then! Come and get it, Heloise!' Bent over and beckoning, Walter dragged his mailbag lightly behind him as he walked down the driveway. Heloise leapt and dashed behind, barking delight-edly at the bag, all the way down the driveway, with Matt and me – now upright – on either side and just behind. Matt still held her leash. 'Keep a light touch on it, hon,' I said. 'We don't want her to feel any pull on it, or it'll inadvertently give her a mixed signal.' He lowered his hand, keeping the leash slack. At the end of the driveway, Walter turned and headed down the sidewalk, still dragging his mailbag, Heloise trotting after it. Matt started giving color commentary, as if it was a horse race: 'And she's *off*! Heloise is out of the driveway, in great form. Her training has paid off, folks!'

We continued our little processional from one house to the next, stopping at each one so Walter could deposit the mail. Matt kept on. 'The young filly "Mom's Little Heloise" is a long shot, but she's looking good on the first turn! Whoa! Distracted by a bug! But, no, she's off again! Blazing down the final stretch!' I was laughing so hard I was afraid I'd have my own little accident.

But we did it. We'd gotten Heloise out of the driveway without carrying her. Twice! And we'd managed to *keep the exercise fun for the puppy*. And the trainer. And the son. And the mailman.

CHAPTER 12

'**M**ah-*ammmm!* Where're my soccer shorts?'

Lainey's voice careened down the stairs and into the kitchen, where I was preparing breakfasts and lunches. The urgency in her voice sounded more like she'd suffered a severed artery, rather than a temporary separation from a piece of athletic clothing. I wiped my hands angrily on a dish towel, Heloise jumping and biting at it.

'Uh-uh, girl!' I said sternly. Heloise sat. She now defaulted to a sit every time I corrected her, knowing I would praise her for sitting. I did.

It was the end of May, the second-to-last weekend before school let out for the summer, and both kids had full plans for the day, then home to study for finals. I headed toward the basement door, to look for Lainey's shorts, but stopped, my hand on the doorknob. 'No,' I said to myself. Heloise looked up, confused. I had to watch what I said around her every minute; she was like a sponge, soaking up knowledge. From me.

I walked to the bottom of the stairs to the bedrooms. 'Lainey!' I shouted up. 'You're going

160

to have to find them yourself. Check your dresser, then check the basement.' Silence. My fingers gripped the banister, white knuckled. I had a fleeting moment of wishing Neil was here to help out. He was at the clinic, painting walls. For better or worse, I had grown used to his absence. The rare moments we were home at the same time, we just seemed to get in each other's way. Not like the old days. What had once been a well-choreographed dance around each other, getting things done, laughing, had now become a collision course, both physically and emotionally. If he were here now, he'd offer to put the lunches together, but in his methodical way, lining things up like a damn surgical tray, taking forever, his breath whistling through his nose hairs the whole time. I'd have to tell him what to put in, what to leave out for each kid. It was far better, I told myself, that he's not here.

The doorbell rang. Heloise was immediately on the baby gate, yapping, tail wagging frenetically.

'Oh! Amy. Hi,' I said pleasantly, despite my astonishment at finding Amy Kellerman on my doorstep. 'Is everything all right?' I could hear the hint of panic in my voice. I almost laughed as soon as the words were out of my mouth. I sounded just like my mother; nothing about Amy suggested any emergency. She was wearing an orange velour zip top and matching pants, hair and makeup done, but subdued, for her. On her feet were orange sandals; they reminded me of Barbie shoes, tiny, delicate. Each had an orange jewel on the toe strap. Their spiked heels gave her that same Barbie pitch forward. Amy smiled, almost coyly, as she held up a large, empty Tupperware container. I was pretty sure it was my container from two years ago, when I'd brought soup over when they'd all been ill. I'd wondered what had happened to it.

'I'm sorry to bother you so early. Can I borrow a couple of cups of dog food, please? We ran out.'

'Sure, come on in.' I stepped back from the door, taking the container from her. I realized that with the divorce and all, she'd probably had to cancel the grocery shopping service. I left her in the hall and stepped over the baby gate, into the kitchen. I filled the container, Heloise sitting at my feet obediently, but her whole body quivering with anticipation at the sound of her chow. I dropped a couple pieces in her bowl and she devoured them. It wasn't fair to *hear* your food and not actually get any. I pressed the lid closed on the Tupperware. When I returned, Amy was peering around the corner, surveying my living room, and smiling. I peeked in too, curious what she was looking at. Someone had drawn a heart in the dust on the lamp table.

I handed her the Tupperware. 'It's puppy food, but I don't think that amount will be a problem for Melba.'

Amy looked back at me, still smiling. 'No. I'm sure she'll love it. Thanks a million, Deena.' She left, walking down my driveway with the Tupperware of puppy kibble resting on her hip. Only Amy could make dog chow look sexy.

'Mahh-*ahmmm!* They're not in my drawer!' Lainey's voice screamed out from her bedroom again.

I wheeled back around, yelling up the stairs again, 'Lainey! I said check the basement. Do you hear me? *Come here!*' If she had those goddamned headphones on . . .

Heloise started barking again. I strode to the kitchen and saw Hairy on the counter. I was sure he'd been taunting poor Heloise. His new technique was to sit above her and stare at her, vulturelike and unblinking. I grabbed him off the counter, gave Heloise her dinosaur chew toy, and, Hairy in my arms, returned to the bottom of the stairs.

Lainey was at the top, headphones on, but she was holding one earpiece up. *'What?!'*

'Argghh! Lainey! Take those things off. Now.' I stared at her. She stared back. I stepped up on the first step. An unblinking mother wolf. She pulled the headphones off, settling them around her neck, the surprise evident in her eyes.

'Good girl! Now, I'm trying to get your brother out of here first. You don't have to leave for another half hour, Matt's ride is coming in—' I glanced at my watch, spun back around again, looked out the window. Josh's red beater was in our driveway.

I yelled up the stairs, *'Matt!* Josh is here!' More calmly, but still firmly, I barked: 'Lainey! Shorts!

163

Basement!' I pointed at her, then pointed down-ward. I put Hairy on as high a step as I could reach. 'But first, put *him* in your bedroom!'

I ran into the kitchen to finish packing Matt's lunch. The boys had been researching Eagle Scout projects for the summer. They'd narrowed it to three possibilities: building a garden at a low-income housing project, rebuilding a crumbling bridge at a park, or painting a mural at a Head Start center. They were visiting them all today.

I loaded his backpack with two sandwiches, a bag of chips, two bottles of Gatorade, some snack bars and an apple, which I knew would likely come home bruised and uneaten, but a nod to nutrition compelled me. As I zipped it up, Heloise sniffed around the floor for any morsel I might have dropped. She and I would eat later, in peace and quiet.

Matt came thundering down the stairs. I handed him his backpack at the door. 'Thanks, Mom.'

'You're welcome! Uh, Matt?' He turned, one hand on the screen. 'Um, have a good day,' I said. 'Thanks for thanking me.' He nodded, stepped onto the porch. 'Matt?' Heloise barked from the kitchen.

'Mom! I gotta go!'

'I know, I just— Well, if you guys decide to do the mural thing? I could, maybe, help you a bit.' He stared at me. 'I mean, we have a lot of paint in the basement. Brushes, too.'

''Kay.' He walked out the door. Heloise barked

again from the kitchen. I closed the door, one palm on the cool glass, and watched him climb into the car.

Several days later, on another sunny morning, Heloise and I were returning from our neighborhood walk, when I again saw Amy outside her house. This time she wasn't getting her paper, she was sitting on a beach towel on her overgrown lawn. She was wearing crisp yellow Capri pants and a fitted white tank top. She had one hand on the towel, propping herself. With her other hand she was running an old hairbrush over Melba, but she seemed to be avoiding the mats. Amy's perfectly aligned legs were bent to one side, her feet today adorned with a pair of yellow flip-flops with little daisies on the toe strap, her toenails a bright pink. Her pose and outfit made her look like a blonde 1950's bombshell. But her companion was considerably more canine. In all the years they'd lived across from us, I'd rarely seen Amy with Melba, much less brushing her.

'Hey, Deena!' she said, leaping to her feet as Heloise and I neared. 'Howdy, neighbor!' Her smile was too big, affected. 'She's getting real big, isn't she?'

'Yes,' I said, glancing at the knee-high Heloise. 'She's growing fast. That's for sure.' I checked my watch. 'Well, I—'

'How are your girls? Um, hee, hee—' Amy flushed, made a mock slap of her cheek. 'I mean, your kids! Matt and Lainey! Lots of plans for summer?'

'They're fine. Yeah. Mostly they're looking forward to school being out, I think.' Uh-oh. Was that what this was about? Asking me to look after her girls this summer?

'Yeah. I think Nan and Sara are, too.' Neither of us spoke for a few seconds. I was just about to ease myself into a departure when Amy mumbled, 'I hardly see my girls anymore. You know, since Marty left. Are they over at your place a lot?' Her voice was fragile, her smile now searching.

Heloise slumped down on the concrete, tired of sitting.

'Well, not too much anymore, now that you mention it,' I said. 'But my kids aren't around much either. Teens aren't generally known for spending a lot of time around the house.' And then they leave altogether. I forced a smile and shrugged.

'The airline is about to do a round of layoffs,' she said abruptly. Oh, no. Poor Amy. Not after the divorce and all. My face must have fallen, because she immediately said, 'No! It's a good thing. I think. They're offering a really great severance deal if the high-seniority people take early retirement. I'm thinking of going for it. Then I could be around more. For the girls. I'm thinking of getting a real estate license.'

Whoa! That came out of left field. Why was she telling me all this? 'Well, that's great, Amy,' I said, mustering as much enthusiasm as I could, under the circumstances. I guessed it was good. She looked pleased. Scared, but pleased.

'Maybe then, when I do?' Her face was bright again. 'We can walk our dogs together sometimes?'

I nodded, a dazed smile on my face. I'd *never* seen her walk Melba. The girls used to, when they'd first gotten her. Nan still did from time to time. And now Amy – *Amy!* – was brushing Melba and wanted to go on walks with us. No matter how sure I was of how the world worked, sometimes it seemed to tip a little on its axis.

She pointed at Heloise again. The poor dog was now lying with her head resting on my foot, bored eyes gazing up at me.

'God, she's cute!' she said, resuming a languid stroking of Melba with the hairbrush, but staring at Heloise. 'She's going to be a real special gift to someone, isn't she?'

I thought about the chewed cabinets, about all the housebreaking accidents, about the digging, the stubbornness, all of which still happened if I wasn't paying close attention. I looked down at Heloise, looking up at me.

'She already is,' I said. Amy stopped brushing and looked at me. We both smiled.

CHAPTER 13

A week later on a cloudy, threatening day, I was surprised, to say the least, to again have Amy ringing my doorbell.

'Hello again!' she said cheerily. This time she wore high-fashion jeans, a designer T-shirt, and an unbuttoned white rain coat. I wondered if the T-shirt was hers or Sara's. I knew Nan disdained any and all name-brand clothing. Lainey, on the other hand, pined for it, but I'd put my foot down at a forty-four-dollar T-shirt, telling her if she wanted it she'd have to buy it herself.

'Hope I'm not bothering you, Deena,' said Amy. Heloise had stopped barking and now had her front paws up on the baby gate, nearly wagging herself right off.

'No, not at all. How are you?' I opened the door wide. 'Come in.'

'Thanks,' she said, stepping inside. She stood in the hall, nervously twisting her hands together in front of her.

'Um, would you like a cup of coffee?' I asked.

She looked at me, sort of quizzically. Surprise,

168

maybe? 'I'd love to, but I can't. Can I take a rain check?'

'Of course.'

'What I really need is to ask you a favor.' She clasped her hands under her chin, her eyes wide in lighthearted beseeching. '*Another* one.'

I laughed. 'Of course. If I can . . . .' I didn't want to commit before I knew the favor. You never knew with Amy.

'You know I told you I wanted to get my real estate license?' I nodded. Then her words poured out, her hands gesturing wildly. 'Well, there's a class next weekend – all weekend – and I'm still working for the airlines till the end of the month, but I'm off for the weekend, and Marty offered to take the girls but he's flying a red-eye Friday night and, well, *she's* there, and I don't want the girls . . . It's just that I think the girls need . . . Well, Sara just wants to stay home by themselves, but I don't really want them to do that. Not now with, well—'

'I'd love for the girls to come over for the weekend, Amy.'

She heaved a dramatic sigh. 'Thank you sooo much, Deena.' Without stepping forward, she clasped my hands in her hands. 'I'm— You're— Well, I can't think of anyone I'd rather have them with.' Her eyes were tearing up.

Damn. So were mine.

Shortly after noon on Friday the doorbell rang, and Sara and Nan stood huddled on the doorstep, their overnight bags in hand, a steady rain falling behind them.

'Oh! Girls, come in, come in!' I said, holding the door.

'Thank you for having us over, Deena,' said Nan, a drop of rain hanging from her yellow slicker hood like a tiny jewel above her forehead. Sara, wearing a wet zip sweatshirt, looked like she'd been rousted out of bed about five minutes ago, and considerably earlier than would have been her preference. Mornings and sixteen-year-olds got along about as well as Hairy and Heloise. Although this morning, Matt had actually set his alarm in order to wake in time to make an escape to the more masculine environs of Josh's house. Matt was uncomfortable around Sara. She'd had a raging crush for years on Sam, starting when she was only twelve, then when Sam left, she'd transferred it to Matt, who'd been wholly unprepared for that kind of attention. He still wasn't. But I don't think Matt had anything to fear anymore. Apparently Sara was now so completely wrapped up in this Kurt boy that Amy had given me confidential instructions to make sure he didn't come 'sniffing around,' as she put it. But Matt had a good excuse to be gone anyway; he and Josh still hadn't decided on which Eagle Scout project they were going to do. If they were to finish the project by the end of summer, before school started, I'd told Matt that today had to be the deadline for choosing. I knew it was now between two: the garden or the mural.

'I'm delighted to have you girls here, Nan,' I said,

170

once again admiring her manners. I turned to Sara, not wanting to exclude her. 'When did this rain start?' It hadn't been raining when I'd taken Heloise out earlier that morning.

Sara shrugged, scowling at the wall. Clearly she considered that I was babysitting them, and I didn't really blame her for not wanting to be here. Given the situation, however, I didn't blame Amy for making them come over here, either.

Plus, that was a stupid question for me to ask her, I realized too late. She'd seen the first light of day just moments ago.

'It started about an hour ago,' said Nan, her sweet smile melting me again. Nan was an old soul. There was something deeply innocent and compassionate about this girl. 'I guess May showers bring June flowers,' she said brightly, pulling off her rain slicker. I took it from her. 'Thank you,' she said again.

'My pleasure.' I gave her a hug with my free arm. It was sort of amazing to me that Nan and Lainey were both fifteen. Lainey was just about 100 percent attitude these days, while Nan seemed nearly 100 percent gratitude. And Nan had lost so much this year.

'Why don't you give me your coat too, Sara, and I'll hang them up to dry.'

Sara took off her sweatshirt and handed it to me, never looking me in the eye. In the past year the once bright and energetic Sara had become sullen and sometimes even surly. Understandable, perhaps, with everything her parents had gone through, and therefore the girls had had to go through. But Nan and Sara could hardly have reacted more differently to the whole thing. It was another real argument for nature over nurture. Sara seemed to resent both her parents, disdain them, really. Nan seemed to think it was her job to take care of everyone. Which made me want to take care of her.

'Have you girls eaten?'

'I had breakfast,' Nan said. 'But that was a while ago.' She looked past me shyly, then added quickly, 'But you don't have to feed us, Deena.'

'Feeding people is what I do best, Nan!' I put my arm around her shoulders and shepherded them both into the kitchen.

'Oh my gosh!' Nan squealed softly, seeing Heloise curled up, asleep in her kennel. 'Mom said she was cute, but, *oh my gosh!'*

I felt bad that Nan hadn't even seen Heloise yet, but at the same time, I felt a little bud burst open inside my heart. Lainey had not had that reaction to Heloise, initially. What girl didn't love a puppy? Well, perhaps one greeted by her pee and vomit within the first twenty-four hours in the house. Although now both my kids seemed to be growing fond of her, calling her Lil' Girl, or Wheezy. Until she'd chew on something of theirs, or have an accident. Then she became Hellion, or, 'Mom, look what *your* dog did!'

'Lainey!' I shouted up the stairs. 'The girls are here!' She probably had those headphones on

172

again. I yelled up again, louder. Sure enough, she clomped downstairs, headphones around her neck.

'Hey!' She put her arms around Nan and they hugged. She gave Sara a hug, too. I was surprised, but warmed, by their show of affection.

'I think a rainy day calls for grilled cheese sandwiches and tomato soup,' I said, rubbing my hands together. 'How does that sound?' I'd spoken too enthusiastically; Heloise jumped up in her kennel, stretching. Or maybe she just knew I was talking about food.

'Great, Deena!' said Nan. 'Thank you so much. Do you need any help?' I was about to say no, when she added, 'I could play with the puppy for you.'

Lainey looked up at me and asked, 'Can we, Mom?'

I nodded, dumbstruck. Lainey stepped forward to the kennel and pinched it open. My jaw nearly fell. I didn't know she knew how to open it. Lainey gathered Heloise into her arms, and all three girls fell on her with painted fingernails and pink glossed kisses.

'She's getting heavy, Mom!' said Lainey, smiling.

'I'll take her!' said Nan.

'Actually, could you girls take her outside for me, please? She just woke up and probably needs to go to the bathroom.'

'Sure, Deena,' said Nan. 'Can I carry her, Lain?' Lainey poured Heloise into Nan's arms, the smile on both their faces filling the kitchen. Heloise licked Nan's chin like it was her favorite flavor of ice cream. Nan threw her head back, giggling. Even Sara was smiling now.

'Do you know what to do, Lainey?' I asked. She knew how to open the kennel, maybe she knew more.

'Don't we just put her in the grass? She'll go if she has to, won't she?'

'I have to train her to go to the bathroom when I tell her to. So when she goes, you say, "Do your b–u–s–i–n–e–s–s."' I spelled the word because Heloise was so well trained now the mere mention might stimulate her. The girls looked at each other, quick confused glances, then all three burst out laughing.

'*What* do we say?' Lainey asked, her mouth crooked with amusement.

I smiled. 'I don't want to say it because she's really learned it pretty well and it might make her go. Listen, when you put her down, say, "Do your"' – this time I slowed the spelling considerably – '"b–u–s–i–n–e–s–s." Then, hopefully, she'll go. They have to learn to only go when they're told.'

'Well, that doesn't seem fair!' Lainey said, indignant. If she couldn't be indignant for herself, she'd gladly take up the cause for someone, anyone, else.

'Well, think about it,' I said. 'If you were blind and your guide dog was walking you to work, would it be okay if that dog wanted to sniff every bush and tree, and pee on them, or poop wherever it wanted?'

'No . . . I guess not,' she said, stroking Heloise's back.

'And if you think about it,' Nan said, looking at Lainey, 'we don't exactly get to go whenever or wherever we want either.' This time I joined in the giggles.

'Better get her out, she's really awake now.' Heloise was looking intently at each of the girls, perhaps even pleadingly. 'If you stay under the big pine tree, you'll be protected from the rain.' The girls headed toward the door. Suddenly, Lainey turned.

'Mom?'

'Yes?'

'I'm supposed to *say*, "business," not spell it, right?'

I bit my lip, so I wouldn't laugh. 'Yes, sweetie. Thank you.' She nodded, a look of deep concentration on her face as she grabbed the umbrella and opened the door.

'She did it, Mom! She went!' Lainey's cheeks were pink with excitement. I couldn't believe the transformation in her. Just like when they were little, nothing ignites a kid's interest in something forgotten or rejected like a friend's interest in that thing.

'I told her to do, you know, and she peed! She's smart!' The little bud in my heart was fully abloom.

'Yeah? That's great, honey! Thanks, girls. Lunch is almost ready, so tuck her back in her kennel and wash up, please. Tell her the word first.'

Lainey and Nan, their backs to me, looked at

each other, then turned slowly around. 'What word?' they asked in unison.

' "Kennel",' I said. Nan burst into giggles again.

'Oh. Duh!' Lainey slapped her forehead, and for that split second, she looked a lot like me.

After lunch, Nan insisted on helping me with the dishes. The dishwasher had recently started sounding like a cement mixer, so I'd been doing dishes in the sink till I called a repairman. But I knew what would happen when I did. The repair estimate would be half the cost of buying a new one, and I'd agonize, debating over whether to just pay the trip charge and let it go, or pay for the repair, or buy a new one. It was easier to just do the dishes in the sink.

Lainey and Sara were combing through our videos and DVDs to see if there was anything they could all agree on. Heloise was out of her kennel but confined to the kitchen, where I could keep an eye on her. She still couldn't be entirely trusted not to have a little snack of kitchen cabinet. But at the moment she was in the middle of the kitchen floor, lying on her back, almost balanced on her spine, feet up in the air. She was flipping her little white bone from one side of her mouth to the other, her body snaking back and forth.

'She's *so* cute, Deena,' said Nan, staring at Heloise while drying a plate. She placed it carefully in the cabinet, then looked at me. 'How are you ever going to give her up?'

'It's going to be hard, Nan. Although it's hard raising her, too. To be honest? At first there were a couple of times there I was ready to give her up. Puppies chew everything, go to the bathroom in the house, things like that.'

'Oh. Well, I guess it is a lot of work, huh?' I nodded. 'Where do these go?' she asked, holding the dry saucepan and lid.

'In there,' I said, nodding my head toward the spinner cabinet, my arms up to my elbows in soapy water.

Nan headed for the cabinet. 'But she seems real well trained n— Oh my gosh! Oh *my gosh!* How funny!' Nan was stumbling backward from the open cabinet, still holding the pan and lid, beside herself with giggles. I leaned away from the sink and peered in, only too sure what I would see. Yes. There was Hairy, sitting in the cast-iron frying pan. I could see several white hairs against its seasoned blackness.

I had just started to ask aloud how he'd gotten in there, when a tan blur crossed in front of me, followed by a screeching meow. Before I could pull my hands from the suds, Heloise had sent herself and Hairy spinning. Hairy screamed again, leaping out of the cabinet as the spinner came back around. Heloise was splayed across a large glass lid, unable to gain her footing as the circle spun. I reached in, stilled it, and pulled Heloise off, grabbing her with my soapy hands. Hairy had jumped up on the desk, but was standing, back arched, glaring at Heloise.

177

I released Heloise and grabbed the dish towel. I was wiping the suds out of the cabinet when Nan let out a little shriek.

'Uh-oh! Deena!' There was unmistakable urgency in her voice. I whipped my head around to see Heloise, legs spread, a small puddle forming under her.

'Oh, Lord!' I said, grabbing her again, midpee. *'Uh-uh!'*

'I'll get it!' said Nan. She jumped up and grabbed enough paper towel to wipe up a small lake of pee, but I wasn't complaining. In fact, I was thrilled when Sara and Lainey ran into the kitchen to see what the commotion was about. I hoped Lainey was taking note of Nan willingly doing this particular chore. I raced outside with Heloise, where she finished her business.

When we returned, Lainey had her hands on her hips. I steeled myself for another lecture from her about Heloise chasing Hairy.

'Mom, there's nothing we haven't seen a hundred times,' she said. I had to think what she was talking about. DVDs, I remembered, as I put Heloise back in her kennel. 'Kennel, girl!'

I was relieved that Lainey wasn't worried about Hairy, since I was not entirely upset with Heloise for chasing him out of my spinner cabinet. Way more effective than a toothbrush. 'You could play a board game,' I told the girls.

'They don't call them "bored" games for nothing, Mom.' Teenage hilarity followed.

'Well, I have an idea,' I said. 'But you have to listen to the whole plan, okay? It involves Heloise.'

All three girls gave me their full attention. 'Let's go sit in the living room.' They hustled to the couch and sat in a neat line. I was loving this. Heloise gave me cachet!

'We could go to the mall—'

'Yes!' said Lainey, rising.

I lifted my palm. 'Wait! You have to listen to the whole plan, okay?' I stared at her, eyes focused on hers. She sank back down on the couch.

'I could take Heloise on her first real socialization.' I'd mostly just taken her on brief trips to the grocery store. I felt she was ready for more. 'A socialization is when you take the puppy to a public place.' Now all three girls stood up, and I again held up my hand. 'Girls?' They looked at me. 'Sit.' They sat. 'Thank you.' This was going incredibly well.

'But it has to be really short, okay? I want it to be successful, so we have to stack the odds in her favor – have her go to the bathroom right outside, make it short, things like that. One hundred times more effective to praise the right behavior than to punish the wrong behavior.' I smiled, realizing I was sounding like Bill. 'So we'll just take a brief stroll around the mall, and then leave.'

The girls looked at each other blankly, then back at me.

'Couldn't we stay for an hour, at least?' asked Lainey, almost, but not quite, whining.

'No. Heloise and I can't. And I don't want to

drive all the way down there, drive home, then drive back and get you guys again. But I will stop on the way back and let you rent a movie for tonight.'

'Okay. Can we make BYOBs, too?' asked Lainey, rising again, then quickly sinking right back down, but bouncing slightly.

'Make *what*?' asked Sara. I could tell by the look on her face that she knew a meaning for those letters that she doubted was intended here.

'Build your own burrito,' said Lainey. 'Mom makes all this different stuff and then we all get to put whatever we want in our own burritos. Can we?'

I loved how she asked 'Can *we*?' 'Sure,' I said, 'if you'll make the stuff.'

Her eyebrows furrowed. 'We don't know how.'

'I'll show you. So, are we going to the mall?' I asked. They shrugged, then nodded. A classic teenage acquiescence to something they wanted to do, but God forbid they look enthusiastic about it.

I myself would readily admit to both nerves and excitement at the prospect of Heloise's first real socialization. What if she pooped in the mall? Or worse, what if she slipped out of her collar and ran away? I filled the fanny pack with poop bags, a small packet of Wet Wipes, her little white bone, and some paper towels, prepared for any eventuality. And if she got away from us, at least there would be four of us to give chase.

The rain had stopped before we even left the house, and as we pulled into the mall parking lot, the sun was out again. I hadn't even pulled on the parking brake when the girls raced out of the car and around to the back to be the first to get Heloise out.

'Wait, please,' I said, scrambling out of the car myself. I supposed I should be generous, mature, let them take turns with her, guests first, then Lainey, then me. But I was feeling protective of both Heloise and myself. I went to the puppy meetings. I cleaned up after her. I got up in the middle of the night with her. I wanted to be the one to take her on her maiden socialization.

'Let me take her to start with, see how she does.' I set her in the grass and she took care of business. I sighed with relief. I slipped her green jacket over her back, fastening it under her stomach and in front of her chest. All three girls let out a chorus of 'Awww' at the sight of her in her little coat.

If we passed a person who didn't look at us and smile, I missed it. Heloise trotted along on her leash, stopping many people in their tracks, 'Aww' and 'Ohh' and 'Look, look, look!' coming from every direction, many pointing. I felt like I was walking through the mall with Julia Roberts at the end of the leash.

'Now can I take her, Mom?'

'Let's let Nan go first. She cleaned up the pee in the kitchen today.' I shot a proud smile Nan's way. Lainey did too. Surprised, I began to wonder if some of Lainey's 'expected' teenage behavior happened for just that reason, because I expected it.

We all took turns, Heloise trotting happily along,

181

no matter who held the end of her leash. All three girls stayed closely clumped together, often arm in arm so there'd be no confusion that each one was associated with this special puppy, each one of us basking in the attention Heloise drew.

CHAPTER 14

May was going out with a blaze. The sun was already hot at seven thirty in the morning. I surveyed the yard, sipping my coffee from the big, slightly misshapen blue mug that Matt had made for me in a pottery elective last year.

The redbud tree needed pruning. I would get to it eventually. Or maybe not. I'd abandoned the idea of planting a vegetable garden this year. I was growing a guide dog. I stretched my arms out luxuriously to either side, my mug in one hand, Heloise's leash in the other.

My stomach was growling, and Heloise was pulling toward the house.

Now we ate only after everyone was gone. We ate together. She on the kitchen floor, me nearby at the kitchen desk; she her high-quality dog food required by K-9 Eyes, me some high-quality protein required by the new food plan I was trying. I'd bought a book called *A Woman's Guide to Maximizing Midlife*. If ever there was an example of the marketing adage 'If you can't fix it, feature it!' that title was it. But the book was well written, not too preachy or saccharine. It cited studies showing that many women had fewer symptoms – memory loss, fatigue, cravings, aches and pains, even hot flashes, all the ones I was having – when they cut down on refined carbohydrates. So, while Heloise dined on her high-protein kibble, I ate a scrambled egg, sometimes with a bit of salsa over the top. The protein in the morning seemed to stay with me better than the high-fiber cereal I'd been choking down; it could double for garden mulch. No wonder I'd often felt the need for a Corn Pops chaser.

Heloise had finally worked her way around her bundt pan, licking up every last bit. She was now patiently standing at the baby gate. She knew the routine. Eat. Walk. I always made sure to lace up my shoes before breakfast so we could make a quick getaway. I leashed her up and grabbed her little green K-9 Eyes Puppy in Training jacket. I marveled at how an adorable puppy could get even more adorable simply by wearing a little green coat. I felt like I should also have a green jacket, not for any kind of fashion statement, but for a disclaimer identifying me as a Raiser in Training. But I was learning. We both were.

I opened the door and Heloise tried to scoot out ahead of me, but I made her sit and wait. I stepped through the door, paused very briefly, then said, 'Okay!' She bounded out.

She now loved her walks, which were slowly getting longer. She always trotted down the driveway, and in general was much better on the leash, except that she still considered it her job, and pleasure, to vacuum the whole outdoors: cigarette butts, goose poop, rocks, the occasional slow bug. But I loved our morning treks as much as she did. I loved watching her, imagining what she was thinking. But I also loved just thinking my own thoughts, ones that seemed to freely spill themselves only during these long walks.

The cool breeze and hot sun made for a perfect morning, only possibility raining down on us. Heloise and I walked along the sidewalk, winding our way through the neighborhood. We'd wandered out of our middle-class 1960s development into the higher, in both altitude and price, homes above ours. I liked looking at the expansive, professionally designed and maintained gardens. But what caught my eye today were the foothills, rising up dramatically behind the houses, the yellow-green hills almost glowing in the fresh morning light. I turned around, pulling Heloise behind me. She grudgingly followed. She now resisted whenever we headed for home.

'Come on, girl. We're not done yet. Au contraire.' We turned left on Majesty Drive, Heloise bounding ahead again as soon as she realized our walk was really just beginning.

A reasonably wet winter, and now the warm spring, had resulted in abundant wildflowers among the tall mountain grasses. It was as if someone had flicked paint off a brush, splattering dots of nearly every color on the hillside. I racked my brain trying to remember the names of flowers that I knew I once knew. There were those soft blue, tall things. I thought the name began with an F. Bursts of low-growing yellow things that I thought had some sort of French name. Some lacy white things that I was pretty sure were Lacy Somethings. Or Something Lace. I even spied a tiny spot of a flower, rusty orange, blooming in a hollow. I could feel the name circling, invisibly, in my brain. Damn. Menopause was turning my brain into a noun drain. I couldn't come up with a single name. Heloise grabbed the flower in her mouth. She didn't need names for things. Only to take a big bite and taste it. I fished it out of her mouth, worried she would not discriminate against toxic blossoms.

The birds were not to be outdone by the flowers. A black bird with vivid orange-red bars on its wings called from a cottonwood. 'Red-winged blackbird!' I shouted, absurdly pleased with myself for remembering this most obvious name. I pulled Heloise to a stop while I watched several little gray birds flit about, their chickadee-dee-dee call helping me out with their name. Heloise looked right and left for them. She sat, head cocking first to one side then the other, to the point I thought she might tip over.

'Look up, girl,' I said, laughing, gently pointing her muzzle up toward the tree. She stood suddenly, her tail a signal flag of announcement, indicating she had pinpointed the locus of the mysterious sound.

'What a goofball!' Still laughing, I bent and kissed the top of her head, then her velvet ear. She turned and licked my chin, a wet, unconscious kiss. I decided that the scent of her breath was a mix of appetite for life, and unguarded love.

As we continued up the trail, I thought back to my walks here years ago. I'd tuck Sam in the Snugli, pack my bird and wildflower books and a bottle of water in a fanny pack, and spend a morning hour or two strolling, as Sam mostly slept.

Now as I trod up the trail, I tried to recall why I'd stopped my daily walks. Life, I guess. Or lives. My kids'. Theirs had become mine.

I stopped, midstride, stunned. Heloise waited at the end of her leash, captivated by some ants crawling across the dirt.

I had happily, *euphorically*, traded my self for wife and mother. In my twenties I'd pulled off the only marginally fitted self, a mishmash patchwork of experience and imagination, and wife and mother had slid on like a second skin. As though it had been tailored just for me. And it had. But now I felt like I was slithering along, peeling that skin, whether I wanted to or not.

Heloise tugged at the leash, pulling me forward. I tried to prevent her eager sampling of small rocks, sticks, and even pine needles along the way.

But if I was shedding my skin, how much of *me* was coming off? Or more important, how much of me was underneath? I wondered what part of all this was hormones. I could blame a flat tire on hormones. But I was convinced that our twenties biology sends us scouring for mates and pursuing bondage. Okay, bonding. Our thirties biology beats the drum of procreation and nurturing. And in our forties and fifties . . . what? Our biology simply runs out? I knew it was true, in more ways than one.

Although I knew that both Lainey and I felt like we were at the tail of a mean game of crack the mood whip, I couldn't help but notice that everything else she was going through now, I was going through in reverse. Her body was becoming more filled out and pronounced in its firm female curves. Mine was becoming ever more, shall we say, unperky? You would think that putting on a bunch of extra fat over the years would slow that process somewhat, but no. And while Lainey's sexuality was climbing steadily, mine was in an audible nosedive. Clearly an engine out. Any moment I worried I might hear the final crash and burn of my sexual desire.

At least for Neil. Maybe with someone else . . . ? I'd more or less officially moved into Sam's room now. I'd told Neil that I was sleeping better in there, which was true. He'd brusquely replied, 'Well, then, you should stay in there.' So I had. And more than once I'd found myself in the late-night company of

188

the handsome young man with the penetrating stare from a full-page, black-and-white magazine ad. I didn't remember what the product was, but I was sure sold on his smoldering – and youthful – good looks. He was excellent fantasy material. Then there was Bill. Not as safe a fantasy because I saw him nearly every two weeks at puppy meetings.

A loud screech interrupted my thoughts. A brilliant blue and black bird with a sort of Mohawk flew past us, landing in a tall, dense tree. It screeched again at us. Heloise launched into a fit of barking. I laughed, grateful to her for yanking me out of my thoughts. But I still had to correct her with a quick little tug and release on the leash, just enough to get her attention. When she stopped, I patted her head and she looked at me, licked my hand, gently mouthed it. I tenderly but firmly corrected her again. It was hard to correct her for behaviors I knew she couldn't have as a guide dog, but which were, at any given moment, a sort of emotional salve for me. Whenever she mouthed my hand it was almost always gentle, a toothy caress. Like a small child unconsciously slipping her hand into mine. Just wanting some contact. So my corrections were always followed by giving her lots of appropriate contact.

We moved on, both of us slowing at the steep part. I remembered it came just before the turn back down. We'd gone only a half mile up and I was perspiring profusely and noticed there was not enough oxygen for me and Heloise. I was convinced she was taking more than her share as I huffed and puffed, looking for any sign that my fitness level was improving after all our neighborhood walks. But this was different. Steeper. Longer. Harder. Farther from home.

Heloise was taking me to new heights. Literally. Even this little mile loop gained a respectable altitude. Thankfully, I was pulled along by this pup's indomitable enthusiasm for all that surrounded her. *A rock! A flower! A bird call! I'm peeing! I don't know why you love it when I pee but I love it that you love it! Ohh! Up ahead! What's that?!* A puppy's life was full of exclamation marks. There was something completely infectious about her desire to see what was around the next corner.

My quadriceps burning, I set my mental sights on the turnaround point, at the top of the hill. If I recalled correctly, it was just up ahead, then around a bend, then almost all downhill on the way back. Years ago there'd been a bench at the turnaround point. I could only hope there still was. At just a little after nine a.m., I guessed it was already nearing eighty degrees.

As we rounded the bend, I saw my bench at long last, but my whole demeanor sagged at the sight. It was already occupied. An elderly man sat alone in the center of the bench, holding an empty leash wound around his hand. His clothes looked clean but unpressed: khaki slacks, a faded blue button-down shirt, and a white tennis hat with a pale yellow band. He was watching a large silky collie nose around a nearby boulder.

'A beautiful day, isn't it?' I said from a distance, not wanting to startle either of them. Both the man and the collie turned, both with striking, placid expressions.

'Yes indeed,' bench gent replied, removing his hat and wiping his brow with his forearm. 'It's going to be a hot one, though.' He smiled, but his face looked weary. He placed his hat back on his head and called to his dog. 'Come here, Teddy.' The collie immediately obliged, and I could see by his slow gait and graying muzzle that he too was in his senior years. These two had probably grown gray together. The thought gave me a small pang.

'Did you see that, Heloise?' I asked, squatting near her and pointing to Teddy. 'When I say "come," *that's* what you're supposed to do!'

The man smiled. 'Lotsa work training a young pup. We got Teddy here when he was just a little thing, too.' He tenderly massaged Teddy's neck with one hand. 'Laura – my wife – was trying to fill the empty nest.'

Was that what I was doing? It felt like I wanted to eject myself *from* the nest. I didn't know what to say, so I pulled out my water bottle and drank a bit, then squatted and poured some in my hand for Heloise. She lapped it up noisily, licking as much onto the ground as she did into her mouth.

He pointed to Heloise's jacket. 'I see that little gal's got a job to do, one of these days.'

191

'Yes, *if* I can teach her the basics.' She finished lapping up the last bit of water from my hand and immediately became interested in a dozen or more tiny blue butterflies that were flitting around a small stream of water trickling up from a crack in the trail. They looked like turquoise stones swirling through the air. I held Heloise on a short leash so she wouldn't eat them.

'Hopefully she'll make it, but only about half of the puppies actually graduate to become guide dogs,' I said, repeating the statistic from the manual. I rose from my squat, my leg muscles screaming obscenities at me. I lifted my sunglasses and wiped a drip of sweat from my eye with my T-shirted shoulder.

'I'm terribly sorry, miss!' said the man, rising. At first I thought he was apologizing for only half the dogs making it to guide dog status. But he gestured to the bench. 'Where are my manners? Please, have a seat.' He extended his hand. 'I'm Merle Wenzell.' I wiped my hand on my pants and took his slightly gnarled hand, cool and soft in my warm one, his grip somewhat tentative, a handshake a man of his generation gives a lady.

'Hi, Merle, I'm Deena Munger,' I said, sitting next to him. 'That's Heloise.' She was still enthralled with the butterflies. Merle reached down, wiggled his fingers, trying to get her attention. With only barely parted lips, he whistled, a thin, sharp note. Both Heloise and Teddy looked up. Heloise bounded over,

Teddy came in a dignified amble. Merle reached over Teddy's back, patting his massive rib cage with an affectionate thump. With his other hand he scratched Heloise under her chin using just his index finger.

Heloise sat remarkably still, staring into Merle's eyes. I could swear he was saying something to her telepathically, and that she was listening. *Oh, please be telling her to stop eating every single thing on the ground!* I willed. Or maybe Heloise was telling *him* something. *Do you realize how many tasty treats are just lying around, everywhere?!* In either case, I suddenly had the feeling that I'd come to the top of the mountain and met an animal guru of some sort. Okay, not the top. Here was the Half-Mile Dog Whisperer.

After a moment Merle looked up, his filmy eyes set on me. He seemed to be looking into my own thoughts now, which was not entirely comfortable. For something to say, I asked, 'Did Laura train Teddy?'

'Oh, yes! Worked real patiently with him, same as with me and the boys!' He laughed quietly, then looked away, as though studying the tree-tops. Heloise suddenly began barking at the butterflies.

'Heloise, stop.' I tugged gently on her leash and she quieted. 'Those little blue butterflies are beautiful,' I said. 'I don't think I've ever seen those before. Do you know what they're called?'

'Little Blues,' said Merle, his eyes shining.

'Really?' I asked, grinning. 'That's creative.'

'Yep. Sometimes the best names are the simplest. Never forget going to the hardware store one day to get one of those things for the screen door that keeps it from bangin' shut.' He looked at me to see that I registered what he was talking about. I nodded.

'Well, so there I am giving this young fellow a wind-full of description because I don't know what the dang things are called. He looks at me and says, "You mean a door closer?"'

I laughed out loud. 'Was that at McDorn's?' I asked. He nodded and I nodded back. 'A similar thing happened to me when I went in there for some chain that my daughter wanted for a necklace. I'm going on and on about little balls all connected, not really beads, chains like the kind you used to see on old-fashioned drain plugs so that you could pull them out . . .' I looked at Merle, who was grinning and nodding animatedly now.

'Know what it's called?' I asked.

Merle shook his head, expectant, delighted. A thrill raced through me.

'Drain-pull chain!' I said. We laughed more than was warranted, the kind of laugh that is a relief and release, two strangers recognizing a safe oasis in a fleeting chance meeting. I suspected that it was our anonymity that freed us somehow. We didn't know each other at all, didn't have to claim any part of our lives that we didn't want to at this moment.

We could silently abandon our burdens, as if we'd left our weighty packs at the bottom of this small mountain.

As we giggled, both dogs came to check on us.

CHAPTER 15

'Hi, Deena! Look, Teddy, it's that cute little girl in the green jacket!'

Merle stood at the trailhead, leaning against the brown trail sign, wearing the same khaki pants, tennis shoes, and hat as yesterday, but a different shirt. This time he wore a pale yellow short-sleeved that matched the band in his hat.

'Glad to run into you gals again,' said Merle, pulling off his hat with one hand and extending his other. I was completely charmed by his manners. I wasn't sure if a man had ever removed his hat in polite deference to me before.

'We were hoping to run into you two as well,' I said, reaching for his hand. This handshake was different from the one the day before, more the sort friends give when they're not quite on hugging terms, but still affectionate. Slower, more grip, more eye contact, deep smiles.

'Shall we?' Merle asked, his arm extending toward the trail.

'Please,' I said, 'after you.'

The beginning of the path was quite narrow

and necessitated single file. We walked in companionable silence, first Teddy, then Merle, Heloise, and finally me. I watched Merle walk, his gait slow but steady, his shoulders slightly rounded, his hat bobbing slightly as he walked. He reached out every so often to touch a leaf, or look up at a bird. He stopped whenever a tree branch extended across the trail, and held it for me.

Everything about Merle made me want to meet Laura, see their house, peer into their lives. I realized I'd already set up a little fantasy about them. Having long since made it through the roil of raising their kids and sending them out into the world, their home, I was certain, had now distilled down to only soothing things: soup simmering on the stove with last night's ham bone; real, fresh-squeezed lemonade in a glass pitcher in the refrigerator; colorful cloth rag carpets lying in magic swirls on dark floors, their aura of time-lost handiwork still warm and wavering above them. The kind of home that was simply lived in, not managed. An old couple still in love, not in residence.

We emerged from the small glade and stepped up onto the trail, which was almost a narrow road at this point. Merle bent down and unfastened Teddy. 'There you go, old boy. Sow your oats.' Merle looked at me. 'I guess the young lady here is a little young to go off lead just yet.'

'She's not ever supposed to go off lead,' I said, a little forlornly. I couldn't help but remember Rocky and Fordy gallivanting all over creation on

197

the farm. A dog's heart soars in the freedom of running. I couldn't even take Heloise for a run *on* leash because, even though there once was a day when I jogged a bit, that was a lifetime ago. 'Guide dogs in training have to be leashed, unless they're in a fenced area.'

'Ah. I see.'

We walked along, Teddy leading the way, Heloise straining to catch up to him. Teddy, at least, should be grateful for Heloise's bondage, I thought. Without it she was apt to jump about his face, licking and love biting. Not something a dignified old gentleman like Teddy could easily endure.

There was a stretchy silence, so I thought to ask about Merle's wife. I had already begun to imagine a friendship with her, too. An older woman friend seemed extremely attractive to me right now. But I didn't want to appear too nosy. 'Does Laura ever come on your walks?'

Merle looked at the ground, pulling both his lips inward, a clear attempt at control. 'No. No, Deena, she does not. Laura's not well. Her mind has left her. She's had the Alzheimer's for several years now.'

I stopped in my tracks. I shouldn't have, but I couldn't help it. The crystal image I'd had of their life had fallen; shards of my clichéd imagination lay around us. So that was his burden. And a hell of a burden it was.

'I–I'm sorry, Merle. That must be terribly hard.' He nodded, now biting his lip slightly. His pain had bubbled to the surface. We stood in the middle of the trail, silent. Teddy, who'd been keeping a steady twenty yards ahead of us, circled back and pulled up next to Merle, his long snout lightly touching Merle's limp hand. Of course he knows.

'Let's go, Teddy!' said Merle suddenly, throwing a snap of his fingers forward. Teddy dutifully trod on. I kept in step as Merle continued up the trail. Both his speech and gait were energetic now, something to throw over his exposed sadness. 'I take care of her. She took such good care of me and the boys all those years, least I can do. Very least. Leticia, the gal from the nursing service, comes in every morning, to do her exercise, to set with her a while, so I can take Teddy on his constitutional.'

I nodded, my eyes unforgivably welling with tears. I looked down, biting the inside of my lip, not wanting to make his pain worse with my own involuntary display.

'I put her in a home earlier this year. Took her right back out after a couple weeks. I just worried about her all the time. So—' He paused, rubbing his hand over his mouth, pulling at his clean-shaven chin. 'She's back home with me. Harder on me physically, but having her away was hell on me emotionally.'

I wanted to hug him, but knew that wasn't what was needed. This was a long-standing reality for him; only new to me. Embracing him, I felt, would make it all new again for him somehow.

'How long have you two been married?' I wasn't

sure if that was the right thing to say, or even an appropriate thing to say, but I had to say something besides again saying I was sorry.

'Fifty-four years. She was only sixty-nine when the disease hit. For a while she was just a little forgetful. She thought it was, you know, just age. Anyway, the boys sent us on a cruise for our fiftieth anniversary.' Striding along, he looked over and grinned at me. 'That was sure something, I'll tell you what. You ever been on one?' A resounding change of subject. Deft. But I still felt at a loss.

I smiled, shaking my head. Heloise had wandered down the side of the grassy slope, which was dropping steeply beside us, and I tugged her back on course. 'Come here, girl.' She climbed back up, trotting next to Teddy, who'd come over at my call. I slowed, glanced at Merle. 'Neil – my husband – and I used to talk about going on a cruise, once all the kids were out of high school. But now that we're getting close, we don't talk about it anymore.' I didn't want to go down this road. 'College expenses looming, I guess,' I hastily added, picking up the pace again, Merle keeping by my side.

'Well, I tell you what! You don't need to feed yourselves for about a week and a day before you go and after you get back. They feed you till the cows come home!' He patted his trim stomach and laughed.

'Where did you go on your cruise?'

'Oh, a few places in Mexico. It was—' He paused, tipped his head briefly. 'The ocean was very pretty.'

I suspected that he and Laura had felt a little out of place in the ritz and glamour of a cruise, and especially the touristy port stops.

'Where are you from originally, Merle?'

'Right here in Colorado. Grew up on a big farm near Hernsdale.'

'No kidding! Me too! Well, not Hernsdale. I grew up on a farm in southeastern Colorado.'

He turned, his face a solar flare of enthusiasm. 'Cantaloupe country!'

'Yes sir! The best!'

'Rocky Fords!' he said. I felt my own face light up at this man's recognition of my hometown pride. 'Yes indeedy. Laura and I always ate a couple of cantaloupe every week of the season. We'd get them at the farmer's market, or roadside stands, or just at the grocery store, and we'd rate them.' He grinned at me again. 'We had a scale of one to one hundred. Best we ever did was a ninety-eight.' He was thoughtful a minute, but still smiling. 'But, you know, to tell you the honest truth?' I nodded, as expectant as he had been yesterday at my deliberate revelation of the name of the drain-pull chain. He winked and said, 'I think that the ninety-eight *was* a perfect one. Sweet as heaven. Juice just about spillin' out of it. Gorgeous deep orange color. Firm texture, perfume scent. Any better and it'd been too perfect, you know what I mean?'

Too perfect? But I nodded.

'Plus, that way we could keep on searching!'

Both smiling now, we looked up to see Teddy

201

nosing around the same boulder he'd been investigating the day before. We'd arrived at the bench already. Merle and I sat down together, and immediately drank from our water bottles.

I couldn't believe we'd arrived so quickly. Chatting with Merle had made the uphill walk nearly effortless. I was sweating, but not huffing and puffing quite as much this time. We gave our dogs water out of our hands. Teddy lapped demurely from Merle's cupped hand; Heloise didn't really get the concept. She kept trying to lick and chew the tip of my water bottle, trying to get the water at its source.

'Allow me,' said Merle, taking my bottle from me and nodding toward Heloise. I cupped both my hands, and Merle held the bottle high, pouring out a small stream. I bent over and slid my filled hands under Heloise's nose, and she lapped up the water. As she did, I turned, looking at Merle, both of us smiling.

When Heloise had finished, Merle handed my bottle back to me, then reached in his pocket and pulled out a small rectangular white box. 'Lemon drop?' he asked, holding the open box toward me.

'I'd love one!' What I really wanted was to accept Merle's offer. Any offer. I popped the drop in my mouth, its sweet-sour mix a delightful memory. How long had it been since I'd had a lemon drop? It struck me profoundly how this single lemon drop was much more satisfying than a whole bowl of sugary cereal.

Heloise jumped repeatedly at Teddy's shoulder, determined to have just a small taste of his ear. Teddy looked over his other shoulder at us with a doleful but patient expression, clearly understanding and accepting that the whimsy and energy of youth must simply be endured. With some urging from me, Heloise relented and sat down, splay-legged as ever, leaning against my shin. Merle placed a lemon drop in his own mouth and then patted Teddy. We both leaned back on the bench, and both laughed again when we said 'Mmmm' at the same time.

The two July puppy meetings were both held at the Cottonwood outdoor pedestrian mall. We always drew a crowd when the dozen or so dogs, all in their jackets, strolled along the busy mall. The first meeting happened to be on Matt's birthday, and he asked to come with me. Lainey, too. Neil came home for dinner, gave Matt a book, *Colleges That Change Lives,* and headed back to the clinic as we headed to Cottonwood. But the kids and I had a great time. They loved seeing all the other dogs; I loved introducing them to the group. We took turns with Heloise, practicing ignoring distractions by walking by statues, over grates, and through the thick crowds, which were laced with Rollerbladers, baby strollers, and bicyclists. The dogs had to learn not to react to any of it. But the toughest distraction by far, from the dogs' perspective, were the very small people with very large ice cream cones. Our canine and human group overwhelmed the ice cream shop when we stopped in for a treat and sang a rousing 'Happy Birthday' to Matt.

Seventeen. Little Mattie. He'd decided to start practicing driving again, but only with me. He drove us home that night, flawlessly. At home, I gave him my present, a fifty-dollar gift certificate to the Art Department store.

By August, the puppies in our group were dogs, including my own. I'd lost a bit of weight, Heloise had gained substantially more, but we were both getting nicely muscled from our long walks. We often walked with Merle and Teddy, but often alone as well. With my weight loss, I'd begun to dress a little more nicely for the puppy meetings, but I didn't think Bill had noticed. Fashion statements were futile anyway; everyone was pretty much covered in dog hair by the end of every meeting.

At our first August meeting, we returned to the cool of the warehouse building.

'Okay, we're almost out of time, but who's got issues?' Bill asked. The group laughed appreciatively at his phrasing.

The teen girl who was raising one of the golden retrievers raised her hand. 'Bernadette is so hyper whenever I take her out on socialization trips.'

I reached down and gave Heloise, lying quietly by my feet, a thump of appreciation. She was a gem whenever I took her out, although we had a fairly limited repertoire, mostly of grocery stores, sometimes the mall, bookstores, once to the post office.

'Where are you taking her?' asked Bill.

'Well, Mom and I went to the mall with her, but she went ballistic by the outdoor fountain, so we didn't even go in. We tried about four or five times to get past that fountain, but she was totally freaked so we just went home.'

'Okay. I'm glad this came up. When your dog is freaking out, you simply can't give up. That tells her two things, neither of which you want to be telling her: One, that fountains really are terribly dangerous and scary, and should be avoided at all costs.' Everyone laughed, including me, but it also gave me pause. I'd done that with my kids – and maybe even Neil – given in too often to their fears or fits. Or my own. 'Two, it tells her how she can get *you* to do what *she* wants. You've got to stick it out. Calm, loving, reassuring. Distraction, different tactics. Your dog will usually only try to lead if they don't have a confident leader to follow.'

Everyone was giving Bill their full attention. Except the dogs. Several had fallen asleep. Heloise was chewing on my shoe. I couldn't help but smile. She'd relieved herself outside before the meeting, so I knew it was the dog version of when my kids were little and they'd pull on my pants leg or skirt hem when they wanted to hurry me along at the grocery store. I pulled my foot away and slipped a toy in her mouth. 'Good girl,' I said quietly but enthusiastically as she began chewing the toy. I didn't look up but hoped Bill had seen.

'Exactly, Deena! Good job.' Bill winked at me and I almost wet my pants.

Thankfully, Bill clapped again and got everyone's attention. 'Okay, time's up for tonight, but I want to make a quick announcement. We have an opportunity for a very special group socialization. You've all heard of John Abrams, who owns car dealerships all over Denver?' We all nodded. 'He's a big K-9 Eyes supporter. His sister is blind and has had three working guides from K-9 Eyes over the years. Anyway, John's donated a dozen tickets to our group for Thursday night's Rockies game against the Padres. I'm not much of a sports fan myself, but this is as close as our pups can come to playing ball.' More laughter. He had us all in the palm of his hand no matter what he was talking about. Pure charisma.

'Plus,' he continued, 'it's a good crowd socialization. First come, first serve, but I think we'll have plenty, given it's on a Thursday night.' He pulled a small piece of paper from his pocket, unfolded it, and began reading. 'We'll meet at the Park-and-Ride bus garage on Mesa Drive at four. First pitch is at five thirty.' He looked up. Again that disarming smile. 'Who wants to play ball?!'

A few hands shot up. I knew nothing about baseball. Had never been to a game, had never had a desire to go to a game. I looked at Heloise, lying quietly on the floor. Lainey had soccer practice

Thursday, but she could ride with Sara. Matt might need a ride home from his scout project. No. Josh said he could bring Matt home. What if Josh's old car broke down? And Neil was coming home Thursday night from his medical conference. I should—

Stop! Stop making them need you. They don't. It's Heloise that needs to get out. And you.

I leaned down, gently fondled Heloise's ear with my right hand. Slowly, I stretched my left high in the air.

CHAPTER 16

I'd left Neil a note on the kitchen table saying where I was and not to wait up, as I had no idea how long a baseball game lasted. I'd told Matt, twice, that Heloise and I were going to a Rockies game. He stood incredulous and slack-jawed in the kitchen, watching me assemble my fanny pack.

'Are you and Josh working on the mural today?' I asked. I was thrilled with their decision.

'Josh is coming over here 'cause they're resurfacing the parking lot at the center. We're going to firm up the sketch and figure out our paint situation.' So, I wouldn't have to worry about Josh's car. 'You're really going to a baseball game, Mom?' he asked, for the third time.

'Yes! Now, shoo!' I said, playfully swatting him on the rear.

'Lainey!' I shouted in the general direction of the stairs. It was the second time I'd called her. I turned to Matt again. '*What* is your sister doing up there?'

'Deena Munger, my mom, going to a *Rockies game,*' he said, laughing. 'Can I ask why?'

'I have a secret passion for the thrower guy.'

Matt bent over his knees, laughing. 'Mom! He's called a pitcher!'

I swatted him again, this time on the arm. 'I *know*, Matt. I'm just teasing you. I'm going because it's good exposure for Heloise and, who knows, I might just love baseball.' I continued jamming things into the fanny pack. I was running late, plus I was a tiny bit peeved at Matt's persistent disbelief that I, his boring old mother, could be going to a professional sporting event. Matt wandered out of the kitchen with three granola bars in his hand, muttering, 'Mom. At a Rockies game. Unbelievable.'

'Matt!' I called to him, truly feeling hurt now that he wouldn't let it go. 'I'd like you to go through all the paints in the basement, find out what's good, what's dried out. Put the old stuff in a box in the garage.' He stared at me from the hallway. I stared back. He turned and walked up the stairs, his head shaking side to side. 'And clean your room!' I wanted to keep adding more. Make dinner! Mow the lawn! Scrub the toilets water the plants do the laundry shop for groceries vacuum a rug pay the bills call the plumber. And oh yeah! Take the cat for a haircut.

Instead I called for Lainey again. This made the third time. What was it with my kids that they needed everything in threes? I cringed. I suddenly realized that, just as with Heloise, I shouldn't repeat things. Then they'd have to learn to listen the first time. Finally Lainey came trudging down-stairs from her bedroom, her headphones still on her ears. I mimed taking the headphones off, just once, and waited, keeping my eyes on hers. I put my shoulders back, pulled up to my full height, just a hair taller than my daughter. Lainey furrowed her brow, then pulled off the headphones, leaving them on her neck.

Lainey, it turned out, was less incredulous about the ball game, more incredulous at my blatant abandonment of her. 'You *have* to drive me to soccer!'

'I'm sure you can ride with Sara,' I said. The girls, while on different teams, both practiced at the same sprawling soccer fields north of town. She'd ridden with Sara once before.

I stood at the sink, filling a large water bottle so both Heloise and I would have something other than beer or soda to drink. I checked to make sure her collapsible water bowl was in the fanny pack.

'God, Mom! Sara quit soccer weeks ago!'

I wheeled around. 'No! Sara quit soccer?' Now I was incredulous and repeating things.

'Yup,' said Lainey, smirking slightly, reveling in the power of prior knowledge.

'Why? She's lived and breathed soccer for—' As I tried to estimate the years, my mind flashed to when Matt went to Sara's sixth birthday party, back when boys and girls could just be friends. We'd bought her a soccer pillow and soccer tote bag. Virtually every present at that party, and for many after, was soccer-themed. 'Forever! She's so talented! She was one of the stars of the state team last year!' I'd really thought this girl would be the next big soccer superstar.

'Maybe she just had enough,' said Lainey, squatting to stroke Heloise's head. 'Besides, she has Kurt now.'

Suddenly I wasn't late. Warning flares went off all around me. Heloise looked up at me, as though she too could see them.

'What do you mean, "besides, she has Kurt now"? That's a non sequitur if ever I heard one.'

She stood, and Heloise did too, pushing her head into Lainey's limp hand. Heloise would take passive petting over no petting at all. 'What's that? Someone who doesn't suck but still quits?' She unconsciously began rubbing Heloise's head again.

I smiled. 'No, but good guess, sweetie. It's when one statement doesn't logically follow the previous. What does dating Kurt have to do with Sara quitting soccer?'

'Well! Duh!' Lainey gave me her infamous eye roll again. I swear those orbs were going to roll right out of her head one of these days. What fun Heloise would have chasing them as they rolled around the kitchen!

With a deep sigh of resignation, Lainey clarified the matter for me. 'Obviously he wants to spend more time with her, Mom. I think it's nice. I wish I had a boyfriend.'

211

Now the whoop whoop of air raid sirens joined the flares. Amazingly, Heloise cocked her ears, although I was pretty sure she was just sensing my emotion ratcheting up.

I took Lainey's hand in mine. She reluctantly let me. Heloise sat near us, looking like she was watching a tennis match. 'Honey, you *will* have a boyfriend, probably lots of them, probably all too soon. But tell me you understand how important it is not to give up your dreams for—' I stopped. 'For anything.'

Lainey looked at me blankly for a moment, absorbing the concern in my face and voice. Then she pulled her hand out of mine, gave me another eye roll, this time combined with a single but sharp *tsk* from her tongue. 'Mom, they're really in love. You wouldn't understand.'

My mouth opened, then shut, then opened again. But I couldn't speak.

Was she saying she thought I didn't love her father? Did I? Or was she just giving the standard teen line given by all adolescents when they are so self-absorbed they assume no one else has ever been through anything like what they're going through? It occurred to me, mouth-breathing there in my kitchen, that there are several times in our lives when we are so wrapped up in ourselves that a worldview becomes difficult, if not impossible. When we rather suddenly have some sort of new power, and with it, new vulnerability. Two-year-olds are often like that. It happens again, big time, in adolescence. I thought a minute. And yes. I was like that when I was pregnant, too.

Maybe menopause was another self-absorbed time. Were all these times in our lives determined by our hormones? Some biological imperative to concentrate wholly on the self?

Or were these just the whiny times of life?

'Yo. Mom.' Lainey was waving her hand in front of my face. 'How'm I gonna get to practice?' Heloise had slumped onto the cool tile floor and put her head on my foot, letting out a small groan. Her way of saying, 'Humans take *forever* to get out the door!' I looked at the clock. Damn.

'Uh. Okay, look, I'm running late. Let's see . . . Do you know anyone else who could give you a ride? And Lainey?' I looked at her hard, held her shoulders in my hands. 'I want to talk about this again. I want to tell you some things about—'

What? Life? Oh, that'll go over real well. Just what a teenager wants to hear. *We need to have a life talk, darling.* 'I want to tell you about some mistakes I made.' Her eyebrows shot up in genuine surprise. *This* she wanted to hear. 'But for now, is there anyone else who could give you a ride? I'm already committed to go to the game and I've got to scoot to catch the bus.' I grabbed the fanny pack, my purse, then wheeled back toward her. 'The bus! *You* can take the bus!'

'The buh-us?' She gave it two heavy syllables of disdain.

I was already digging through my purse for bus

coupons. I lifted out the packs of gum, the rolls of LifeSavers, and a tin of mints. 'Here,' I said, setting one after another on the counter, 'you want these? I'm off sugar.' She looked at me like I was an alien in her mother's body. 'Ah! Here they are. Say, you know what, Lainey? I saw a sign at the bus station. They have very affordable monthly teen passes. Then you can go wherever you want, whenever you want!' I handed her two coupons. 'I'll pay for it!' Her favorite words. 'For now, go online right away and get the schedule for today. Here. The site is on the coupon.' She stared at me. I stared back. 'Now.'

She blinked as she took the coupons, pulling her head sharply back, as though I'd flicked some water at her. She recovered quickly, and with a loud 'pfffft' lifted her headphones back over her ears. Coupons in hand, she headed to the den. To the computer.

I only had a moment of satisfaction before dread washed over me as I headed out to the car with Heloise. What was I going to tell her later, when we had our 'talk'? That my marriage to her father was a mistake? Was it? No. I knew that much. We'd had some really great years together. Was it that I married too young? Or was it that even some successful marriages only had a couple of decades of natural life?

Doubting that baseball would provide any answers, it was nonetheless time to go. I turned the key in the ignition, looking in the rearview mirror at Heloise. She no longer rode in the kennel, she now owned the back end of my wagon. She had her head draped over the edge of one of the backseat headrests, her ears up, ready to copilot. I backed the car out of the driveway and said to her, 'Let's go watch a ball game, girl.'

'Mind if we join you?' Bill asked me, coming up the bus aisle with a huge German shepherd in tow. Heloise jumped to her feet and so did my heart. I'd arrived late and had gone to the back of the bus, to the only empty seat. There were seven other raisers and dogs among the regular baseball faithful. Bill had come on only after the last person from our group was on. Namely, me.

'Sure,' I said to Bill. 'Sit, Heloise.' I realized I'd reversed the order for giving a command. Name first, then command. 'I mean, Heloise! Sit. Sit!' *Oh! Shoot! Don't repeat the commands.* Wrong again, in front of Bill. Heloise sat anyway, bless her heart. I patted her shoulder.

Bill sat next to me, and the shepherd settled like an old pro in the bus aisle.

'Who's that?' I asked, nodding to the shepherd.

'Belladonna. She's from the Colton group. I'm doing a little work with her while the raiser's on vacation.'

'How old is she?' I asked. 'She's huge!'

'She's seventeen months. The shepherds take longer to mature than the Labs.' He settled back in the seat. I could feel our arm hairs touching.

215

'So, how are things, Deena?' he asked, as the bus pulled away. 'Heloise seems to be doing really well.' She had settled down again, working hard on Bumpy, her hard plastic dinosaur covered with small spiky bumps. It hurt my mouth to watch her chew it, but she loved it. Bill reached down and rubbed her ear. His forearm gently touched my shin; the contact felt hot, electric.

'She's doing great,' I replied, with a ridiculous amount of concentration. 'She's smart as a whip. And you're right, she really does want to please me. In fact, here's how smart she is: If she does something wrong and I catch her, she immediately sits, and then looks expectantly at me, waiting for the praise she knows she'll get for sitting.'

Bill's laugh sent ripples of pleasure through me. 'She's a cagey one all right,' he said. His eyes crinkled in amusement. The guy could be an advertisement for a cream to *give* you crow's-feet. I looked down at Heloise so I wouldn't blush again, several strands of my grown-out bangs falling across my eyes. I had to get this mop cut!

I pushed the hair back behind my ear and asked, 'While I've got you here, Bill, sort of a captive audience, I do have a question. Or two. Or three.' Again, his wonderful laugh. I was feeding on it.

'Fire away. I'm all yours.'

I kept the swoon deep inside. 'Okay. You know how you told us not to put them in their kennel to punish them?' Bill nodded. 'But you also said it was okay to put them in there if they're driving us crazy, and we just need to get something done?' He nodded again. 'So doesn't that feel like punishment to them if we put them in there because they're driving us crazy?'

'Well, you're probably thinking about this a little more than Heloise is.' There was that grin again.

I laughed. Charmingly, I hoped.

'Just do it in a real happy voice. "Okay,"' he said, demonstrating in singsong, '"Kennel."' Heloise looked up at him, her head cocked.

I nodded. 'What about the opposite? I mean, sometimes right when I'm coming to let her out, she starts whining. So doesn't that make her think I'm letting her out because she was whining?'

'Same thing. You're right not to reward the whining. Start talking to her a bit as you're on your way, real upbeat, praising her. But don't worry too much about it, Deena. She's doing great. *You're* doing great. Trust yourself.'

If only . . .

'Okay, thanks,' I said, looking at the back of the seat, still unable to look directly at him. 'One last question,' I said, rather apologetically.

'Deena. I love it that you ask questions. I wish everyone was as thoughtful and careful as you are.'

I managed to look at him, and fell right into his blue eyes, every thought in my mind flowing out. Between menopause and a handsome man looking at me, my brain just seemed to flush like a toilet, all those verbs and nouns whooshing down my cerebral drain, leaving me only with subjects. 'I – You –' I blushed. Again. 'I forgot what I was going to ask you.'

We both laughed. The two girls ahead of us turned around to see if it was a dog doing something adorable. Disappointed, they turned back around.

Bill began chatting about his upcoming trip to the K-9 Eyes campus in California for the graduation of one of his pups. I leaned back against the window, listening to his smooth voice. He told me about the different dogs he'd raised, and some of the different blind people they'd gone to: a banker in Wichita, a teacher near Seattle, a CEO in Chicago. I could listen to him forever, I thought. Such a giving, generous man. Not that Neil wasn't. It was just—

As I was listening, Heloise had repositioned herself and fallen fast asleep, nestled on my feet. Her front elbow was digging into my right foot. I could feel the pins and needles starting in my leg. But as Bill and I talked, never had the old adage about letting sleeping dogs lie been more true.

I almost gasped as the bus pulled up to the ballpark. With Heloise asleep and Bill next to me, the hour-plus ride had seemed mere minutes. My right leg, however, was profoundly numb.

As the bus emptied, front to back, Heloise and I at last stood, following Bill and Belladonna. Heloise was pulling at the leash, eager as always to be on to the next adventure. But I was slowly limping along, grabbing on to each seat back, trying to take the pressure off my nearly worthless leg and foot. At the bus steps, however, Heloise balked, her front legs spread and stiff, her head and tail down, ears flat. I looked at Bill, already off the bus, watching me.

'Go ahead and pick her up, Deena. Don't push it if she's afraid.'

I scooped her up awkwardly. She was getting so big, and the bus stairway was quite narrow. I limped down one step, my right leg filled with jelly. Heloise stiffened in my arms, all four legs sticking stiffly out to the sides. Hang the next adventure. She now clearly didn't want to leave the bus, and knew exactly how to make it difficult for me to carry her off. I carefully threaded her splayed legs through the doorway, one at a time.

Finally, I set her down on the ground with an audible 'Ooff!' and remained bent over to untangle her leash from around her foot and my wrist. My leg had now reached the electrocution stage of waking up, completely useless. Heloise suddenly ducked through my legs and around Bill to lick at Belladonna. The leash did a neat lasso around us. My worthless limb buckled and I tipped over, the leash pulling Bill down on top of me. We were face-to-face on the ground, bound together by Heloise's leash, the end of which was wrapped tightly around my wrist. My wrist being under

219

me. Me being under Bill. Heloise pulled to within inches of both our faces.

'Are you okay?' asked Bill, sliding off me, as best he could, given the restraint of the leash. Heloise looked like she was trying to decide if this was fun or not.

I nodded to Bill, unable to speak, heat pulsing through me. Either the hot asphalt was slowly cooking me, or another hot flash was coming on. Or else dying of embarrassment felt exactly like a hot flash.

Heloise's head suddenly appeared over my face, and she started licking my nose and mouth, then Bill's, ecstatic that these two faces were now reachable. We both started laughing, pushing her away with what little mobility we each had.

Marilyn rushed over, unthreaded Heloise's leash and pulled her away. I gave both Bill and Marilyn a weak smile. 'I'm so sorry,' I said finally, sitting up and pushing my wet hair off my face. 'My leg's asleep.' One advantage of sweating this much was that I could now paste back my ornery bangs.

'You sure you're okay?' Bill asked, touching my shoulder.

Even though he was now completely off me, I felt like I couldn't breathe. Mute again, I nodded, staring into his eyes.

'Come on, girl,' said Marilyn. I assumed she was talking to Salsa, till she took my hand and pulled me up and over toward a grassy area where our group had assembled. I stood in the shade and massaged some feeling back into my leg while Marilyn took both our dogs for a pee break. Bill gently took my elbow in his hand. 'You sure you're all right? You look a little flushed.' I nodded and suddenly, miraculously, found my hand on his. 'Yeah, thanks.'

Just as suddenly, Marilyn was back, grabbing my hand again and lunging forward. 'C'mon, gang! Let's go play ball!'

The fourteen of us, seven canine and human pairs, joined the crowds heading for the gates. I nervously watched over Heloise's feet in all the jostling. Most people were paying attention, smiling and giving us as much room as they could. But one unkempt man in a dingy white T-shirt that barely covered his enormous belly *tried* to step on Heloise's toes, muttering, 'Damn dogs don't belong at a ball game.' Bill quickly and deftly switched places with me and Heloise, placing the hundred-and-ten-pound Belladonna between Bill and Creep. Creep said nothing more and gave the shepherd a wide berth.

The team's losing season had translated into a less-than-sold-out crowd. We had the entire handicap area to ourselves, so there was plenty of room for all the dogs at our legs. The delicious smells somehow both preceded and followed the various vendors walking the aisles. I thought I might actually have to buy myself a hot dog later on, just because it didn't seem right to go to a ball game and not eat a hot dog.

221

Marilyn and Salsa sat on one side of me. Jack, Marilyn's ex-husband, was on the other side of her. Bill was on my left. Jack bought all four of us beers. I gave mine to Bill. By the end of the first inning I'd already learned something important about attending a baseball game: most people only watch intermittently, chatting throughout. I'm not sure what I'd expected, but this was a pleasant surprise. My companions, Marilyn especially, taught me just enough to keep me modestly involved in the game, but Heloise required a fair amount of my attention, till she fell asleep again late in the third inning.

By the seventh inning, Marilyn and Jack had had several rounds each. After one egregious call in the eighth inning – even I could see the pitch was clearly wide, and it was called a strike – Marilyn joined the catcalls and jeers, then stood up and bellowed, 'Hey, ump! Wanna borrow my seeing eye dog?!' eliciting howls of laughter and applause from everyone within earshot. In fact, Marilyn had me laughing and entertained much of the game. We found that we had several things in common: three kids, though her youngest was the age of my oldest; we'd both grown up in Colorado, though she in Denver versus my rural upbringing; and we'd both been married the same number of years, twenty-three. Although that was four years ago for them. That was the year she and Jack had agreed to divorce, live separately, but remain close friends. After twenty-three years of marriage.

'It works for us. I think we have an unusual situation though.' She left it at that and I didn't want to pry, so I didn't ask for the details. But I was dying to know.

At the beginning of the ninth inning, Marilyn invited me to join her on a trip to the ladies' room. 'If you wait till after the game's over, the line's out the door.'

With our dogs at our sides, we strolled down the long concourse toward the restrooms. We were stopped twice as we walked, the questions the same as always: How long do you keep them? How can you bear to give them up? We answered politely but quickened our pace after the second.

'May I ask you something personal?' Marilyn said abruptly.

I was caught off guard, mostly because I was debating whether to pose the exact same question to her.

'Sure.'

'Do you have a thing for Bill?' My heart pounded and I could feel my face immediately flush.

'I thought so,' she said, not needing more response from me. 'We all do, in our own way. But look, I've known him for years, and I just want to let you know, he's kind of a tortured soul, Deena.'

I stared at her, all my senses on alert.

'He's gay.'

I gasped. I immediately regretted it, mainly because I didn't want Marilyn to think that I thought that being gay was a bad thing. Which is exactly what she seemed to think. She stopped walking, gauging my reaction. I stopped too, tried to explain. 'No, I'm just surprised is all. I don't think that's bad. I mean, not that it's good,' I stammered. 'It's *fine*. My best friend is a lesbian.' Oh, that sounded so lame, even though it was true. I couldn't think clearly. I was definitely feeling at a loss here, but it was all stirred up with shock. I'd had such a . . . crush. A schoolgirl crush. A fantasy. Nothing more. And nothing less.

Marilyn started walking again, and thankfully, talking. 'He doesn't broadcast it. He's less than accepting of it himself. He probably always knew he was gay, but because of his background – his father's a minister, very conservative and all – he couldn't be honest. So he dutifully got married, had kids, faked it reasonably well for a while, then battled a deep depression for about eight or nine years, till his wife left and got custody. Now he lives alone, with his dogs. His family and religion can't accept what he is, so neither can he. He's just decided not to have any sexual life at all. He keeps everyone right about here.' She held her free arm stiffly in front of her. 'At least in terms of intimate relationships.'

As we headed into the ladies' room, she said quickly and quietly, but with vehemence, 'He's such a dear, charming man, and it's a goddamn shame our society is so screwed up about love.'

The restroom was not crowded, but someone was

in the handicap stall and I really had to go, so Heloise and I crammed into an available narrow one.

Bill. Gay. Well, in some sense, now that it was sinking in, it didn't surprise me. Wasn't it conventional wisdom that a gay man made for a straight woman's best friend?

I struggled with holding Heloise's leash and getting my pants unzipped and pulled down, while keeping Heloise at even a minimum discreet distance from my privates. We'd had some experience with this at the grocery store, but mostly I tried to avoid it. The stalls in most ladies' rooms are just not made for lady plus dog. Especially when dog is a little too interested in the tinkling sound and keeps trying to sniff under lady's butt. I held her by the collar, at arm's length, so she couldn't intrude on my privacy any more than she already was, just by being in there with me. My stiff-arming her made me think of Marilyn describing Bill.

It had felt like a small bombshell of information. It wasn't just that he was gay; I didn't really think I would pursue a relationship with him anyway. Did I? But for him to feel like he had no options was . . . heartbreaking.

When Heloise and I emerged from the restroom, Marilyn and Salsa were waiting for us in the concourse. We had taken the dogs outside in the fifth inning, but I wasn't sure what the protocol should be, so I asked Marilyn, 'Should we take the dogs out again?'

'No, they'll be fine till we go out to board the buses. Game's almost over.'

We walked silently back toward our section. Finally, Marilyn spoke.

'Hope that was okay to tell you that. About Bill.'

'Oh, yes! Of course. I didn't really have a crush on him or anything. I'm married! I just think he's a lovely man.' I tucked my bangs back behind my ear, looking straight ahead. 'Thank you for letting me know. It's just so sad, though. About him. No one should be in a position where they have to choose to not love at all.'

'Yeah. If there's one thing you'd think people could accept, it'd be one person genuinely loving another person. It's not like we have too much love in the world or anything.' I nodded.

We rejoined the others, and Marilyn put her index and middle fingers of each hand in her mouth and whistled at the food vendors. As two of them climbed the steps, I turned to Bill. 'Can I buy you a hot dog?' I asked. 'Sort of a thank-you for all your help, to the group.' I took a deep breath. 'But especially to me. For giving me a chance.'

He smiled, putting one arm around my shoulders and squeezing. 'Deena, you're doing a fantastic job with Heloise. How's the housecleaning?' We both burst out laughing, then Bill looked at the two vendors. 'That's a nice offer of a hot dog, but can I have a bag of peanuts instead?' He grinned.

'You bet!' I paid the vendors for my hot dog and Bill's peanuts, warm and in the shell. Marilyn bought a box of Cracker Jack. I smiled at the cliché of it all. Bill thanked me again for the treat, and switched places with Marilyn so he could chat with Jack.

'So, Deena,' said Marilyn. 'You must love the outdoors, growing up on a farm and all.' She slid a handful of Cracker Jacks into her mouth.

'Well, yes and no,' I said. I lifted the hot dog out of its bun and took a small bite. I'd always heard that there's no better hot dog than one eaten at a baseball game, and it was true. It was delicious.

I licked a little mustard off my lips and continued. 'Actually, I really haven't been much of an outdoors person, most of my life. But I've started hiking the foothill trails near my house with Heloise and I really love it. It feels like I can breathe when I'm up there.' I thought of all my treasured walks with Merle and Teddy. I'd seen them just a few days earlier up on the trail, but Merle said he was going to take a little break from walking Teddy because the old collie was having trouble with the heat. It had been ninety-seven degrees on that day, though. I think we'd all had trouble with the heat during that hot spell.

'I can't get enough of the mountains, myself,' said Marilyn, shaking out more Cracker Jack. The prize came sliding out too. 'I love to hike and mountain bike. But my real passion is fly-fishing.'

I looked at her. She had to be in her mid to late sixties! Mountain biking? Fly-fishing?

'No kidding? Fly-fishing. I don't think I've ever met a fisherwoman. Not that I know of anyway.'

She peeled back the red-and-white paper, concentrating on unwrapping her prize, and said to me without looking up, 'Want to try it? I'd be happy to show you sometime.' She pulled at the prize, stuck in its wrapper. 'I've got a rod you can use. I bet you'll love it. It's very meditative. I'll give you my prize if you'll say yes.'

Meditative. That sounded good. Up in the mountains. That sounded good, too. But the fly part was a little dissuading. The fish part, even more so. But I was intrigued by Marilyn, how she'd gotten to this place in her life. 'I'd love to go. Do you take Salsa with you?'

'Oh, sometimes. It's a lot more meditative without her though.' We both grinned.

'Shoot,' she said, handing me a mini baseball card. 'I was hoping it'd be a decoder ring. You could use one.' We both burst out laughing, until the sharp crack of the bat connecting with the ball made us look up as the crowd erupted.

CHAPTER 17

'Okay, now you try it.'

Marilyn had just finished showing me how to cast on to the languid, meandering river. We'd left our dogs with puppy sitters for the day, packed a lunch and headed to the high country. The air was crisp, the sky azure, and the grasses, water, rocks – everything – seemed to pop with vibrancy. Plus, it was in the pleasant upper seventies up here, about fifteen degrees cooler than in the valley.

I felt like I was playing hooky. There were dozens of things on my to-do list at home. A dozen more on my should-do list. At the very least, I should be with Heloise. This felt remarkably like the first time I used a VCR and paused the movie to go get popcorn out of the microwave. This was even more powerful. Like I'd put the world on pause and magically stepped into another reality. Or maybe put my reality on pause while I stepped into the world. I breathed a deep lungful of mountain air and smiled. Maybe that was really the only should that should be on my should-do list.

'Let me watch you one more time,' I said timidly.

Marilyn grinned, but picked up her rod and walked toward the river's edge. As she began, I shook my head in admiration. She was a visual symphony, her instruments the rod, the line, the fly, and her body. I had at first expected a whipping sound, but her moves were so deft that the line silently sliced the air. It danced slow, almost hypnotic arcs, her arm flexing then straightening, her movements fluid, cohesive, like a bird flying in slow motion. Finally, just a hint of concentric rings spread on the water as the fly landed in a small dark pool on the other side of the river. The rings disappeared in the gentle current, and the fly drifted lazily downstream.

'Okay, now I'm going to amend.' She twitched her forearm and the line in the water magically jumped over the fly, and lay upstream. 'Your turn, Deena. You can do it!'

I couldn't help but feel like Dumbo being told by the mouse that he could fly. For the first time that morning, I genuinely wished Heloise was here. My magic feather.

I readied my fly, uncoiled some line, inhaled again, and began the dance. But instead of a bird in balletic flight, I'm pretty sure I looked more like I was doing the funky chicken. I had two passable flicks, but on my third backward reach, the fly remained behind me as I brought my arm and rod forward.

'Heeyyy! Congratulations, Deena! You've caught your first bush!'

My face reddened. 'Oh! I'm sorry!'

She laughed. 'No! That's a good thing! Every fly-fisher worth her salt has caught a shrub or two. Or twenty. Just hang out there a minute.' She reeled in her line and went to retrieve mine.

As she first located and then worked on freeing my fly and line from the bush, I was as astounded at myself as Matt had been at me the other day. I, Deena Munger, was up in the mountains fly-fishing. *Fly-fishing!* Or attempting same. I wasn't sure, especially at this point, that it was something I'd ever do again. But this, and the baseball game, and even the dog raising – it was like I was in college again, 'trying on' all sorts of things, even some things I was pretty sure wouldn't fit. I felt, if not young, daring. And all of it was causing my family to wonder if I hadn't lost my mind.

Neil had seen me packing a backpack the night before in the kitchen. 'Fly-fishing?' he'd asked, wide-eyed. '*You're* going fly-fishing?' I simply nodded. 'Why? And with whom?' I could hear the mistrust in his voice. I didn't want him to flounder in this abyss, but then again, maybe I did. When it came to Neil, I didn't know what I wanted. I didn't want to be cruel. I just wanted to *be*.

'I'm going with a friend from the puppy-raising club.' His face was filled with questioning, with hurt. 'A woman friend,' I added.

I knew my family was wondering what had happened to their mom and wife. Odd how when I'd felt most lost and undefined, they were most secure in their knowledge of me.

'Almost got it . . . ,' yelled Marilyn jubilantly from behind me. 'Just hang there a minute longer. And hold your rod up a little, please.' Without turning, I lifted my arm and held the rod high. A little breeze ruffled the tall grass, first from across the river, then rolling toward me like a soft tide. I watched a fat bee near my feet in its floaty dance, regularly pausing and hesitating in midair for reasons I couldn't discern, its languorous hum the perfect score to the morning. Up and down and around the bee flew in a circular hover. Was it tasting the air? Was it getting signals from a friend or the home-base hive as to where the good flowers were? *To the left, no, too far, now right, up a little. There! Straight ahead!* Finally it landed on a gently swaying black-eyed Susan and began crawling toward the red-black center.

'Ta-da!' yelled Marilyn. I turned to see her white smile flash in the clear morning, and met it with my own. She held the fly and untangled line aloft in victory. 'You're free!'

Marilyn and I packed up in midafternoon, headed for home, but talked each other into stopping for ice cream in Danner, a tiny old mining town that still had an active mine, probably just to draw tourists. But a little shop there, Naz's Treat Shoppe, made their own ice cream and pies and drew locals for miles around. As we finally headed down the canyon again, the air temperature seemed to increase a degree with every foot we lost in altitude. Blocks from my house we passed the First Bank of Fairview. Its sign blinked *94*, alternating with the time, 5:58.

At home, the kids foraged while I took a needed shower. They were already in the cool basement den by the time I emerged, dressed, in the kitchen. I made myself a small salad, ate alone at the table, reading a novel. After dinner, I plopped down on Sam's bed under the ceiling fan, continuing the novel, which carried me back into the mountains with a woman park ranger.

'Deena?'

It was Neil, just outside my bedroom, Sam's bedroom, dark save for the soft glow of the reading lamp. I realized I must have dozed off.

I held my eyes closed, my book still splayed across my chest, the ceiling fan lazily whirring above. The hot night was almost muggy, by Colorado's usual dry standards. I lay motionless under the sheet, except for my breathing, which I was hoping sounded like that of a person solidly into REM. Even though it was only eight thirty, I felt like I actually could drift back to sleep, if he didn't say anything else.

'Are you asleep?' he asked softly. He'd come into the room. He waited. I breathed. 'Are you asleep?' he asked again, louder.

Goddamnit. A person couldn't even fake sleeping here, much less actually sleep.

'No! Not anymore!' I said, angrily throwing back

the sheet. I stood, suddenly realizing I was still fully clothed. This no doubt somewhat weakened my position as Disturbed Slumberer. Heloise whined from her kennel, probably thinking: *Salvation!* I normally put her in her kennel for the evening at about nine thirty or ten. When I'd put her in there at seven thirty this evening, she must have felt her bladder swell at the very idea.

'What do you want, Neil?' I asked.

'Well, dinner. There's nothing in the oven, nothing in the fridge.'

I tried not to fume. 'Neil, I didn't cook any dinner tonight. It's too damn hot. I told the kids to forage. Can't you make yourself a salad?'

'A salad's not a meal.'

'Well, toss on some tuna or something! For heaven's sake, Neil, you better start learning how to take care of yourself.'

He paused, pulled on one of the starched cuffs of his white shirt, then looked at me. 'Meaning what, exactly?'

Heloise whimpered.

'Nothing. I have to take Heloise out,' I said, opening her kennel. 'Let's go, girl.' I patted my thigh as I headed out of the room. Heloise exited her kennel, but instead of coming to me, she made a beeline for Neil.

I stopped at the top of the stairs and called her again. Neil reached down and scratched her ears with both hands.

'Can I come with you on your walk?'

'I'm not walking, just taking her to the yard.'

'Oh. Guess I'll just go make a salad, then.'

I waited for Neil to go downstairs and into the kitchen before I went to the top of the stairs with Heloise. She was now comfortable going up and down nearly all stairs, except those leading to our basement. I didn't know why, but she steadfastly refused to go down there, unless I carried her. And she was getting too heavy for much of that anymore.

'Wait,' I told her, walking down. At the bottom I turned. She watched me, intent. 'Okay!' She joyfully skittered down the stairs. 'What a good girl you are!' I told her as I clicked on her leash and we stepped outside.

I really *hadn't* planned to walk. But once on the front lawn, Heloise did her business then headed for the driveway, pulling hard on the leash, clearly thrilled to have escaped from the hot bedroom into the summer night. I followed on the other end of the leash as she trotted down the driveway and onto the sidewalk.

The evening was warm but still noticeably cooler than the house. Or my temper. I took in and released deep breaths till I felt my anger subside somewhat. Heloise seemed oblivious of my mood, alternately trotting and leaping forward, barely aware of the anchor of me behind her.

I was angry at Neil for expecting, almost demanding, dinner. I was also mad at myself for having created an environment over the past near-quarter century where he'd almost never had to fend for himself. I'd always been prepared for any time I might not be able to perform my duties. Even when I was sick or just after delivering the kids, I'd always had a freezer full of casseroles, a pan of enchiladas, and/or containers of soup in the freezer. In college, Neil had cooked for himself, but when we'd married, it had become 'my job,' part of it anyway, and I'd guarded it fiercely. Fierce, I realized now, not because I didn't want him to cook, but because I felt I was shirking my responsibilities if I didn't. I'd lived for too long now with a never-ending list, either in my mind or, more often, on paper. A statement of what I had to do to be worthy, and the list was never, ever, ever done. If I was doing one thing on the list, I felt guilty about not doing another.

Heloise and I crossed the street and headed for the path around the lake. It was mostly dark now. Normally I never ventured out in the dark. I'd always been too fearful, my imagination too great. There were muggers on every street corner, rapists behind all the dark bushes.

But there was little room for fear with the hulking anger inside me now. Besides, I felt oddly protected by this fifty-pound bundle of love, whose main weapon was a manic tail. Okay, that and a few small daggers in her mouth that I'd finally taught her were not to be used for kisses.

The lake shimmered under a nearly full moon. I looked up, wondering if it was waxing or waning.

I guessed it was waning because it seemed like it had just been full a day or so before. But every full moon surprised me lately. Again? Already? Full moons seemed to come much more often than they did in my childhood, now rushing by like headlights on life's busy road.

A small breeze ruffled the leaves. Something larger rustled the reeds on the shoreline. Heloise and I both jumped, veering away, giving whatever it was a wide berth. *Probably just a goose settling in*, I told myself. My anger was abating, changed by the startle into something resembling determined boldness. I was amazed, and proud, to be out walking alone at night. Well, alone with Heloise.

A cloud scudded over the moon, darkening our world momentarily. The dusky light that had shimmered on the water disappeared, making the lake a viscous black.

Now the heebie-jeebies overtook me, and I tugged on Heloise's leash. 'Let's go, girl!' It didn't take a lot of convincing. We left the path and cut across the grass toward the street as the moon popped back out. I tried, mostly in vain, to spot and avoid the myriad goose poops. Heloise tried, all too successfully, to snack on them before I could pull her head up. It was times like these that made it difficult not to put constant pressure on her collar, trying to keep her head up, but I dutifully tugged and released, tugged and released. Bill had impressed upon us how constantly pulling on the leash was like giving constant demands, making them ultimately ignore you altogether. We reached the sidewalk across the street just as another large cloud drifted over the moon.

Heloise barked suddenly. I followed her line of sight and could just barely make out a figure well ahead, but coming toward us. 'It's okay, girl. Just someone out for a walk.' I looked at the houses as we passed, gratefully noting the lights on in most of them. Heloise lunged forward, then checked herself, backing up and barking again. I stopped. The figure was now a block away, striding quickly toward us. A ridge of hair along Heloise's back stood on end and she growled. I pulled her close to me.

Suddenly her tail started wagging frantically and she lunged forward. A few more paces and I too recognized the familiar, swinging, long-legged gait.

'Neil?!' I said, loud enough to cover the distance. He'd come after me. The thought, far from pleasing, filled me anew with anger. I stopped. 'What are you doing here?'

He stopped. 'You said you weren't going for a walk.' I couldn't see his face, but the edge of his words cut through the night. 'You shouldn't be walking alone. I came to walk you home.' I let Heloise pull the leash to its length, allowing her to reach Neil. She jumped up on him, delighted the monster had turned out to be Neil. Her front paws on his knees, he scratched her head till I pulled her back a few feet.

'Don't let her jump on you like that,' I said.

'She's not supposed to.' I reeled her in, and she turned her attention to sniffing a mailbox post.

Neil's protection of me had always felt comforting, affectionate. Until recently. Now it felt controlling, diminishing. I couldn't breathe in the air allowed me.

'I'm not alone. Heloise is with me.' He took several steps toward us. I felt an anger boiling in me that didn't seem proportional to the situation. Or maybe it was proportional, needed even. A rocket needs to burn dramatically on the launch pad in order to break free.

Neil stopped, maybe sensing my anger, maybe harboring his own. The cloud slid off the moon and in its milky light our shadows stretched up over the manicured lawn, long and looming, like fence posts at their inexorable distance. He turned finally, walked toward home. I stood, waited. Then Heloise and I turned left, choosing a different route entirely.

CHAPTER 18

'Can I do the gowns, one red, one white, Matt?' Lainey yelled from her end of the mural. She had on a white painter's cap, her hair in a long ponytail, her thrift-store white overalls dotted with various colors of paint, as were her face and hands. She looked adorable.

Matt glanced at Josh, who was putting the finishing touches on one of the dogs, painting in black toenails. Josh shrugged, only briefly looking up from his work. 'We'd planned on purple, but I don't think we have enough purple paint, and at this point, I don't care. I just want to get it done.'

'Sure, Lainey. Go for it,' Matt yelled to her.

'Who's got the red?' Lainey said, jogging down the length of the wall, peering into the various open paint cans.

'Over here!' Amy raised one hand, while concentrating on painting in a flower along the base of the wall. A dried streak of yellow paint blazed across her forearm.

Matt and Josh had spent too many weeks of the summer planning and sketching designs for the wall. Then there was the asphalt resurfacing delay.

Now they were up against the deadline. School started on Monday. Their school and this Head Start school. They were determined to have the mural finished, ready to greet the kids on the first day. They'd opted for this sketch, feeling that it was fun, yet would still encourage the Head Start kids to aim for graduation, a request from the director. I thought the boys' idea was fabulous.

Matt and Josh had asked me for a little help on parts of some of their sketches, but mostly I'd tried very hard to stay out of it, to let it be their project entirely. It was hard for me, but I was learning. Besides, my son's talent in drawing was humbling. And inspiring.

But Heloise's influence was undeniable. Although she wasn't here with us (I'd left her with a puppy sitter for the weekend, fearing multicolored paw prints across the new asphalt), she was with us in spirit. The boys' 8½-by-11 sketch was now a wall-sized mural of two children and a dog, shown in five stages of growing up together, beginning with the boy and girl as babies, the dog as a small puppy. The last illustration showed the boy and girl in their graduation gowns, which Lainey was now painting red and white. Matt was putting the final touches on the last dog, fully grown and sitting, a dog-sized mortarboard and tassel on its head.

Because of the deadline, Matt had asked me and Lainey to help them finish painting over the weekend. To no one's surprise, Neil was at the clinic all weekend. It was actually serving patients now, but they couldn't afford to hire all the labor needed, in either medical or administrative, and the construction budget had run out before the work had. So Neil was working on every aspect.

But we did have another helper. When we'd been loading the paints into the back of my wagon on Saturday morning, Amy had come over, inquired about the project, and offered to help. While the kids were inside packing drinks and snacks, Amy told me that Sara and Nan were with Marty for the weekend, after he'd given Amy assurances that 'she' wouldn't be there.

Amy had run back home and returned in record time with her hair pulled back into a ponytail, wearing a pair of old cutoffs, a McDorn Hardware T-shirt and Sara's old red high-tops. I'd told her she looked fabulous, and meant it.

On the ride over, she'd told me she'd gotten a 'pretty darn good' severance deal from the airline, both monetary and 'more free miles than I care to think about,' and was now taking a couple weeks of vacation before she started her new job with Fairview Realty.

We'd had a really nice weekend working together. On Saturday, the two of us even went to a little café for lunch while the kids walked to a Taco Bell. We'd had a great day today, too, though long.

Finally Matt was putting on the last dabs of paint (black, darkening each of the dogs' noses). The mural finally complete, we all five piled in the car, paint-covered and dog tired. I steered the car across the pristine parking lot, then braked. We all stared at the wall, smiling.

'It's really great,' said Amy softly.

I nodded, so proud of my kids, and us, that my eyes welled up again. I pulled the car forward and into the street, noticing Amy brushing away a tear. We both laughed.

'Hey, Amy?' Matt said, leaning forward.

Amy turned to look back at him. 'Yes?'

'Thank you for helping us. We couldn't have finished without you. You too, Mom, Lainey.'

'Yeah, thanks a lot,' said Josh.

My hands involuntarily squeezed the steering wheel, grateful as only a mother can be when her child remembers to say thank you.

'You're welcome, boys. It was fun!' said Amy. 'That wall's something you can be really proud of. That's going to inspire a lot of people, I bet. Not just the little ones. It inspires me!'

I glanced over at her, careful not to take my eyes off the road too long. I was struck by the change in her these past few months. She looked like a different woman, relaxed, happy.

'Amy, really,' I said. 'Thank you so much. I can't believe you spent a whole weekend of your vacation painting a wall. With all those free miles, you could probably be anywhere in the world right now!'

She leaned back against her seat, a satisfied grin on her face. 'Flying somewhere, anywhere, is not currently my idea of a vacation! Helping you, your family – finally! – is exactly what I want to be doing.' She let loose a light and genuine laugh, then turned suddenly and stared at me. She grinned, leaned back in her seat, saying nothing.

'What?' I said, smiling, curious.

'Nothing,' she said. My quick sideways glances told me there was something, but I let it go. I figured I had paint in my nose or something.

'Hey, Amy,' I said. 'After we get home, Lainey and I are going to go over to the rec center to shower and have a soak in the hot tub. Want to join us?'

Her eyes sparkled. 'Well, I'd love to, Deena, thanks for asking, but I can't.' She took a dramatic deep breath. 'I have a date. He reminds me a little of Neil. We'll see.'

Now my fingers went cold on the steering wheel. My eyes involuntarily darted to the rearview mirror. Lainey's eyes were perfectly framed in the rectangle, squarely focused on mine. I quickly looked back at the road. 'That's wonderful, Amy. I hope you have a great time.'

I slowly eased myself into the hot, bubbling water. Lainey was already in, watching my protracted descent. Even though hot tubs always made me feel like I was a lobster being plunged into a boiling pot, the steaming water felt wonderful on my aching arms and back. As I leaned back against a jet, my suit, now too big and stretched out, immediately filled with air.

'Mom,' said Lainey, laughing, 'you look like the blueberry girl in *Charlie and the Chocolate Factory*!'

With the bosom of my suit ballooning up to the surface, we both cracked up. I pressed the air out with my hands, releasing big jellyfish-shaped bubbles into the water.

'Have you lost weight, Mom?' she asked, surveying me.

'Yeah, some,' I said, slightly embarrassed, but also thrilled that my daughter had noticed.

'You look good,' she said, nodding.

'Thanks, Lainey.' I submerged down to my chin, smiling. Lainey rested her head back on the edge, eyes closed. The center was closing in twenty minutes, so except for the lifeguard and one lone swimmer in the lap pool, we had the place to ourselves.

'Lainers?' I said. She opened her eyes. 'You know that talk I wanted to have with you?' She shook her head. 'About mistakes I made?' She shrugged, then nodded. 'Can we have that talk now?' She closed her eyes, nodded again.

'I just want – Well, it's not that I made a mistake, really. Well, I kind of did. Of course I've made mistakes, lots of them!' I laughed nervously. 'I don't know, it's just that—' I hadn't thought this out. It occurred to me that *this* might be another of my many mistakes.

'Lainey, you know how Sara has changed since she's been dating Kurt? Just wanting to be with him all the time, doing everything to please him?' Lainey shrugged again, then nodded. 'Well, you might be surprised to hear this, but I think it's actually pretty easy to lose yourself in love like that. I think it happens to both boys and girls. But girls especially. We tend to sometimes give up our own identity when we're in love with someone else, I guess because giving feels so good. But you really can give too much. One of the most addictive things in the world is helping someone to achieve their dreams, and that *is* a wonderful thing. But not at the expense of your own dreams.' She was watching me now, listening. I touched her head lightly with my finger. 'You have to stay conscious, work at it, work at being you, your whole life. You can and should be able to put yourself aside now and then, but not for too long. Think about who *you* are, and what *your* dreams are, and how you're going to achieve them.' I waited, then asked, 'Am I making any sense here?'

'Mom?'

'Yes, honey?'

'Do you think it was a mistake to marry Daddy?'

I closed my eyes, briefly. Boy, teenagers could really cut to the chase. I took a deep breath, then slid close to her. I gently held her chin in my hand, looking into her watery eyes. 'No, sweetie. Marrying your dad wasn't a mistake. Not cultivating my own dreams, my own passions, was a mistake. It's like – well, I guess like a garden. Everybody is born with a garden of possibility, and we all, but maybe especially mothers, sometimes see everyone else's garden better than our own. So we forget to tend it. And like any garden, it can wither. And then, we do.' Her eyes were fixed, staring straight ahead, at nothing. At everything. 'Sweetheart, your dad is a wonderful person and we've had a great marriage. For over twenty years!' I added, maybe too brightly. For over twenty years, it *had* been good. But somehow, in the past few years, it had withered. But I didn't want to lay that on Lainey now.

Finally she looked at me, her brown eyes pulling in meaning. Her eyes at that moment could have been Heloise's. 'So you and Daddy don't hate each other?'

She'd pulled her knees up to her chest, hugged them tightly. I felt like I was cracking open. Not a lobster at all. An egg. Bumping up against the other boiling egg, my soft white insides spilling out.

'No, honey. No, we definitely do not hate each other. We're just in a hard place right now.' I rubbed at a tiny spot of paint on my wrist that I'd missed in the shower. I looked at my daughter. My baby. She looked both older and younger than her fifteen years. My heart swelled with love, and an overwhelming need to try to convey to her some wisdom, hard won.

'Lainey? Look at me, hon.' Reluctantly, she did. Her eyes were glistening with tears again. 'Sweetheart, in a way I guess it's kind of like the mural. You have different stages of your life, your whole life long. The growing and changing doesn't stop at high school graduation. Or even college. You have graduations your whole life – like when you get

247

married, when you have babies, when *they* graduate, when *they* get married, have babies.' I poked her gently in the ribs with my elbow, smiling. She jerked away. I immediately felt stupid. I shouldn't have done that, this was serious. Wrong again.

'I'm sorry, Lainey. Look, sweetie, your dad and I are kind of at another graduation. We just haven't figured out to what, exactly, yet.'

Neither of us spoke. The only sound was the roil of thousands of small pockets of air bursting to the surface.

'But we will,' I said, forcing a smile. I knew I'd too often overprotected my kids throughout the years, but I was confident that this time was crucial. And I knew Neil and I would work something out, I just didn't know what that something would be, and I sure as hell didn't have to drag my poor daughter through any more confusion than necessary. I could pretend to be the confident pack leader. I put my arms around her and she let me, tipping her head onto my shoulder. 'I love you, Lainey. We both do. Very much. Dad and I will figure it out, honey. It'll be okay.'

There I went again. Telling a frightened young thing that it would all be okay, when her fate lay in my uncertain hands.

CHAPTER 19

The kids started school again on August 24. It seemed to get earlier every year. Their first day back, Amy and I had a date to walk the dogs around the lake. We'd done this two or three times already, but this was her last day before she started full-time at her real estate job. It was hotter than Hades again, so I figured Merle and Teddy would likely be staying home.

After two power-walking circuits around the lake, Amy and I started our cooldown, the dogs grateful to be walking rather than trotting. They lagged behind us, their long tongues hanging out. Heloise was so hot and tired she wasn't even trying to eat the goose poop.

We headed for home, and I felt a sudden sense of being on a precipice. A takeoff point. Maybe it was the kids being back in school. Maybe it was all the signs that fall was just around the corner, the yellow leaves already dotting a few cottonwoods, the mums in gardens giving summer's last hurrah, the ragged Vs of south-bound geese honking overhead. Or maybe it was that Amy was starting her new job tomorrow, and her excitement had been bubbling up all morning.

'Amy?' I said, when I'd caught my breath.

'Yeah?'

'I just want to say how much I admire you. I mean, you've really taken your life by the horns, y'know? Your new job and all. I know it hasn't been easy, this past year.'

Her eyes welled up, which made mine well up, and we both laughed.

'Damn, but we're leaky!' she said, wiping her eyes with the dangling sleeves of the sweatshirt tied around her waist. She turned, took my wrist tenderly. 'That means the world to me, Deena, considering how much I admire *you*.'

'Me?!'

She nodded. 'God! Yeah! You're just so – grounded, y'know? You can do a million things, all well, for so many different people. And you've got such a great relationship with your kids and husband.' Before I could even close my open mouth, she began jumping up and down, clapping her hands. 'I can't wait anymore! Come on!' We'd just turned onto our street, and she pulled poor Melba back into a trot. Heloise and I hustled behind, following her into her house.

'This was supposed to be your Christmas present,' she said, giving me an exaggerated grimace, 'but I can't wait *four months*!' She trotted into her living room, calling over her shoulder, 'Besides, you might want to go somewhere over

Christmas.' Both dogs found the water bowl by the kitchen door and began drinking noisily, side by side. Amy pulled open a small drawer below a built-in bookcase, then walked toward me, her hands behind her back.

'Okay, Deena,' she said sternly, 'I'm *not* going to cry!' She took a deep breath. 'This is to say thanks for everything over the years, especially this past year. I'm really glad—' She paused, teary-eyed again, her voice squeaking up an octave as she forced the words out, 'that we're friends.' I felt my own eyes filling.

She brought her arms forward, handing me something that looked like brochures. I took them, studying them a minute. There were four. Four vouchers for round-trip airline tickets.

'You can all go see Sam! Or go to Disney World! I have coupons for rides and stuff there, too!' She was jumping up and down again, speaking rapid-fire, like a ten-year-old on Christmas morning. 'Or anywhere! In the U.S.' She stopped jumping. 'Except Hawaii. Well, or Alaska or Puerto Rico.' Her eyes were shiny with joy.

Airline tickets. To *fly* somewhere. Of all the things Amy could give me. Us.

I hugged her, and she hugged me back. For the first time, we held each other in a tight embrace.

'Deena?' It was Neil, poking his head in the door of Sam's room. I looked at the clock: 11:10 p.m. I was sitting at the desk, doing my *Maximizing*

Midlife workbook, specifically the chapter that was supposed to evaluate my skills and personality for 'My Midlife Career Potential.' At Neil's voice, Heloise immediately woke, and jumped out from under the desk, where she'd been lying on her new red-and-black-plaid bed. She no longer slept in her kennel.

Before Neil could even step in, Heloise had her head thrust at him, her tail thumping out a steady beat on the open door.

'Come on in,' I said. I turned my chair toward him. He stepped in, the airline vouchers in his hand. I'd left them on the dining room table with a note of explanation.

'Can I talk to you about these?' he asked softly.

I nodded. 'Sure. Have a seat.' He closed the door, sat on the bed. Heloise sat next to him, leaning partly against the bed, partly against him, looking at me. It was as if she was trying, in her own way, to bridge the distance.

Neil cleared his throat. 'As you know, I have another conference over Labor Day,' he said. I nodded. 'In Florida?' I nodded again. 'For Health Justice?' Again, I nodded. There was still a part of me that was proud of his national work trying to get political action behind low-cost health care for the poor. It *was* important work.

Ahh. Suddenly I knew what this was about. Of course. He always paid his own way to the Health Justice things. Using a voucher would save us that fare.

'I'd like to use one of these for that.'

Bingo. I nodded.

'And I'd like to take Matt and Lainey with me.' I felt my eyebrows shoot up. 'Even take them out of school an extra day or so around their long weekend. I'd like some time with them. I—' He was looking down at his hands, clasped between his knees, one thumb rubbing the other. 'I haven't been around much and *they're* not going to be around much longer. I thought I'd seize this opportunity.' He looked up at me. 'I feel like I've missed a lot of opportunities.' He dropped his gaze downward again, stared at the carpet. 'With Sam and all.' He inhaled sharply, then looked at me again, also sharply, I thought. And, though he spoke softly, his words had an edge. 'I thought about just you and me going somewhere, Deena. But I know you wouldn't go, hating to fly and all. And I know—' He stared at his hands. He couldn't keep his eyes on me for more than seconds at a time. It used to be he couldn't take his eyes off me. 'I know now isn't a great time for us.' He looked up again, a manufactured energy to declare that tangent of conversation closed. 'So, you get your wish. You'll have a few whole days of that solitude you've been wanting. House to yourself.'

I opened my mouth to speak, but he hurriedly spoke again. 'And I thought I'd send the fourth ticket to Sam. See if maybe he'll come home for a visit, either Christmas or spring break this year.' Sam had chosen to stay at Stanford for the summer, taking a couple of classes and, not entirely coincidentally, volunteering at a low-cost health clinic.

The fourth ticket. My ticket. On the surface, everything he'd said was good, considerate. Time with the kids, time for me. Getting Sam home. But he hadn't so much *asked* me as *told* me all this. And that solitude comment felt almost antagonistic. *What if he* had *asked you on a romantic trip, Deena?* I asked myself. What if he had?

It was true that everyone, except Amy apparently, knew that I hated to fly. I couldn't imagine myself in any sort of paradise without also imagining a flaming plane, plummeting from the sky. I looked at Neil.

I didn't know what to say. So I simply nodded again, swallowing hard.

When the airport shuttle had disappeared from our driveway, Heloise and I wandered around the empty house for a few minutes, going from room to room, walking through the silence. Hairy followed us, at a distance, like a secret agent trailing his mark, darting from one hiding place to another. I pictured him in a little trench coat, tiny sunglasses perched on his flattened nose, making myself laugh out loud. We all three walked upstairs.

I was amazed at myself, looking at my children's empty rooms, the house itself looking large and empty. But I wasn't lonely. I wasn't scared. *I was happy.* We walked back down again. The sun was now streaming in through the tall windows of the living room, striping the oak floors with the young light of early morning, ever-hopeful, everything yet to come.

'Let's head for the hills, girl! Walk?' Heloise's ears immediately shot up at the sound of her second favorite word. We jumped in the car and headed west. I thought if we drove we might still be able to catch Merle and Teddy, if they were walking on the same schedule.

It'd been a while since Heloise and I had walked the trails, usually preferring the shade of the lake on the hot days, often joined by Amy and Melba. But now Amy was at her new job. My family was gone. I was on my own in a way I'd not been since . . . when? Ever?

When I thought about it, I realized I'd never been on my own like this. I'd gone from my parents' house, to a dorm, to an apartment with Elaine, to Neil. Never really on my own.

The freedom was intoxicating. I felt like running up the hill, my arms spread wide, singing at the top of my lungs, à la Julie Andrews. I decided I'd spare the pristine setting.

The gorgeous autumn day only added to my sense of freedom. Pockets of yellow-gold aspen shouted their glory from the evergreen hillsides. The dry, cool air made for a sky so blue you could swim in it.

I'd broken down and bought myself a nylon pants and jacket set for these cool mornings. I'd finally gotten rid of my dingy gray sweats. But it hadn't been easy. I'd again wrestled with myself over the 'need versus want' thing, but when I'd found this set at a discounter for eight dollars, I couldn't resist. Eight dollars! For the set! So it was too big. So it was neon green. It was a bargain!

Heloise was biting at the leash as I walked toward the trailhead. I removed it from her mouth and walked more quickly. As usual, it worked. At a fast clip, Heloise trotted alongside me like a show dog, head up, tail high. She was seven months old. She had some filling out to do yet, but was nearly at her full height now. Weeks ago Bill had brought over one large kennel, to swap out for the two small ones. We only needed one, now that she slept on her red bed. I was so proud of her many accomplishments and milestones. She'd also graduated to her thick adult collar, its embossed golden plate identifying her as a K-9 Eyes dog. The collar was still a bit big for her on its tightest notch, but she'd outgrown her puppy collar completely. She had also gone through two size upgrades in jackets, though I now had her wear it only on socializations, not on walks. Heloise was beautiful, sleek and strong, lighter-colored than most yellow Labs, almost white, with just the tips of her ears, tail, and backbone a reddish tan.

I glanced at my watch: 8:41. I had to hurry! If Merle was still walking on the same schedule, he'd be well started on the trail by now. I quickened my pace and Heloise stayed with me, eyes bright,

256

ready for today's adventure. We rounded the trail-head and crossed the bridge. As we emerged from the thicket onto the road, I thought I saw Merle rounding a bend a couple hundred yards ahead. I didn't want to shout, in case it wasn't him, so I quickened my pace. Heloise broke into a fast trot up the hill, and I walked faster too, pulling back on her a bit to keep her from a full run. 'Stay with me, girl.' She jogged beside me again. 'That a girl!' I said, between sucking in lungfuls of air. It was then that I realized *I* was jogging. It felt good! Even though I was pretty sure that in my new outfit I probably looked like Shrek on his morning exercise rounds. I didn't care. I was ecstatic! 'That a girl!' I repeated softly.

I jogged the whole way, uphill, and was fairly short of breath by the time I reached Merle. 'Hi . . . Merle!' I gasped, as Heloise and I came up behind him.

He stopped and turned, his expression bright-ening. 'Hello, ladies! Good to see you again.'

Heloise bounded toward Teddy, both dogs tails waving like allied flags. I let her get close, and she showed her maturing social wisdom by doing a dog version of a curtsy – stretching out her front legs, lowering her head, wagging her tail. Teddy raised his majestic snout as though to dismiss her, but then lifted his front paw and gently batted at her shoulder. I put my hands on my knees and tried to breathe.

'You okay, Deena?' Merle asked, his voice tinged with alarm.

I immediately rose. 'Fine!' I said. 'Just a little out of breath. Whew! Feels good though.' I took off my jacket and tied the arms around my waist. 'Heloise's got me on a rigorous conditioning program. But a middle-aged, overweight woman can only do so much.'

Merle laughed. 'You aren't overweight! Fact is, you appear to have lost quite a bit. Anyway, you just stick with this old guy,' he said, patting my shoulder, 'and you'll be just fine.' He snapped his fingers and said briskly, 'Let's go, old boy!' and Teddy ambled on up the road. I reeled Heloise in, and the three of us set off after the big collie.

'I'm glad you're back,' Merle said. We were in step, left, right, stride for stride. 'Teddy and I missed you ladies.'

'Thanks, Merle. We missed you, too. I got pretty busy, with the kids and all.' I was pleased at how quickly I'd recovered my breath, even though we were still striding up the hill.

Merle nodded. 'I remember.' A sly sort of smile slid across his face. He rubbed his chin with his index finger. 'The fall was always Laura's favorite time of year. She said it was because of the weather, but I think it was finally having those boys out of her hair.' Now he had his chin between his crooked index finger and thumb. I almost laughed as I recognized a story coming on.

'One year, I think it was when our five boys were in three different schools – one in high school, two in junior high, and the twins in elementary school

258

– I came home from work at lunch to surprise Laura. It was during that first week of school, I think.' He looked at me, a Cheshire cat grin on his face. 'Know where I found her?' I dutifully shook my head, uncontrollably grinning back. 'Right smack in the middle of the backyard! Just sitting there on the grass, all up tall, with her legs crossed, her hands in her lap, her eyes closed. She looked like one of them gurus. So I ask her what she's doing.' He gestured, palms up, a quizzical expression on his face. 'Real quiet-like she says, "Just sitting." That's all! So I said, "Why are you just sitting?" She didn't even open her eyes or twitch a muscle. She just says, in that same quiet voice, "Because I can." Merle chuckled and shook his head. 'Poor woman. First peace and quiet she'd had in three months.'

'I can't imagine raising five boys,' I said. 'That's a herd!'

Merle chuckled. 'Yep. That's exactly what they were. But Laura was chief wrangler and they knew it. They toed the line for her. She was gentle but firm. She had a sense about her that she always knew what to do. She had good instincts about kids—' He glanced at the dogs, trotting alongside one another. 'And animals. With both of them, she had a sense about when to goose 'em, when to let them raise theirselves a bit.'

I realized I was only just learning how to let my kids 'raise theirselves a bit.' Suddenly Merle chuckled again. 'The next week? After that backyard thing? She volunteered at a day care for low-income single

259

moms! Then she took up photography. Took pictures of the moms and the kids. She was good. Even had a little show at church. It never took her too long to get back her get-up-and-go. She was always real thirsty for learning new things. She maybe didn't get famous or nothing, her gift was more how she could see people, help them see themselves as good, help 'em grow, I guess. Plants, babies, kids, neighbors. Me.'

'She sounds remarkable, Merle.' He nodded, his eyes shining. Heloise suddenly veered over to a cactus that she was intent on investigating. *Look! Another great thing!* Not. I reeled her in and she spotted Teddy, already at the bench. She pulled toward him.

Merle chuckled and shook a finger at Heloise. 'Stay away from them cactuses, girl. Porky-pines, too!'

We sat down and Merle poured water into my cupped hands for Heloise. 'I put Laura back in a home,' Merle said suddenly, his voice barely audible. 'Took her out again last week.'

He stopped pouring and looked at the ground. I looked at him, his weary profile. He looked at me. We didn't need words. He knew that I knew what it was to give until you had no more to give, but love and a sense of duty whipping you on.

'It must be so hard, Merle.' I wiped my hands on my shorts and touched his shoulder. His elbows rested on his thighs, his right hand still clutched the water bottle.

'It's hell on me physically when she's home. It's hell on me emotionally if she's not.' In his weariness, he didn't remember he'd already said these very words to me. Or maybe he did remember, but who else did he have to say them to? I suspected he couldn't or wouldn't say this to his sons, who were probably already torn by their distant lives keeping them from their ailing mother and worn-out father.

My hand was still lightly on his shoulder. I gave it a small squeeze. I tried to picture Neil needing that level of my help 24/7. Especially if I was in my late sixties, early seventies. Somehow, the picture made a kind of sense that our life together now did not.

'I'm sorry, Merle,' I said. 'I bet you're exhausted.'

'Well, she took such good care of me and the boys for so many years. She was probably exhausted a lot of the time!' He managed a small smile. 'She did everything. Lots of things we didn't notice or appreciate till she stopped doing them. If it'd been me sick, she'd be there, you can bet on that. She's my partner. For life.'

'Is there anything I can do to help, Merle?'

He shook his head.

'Can you get Leticia to come to the house more often?' I asked.

He lifted his head, blinked, and took a deep breath. 'Sometimes Laura gets upset when I'm not there, Deena. She even got upset when the boys came to visit last time, didn't seem to know

261

a one of them, so I told them not to come anymore. Too hard on her. Too hard on them. As it is, I only have Leticia so I can get Teddy here out every day.' He rubbed his eyes vigorously, then forced a smile. 'Aww! Listen to me! What have I got to complain about? Best damn life on the planet, I'd say.'

I smiled at him, understanding his need to move on. He was stuck between the decades of rock-like love for Laura, and the hard, hard place of a debilitating illness that had robbed them both of something they'd believed could never be stolen.

There was silence again, then Merle pointed. 'Look at that boy! Thinks he's king, he does.' I followed the line of his finger and saw Teddy lying in the cool shade of a small aspen glade twenty yards away. He did look regal, his head up, and with just a hint of sentry about him. I looked down to see if Heloise was admiring him, too, or again chewing my shoelaces. My heart stopped, my fingers clenching around the lead. Lying in the dirt at my feet was the ring of Heloise's empty collar.

CHAPTER 20

'Oh, no!' My insides felt as white-knuckled as my fist looked on the empty leash. 'Heloise!' I desperately scanned around us.

Merle stood, and whistled for Teddy. The collie immediately rose, but uncharacteristically refused to come.

'Deena,' said Merle, tapping my arm, pointing again. There behind Teddy was a perfect tan circle. Heloise's head was tucked neatly into her folded legs, a tight donut, rising and falling in contented slumber.

Leash and collar in hand, I took a step toward her, but Merle touched my arm. 'Can she stay just a minute, Deena? She's just napping. Teddy won't let her go anywhere.' He chuckled. 'Look at her, snoozin' away. She doesn't even *know* that she's free. You trust that pup. She'll come back to you.'

I looked at Heloise, and Teddy, then back at Merle. I nodded, sat back down, a welling of emotion rising in me. Neither Merle nor I could quite loosen the ties and restrictions that had become binding in our own lives, but we could allow a little collarless dog a nap under a tree, unrestrained.

Merle motioned to Teddy. 'Go on back, boy. Down.' Teddy settled next to Heloise again.

We sat quietly, the four of us, breathing in the clean mountain air, tinged with pine and earth and contentment. I leaned back, stretched my arms over my head, the stretch pulling down to my toes, like a full-body yawn. I watched a hawk floating above us, slow, hypnotic circles, lifted by a mere difference in air temperatures, hot and cold colliding. He drifted round and round, without a single beat of his wing.

I glanced at my watch above my head. 'Wow! It's quarter to ten!'

Now Merle looked panic-stricken. 'Lord! Leticia's got to get going. I had no idea it'd gotten that late!'

We both rose, and while Merle hastily packed up our water bottles, I retrieved Heloise, easily slipping her collar back over her head as she blinked her heavy, black-rimmed eyes at me.

We began walking briskly down the trail, Heloise dragging sleepily behind me. 'I'm sure it'll be okay, Merle. Leticia won't leave Laura alone.'

'No, you're right, she won't. But she has other patients. I've never done this to her.'

'What time does Leticia normally leave your house?' I asked as I urged Heloise into a trot to keep up. She looked dolefully at me, but gamely picked up her pace.

'I'm usually back by nine forty-five; she leaves around ten.' He was walking so fast I was worried one of us would slip on the pebble-strewn trail.

'Well, we're okay then, Merle,' I said, slowing. 'I drove to the trailhead today. I'll drive you home. Do you live far from here?'

He slowed now too, looking at me. 'No, just over on Columbia. By the lake?'

'No problem then. We'll have you home in a matter of minutes.'

He smiled that lovely smile, exhaling relief. 'You, dear Deena, are an angel.'

I pulled up to Merle's house; it was right across from the lake where I often walked with Heloise. It was, unlike the old Victorian I'd imagined, a 1960s two-story, similar to my own, just blocks away. A small, black, wrought-iron fence bordered the sidewalk, a bubbly blanket of big orange marigolds behind it. Yellow roses climbed a wooden trellis next to the front door.

'Would you like to come in?' Merle asked, unbuckling his seat belt. There was apprehension in his voice. Was it because he really didn't want me to, or because he was afraid I wouldn't want to? I took a gamble, knowing how most people shun illness.

'I'd love to,' I said, 'if you're sure?' That ought to cover my bases.

Merle nodded deeply, smiling. 'Yes, indeed. Think I might even be able to rustle up some lemonade.'

We got the dogs out of the back and headed inside.

An attractive Hispanic woman in her thirties came to greet us. 'Oh, Meester Merle! I was worried!'

'Leticia, I am so sorry—'

Leticia raised her hand and turned her head. 'Eep! No problem, sir! No problem! I jeeste worry about Teedy.'

Merle turned to me. 'Teddy's had one or two sorta fainting spells recently. I think it was just the heat, but Leticia's been worried about him.' Merle turned back to her. 'Leticia Cruz-Gomez, this is Deena—'

'Munger,' I said, extending my hand.

'Please to meet chu!' Her broad white smile made her even prettier. She turned back to Merle. 'Meese Low-rah is asleeping, in dere.' She pointed to an arched entryway, which I assumed led to the living room.

Merle nodded, pulled out his wallet. 'Here, let me give you something extra—'

Leticia again held up her hand like an officious crossing guard. 'Eep! Chu put that back!' she barked. She stepped toward him and gave him a little hug, then picked up her purse and headed for the door. Halfway out she turned, one hand on the screen door. 'Nice to meet chu, Meese Deena. Please you make him eat asomething besides his weenies.'

I bit the inside of my cheek to stop from laughing, and nodded dutifully.

But Merle laughed out loud. He looked at me. 'I happen to enjoy cocktail franks. Not s'posed to have 'em though. Too much salt. Good-bye, Leticia! Thank you!' Leticia waved over her head without looking back. Heloise was pulling on her leash, anxious to get the lay of the land in this new place.

'You can let her off in here, can't you?' Merle asked.

'Merle, I don't dare. She still chews on things if she's anxious.'

He nodded and led us into the kitchen. 'Would you like some lemonade? It's only that powder stuff, I'm afraid.' He pulled a canister from the cupboard.

'I'd actually love just a glass of water.'

He smiled. 'Me too. Let me go peek in on Laura first.'

'I'll get the water,' I said. 'Where're your glasses?' He pointed toward the cabinet to the left of the sink.

I was filling the second glass when he returned.

'Still sleeping. That's one saving grace of this illness, she sleeps a lot. Here, let me shut the kitchen doors, then Heloise can stay in here with us.' He closed a sliding wood pocket door on one side, and an old accordion door of dark wood veneer on the other. It clicked shut on a magnetic clasp. I reached down and unfastened Heloise's lead.

'There you go, girl!' She immediately found Teddy's water bowl and began loudly lapping. Teddy looked at her from where he had settled, in what was clearly his corner of the kitchen. He rested his head between his front paws again, and closed his eyes.

'Both my companions here sleep a lot these days. Don't you fall asleep on me or I'll feel like it's my company putting everyone to sleep!' He smiled, holding his glass as we both took a seat at the kitchen table, a massive slab of oak with thick carved legs. The top had grown dark with age and use. Several gouge marks on the top, no doubt from the various projects, sanctioned and otherwise, that their boys had undertaken over the years, far from marred it. They were almost a kind of artwork. There wasn't a single mark in my like-new but decades-old cherry table. It was smooth and polished, albeit maybe a bit dusty at the moment. As I ran my fingernail idly along one of these marks, I became almost dizzy, seeing these boys, Laura, Merle. A rush of memories that weren't even mine came like ghosts, passing right through me.

Merle and I had our first awkward silence as we sipped our water. I watched Heloise nosing her way around the ancient, redbrick-patterned linoleum. In front of the sink, refrigerator, and stove were black depressions where the linoleum had worn through. No doubt it was Laura's labors those spots bore witness to. I surveyed the dark, den-type wood laminate cabinets, the harvest-gold stove and refrigerator. Here was a woman who hadn't needed her kitchen remodeled – ever? I looked at the black hollows, and felt something like envy.

Heloise continued circling the kitchen, looking for any morsel of food – morsel of anything, actually. But she found little. Either Merle was a good housekeeper, or Teddy had already seen to any crumbs.

'Are you hungry?' Merle asked, rising slightly. I could tell he was uncomfortable, too. Our conversation had been so easy up on the trail, now neither one of us knew what to talk about. We had trespassed our borders of anonymity.

'No, thanks. I'm fine,' I said. 'I really shouldn't stay long. I've got to get to the grocery store.' As if I had a standing Wednesday ten thirty appointment there. Well, I kind of did. The sales always began on Wednesdays, so the stock was good. Plus, if I got there much after eleven, I'd run into the deluge of high schoolers arriving to buy their candy bar lunches. It was impossible to make any progress through the store with all those teenagers wanting to pet Heloise. But now I felt as though I was cutting out on Merle.

A staccato grunting came from the living room.

'It sounds like Laura's awake. Would you like to meet her before you go? You don't have to, a'course. I know it's uncomfortable for some folks. It's just that, I feel like she knows you, too, somehow.'

I smiled, but felt compelled to ask, 'If it wouldn't upset her, meeting someone new?'

'I don't think so. I've been telling her about you. I often think what upsets her is seeing people that

269

she knows. People she knows she should recognize, and she doesn't.'

I nodded. 'I'd love to meet Laura, Merle.'

His expression was full, happy. I couldn't tell if it was gratitude or pride. Maybe both. 'This way,' he said.

I followed him into the living room. Laura was at one end of the long, narrow room, sitting slumped in an old sixties-style upholstered orange armchair. Like most of my fantasies, I'd been wrong about this room. Mostly. The details were different, but the warmth and comfort was there. Or had been. There were no hooked rugs. Instead, against the far wall, several worn-looking oriental rugs lay rolled up and stacked on one another. The dark hardwood was worn and bare, nothing to trip over. A hospital bed was at one end, facing the window and the mountains. At the other end, an antique rocking chair with a sagging caned seat, an old and faded rose-colored love seat with two pillows, one tatted and one tie-dyed, and Laura's orange chair, all circled around a television.

Laura sat slumped in the armchair, facing the television, a colorful crocheted afghan draped over her knees. Her white hair was short and flattened down on one side, a bare spot in the back, clearly from where it must so often now rest against the chair or bed. At the moment, though, her head hung forward, cocked slightly to the side, as if she was watching the show out of the corner of one eye. The picture was on but there was no sound.

It was an old black-and-white episode of Andy of Mayberry, just starting. I smiled at little Opie throwing that rock into the lake.

'Now, she can't respond in any way, but I'll introduce you,' said Merle. He moved in front of her, then elegantly went down on one knee, taking her hand in his. He looked for all the world like he was about to propose to her.

'Laura, dear, I'd like you to meet someone.' It was clear she couldn't lift her head or raise her eyes, so I followed Merle's lead and knelt in front of her. 'Laura, love of my life, this is Deena. We met on the trail, near Ute Rock. Where the bench is.' Her mouth was open, limp, her breathing raspy. With considerable effort, she moved her blank stare from Merle to me. Her eyes widened slightly, confused, then looked past me.

I looked into her vacant eyes and smiled. I gently touched her arm. 'It's nice to meet you, Laura.' Her only reaction was to, again with great effort, turn her head back toward Merle.

'Are you thirsty, love?' he asked. He reached for the glass of water on the table beside her and brought it carefully to her lips. He held one hand underneath her lower lip, supporting the rim of the glass. Slowly he tilted a small amount into her mouth. She choked a little, swallowed some, some dribbling down the side of her mouth. He dabbed at it with a cloth kept on the arm of her chair. 'There you go, my sweet.' He took the corner of the now-damp cloth and ran it tenderly over her

271

brow, then leaned in slowly and kissed her flaccid cheek, lingering there, eyes closed. If they had been younger, something like electric current might have passed between them. Now, it must be currents of time. It might have been the millionth kiss he'd bestowed upon that cheek, yet it looked like the first.

I suddenly felt like an intruder, that Merle was making love to his wife in the only way they could both accommodate and understand. I rose and walked back into the kitchen, and sat at the table. In a moment, Merle joined me.

'Thank you,' he said, his voice cracking slightly. My throat stung, my eyes filled. I reached across the table, took his hand, and silently mouthed the same words back to him.

I rose, still holding his hand. 'Walk tomorrow?' He nodded, squeezing my hand. I reached for the accordion door and saw that it was already open. I shot a glance over to the dogs' corner and saw only Teddy. Damn! All Heloise had to do was push open the magnetic clasp; I'd just bargained on her not figuring that out. Wrong again. And she'd had all that water. She was undoubtedly anxious, having to pee.

Envisioning a mauled chair leg, or at the very least a slobbered-on sofa, I strode through the hall calling her name softly, so as not to disturb Laura. Laura. Oh, dear. I turned the corner into the living room and saw the back of Laura's head in her orange chair. Heloise's bottom and her little yellow tail stuck out from the side. Oh, God! What if she was chewing on Laura's robe or slipper?! Merle suddenly appeared at my elbow, smiling. *She's okay*, he mouthed to me.

Silently, I stepped just close enough to see.

Heloise was sitting quietly at Laura's side, not chewing at all, but with her head gently resting on the old woman's thigh. One of Laura's trembling hands slowly stroked Heloise's head. Laura's eyes were closed, a look of peace on her face, completely counter to the confusion of meeting me. I stood silent, watching. I wondered, if in the tatters of her memory, she'd found a long-ago shred, a beloved childhood pet, and was stroking his head, being so unconditionally loved that she was bound by neither time nor memory.

Whatever she recognized in Heloise, Heloise recognized something in Laura, too. Heloise's brown eyes looked up at her, blinked once, but otherwise she was utterly still, absorbing the caress of a soul in need.

I backed away and leaned against the wall of the arched entryway, staring at the back of the chair, the top of an old woman's head, and the small part of my pup that I hadn't seen before.

CHAPTER 21

I took Heloise to the movies that night. Or maybe she took me. I'd never been to a movie theater alone before. We saw a chick flick, full of sappy romance and happy endings. I loved it. Heloise loved the sticky-sweet floor. Afterward we went to a nearby café and had dinner on the patio. It was a very warm evening, but pleasant outside there, and lovely, with ivy-covered lattice, masses of graceful, shading tree branches arcing over our heads, great tubs of pink and red petunias. Heloise literally had her dinner on the patio, as I had remembered her kibble, but not her bowl. I took my time ordering, enjoying a glass of wine first, reflecting, breathing, trying to not feel awkward, dining alone. After just a few sips of wine, and a lot of patting of Heloise, I felt relaxed. Even sort of thrilled. Nobody was staring sympathetically at me. The other diners mostly went out of their way to smile at me admiringly, heads nodding, acknowledging both Heloise in her jacket and me.

The only mishap of the evening was when a squirrel leapt onto a low branch above us, and

Heloise jumped up and I knocked my salad into my lap, reaching for her. But she didn't bark, and immediately settled down again at my command. Otherwise the evening was like a perfect first date. It wasn't the first time I'd ever dined out alone, but it was the first time I enjoyed it.

A little after nine, Heloise and I returned to a quiet, deserted house. As soon as we walked into the kitchen, Heloise stepped into her kennel, and went to sleep. I listened to the silence. I felt along the wall to the light switch, but then didn't flip it on. Instead, I walked through my hushed, empty house, my eyes adjusting to the dusky illumination from streetlights and moonlight seeping in through windows. The chairs, couch, bookcase, desk, rugs all seemed to be asleep, frozen in time even. I felt like I'd snuck into a museum after hours.

It used to scare me, being alone at night in my own home. Now it felt magical. I stepped into the moonlit sunroom, held my arms out, and slowly turned circles.

I'd had a single glass of wine with dinner, but now I was in the mood for more. I walked back into the kitchen, flipped the switch, blinking in the now-harsh brightness. I rummaged in the liquor cabinet till I found one of our bottles we kept for special occasions. As I wiped the dust off with a paper towel, I noticed the drops of oil on my shirt and jeans. I knew I should stain-treat them right away, but I didn't want to. I wanted this wine. A Shiraz. I was by no means a wine connoisseur, but I wanted something deep, strong. Gutsy even.

I opened the bottle and left it to breathe on the kitchen counter. I flicked the kitchen light off, leaving only the geometrical shapes of outside light patterning the floors and walls. In the dining room, four slanted rectangles of streetlight spread across the wood floor, making the room look holy. I pulled open the china hutch, carefully fingering the stems of several of our huge, but elegant, crystal goblets, our wedding gift from Elaine. I treasured these glasses, so I rarely used them, which now struck me as slightly absurd. They were big and round, voluptuous, Rubenesque even, each with a different-colored beveled stem. I picked one, held it in a square of light. It was the purple stem. Perfect.

Back in the kitchen, I filled the glass, and as I was pouring, Hairy walked silently into the room, warily watching Heloise. She opened one eye, but didn't flinch.

'Good girl, Heloise,' I congratulated her. Her tail tipped softly behind her and she went back to sleep. Hairy jumped up on the desk and began crunching his kibble.

I lifted the glass to my mouth, loving the feel of the crystal's expensive edge and coolness against my lips. I sipped again, clicked on the ceiling fan to move some air. As it whirred above me, my skin came alive; I felt the air currents move over my arms, the cool of the tile on the hot soles of my feet, each hair where it was rooted in my scalp. I took another sip. A little ripple of heat pulsed through me. I thought it might be another hot flash. But then, no. Maybe just the hot night.

I set my wine on the counter and slowly began unbuttoning my shirt. I stopped, looked over my shoulder, then nervously laughed, making Heloise briefly open her sleepy eyes again. I finished unbuttoning, let my shirt drop to the floor. I reached both arms behind me, unclasped my bra, dropped it on the shirt. I took another sip of wine, set it back on the counter. Deep breath. I slid my jeans and panties off. I remembered the stains on my shirt and pants. I stoppered the kitchen sink, filled it with warm water, squirted in some dish soap. I pushed the shirt into the suds, then gathered up my jeans and underwear, pushed them in too, smiling at the mixed fabrics and colors. Washing a bra with jeans. I really was expanding my horizons.

I wiped my hands on the dish towel, lifted my glass, both hands cradling the bowl, and sipped. I carried it reverently in my cupped hands into the living room. I ran my finger up and down the CD tower, searching.

The phone rang. It was as if someone had screamed. I jumped, nearly spilling my wine.

'*You are naked!*' the phone screamed a second time.

A drumbeat in my chest. Who would call at this hour? Neil. The kids! I set my wine down and ran into the kitchen, grabbing the dish towel as I passed. I lifted the phone with one hand, hurriedly covering my boobs with the damp dish towel in the other.

'Hello?' I said meekly. My hands were shaking.

'Hey, girrrrlfriend!'

'Oh! Elaine. Hi. Hello.' I let out a huge breath. The dish towel slipped off of one boob.

'Are you okay?' she asked. 'Did I catch you in the middle of something?'

'Uh, no.' I shifted the dish towel so it was covering both boobs again. I had to sort of lean backward to keep it there. 'No. I was just, uh, cleaning,' I fibbed. Besides, I didn't know the exact term for drinking wine while wandering nude around one's dark house.

'At this hour? Well, put down the damn tooth-brush, girl! I've got news!'

I sat on the desk chair, wheeling it backward with my feet. I bumped up against the wall, where I felt less exposed in my dark, empty house. 'What news?' I asked Elaine, distractedly. The upholstery of the chair was scratchy on my bare bottom. And it felt . . . unsanitary.

'Well . . . ,' she said dramatically. 'It has to do with my arrrrt . . .' She was baiting me to guess.

'Uh, let me think.' I stood, walked to the stove. I grabbed two oven mitts, brought them back to the chair and placed them – strategically – on the seat. I lowered myself carefully onto them. Much better. 'Uh, you're going to have a huge art show in Gallery One.' I was trying to come up with something outrageous, to play along. Gallery One was a nationally known gallery in Madison. But I really just wanted to get off the phone.

Elaine didn't respond. I put my feet up on the desk and a mitt thumb slid where it shouldn't. I carefully changed position in the chair. 'Elaine?'

'*Yyyyesssssss!*' she screamed.

I stood up, my mouth open. My dish towel dropped to my feet as I grabbed the phone in both hands, switching ears. 'Are you kidding me?! Gallery One? Really, truly, Elaine?!'

'Yes – No! Yes, it's true, and no, I'm not kidding! The Saturday after Thanksgiving. That's like one of the hottest dates you can get for an opening!'

Then *I* screamed, waking Heloise. 'E, that is fucking fantastic!' I walked into the living room, retrieved my wine.

'Wow.' Elaine's tone was stunned, but amused. 'I haven't heard you swear in, oh, I don't know, about twenty years.'

I laughed, sipping on my way back to the kitchen. 'True.' I set my wine on the desk, picked up the dish towel, placed it neatly over the back of the chair, sitting down again on it and the mitts. I propped my feet back on the desk, wine in hand. 'It's in the parent handbook. You have to give up swearing. And every other guilty pleasure. But nobody's home. I'm a free agent.' I sipped again.

'That is so cool, E. Gallery One! Hot damn.' I dangled my hair over the back of the chair, swinging it back and forth.

'I am soooo excited,' she gushed. 'I just found out this afternoon. Biggest damn thing that's happened to me since – Wendy!'

I smiled. I was truly happy for her. Like, happy-happy. Her happiness was my happiness. The wine didn't hurt, either.

'I don't suppose I could talk you into coming out for it?'

I sat up. I stared at my boobs. They looked tired. Depressed, even. I put my thumb and middle finger above them and pushed upward, giving the girls a little temporary lift. I sighed into the phone. I didn't have the energy to do the whole fear-of-flying conversation now, so I simply said, 'You know what? I'll think about it. I really will.'

After I hung up with Elaine I returned to the CD tower. I finally found the one I was looking for, long-ignored at the very bottom. Neil had gotten me the CD just before we'd moved into this house, after we'd decided not to haul our record albums around anymore. We'd chosen only a few to replace on CD.

I took another sip of wine, set it down, lifted the silver disc out of its case. I studied the buttons on the player. I rarely listened to CDs, easier just to flip on talk radio or the TV. I found the button, and the holder slid out like a tongue. I set the disk in the circle, pushed the button and watched it disappear. In the dusky light I walked to my grandmother's desk, opened the drawer, picked up the remaining airline voucher. The only sound was the hum of the machine finding the lone disc. As the music started, I slid the voucher back into the drawer and closed it.

I took another sip, rolling it around in my mouth. My eyes closed momentarily as piano notes began floating out into my night. Each note, a chord of memory.

I lowered myself sideways onto the recliner, my knees over one of the arms. The feel of my bare skin on the soft, cool leather was deliciously deviant. Much better than the desk chair. I sipped, listening to Carole King sing the long-forgotten words of my long-forgotten life.

My throat tightened on the wine and, afraid I might choke, I set the base of the glass on my knee, swallowing the sip down hard. The music had brought Heloise into the living room. I hung my hand over the edge of the chair; she gave it a few licks, then wandered off. I let her. She was pretty trustworthy now. She would usually only chew something if she was anxious, or had to go to the bathroom. She'd gone just before we'd come into the house, and, since I thought we were both feeling about as relaxed as possible, I figured she was set for the night.

I ran my finger over the rim of the wineglass,

my thoughts pulled back in time by the deeply set hook of the music. How Elaine and I had loved this album! All these mellow songs about love found, love lost. Love we had no clue about. A romantic fantasy, perfectly summed up by the album's back cover photo of Carole King wearing a long, diaphanous skirt, riding a big, handsome thoroughbred on the beach at sunrise. Or was it sunset? And, for the first time out of the hundreds I must have stared at this most romantic of pictures over the years, I acknowledged that she is, in fact, alone.

I remembered dancing, alone, in our apartment – Elaine's and mine – to this song after Neil had left after our first date. Bowling. Terribly unromantic, and yet it was. Sweetly romantic. Neither of us could bowl worth a hoot. Our reasoning had been that if we did something we were both bad at, it would break the ice. It had. We'd laughed until we'd cried, first at Neil's orange-and-green clown shoes they'd given him (they'd handed me a much more subdued red-and-tan pair), and then at our gawky form and myriad gutter balls. After our date, we'd gone back to my apartment – Elaine graciously absent – for a simple Crock-Pot dinner. It happened to be pot roast. The day before, in my pre-date jitters and near-frenzied anticipation, I'd made a wildly impressive-looking cake that required no skill whatsoever – basically it was chocolate wafer cookies glued together with whipped cream, then frozen. I'd originally gotten the recipe from the box of cookies. So, when Neil had asked me what it was called, as he cut his fork into the many tender layers of chocolate and cream, I'd been too embarrassed to say I didn't know, so I'd simply said, 'Wafer cake.'

'Wayfarer Cake. Sounds so literary, and . . . romantic. I'm very impressed!' he said.

'I'm glad you like it,' I said, trying not to grin like the fool in love I already was.

When he left my door that night, I secretly watched him walk to his car, whistling, a lightness in his step. Then I closed the door, dancing into our living room. Maybe not so much dancing as swooning. I was enraptured. I'd put Carole King's *Thoroughbred* on and danced with Neil. So completely imagined was he that the real thing might have been less physical. As Carole sang, I'd recounted to her his infinite good qualities: his long and elegant yet strong hands, his square chin, his fine sandy hair, his brown eyes. His dimple. His intelligence. His charm. His sense of humor. His sensivity. Even his car was perfect – an old VW bug. I'd found 'it.'

'Carole,' I said, out loud now, making Heloise look up from her sniffing exploration of the living room. 'People don't realize that they're on drugs when they fall in love. Big, scary, mind-altering, hallucinogenic, addictive drugs. Their judgment is impaired. Everything looks and feels . . . *incredible.*' I aggressively sipped my wine. 'People probably shouldn't operate machinery when they're in

283

love. They shouldn't make important decisions in that state of mind. Decisions like getting married. Having children.'

Carole didn't listen to me.

Suddenly the lyrics made me smile, in love again. With Heloise.

Heloise. Where was she?

I called her name. She raised her head from the other end of the bookcase, undoubtedly going after the cobwebs behind it. She sneezed, then looked up at me, licking cobweb from her nose. Ears up, eyes bright, she came over to tell me how wonderful it was. I scratched her ear for a minute, then let her wander off again to find more cobwebs. God knows I wasn't keeping the house free of them, she might as well. She lowered her front to sniff under the couch, her tail wagging.

'Are you trying to get the dust bunnies to come out and play, girl?' I burst out laughing. Then the second track started up. It turned out to be the perfect accompaniment to watching my dog. 'Daughter of Light.'

Just like that, tears. From laughter to tears, 1.2 seconds. Middle-aged women were the Maseratis of emotion. Or at least I was. I felt guilty that this song no longer made me think of Neil, or even Lainey, but instead, with a sharp poignancy, Heloise. I marveled at the power of music to profoundly become the soundtrack to one's life.

Funny thing was, this had felt like the soundtrack to my life when I was *twenty*. How could it feel like it *now*, when my life was so utterly different? Despite my tirade to Carole, I wished out loud that I could feel that first love again. I took another swig of wine, this time not caressing its many virtues along the way, merely slugging it down as the next track played on. I cupped the glass in both hands, swirling its contents, then drank again. This wine was really very good. Getting better all the time, as one track followed another.

As I poured a second glass, Carole was singing about old love's embers, making me think of Merle and Laura. I walked back into the living room humming along, my throat too tight with emotion to sing.

Yesterday's gone, but today remembers.

I danced on the hardwood floor, sat on the recliner, reclined on the couch, and, finally, lay spread-eagled on the living room rug as the songs played on.

Something hard and light smacked my face and my eyes flew open. There was a harsh light, making me squint. The lamp was on, the security timer ticking away on the floor. Neil must have set it before he left, as if no one would be home. It was too bright, unwelcome. Like Neil himself had shown up and was shining a flashlight in my face.

Heloise's head suddenly appeared directly over mine, her ears up, mouth open, her skin wrinkling comically around her eyes from hanging her face over mine. Her eyes were sparkling and her mouth was the cutest baby blue—

I grabbed her collar and sat bolt upright, my eyes blinking in the light, my head pounding. It was dead quiet in the house, the CD long since ended. An uncapped mangled marker lay on the rug next to where my head had been. I picked it up: Skylark Blue.

'Uh-oh, this can't be good.' My speech was a little slurred. I carefully refocused my eyes on Heloise. Her Skylark Blue tongue, mouth, and right front paw suggested she'd thoroughly explored the marker's possibilities as a chew toy. She must have found it under some piece of furniture as she was sucking up spiderwebs. This dog's oral fixation was limitless.

I heaved myself up, but realized with a start that with this stupid light on, I was visible to the outside world. Whatever part of the world might be passing by at two a.m.. I dropped to my knees again, crawled quickly across the floor, my boobs wobbling against my upper arms as I went. Heloise was eyeing them in a way that made me nervous. I reached up from the floor and grabbed the cords, closing the blinds. I stood, stretched, then collected my empty glass, the half-empty bottle, the marker, and stumbled into the kitchen, flipping on lights as I went. I set glass and bottle on the counter next to the sink, tossed the marker into the trash. I leaned back against the counter, holding my head in both hands, rubbing my face, trying to clear the fog of wine and sleep from my head. When I looked up, I gasped. The front hallway. Down most of its length, and precisely at Heloise's mouth level, was a wobbly blue line along my ecru wall.

I pushed off the counter and entered the hall, bending to inspect her artwork. She must have found the marker in the living room, taken it excitedly to her kennel for a proper chew session, in transit bumping up against the wall as she trotted around the corner. I walked back into the kitchen and peeked in her kennel. Sure enough, there was blue on the pillow, blue on the plastic wall of the kennel. I looked around the kitchen. Even the small amount of water remaining in her dish was tinted blue. Markers must make you thirsty.

Heloise was by my side, her blue tongue happily lolling out of her mouth, her familiar 'What's next?!' smile on her face. Suddenly her expression changed, as if some thought just occurred to her. She trotted to the door, stared at it, then looked back over her shoulder at me.

Oh, dear. God knows how long ago she drank all that water. 'Hang on, Heloise!' I squawked, looking at all my clothes still submerged in the sink. I ran downstairs, figuring it'd be quicker to grab something off the laundry pile than run upstairs with Heloise behind me. She still refused to go down the basement steps, which made trips down there more expeditious than upstairs. Like a toddler, Heloise wanted to 'help' with most everything I did.

In the basement, I was greeted by mounds of dirty laundry. I quickly grabbed a pair of jeans and pulled them on. They were too tight! I couldn't even button them. How could that be? I wondered, stunned. But I had to hurry or Heloise would have an accident, and we hadn't had any in so long. I grabbed a sweat-shirt off the pile, yanking it over my head while running up the stairs. Heloise was at the top, looking at me with a patient but needy expression. I grabbed her leash. 'C'mon, girl! Let's go!' She trotted ahead of me, bolting out the door as I opened it. This was not the time to make her wait at the threshold. She barely made it to the lawn before she was squatting.

'Good girl! Do your business. I'm sorry, girl. What a good dog you are.'

I yawned, stretched. My mouth felt like I had fairly recently stored washcloths in there. Heloise was still peeing, off leash. I had it in my hands but felt no need to hook her up. She wasn't going anywhere. It had gotten chilly; the breeze was slicing right through my jeans. I looked down at my cold, bare feet, which were mostly covered by a small pool of denim. Why are my jeans too tight and too long? I twisted, looking at the back pocket. I laughed out loud. 'These are Lainey's!' I glee-fully told Heloise. I was wearing Lainey's jeans! Well! I glanced up. Heloise was *still* peeing. I fit into my *daughter's* jeans! Well, fit might be too strong a word. In fact, they were mostly undone and still tight. I unzipped the few teeth I'd managed to zip downstairs, relieving a bit of the pressure.

Heloise, bless her heart, finally finished peeing. She stood gazing sightlessly forward, her black-rimmed eyes heavy with relief.

'I'm so sorry, girl,' I said, pulling her to me and hugging her. She wagged her tail and licked my wrist. Every reason to be mad at me, but she didn't know how.

We headed inside and I put some kibble in her bowl, figuring it might be good to soak up some marker ink in her stomach. Fortunately, the marker was both nontoxic and washable, so I was pretty sure it would do no real harm to either Heloise or my wall. I just needed to remember not to panic in the morning at what would undoubtedly be her blue Smurf-turds. Heloise finished her snack and I carried her downstairs, laboring under her size and weight, but wanting her company while I did laundry. I figured I had to take the jeans back down, I might as well throw in a load.

Downstairs, my first order of business was getting out of the tight jeans. I peeled them off and found a pair of my own in the pile. Much better; quite loose, in fact. I grabbed a bra from the rack, wistful for the days when I felt more comfortable without one. Those days were long gone. I stared at the mounds of three people's laundry heaped on the floor in front of me. I listlessly picked up one of Matt's T-shirts and started a whites pile. Heloise stood over it with predator eyes, clearly thinking, Ooooh! Fabric to chew and tear!

I was thinking: In what way will placing these

clothes in their discrete little piles, then into just the right temperature and agitation, with just the right kind of soap, for the proper length of time, contribute to . . . anything? Me? My relationship with my family? They didn't appreciate clean laundry, they just expected it. Will anyone in the world know that I have lived because my children never wanted for clean underwear? I looked at Heloise again. She was looking up at me, and I realized she was showing remarkable restraint. I knew she wanted to grab, at the very least a dish towel, and run through the house with it.

I bent, thumped her rib cage affectionately. 'Come on, girl. Let's get out of here.' We headed upstairs. Heloise was always willing to go up, just not down.

As we stepped into the kitchen, I checked the time on the microwave: 2:38 a.m.. Heloise and I climbed the second set of stairs. I stood in the hallway a moment, deliberating whether to sleep in Sam's room or the master bedroom. Neither one felt like my bedroom. I walked into Sam's room, fell onto the bed. Heloise nuzzled my arm. I desperately wanted her to sleep up on the bed with me. Completely against the rules. I got up, pulled the quilt and blanket off and made a nest on the floor for us. I lay down, patted the floor, and Heloise lay on her side next to me, and I spooned her, my arm over her shoulder, my hand gently stroking the thick fur on her chest. She gently mouthed my hand. I smiled, but stopped her. Instead, I grabbed one of her chew toys, Bumpy, from under the desk. I held one end for her; she chewed the other, her eyes mostly closed, small contented grunts coming from her, as if she was nursing. I had to admit, I felt a similar satisfaction.

CHAPTER 22

'I really did! I swear to God! The ticket is in my hand!'

Laughing, I pulled the phone away from my ear as Elaine screamed jubilantly, her each and every decibel flying across the miles. I set my ticket on the desk, ran my finger over the name. Ms Deena Munger, party of one. It had been so easy. I'd given the voucher to the travel agency Amy had recommended, and they'd done the rest.

'When? How long can you stay? What will you do with Heloise? Can you bring her?' Elaine breathlessly fired questions at me. I half sat against the desk, grinning, and watching Heloise at my feet; she was making loud squeaking noises chewing her new giant blue rubber bone. It looked like her old bone on steroids. It had, at least temporarily, replaced Bumpy as her favorite.

'If it's okay, we'll arrive on Wednesday, the day before Thanksgiving, and yes, I'm bringing Heloise with me. Bill said it was okay, and the travel agent cleared everything with the airlines. She even arranged for Heloise and me to sit in the bulkhead – that's the roomy row.'

'Yes, I know, silly. You're probably the only person who doesn't. Well, and anyone else who doesn't fly. Who's Bill?'

'You know, the puppy-raising leader. The great guy? Charming, handsome!' I laughed, but there was no response. 'Elaine, he's gay.'

'Oh. Okay.' I knew she was worried about not only me, but me and Neil. Elaine was our biggest matrimonial cheerleader. She'd always loved Neil, said if any two people were soul mates, it was me and Neil. But I think she, like Amy, had her own fantasy going about my perfect marriage.

'Deena, I'm sooo excited that you're coming, but, I'm sorry, I've got to get to the gallery now. I'm already late.'

I smiled. Elaine was always late to everything. 'No problem.' Neil and the kids would be home soon anyway. 'I've got to go, too, get Heloise out on her walk.' I wished I had a gallery to go to with Heloise.

'But real quick, give me the specifics,' she said, the bounce back in her voice. 'What time does your plane get in?' I relayed all the logistics with one finger on my ticket, my heart beating with both excitement and panic.

I hung up, then checked for messages, surprised at the stutter tone indicating there was one. Surprised, but not excited. I no longer even let myself think it could be Sam. Just reminded myself every time not to even hope. I dialed in the voice-mail number and then our code. Probably one of

293

those recordings from the library saying someone in the household had overdue materials.

The time stamp confirmed that the call had come just minutes ago, while I was on the phone with Elaine. 'Hey. We're on our way home.' It *was* Sam's voice! My heart raced with adrenaline. 'We're in the shuttle now and just getting onto the turn-pike' – It was Neil. Their voices . . . so alike – 'so we should be there in about thirty minutes or so, depending on traffic. See you soon.'

I glanced at the clock. They'd be home any minute. I did a quick survey of the house. I'd cleaned for hours yesterday, after dropping off the voucher at the travel agent. I'd been so nervous I'd taken it out on the accumulated dust and debris. The house once again shone, but it wasn't quite as satisfying to me now. It made me remember the time I'd stumbled upon my very remote Swiss grandmother in the hallway early one morning when I was about ten or eleven, seeing her for the first time without her makeup and complex coiffure, having a wonderful little chat, right there in the hallway, only to see her reemerge later with all her rouge and bobby pins and social fences back in place.

But I'd thought maybe a clean house would help pave the way for telling Neil that I was going to use the ticket after all. That I would not use it to go on a trip with him. Or the kids. That it would not be available for Sam. That I was using it to fly, alone with Heloise, to Madison, the place where Neil and

I had met, fallen in love, and gotten engaged. He would undoubtedly be hurt. I slumped into the desk chair again, imagining the confrontation. I'd done this all wrong. I should have spoken up when he was in my bedroom, Sam's room, telling me his plans for all the tickets. When I wasn't around my family I felt whole, paddling my own course, able to make thoughtful decisions. But somehow their mere presence made me feel swept away in the currents of silence and self-sacrifice.

Heloise trotted over, dropped her big blue bone in my lap, took a step back, ears up, tail wagging. She backed up farther, looking expectantly from me to the bone. 'Not now, girl,' I told her, setting the bone on the floor. I was not in the mood to play. But she wasn't giving up. She picked the bone up, again setting it in my lap. 'Uh-uh, Heloise,' I said more firmly, putting the bone on the floor again. She rushed in, grabbed the bone, plopped it in my lap, and, without a doubt, smiled. I put the bone firmly on the floor, pressing my fingers to it and holding eye contact with her. 'Uh-uh,' I told her, struggling to not laugh at her enthusiasm and persistence. I sat up slowly, my fingers equally slowly lifting off the bone. She immediately moved in. I knew I shouldn't, but I couldn't help the chortle that slid out as she plopped the bone in my lap a third time, her whole body wiggling in happy invitation, saying, 'Your turn!' This dog could make even behavior correction a game.

A sound on the front porch made us both freeze.

We separated slightly, looking at each other as we listened to the front door pushing open.

'Mom! We're home!' shouted Lainey.

Heloise ran so fast for the door that she slid across the tile, her hindquarters going out from under her. She immediately righted herself, no less frantic, and ricocheted off walls in her frenzy to get to the returning pack members. I set her bone on the floor again, then rose to follow. My hindquarters did not slide out from under me as I walked slowly toward the true and final end of my solitude. At least till Thanksgiving.

Heloise greeted Lainey, Matt, and Neil as they each tried to maneuver their way with suitcases and bags, not only through the door, but also past a manic dog. Heloise went from one to the next, her wagging body weaving in and out, trying desperately to keep 'four on the floor,' as she was supposed to, but only partially succeeding. She was determined to sniff and lick each of them – repeatedly – bathing them in her reunion euphoria. Wal-Mart greeters could take a page from her book.

'Hello, Hell-oh-wheezy!' said Matt, trying to reach down around his sister's suitcase to pat her.

'Hello, sweet doggie, how ya— *Heloise!* Cut it out!' yelled Lainey. Then again, seeing the part of anatomy that Heloise was most interested in greeting, a Wal-Mart greeter doing the same would be arrested.

I pulled Heloise away from Lainey. 'Uh-uh!

Heloise, sit!' She sat, looking apologetic but still gleeful. 'Good girl. Okay,' I said, releasing her. She swirled amongst them again, still saying 'Welcome home!' but in a more socially acceptable manner.

I turned to the kids, a trained smile on my face. 'Hey, travelers! How was it?' I was glad to see them. I just wished they could see me. The me that I'd been for the past four days. But I knew they wouldn't. They'd see Mom. Neil would see Wife. The Invisible Doer. That's all I'd ever let them see. But even as I stood here, I felt the authentic self I'd been for a few days rapidly fading, already dreading telling Neil that I'd last cashed in the voucher on a ticket for myself. He'd ask, with both hurt and anger in his eyes, if I was willing to fly, why didn't I want to go somewhere with him? And I had no good answer, except that I needed to do this trip on my own. To break out of something very hard and dark and encasing.

Neil was looking left then right, his face red with frustration, trying to see on what he'd caught his jacket. Amid Matt and Lainey's replies to me of 'It was great!' and 'Fun,' Heloise, evidently satisfied she'd anointed each sufficiently with her welcoming slobber, dashed into the kitchen. Neil replied to my inquiry with a tired smile and shrug. 'Kids were great, the meetings long, the prices outrageous. But all in all, a great trip.' He winked at Matt and Lainey.

'How was the flight?' I asked, stepping toward the kids, wrapping my arms around both of them at once.

'Cool! At least the flight home,' Matt said, giving me the most perfunctory of embraces, then pulling away, but eyes shining. 'They showed *Profound Justice.*'

'Ugh!' said Lainey, returning my hug with surprising vigor, then she too pulled back to show me her eye-rolling review of the movie. 'It was so violent! But on the flight over we got to see *Until Venice,*' she said, sighing romantically. 'We should rent it, Mommy. It was sooo cute.'

'Aww, c'mon!' moaned Matt. 'It was sooo lame! *Profound Justice* at least had a *plot*!'

Lainey looked at Matt, he at her, then both simultaneously poked an index finger into their downcast open mouths. I laughed, holding on to a sleeve from each of them in my hands.

'Well, that's good that you each saw a movie you liked on one of the flights,' I told them, feeling a freshness to my love for them, how they were growing into these wonderful unique people.

Heloise returned from the kitchen with her bone. She dropped it at my feet, backed up, expectant, tail wagging, her message clear: 'Your turn.'

I stared at the bone. Yes. *Yes.* I smiled at Heloise, then looked up at Neil. 'I guess it's my turn to go now, eh?'

Neil set his suitcase down and unhooked his jacket pocket from the screen door handle. He gave me a self-satisfied grin, and said, 'Okay,' stepping forward to bestow the hug he thought I'd asked for. As his arms wrapped too tightly around me, my eyes closed, and the mortar of misunderstanding filled the small crack I had made in my hard, dark shell.

Late that night, Neil and I sat in the living room, me on the couch, he stiffly in a chair. The exact hurt and anger I'd expected was on his face. 'So, what do *we* do for Thanksgiving?' he asked accusingly. 'I couldn't cook a turkey if my life depended on it.' There was a brief silence, then he added pejoratively, 'What, Sam's room isn't far enough away from me?'

It was bad enough, in Neil's opinion, that I was 'abandoning' them, but worse, that, as he'd put it, I'd 'chosen to leave on the most important family holiday of the whole year.' I'd wager the kids would put not only Christmas, but their birthdays, and even Halloween, well above Thanksgiving. And there were certain arguments to be made for Easter, too. But no matter. It was hopeless. He was determined to take my trip, for myself, as a personal affront.

I'd tried to do it right, using the 'I' statements that all the relationship articles said to. 'It's probably the biggest day of Elaine's life and I want to be there for her,' I told him. 'She's come out to visit so often; I never have. Plus, I just need some time now, Neil. I really need to face my fear of flying alone, well, with Heloise. Plus, it'll be good training for her.' He was staring at his clasped hands in his lap, a beleaguered expression on his

face. I wondered why they called that hangdog –
I'd certainly never seen anything like it on the
exuberant Heloise. I didn't want to, but I added,
hoping it sounded more sincere than it felt, 'And
after I do it – fly – we can maybe go somewhere,
together.' Still, nothing.

I tried again. 'I need a little perspective is all, a
change of environment for a few days. And you
know, Neil?' I waited for him to finally look at
me. 'As hard as it is in some ways for me to not
be here, I think it's probably good for me to not fix
Thanksgiving dinner this year. You know I always
tend to overdo it a bit and get pretty stressed out.'
Last year Neil's folks and two doctors from work
had joined us, and I'd made a nineteen-pound
turkey, *and* a six-pound ham, and peas and pearl
onions (Lainey's favorite) and mashed potatoes
(Matt's favorite) and twice-baked yams (Neil's
favorite) and pecan pie (his father's favorite). The
only thing I didn't make was the lime sorbet, Neil's
mother's favorite. I'd bought a carton from the
store, only to have Helen arrive and be on a low-
sugar diet. But she was grateful, just the same. I'd
intended to make cornbread too, Sam's favorite,
even though he wasn't going to be with us. But
I'd simply forgotten. When I'd realized it, moments
before the guests were to arrive, I'd fallen apart.
I'd hidden in our bedroom closet, missing my son
so acutely I'd felt a literal hole in my chest. I was
sobbing, even as the doorbell of our first guest
rang downstairs. Neil had coaxed me out finally

with a shoulder rub and assurances it would be fine for me to shower, that everyone would have a beer or glass of wine and watch the rest of the football game. 'When you come down, we'll turn it off and go for our walk.'

Our Thanksgiving walk before we ate was tradition. Just over to the lake and back, but we took a moment on the dock to one at a time throw a leaf onto the water, and say out loud something we were thankful for, then silently make a wish. We'd added the wish part after years of arguments stemming from one wishbone and three kids. But the kids had added the part about if the leaf floats you get your wish, if it sinks, you don't. Since leaves nearly always float, and/or the lake was often frozen by Thanksgiving anyway, we'd all leave feeling pretty hopeful.

Maybe I *should* stay home, I thought.

I looked at Neil sitting stiffly in the stiffest chair in our living room, staring at me.

'Neil?'

His anger was palpable now. Eyebrows arching in over his darkened eyes, he said, 'It feels like you're leaving me. Are you leaving me, Deena?'

I exhaled slowly. 'No, Neil.' I rose, crossed to where he sat, offering my hands to him. It was the truth. It was not my intention to leave him now. He looked up at me, and I saw the face of a frightened little boy.

Part of me was heartbroken, but part of me recoiled. I wondered if it would pull me toward

301

him, rather than repel me, if he could find a way to step back from this. Let me go with good tidings. But I had to admit, we both knew our marriage was in trouble. But the more he lashed out, or even grabbed for me, the more I felt a need to step away. A thousand miles away.

In mid-September, I was paying bills when Matt came home from school breathless, explaining that he'd missed the deadline for turning in his form – which I had dutifully signed and returned to him – for a field trip the following week for his art class. He'd lost the form. He asked me to call the teacher and intercede. With the phone in my hand, halfway through the numbers, I suddenly stopped. I handed him the phone. '*You* need to call Ms Zeckser, and explain, apologize, and ask her what you should do. This is your responsibility, Matt, not mine.' He put the phone back in its cradle, glared at me, and went up to his room. But that night at dinner, he proudly told me of his accomplishment.

'I called Ms Zeckser,' he announced, taking a grinning gulp of milk. It was just the two of us. Well, three. Heloise was asleep in her corner of the dining room. Lainey was at a slumber party. It went without saying that Neil was gone. But I wasn't even sure where.

'Good,' I said, smiling. 'You got it worked out then?'

'Yeah, she was pretty nice about it actually. Said

she'd give me another form on Monday. I have to come home after school, get it signed, go back, and go through all the forms and help her plan and stuff.'

'Good, Matt. I'm glad you get to go. So now what's going to be your system in the future for not missing deadlines?'

He looked at me, his spoonful of stew halfway to his open mouth. 'System?'

I shook my head, exasperated, but laughing. I couldn't help but think of Heloise, when she'd do something she knew wasn't right, but maybe didn't quite know how it was wrong. Now I could see that same bewilderment in my son, despite the many discussions about writing things down that I'd had with my kids over the years. But, unlike with Heloise, I knew that I'd never really made my kids stay the course, go back, do it again, get it right themselves. Instead I swooped in to save the day – drive the form up to school, wake them when they forgot to set their alarms, finish typing up their procrastinated reports in the wee hours. Not once or twice, but nearly every time.

'Yes, a system, a way to remember next time. You've got to have some sort of system that works for you. Y'know, sweetie, I've realized that you and your sister are too dependent on me to remind you of things, to do things for you. And a lot of that is my fault. I've probably jumped in too quickly to help you guys.' I took a small sip of broth, the reverberation of my admission ringing

303

in my ears. Matt's spoon was still suspended in midair, his mouth agape, his wide eyes still trained on me. 'Look,' I said, pointing my empty spoon at him. 'You're going to be out there on your own pretty soon. I'm not going to be there to remind you to get up, do your homework – *to turn in forms.*'

'True,' he said, shrugging and shoving his laden spoon into his mouth, chewing and bobbing his head from side to side good-naturedly. The difference between my son and daughter was endlessly fascinating to me. Lainey had to get to acceptance through a novella of argument and discussion, and/or knee-deep in drama. Matt went from point A to point B with little more than a shrug or grunt.

'So, what will you do?' I asked, as he thoughtfully chewed a piece of stew meat, staring blankly ahead.

'Huh?'

'A system?' Same blank stare, now directed at me. 'So you don't forget things?'

'Oh. Uh, I guess I need to write it in my planner.'

'That sounds like a good idea, honey,' I said, nodding, silently applauding my own restraint.

I took a sip from my water glass, then folded and refolded my cloth napkin in my lap. 'Matt?' I said, finally. Peripherally I watched him look at me. I briefly glanced at him, then back to my lap. 'I think that's kind of why Sam hasn't been in contact much since he left. It was a really hard transition for him, and he was determined to, I don't know, cut the ties altogether, I guess.' I breathed, looked up.

Matt gave me a crooked smile. 'Yeah. He told me.'

I struggled not to let my own mouth drop open. *Act nonchalant.* 'He did?' I picked up my spoon, dipped it into my bowl, slowly pushed a slice of carrot around, dying to ask what I'd done wrong, specifically. Matt didn't pick up on the forced silence. He, like his father, was fine with silence.

I bit my tongue, but still the question came out. 'What'd he say?'

Matt shrugged, concentrating on fishing out the meat chunks and potatoes, avoiding the carrots and peas. 'Oh, you know. Just Sam stuff.' He chuckled suddenly, looking up at me again. 'He's just going through his "I'm-a-man-now" phase, Mom. He's like a rabbit or something, if you keep chasing after him, he's gonna keep running. He'll get over it if you leave him alone for a while.'

I looked at him, his tousled tawny hair, his jaw, so suddenly squared into a man's chin, his hands large, strong. Then I actually checked in the corner of the dining room to confirm that Heloise was still sleeping, and not delightedly chasing around the dining room floor after the pearls of wisdom my son had just so casually dropped.

November came in as one of the snowiest on record. During one of those storms, Lainey and

I were baking cakes for the holiday bazaar for the school choirs, coincidentally to be held on her sixteenth birthday, when the heavy, wet snowstorm took out the power less than fifteen minutes into the baking process.

'*Mom!*' Lainey'd yelled at me, stomping out of the kitchen.

'Lainey! It's not my fault,' I yelled after her. 'The power's out!'

'Can't you take it over to the Kellermans', bake it there?' she yelled from the living room, her voice choked with tears.

'Honey, I'm sure their power's out too. We'll buy a cake.'

She stomped back into the kitchen, face red, eyes narrowed. 'We told them we'd *bake* a cake, Mom!' She stomped back out to the living room.

I tried to breathe. I'd read the books, knew that a teenager was just as caught as I was between independence and attachment, that their brain development was somewhere between functioning and not, that everything was black or white, that adults, parents especially, were to be praised for nothing and blamed for everything. In fact, for her birthday I'd bought her a book for teen girls, from the same publisher that did my *Maximizing Midlife* book and workbook, hers called *Ready to Roar – A Teen Girl's Guide to Decisions, Debates and Dilemmas*. I thought about running upstairs and giving it to her, unwrapped. But I'd finally backed into my last wall in my dance to avoid confrontation. I'd run out of calm. Clean out of understanding. My blood pounded through me like angry surf.

I'd taken just two steps toward the living room, where Lainey was screaming on the couch, when Heloise stepped in front of me. That's all, just stepped in front of me, not looking at me or wanting me to play. Just standing there. Suddenly the camera that filmed the movie of my life backed way, waayyy up.

My balled fists opened. I realized this had little to nothing to do with me. I said quietly, 'Honey, I'm going to leave you for a minute to think about this situation. Come find me in the basement when you've gotten some perspective.'

I walked down the stairs; I'd forgotten there'd be no light at all down there with the power outage. I glanced back. Heloise stood at the top, looking more worried than ever for my safety down in the black depths. I wasn't going back up. 'It's okay, girl.' I felt my way to the laundry room, crawled across the floor and settled onto a big pile of laundry, clumping some together for a pillow. It was surprisingly comfortable.

Lainey's tentative voice calling from the stairwell woke me. 'Mom? *Mom!?*'

'Yes. What. I'm here,' I said, groggily.

She was at the bottom of the stairs, cautiously shining the flashlight around the corner onto me in my nest. 'Are you *okay*?'

I sat up, shielding my eyes from the beam of light in my face.

'Sure.' I rubbed my eyes, she lowered the beam. I stretched, long and luxuriously. Actually, I was better than okay. A lovely, refreshing nap it had been.

'Were you . . . *sleeping*?'

'Uh, yeah. How long has it been?'

'I don't know, half hour or so.' A beat, then, 'Mom? Why're you sleeping – *here*?' She slowly stepped toward me, the dual beams of the light and her astonishment shining on me.

I sat up, straight and tall on my laundry pile, suddenly almost laughing. 'Because I can.'

Her face was illuminated in the back glow of the flashlight as she stood in front of me, her expression a mix of confusion and amusement. Her long hair looked shiny, just brushed. She was wearing a simple, tailored white blouse and jeans. Her long, slender bare feet, toenails painted pink, looked like a model's. She was tall, curvy, fit. Really very pretty. Her eyes softened. 'I'm sorry, Mom,' she said. 'It isn't your fault the power went out.'

I stood. 'No, it isn't. Thank you. I accept your apology. And you know what?' I smoothed my clothing, looked at her. She cocked her head. 'I think you just had your own little power outage up there. Me, too. That's why I took a nap, I guess.'

She nodded.

'Can I have that a minute, please?' I asked, holding my hand out for the flashlight. She gave

308

it to me and I put the lit end in my mouth, puffing out my cheeks, monsterlike, as we'd done for the kids each Halloween when they were little, to their high-pitched shrieks of delighted fright.

Lainey pulled back in surprise, then burst out laughing. 'I don't know about you lately, Mom,' she said, taking the flashlight from me and slinging one arm around my shoulders. Still smiling, she guided me toward the stairs.

It was Neil with whom communication seemed to break down completely. Just days before I was to leave, I invited him to walk around the lake with Heloise and me. I'd already taken her on a long walk with Merle and Teddy in the morning, but the tension in the house with Neil home was too big for the walls to contain. I thought maybe outside we could finally talk.

It was a Sunday afternoon, gray and cold. We both bundled into our big parkas, mittens, hats. We were as sealed off from each other now by our clothing as our respective fragilities.

The lake was frozen, the remaining ducks intrepid on their comical treks across the ice. Neil stared at the ground as we walked through the brittle stillness, but Heloise and I both watched the ducks, their little triangular feet slipping out from under them as they tottered out, Chaplinesque. They made me feel lighthearted. That, and my freedom on the near horizon.

I broached my impending departure once

more, trying to take the weight out of it with a light tone. 'It's just kind of a fiftieth birthday present to myself, Neil. A little time alone to contemplate the downhill slide.' I laughed brightly as I slid my hand downward in front of us.

Neil remained silent. His only response was to turn his head away from me and look toward the mountains, shrouded now in the low, dark, broken clouds of the back edge of the storm. Neil had become more and more sheathed in his own hard existence. He was spending more time with Lainey and Matt since their trip together, but generally steering clear of me. It was as if both of us refused or just didn't have the energy or just didn't know how to bridge the gap between us. I knew part of it was the absence of sex, of sharing a bed. But my need now was for my own bed, my own space. For once, I was learning how to tend to my own needs.

So then and there, with my boots shuffling through a couple of inches of snow, Heloise's paw prints dappling a path at my side, I gave up. I knew he wanted me to keep reaching for him. I'd tried with this walk, but there was nothing from him. Years ago I would run as far as it took to get to him, to retrieve 'us.' And he'd had his own charming ways to beckon me back, drawing me a bath, bringing home the occasional flowers. Coffee in bed. At one point, it *had* been give-and-take. But for years now, as he became more enmeshed in work, and then the clinic, it had become my responsibility to charge and recharge our marital batteries, along with everything else. I'd prepare a romantic candlelit dinner when the kids were gone, or just listen to his long stories from work, with too many of the wrong details. Years ago, I'd even taken on the responsibility for scheduling midweek, midday sexual trysts, not out of my own lust, but to pull him back. Reconnect. But now my own batteries were so low they would barely register on the meter.

As we headed toward home in silence I thought how nice it would be if there were some sort of marital filling station, some external source to fill us up individually, so we could hang on. Maybe then we wouldn't be coasting on empty down the steep hill into divorce.

CHAPTER 23

'Hurry, Deena! Time to go!' Neil yelled from downstairs as I frantically scanned the bedroom. I'd told him I wanted to take the shuttle, like he and the kids had, but he'd insisted on driving me, said he'd already arranged for the afternoon off. The afternoon off on the day before Thanksgiving. A day that *was* a holiday itself for a lot of people. But it was something for him, so I didn't argue.

I looked out the bedroom window. It had been spitting bits of snow earlier, but had stopped completely now, the gray sky opening here and there to a soft blue. I was grateful the roads would be clear, and that I wouldn't have to worry about the wings of the plane icing up. I could cross one off the list of my dozens of fears about flying.

I looked around the bedroom once more, ran into the bathroom, grabbed a bottle of Pepto-Bismol from the medicine cabinet. There might be a shortage of it in the Midwest. I ran to my dresser, grabbed my swimsuit from the bottom drawer. So it was subzero in Wisconsin right now, you never knew. I stopped on the stairs, ran back into Sam's room, snatched my lip balm from the bedside table, and hurried downstairs.

Packing sanity alighted on me just before I walked out the front door. I left my swimsuit and the Pepto-Bismol on the entryway table, but slid the lip balm into my purse as I pulled the front door shut behind me. Neil and Heloise sat in the car waiting, one drumming his fingers on the steering wheel, the other wagging her tail at my approach.

The drive down to Denver was awkward. Neil asked about any plans Elaine and I had. I told him as far as I knew, it'd be just the three of us for Thanksgiving, then the opening on Saturday night. Beyond that, we were leaving it open. He nodded, his lips tight, as if I really did know of other plans, but wasn't telling him.

'Did you prepare anything?' he asked.

'Prepare? You mean for flying?'

'No, for us. Dinners—' He bit his lip, I think finally hearing himself. 'Never mind. We'll manage.'

The mixed waters of guilt and anger surged in me, a dangerous high tide. I should have left long ago, I thought, but didn't say it.

Finally, we were on the last stretch of the drive, the forlornly straight and long Peña Boulevard, nothing but the absurd Saharan-like white tents of the airport looming in the distance. We were once again silent. I didn't know why he'd wanted to drive me. Thankfully, the heavy holiday traffic moved relatively well along Peña, and I breathed a sigh of relief when Neil put on the turn indicator at the sign to the parking area.

'Neil?' I said suddenly. 'Could you just leave us at the drop-off lane? I've only got my carry-on, and, with the crowds and the security, it'll be nuts in there.' His head dropped slightly, but he slowly redirected the car into the circle drop-off lane. He double-parked next to a packed minivan with what looked like a family of nineteen piling out. He lifted the parking brake slowly, his eyes determinedly forward. As I moved to undo my seat belt, he put his hand on mine, stopping me.

'Deena?' *Not here, Neil. Please, let's not do this here, now.*

'I want you to take this.' He reached into the inside pocket of his down vest and pulled out a folded bill. He pressed the rectangle into my palm, closing my hand around it. 'For emergencies.'

I was relieved he didn't want to talk about 'us,' but did he think I was twelve? I had cash, credit cards, an ATM card. I tried to pull my hand away. 'Neil, I'll be fine.'

He kept his hands clasped around mine and forced a weak smile. 'Then spend it on something for yourself, something you wouldn't ordinarily get. Go a little crazy.' He leaned over, tentatively kissed my cheek. The scent of an unfamiliar aftershave wafted over me.

The fact that he didn't want to 'discuss' us right then and there, that he, in fact, decided to make the cash a gift instead of protection, that he'd taken the afternoon off, that he had a new after-shave on, all made me feel more than a little guilty. But it all also made me feel, again, like I should have done this years ago. For both our sakes. I slipped the folded bill into my jeans pocket and kissed him back on the cheek. 'Thanks, Neil. Oh, I left *The Joy of Cooking* on the counter by the stove; it's got all the information you'll ever need. And Lainey knows how to make BYOBs.' He looked like he was about to cry. 'I hope you guys have fun this weekend,' I said, as cheerily as I could. I looked down, pretending to wind a watch that didn't need winding. 'I'd better go.'

The long halls of the airport were already fully decked for the season. Long, thick gold garlands dipped and rose near the ceiling, giant wreaths on nearly every wall. But the crowds seemed less than merry. Heloise trotted through the thick, tense mass of humanity, her effect that of a clown at a rodeo, drawing smiles and momentarily distracting the bulls from their particular anxieties. We stepped out to a small, grassy pet courtyard. A woman was there with a small reddish dog, whose pushed-in nose made it look like Hairy's canine counterpart. The woman kept imploring it to go to the bathroom before their long flight. 'Come on, Fergie! It'll be over four hours. *Please* go tee-tee for Mommy.' I gave Heloise the command and she immediately relieved herself, much to my relief.

Heloise was also superbly patient as we stood

315

in seemingly endless security lines. As it was finally our turn to walk through the portal, my shoes already removed and handed over, they pulled us aside. 'You'll have to step through separately, ma'am,' said a young female agent. 'Hand the leash through to him.' She pointed to an attractive black man, who smiled at me and nodded. I handed him her leash and Heloise walked through. The alarm sounded, undoubtedly from the metal plate attached to her collar identifying her as a K-9 Eyes dog, as well as her other tags in an attached nylon pouch, but the agents seemed unconcerned. The second agent waited for me to walk through. I did, no alarms, then I took Heloise's leash again while he squeezed and examined her collar, especially the plate and tag pouch. Satisfied, he then patted her down, every inch. It did seem ridiculous, but then again, *I* wouldn't want to be the guard who'd let the Hijacker Guide Dog in Training through security, either. Heloise, for her part, completely enjoyed the attention and groping. In fact, she kept trying to pull and return to him as I sat with her ten yards away, putting on my shoes. She thought she'd found her new best friend.

We bypassed the moving sidewalk, forbidden by K-9 Eyes rules from using escalators of any type for safety reasons; the hairs in her paws could get caught. A working guide who must use them would be individually trained, and always have her paws carefully maintained. Besides, we both needed the walk. Heloise was a little nervous on the concourse train. I was grateful for her company, as I was a little nervous, too. I obsessively watched the moving digital readout, and listened to the creepy *1984*-like computer voice announcing each stop.

But the worst part by far, for both of us, was after we had lined up at the gate for early boarding, handed over our ticket, walked down the long, snaking gangway, and were faced with the open threshold between the ramp and the plane. I wasn't expecting that I'd be able to see the ground below. The crack was probably just an inch or so, but it might as well have been the Grand Canyon. Couldn't they put something over that?!

Heloise paused, as she was trained to do before going through any doorway, but when I said, 'Okay,' my voice trembling, she balked. Through the crack we both stared at the tarmac below. Out the windows I could see the tiny wheels of the plane, seeming absurdly small for this behemoth vehicle. It looked like they'd run out of real airplane tires and made do with Tinker Toys. Heloise and I looked at each other, neither wanting to step over. The passengers behind us pressed closer. Finally, biting my lip and tightly clutching Heloise's leash, I put one foot across, stepping much wider than necessary, in case it suddenly fell away. 'Okay, girl!' But Heloise pulled back on her leash, legs stiff, ears flat. Her driveway perform-ance of months ago. I quickly hopped back toward her, pulling her to the side, letting the line of other early boarders – mostly elderly folks and couples with babies and toddlers – go ahead.

As people filed by, I squatted next to Heloise, near the wall of the circular end of the gangway. I wondered if the airline personnel had some kind of inside-joke name for this area. Like, the panic point. It seemed expressly made for people who were seriously rethinking their travel objectives. I kissed Heloise, stroking the length of her body, whispering reassuring words to her. She wagged her tail but chewed on my sleeve, a sign she was anxious. I couldn't help but wonder if her dog sense was better than my human sense, if she somehow knew that in this big metal tube we were going to be hurled through the air, thousands of feet off the ground. Or if she was just picking up on my anxieties.

I thought of returning home. To Neil's satisfaction at my failure, to the kids' jokes. I stood. Confidently I said, 'Let's go, Heloise!' We stepped into line, people smiling and stepping back for us. Heloise again paused at the crack, looked down at the tarmac below, then up at me with woeful eyes, as if to say, 'Must we?' I gritted my teeth and encouraged her on gaily, resolutely. 'Where's Elaine, girl? Let's go find Elaine!' I chirped, knowing that her eagerness to locate someone, anyone, would send her willingly forward. I was determined not to show my fear again. Right. Like I couldn't feel my terror seeping out of my every pore. But we both did some version of a gulp, then stepped across the threshold together.

The bulkhead, it turned out, was the first row behind the wall separating first class from the rest of the plane. It was a bit more spacious, especially welcome since the plane was certain to be full. Already, our row was. With us was an elderly couple, she in the middle next to me, he with his cane in the aisle seat.

'That's a beautiful dog,' said the woman, elegantly dressed in a pale pink wool suit with a gold-and-pearl brooch on the lapel. I sighed with relief. Not everyone would be happy to share a plane trip with a dog at their feet.

'Thank you,' I said. After the requisite conversation about raising her, we all settled in, the woman reading a novel, the man a business magazine. Heloise had plenty of room at my feet, and was physically comfortable, but emotionally a little shaky. I handed her the dog equivalent of a good novel – her big blue bone – but she ignored it. She cast nervous glances up to the ceiling, over to the aisle, up at me. Finally, the plane full, the flight attendant talk given, the emergency card in my lap, we began rumbling down the runway, the roar increasing. I bent down, patting Heloise, grateful that I could disguise the Crash Position as the Comforting Dog position. Heloise listened intently, panting – another sign of stress – and fear in her eyes, to the loud roars and rumblings

319

from the belly of the plane. She kept looking at me for reassurance. My jaw clenched, my breathing fast and raspy through my teeth, I whispered, 'It's okay, girl. You're okay.'

As the nose lifted, the increasing gravity from the g-force pressed Heloise onto the floor, me against my seat. I looked at her; she looked at me, and cocked her head, as if to ask me: 'Why are we gaining weight?' Then a squeal and *ca-chunk* as the wheels tucked into their housing right below us. We both flinched. Still panting, she looked at me and I scratched her stomach, trying to breathe myself. As we rose higher and higher, then finally leveled off, the sounds too leveled off to a steady hum. I sat up, forced my breathing to slow, my muscles to relax.

When the seat belt sign dinged off, I left mine securely buckled, but heaved a sigh and reclined my seat. Miraculously, Heloise almost immediately put her head down and went to sleep. I figured sleeping was her coping mechanism. The flight attendant, a clean-cut handsome man who looked to be in his late thirties, worked his way down the aisle with his cart, taking drink orders. Just in time for a little coping mechanism of my own.

Both of my seatmates ordered Bloody Marys. 'Double vodka, double lime, please,' I said, trying to sound like someone celebrating, not medicating. I was looking at his name tag – Kyle, it said – and he winked at me, then scooped some ice into a plastic cup. Was that an 'I find you attractive' wink?

Or a 'Double vodka? So you're another fear-of-flying customer!' wink? Or an 'I'm gay and wink at everybody!' wink? I paid him, hoping I was not as red-faced as I felt, and he handed me my glass of ice, with two lime wedges, and two small bottles. The woman next to me had to show me how to pull up my tray from the armrest.

I leaned back and thought about what kind of a wink I wanted it to be. I listened through the crack between the seats as he asked the couple in the row behind us what they'd like. They were trying to quiet their fussy baby, alternately shushing each other for perceived imperiousness. I wanted to turn around and tell them, 'Stop worrying your baby! Have a brandy! Relax!' I glanced up at the flight attendant. He caught my eye, and winked again. I spun around, feeling the blush returning to my cheeks. I looked at my own fists gripped tight, one on Heloise's leash, the other on the armrest. Oh, wasn't I the one to tell folks to relax! The couple finally ordered Sprites.

Still feeling the heat in my face, I turned toward the window, hunching my shoulders. Relax. Pretend you're not you. I took another deep breath, then, shielded by my body, I carefully pulled off my wedding rings, pushing them into my jeans pocket. They bumped against something. I remembered the bill Neil had given me. Guilt swept over me. I shoved the rings back on my finger, an accusing pulse pounding in my ears. Slowly, I reached in and pulled out the bill, which I was pretty sure would be a twenty, knowing Neil. Like my own hairstyle, his sense of economics had changed little since the seventies. But even with a twenty, I could get flowers from the grocery store for Wendy and Elaine. If it was a fifty, maybe some champagne too. As I unfolded it, my heart skipped a beat. It was not one but two bills: two one-hundred-dollar bills. I was momentarily stunned. What was Neil *thinking*?

I shoved the bills back into my pocket. I poured both little bottles into my glass and took several quick, grimacing sips. After that I sipped more slowly, chewed on the limes, and looked out the window, still holding tight to my sleeping dog's leash. Less than halfway through my drink, I too fell asleep.

We were both awakened by the announcement of our approach to the Madison airport. The empty vodka bottles had been cleared away as I'd slept, but my glass of watery vodka remained. As I rubbed the sleep from my face, a tall woman in a business suit returning from the bathrooms stopped by our row. With one hand on the partition she leaned in and said, 'I'm amazed! That dog has been so good!' Lowering her voice to a whisper, she added, 'Unlike the baby behind you.' Funny, I hadn't heard a thing. She straightened up, again smiling, and said to Heloise, 'What a good dog!' At this, Heloise wagged her tail, then stretched mightily on the floor, legs stiffly out front, head arching back, body trembling slightly with the pleasure of the stretch, and let out a high, hissing fart.

'Gotta go!' said the tall woman, laughing and leaving. I cringed, felt the blood rushing into my face again as the nice elderly couple and I became engulfed in noxious Lab flatulence. I reached up and twisted on the air nozzle. They did the same. Then I grabbed the emergency card, fanning the air above her butt. The woman used her novel, the man his magazine.

'I'm so sorry,' I said.

They laughed. 'Don't worry about it, dear,' said the woman, fanning away. 'Our dog at home is a regular fart factory.' I laughed at this elegant woman's turn of phrase.

Her husband grinned, nodded thoughtfully, and said, 'It's true. Just something you've got to endure. But they make up for it in love now, don't they?'

I nodded, swelling with gratitude at their understanding and acceptance of dog farts, and life. Suddenly bits of an urgent-sounding but whispered conversation carried forward. Still fanning the air, I leaned back in my seat, shoving my ear into the crack.

'For Chrissakes, Jen! It stinks! I think you should change him now!'

'Shhh! Stop swearing! I am not going to wake this baby! Besides, if you don't broadcast it, no one will know. I'll change him after we land.'

I imagined them furtively sneaking glances around them, wondering if anyone else could smell it. I hunkered down in my seat, thanking God for small, blameless babies. Almost before I knew it, we'd landed, those tiny tires somehow smoothly cushioning our return to earth.

We let those in a hurry disembark, and that seemed to be nearly everyone. Finally, Heloise and I worked our way down the aisle, only to be held nearly captive by the captivated crew. I politely answered all the requisite questions. *How old is she? How long do you get to keep her? How will you ever be able to give her up? Won't it be hard?* Finally, I thanked them for the safe flight, and Heloise and I stepped lightly and happily onto the carpeted gangway.

We made our way down the concourse, people pointing and smiling at us the whole way. We passed a blind man with a black Lab in working harness. Heloise pulled toward them, but I held her close to me. 'Leave it!' I said, and she corrected her course and we hurried past. The working guide only barely glanced at Heloise, confidently leading on. We stepped out into the large greeting area. I scanned for Elaine.

'*Oh my Gawd!*' came the familiar voice from our left. Heloise and I wheeled around. 'There you are, finally!' screamed Elaine, running toward us with outstretched arms. 'I was looking for one of those damn phones to page you! I thought you'd missed the plane!'

She looked the same, compact, shorter than me by an inch or so, wild short curly hair, a shock of

324

gray in front, a salting of gray over the rest of her head. Bright red, what she called her 'artsy-fartsy' glasses, on her nose.

'I know, I'm sorry,' I said as I came in for a hug. 'I waited so Heloise wouldn't be in the crush getting off. Then the whole flight crew wanted to—' She enveloped me in strong arms, her embrace feeling immediately healing and energizing, her curly hair brushing against my cheek. Filled with happiness, I hugged her back, as Heloise tried to worm her head in between us, wagging furiously, happy for any reunion.

Elaine held my shoulders, but looked down at Heloise. 'Oh, my God, she is so sweet!' She moved her hands to her cheeks, completely charmed and charming. 'She's huge! I thought she was a puppy. How old is she now?'

'Technically, she is still a puppy. She turns one in mid-January.'

'I forget, how long do you get to keep her?'

'Raisers have them about a year or so, till they're recalled to guide school. Usually it's when they're around fourteen to sixteen months old. So probably April or so.'

'Can I pet her?' she asked, almost breathless.

'Yeah, let me get her to sit first.' I gave Heloise the command, and she immediately obeyed.

'Now?' Elaine asked.

I nodded, grinning. Elaine squatted and held out her flat palm under Heloise's nose, then she scratched both sides of her head at once. If the marble floor of the airport hadn't been buffed to a shine already, Heloise's tail would have polished up a bright half circle.

'Hello, you beautiful girl. I'm your godmother.' Elaine looked up at me. 'Right?'

'Absolutely,' I said.

Elaine stood, but continued scratching one side of Heloise's neck. Heloise leaned contentedly into her hand. 'What a darling dog, Deena. I'm in love with her already.' Elaine looked up at me, her eyes as doleful as Heloise's had been, and I knew exactly what she was thinking. What everyone thought, and most asked. Thankfully, she didn't ask, deftly moving on, pointing to my small suitcase. 'Do we need to go to baggage, or is that it?'

'This is it,' I said, lifting it slightly. 'And Heloise probably would be grateful for the nearest exit.'

Elaine pointed both fingers now, pistol fashion, and said, 'Right!' Then she took my bag from me and, hooking her other arm through mine, led us down the concourse and out into the bright Wisconsin light, and suddenly I felt young again. Not twenty, but young enough.

CHAPTER 24

I licked some powdered sugar off the edge of my cookie, closing my eyes with pleasure at the almost foreign sweetness. It'd been months since I'd had a cookie.

We were sitting at Elaine's colorful kitchen table sipping Constant Comment tea and eating Pfeffernüsse, a tradition we'd shared in college each year, right before we'd each left for our respective homes and holidays. This particular brand and kind of cookie – a sort of licorice flavor – was Elaine's favorite, and only available during the holiday season. She therefore always bought about a dozen of the small boxes, putting most in her freezer, where they'd last for months. She claimed they were as good, if not better, when they were rock hard. Geodes, she called them, come spring. It didn't faze her remnant Jewish sensibilities at either Chanukah or Passover that the box was gaily decorated with distinctly Christmassy art.

I dunked the edge of my cookie in my tea, eliciting a frown from Elaine.

'You're not supposed to do that till they're

geodes,' she said with mock disdain. 'But, since I'm so fucking glad you're here, I'll allow it.'

I popped the soggy sweetness into my mouth with a loud 'Mmmm!' Heloise looked up, hopeful, but sleepy. We'd worn her out on our long walk around Tenney Park, just after we'd arrived. Heloise had snuffled through the snow drifts on the edge of the path, while Elaine and I waded happily through the first layer of reconnecting: what each of the kids was doing, Wendy's job (she owned her own ad agency, which had become one of the largest in Madison), Elaine's upcoming art show, which she said would have some surprises. She'd gotten cheerfully circumspect again at that point, changing the subject. In short, we'd talked about everything but that, and my marriage.

On the way back to her house we crossed a bridge over one of the ponds, stopping to lean on the railing. We watched the skaters below, twirling, falling, laughing. A young, twenty-something couple glided unsteadily under us. The girl wore a fuzzy hat and had a matching muff hanging from her neck. I smiled, inwardly pained at what I was sure was her carefully chosen ensemble for this date. It had to be perfect, to match her fantasies of what a girl on a skating date would wear. The muff went unused, her hands otherwise occupied, one clutching her partner's elbow, the other stretched out to her side for balance. The boy looked equally unsteady, but they were both red-nosed and laughing, their breath puffing in happy clouds in front of them. Tenney Park was even more bucolic than I'd remembered. Currier and Ives. I could picture myself living here again. Alone. Maybe after Lainey graduated. How the fantasies change.

But now, finally thawing out around her kitchen table, I think we both knew that this tea party we were having would eventually lead to a discussion of my marital discord.

Heloise was still staring at my cookie, so I reached into the fanny pack and gave her her blue bone, which she sniffed, then ignored. Resigned, she went back to sleep.

'This table is incredible, E,' I said, running my finger over the colorful designs. The table itself was old, a 1950s diner type, with a silver rim around the edge and metal V legs. It had probably been white when it'd started its life as a nifty kitchen table for the newly sprouting suburban developments all over the country over half a century ago. Now it wouldn't even recognize itself. Underneath the added glass top were myriad small images, virtually every color imaginable, painted from edge to edge. Most of the images were of happy, naked, cartoonish women, in various acts of frivolity – dancing, flying kites, holding hands, swimming, leaping, flying. Each figure was outlined in gold. It was the only cloisonné-looking kitchen table I'd ever seen.

'It's fantastic, Elaine!' I said, swallowing the last of my cookie. I wanted another but resisted. I was enjoying my new body and fitness level too much. 'Did you paint it?'

'Yep!' she said, smiling. 'I got the table at a yard sale. I painted it as a surprise birthday present for Wendy.' She showed off the table with exaggerated hand gestures. 'Voilà! A decadent kitchen table!'

'It's really not decadent, though,' I said, turning my head, twisting ear to shoulder to see more of the women on the other side. 'It's just a lot of naked women having fun. I like it. In fact, I love it! Can I buy it and take it home in my suitcase?'

'Funny you should mention that . . . ,' said Elaine in her singsong voice.

'Seriously?' I looked up at her. 'Are you selling this table?'

'No, not this table, but that's the surprise, so I might as well spill the beans. I made a few other small pieces like it, sold them, word got out, and, well, it's ridiculously popular! I think we've entered the Age of the Goddess.'

Suddenly unsmiling, I said, 'You know, Elaine? I've been thinking that very thing. I think that's why I want to be on my own, y'know?' I looked at my sleeping dog, and sighed audibly. 'Since I've had Heloise I've felt what it's like to be out there again.'

'What do you mean? Like, out of the house?'

'More than that. People – strangers – look me in the eye, talk to me, because I have this adorable dog in a green jacket who's going to be this really

330

vital partner to someone one day. So it's the dog they look at, but then they look at me, like *I'm* something. Someone.' My voice cracked and Elaine gently took my hand. 'I guess because they know I'll have to give her up, or because they think I know what I'm doing – I don't know.' I took a deep breath and looked at my friend, my voice strong now. 'I don't think I've ever really experienced this before. This visibility and . . . respect. I have to say, as hard as raising her has been, and it's been a lot more work than I thought it would be, being a full-time mother is a hell of a lot harder. But rarely does anyone look at a mother with that kind of respect and awe.' Elaine was still holding my hand and looking in my eyes, her expression open. Receptive. She was really listening to me. It made me think of Merle.

'Elaine, I've had to learn so much since my kids were born – it's like the most intense college. You have to learn about behavior, psychology, physiology, medicine, logistical planning, engineering, nutrition, brain development – shit! Everything! But we don't graduate to *anything*. No one ever hands you a diploma. No marching across a stage somewhere with a go-get-'em song playing. In fact, it's the opposite. It's like the elevator music that's been in the background the past twenty years of your life just kind of fades out, and you look up, and everyone's gone.'

I pulled my hand from Elaine's, rubbed my forehead. 'Heloise I will have loved and cared for and taught and learned from for a year, year and a half, by the time she's recalled. You do all that with your kids for *eighteen* years.' I looked out the window, my lungs feeling small, my heart swollen. 'I wish I had a dollar for every time a complete stranger has stopped me, looked at Heloise, and asked, "How are you ever going to give her up?" I doubt any of those people would ever stop and ask a mother that.' Elaine nodded, closed her eyes briefly.

I sipped my cold tea, then stared at the drowned crumbs at the bottom of my cup. I looked at the table again. Really, you could hardly help but. I ran my finger over the outline of a chartreuse woman on a hot pink sailboard on brilliant blue water.

'Elaine? You know how when we were in our twenties and it seemed like we'd survived our teenage angst and now the whole world lay before us, full of glorious adventures and whatever perfect life we could imagine? Like *The Price Is Right*, all those shiny curtains, *something* good behind all of them.' I looked up, she nodded again. 'And then I made a couple of choices, happy choices – I chose the marriage/kids curtain. I don't regret it, I just— I just never really thought that those couple of choices made or precluded just about every other choice for me. I mean, who *am* I? It's not that Neil is bad, or even that I don't love him still, somehow. But by choosing what was behind curtain A, we never even get to *look* behind curtain

332

B or C. I *did* choose to get married, and I *did* choose to have kids and be a full-time parent. I loved that life but – I want to see what's behind B. Or C. For *me*, you know?'

I lay my head on my arm and finally let the tears come. Elaine rubbed my back but said nothing. Never had I been so grateful for anyone in my life. To be comforted only, to have someone hear me, not try to fix me. This is what women want. And this is what women give. Why had I let my women friendships dwindle? Even disappear, spun off by the forces of life, like so much extraneous matter in the centrifuge of marriage and family.

We were both silent. But not Heloise. She stretched on the floor, and farted loudly. Again. I remembered she'd gotten into the trash at home before we'd left – found a half of an old sandwich and God knows what else. That's what was causing all this flatulence. Laughing, Elaine and I both reached for something to fan the air; I grabbed the box of Kleenex, Elaine a bill from the stack by the saltshaker. Heloise, oblivious, relaxed back into her nap. But I couldn't help but wonder how much that dog knew about what was being said, or thought, and the exact moment to, well, interject a note of levity into my life.

We moved the air sufficiently to continue breathing.

'Maybe the curtains are still there, in front of you, just ahead a bit,' Elaine said softly.

'I just . . .' I leaned toward her. 'I swear, Elaine,

I can't see them, not from my house. Not from my life. I feel like I do see some here though. I feel like there's possibility everywhere here.'

'Well, that's what getting out from under your life can do, sweetie. I think you still have a lot of passion in you. But I think you've been ignoring it. You just need to test the waters. You know this is just like me being gay.' My mind frantically searched for the connection.

'*What?!*' I smiled at her, shaking my head.

'Sometimes we avoid our biggest truths. We're afraid of dealing with the deepest parts of ourselves. Our secret passion.'

'Why is that, E?' I asked. 'Why do we go out of our way to avoid doing things we're passionate about?'

'I don't know. I guess because someone some-where told us we can't. Then we tell ourselves that.' She shrugged. 'Humans are stupid sometimes.' She leaned over and kissed my cheek, smiling. 'Even women.'

CHAPTER 25

After a delicious Thanksgiving dinner of chicken and dumplings – I even ate a dumpling, they were Elaine's specialty – I called home, but there was no answer. They were probably on their walk to the lake. I left a message wishing them each a happy Thanksgiving, said I was thankful for each of them, sent my love and hung up, feeling relieved of the obligation to check in. Then Wendy and I washed dishes while Elaine headed out to play in the yard with Heloise.

'I'm glad you came to visit finally, Deena,' said Wendy, handing me a soapy wineglass.

I rinsed it under a small stream of warm water, nodding. 'Thanks. You probably can't begin to know how happy I am to be here.' She smiled. She really was pretty: long wavy red hair, a beautiful complexion, lightly freckled. 'Especially for Elaine's big day,' I added.

'Yeah,' she said, a lovesick smile on her face. She looked out the window at Elaine and Heloise in the floodlit backyard; they appeared to be dancing, Elaine picking up great armfuls of snow, heaving them into the air, as Heloise jumped and barked and snapped at the falling clumps. Wendy and I both watched for a minute, our hands wet and limp in our respective sides of the sink, both smiling at the joie de vivre out the kitchen window.

We finished the rest of the dishes chatting amiably, laughing occasionally at the entertainment in the yard. Wendy was wiping the counter and I was drying my hands when Elaine burst into the little mudroom off the kitchen, Heloise right behind her. They both stopped and shook snow off their coats, both in high spirits.

'It's snowing again, big fat flakes. It's gorgeous! Let's make hot toddies and take a tub!' She rubbed her red hands together rapidly as she smiled alternately at me and Wendy.

Oh, dear. I'd forgotten about their hot tub. It had certainly come up often enough in our many conversations over the years. I even knew it was on the deck, off their bedroom. Damn! How ironic! I should have brought my suit after all. I squatted and Heloise came to me, shoving her cold nose under my arm. I scratched her neck, pondering how to respond to Elaine.

She must have seen a stricken expression on my face. 'What?' she said.

Embarrassed, I rose, stepped close and whispered in her ear, 'I didn't bring my suit.'

Elaine burst out laughing. 'Oh, for God's sake, Deena! You don't have anything we haven't already seen! Dooo you?' she said playfully. 'But look, sweetie,' she said, her voice now soft, sincere. 'If

336

you're more comfortable, you can wear my suit. I think we're the same size again.'

My embarrassment dimmed to more of a warm glow. I *was* probably about the same size as Elaine now! Again. I squatted next to Heloise again, my arm over her back. She licked my chin, tail wagging. I took a deep breath. 'Nah. I'll just go for it. But better make my toddy a double!'

After a long soak and delicious hot toddy, I felt myself nodding off in the hot tub. I excused myself, made as graceful an exit up the tub steps as possible – the alcohol hindering that effort, the handrail pretty much saving my life. The phone rang inside just as I stepped on to the deck. I turned quickly to Elaine.

'Just let the machine get it,' she said, flicking her hand. I quickly pulled a thick terry blanket from the stack in the redwood warming box, wrapping it tightly around myself.

'Now, *this* is a decadent towel, Elaine!' I pulled the toasty terry cloth up under my chin as steam rose from my body into the cold night. It'd stopped snowing, but the temperature had dropped to what I guessed must be around twenty degrees. Too cold for anything save the briefest good night.

'Well, many thanks for everything.' I wormed my fingertips out of my towel cocoon and blew them a kiss. 'Good night, ladies.' Elaine blew me a kiss back (they had snuggled close virtually the moment I'd climbed out of the tub), then they looked at each other and broke into a rousing chorus of 'Goodnight, Ladies.' Laughing, I slid the door open and was joyfully greeted by my own girlfriend.

I awoke the next morning to the amazing smell of freshly brewed coffee and frying bacon. Amazing in that it awaited me downstairs, prepared by someone else.

I hurriedly dressed, and headed down the stairs, Heloise waiting at the top, tail wagging. She could see Elaine waiting at the bottom.

Elaine must have heard our stirrings; she stood in her bathrobe, her curly salt-and-pepper hair a halo around her head. In her outstretched arms she held a mug of coffee and my down coat. What a savior! She knew Heloise would have to go directly outside. I gave Heloise the okay to come down, pulled on the coat and gratefully took the coffee. Elaine and Heloise greeted each other like old friends, Heloise sticking her head between Elaine's knees, blissfully accepting a morning rub.

I took a sip of the coffee, feeling a deep resonance of satisfaction ripple through me. To sleep late, be handed a cup of hot coffee before you're even expected to say a word? Much less do anything? This was heaven. I handed the mug back to her. 'We'll be right back!'

Heloise and I stepped out into the brittle chill and blazing brightness, both of us blinking mole-like eyes. The world had been cleansed and lay before us, white, sparkling, inviting. Snow-lined branches above us seemed etched across the blue sky. The yard lay pristine and untracked before us.

Heloise dipped her paws, then her nose, into the new snow. She was hesitant to do her business. I didn't blame her. I wouldn't want to lower my parts in this either. I stomped a wide circle under the giant oak tree in the center of the yard, then gave her the command. She quickly got to it. Her wonderful expression of sheer relief made me laugh out loud. She finally finished and immediately pulled toward the house. I shared her longing for warmth and food. We rushed through the door, Heloise obediently behind me.

Shed of my coat and boots, we joined Wendy and Elaine in the kitchen. It had the warm, welcoming smell of an all-night diner. Elaine was still in her thick, colorful bathrobe, black terry patterned with big blocks of primary colors. Wendy was in a professional but elegant moss-green pantsuit, which showed off her red hair and green eyes. Elaine nodded toward the microwave. 'Your coffee's in there. Can I feed Heloise?'

'Sure!' I said, retrieving my mug. With my hands wrapped around the ceramic, I closed my eyes and sipped. Not quite as powerful as that first taste, but again, a rush of warmth; an explosion of deep roasted bliss traveled down and through me.

I shook my head, marveling at the taste while dropping into a chair at the table. I wasn't sure if this was really, *really* great coffee, or if it was the fact that I was on vacation, just me with my Heloise, soaking in the hospitality of two great women, in a town I loved and missed, with a party ahead of me. I felt transported back several decades. Alone. Unencumbered. Out in the world. Evidently, a hint of my former self remained. A woman with something to look forward to. I had to admit, that could do a lot for a cup of coffee.

'I gotta go, girls,' Wendy said, rising. She looked at me. 'Better have another cup of coffee and a hearty breakfast, Deena. Elaine has plans for you. Big plans.' She smiled, then leaned over and gave Elaine a brief kiss on one cheek, gently touching her fingertips to her other cheek as she did so. There was enough electricity in their gazes to power a small appliance. How did they do it? After all these years.

Wendy pivoted, midkitchen. 'Oh! Deena. There's a message for you on the machine. That was your kids calling last night.' I thanked her. She saluted and headed out the door.

Elaine punched in the numbers for their voice mail, then handed me the phone.

'Hey, Mom, happy Thanksgiving!' Lainey's voice was cheerful, buoyant even. 'Here, say happy Thanksgiving, Matt.' There was some rustling, then Matt's voice: 'Happy Thanksgiving, Matt.' Laughter, a crowd of laughter, then an 'oof' from Matt, no doubt Lainey punching him, Matt laughing again. 'Happy Thanksgiving, Mom. Hope you're having a blast.' Lainey took back the phone.

I could hear her striding into another room as she talked. 'You'll never guess who showed up at our door with a whole cooked turkey and all the fixings!' A dramatic pause. *Had my mother come up?* 'Amy and Sara and Nan!' Lainey almost shrieked. 'We were gonna have spaghetti! Amy ordered the turkey from the market, already cooked and everything! Did you know you could do that?!' A yelling in the distance. 'What?' Lainey yelled back, loudly, that she was coming. I pulled the phone from my ear, smiling. 'Gotta go, Mom! They're starting Monopoly! Love ya!'

I handed the phone back to Elaine and she placed it in the cradle. How incredibly nice of Amy. I couldn't help but admire her ability to just order a turkey. Her self-worth wasn't wrapped up in her prowess, or lack thereof, in the kitchen. I definitely wanted to get her a Christmas present while I was here. My relief expanded. Now Neil couldn't complain about having to eat spaghetti on Thanksgiving.

I refilled my mug and sat with Elaine at the wild woman table, same places as yesterday. A timer dinged and Elaine went over and pulled a pan from the warming oven, filled with latkes and bacon. Classic Elaine contradiction. My dear Jewish Ham.

'Can I help?' I asked, as she next grabbed a frying pan of scrambled eggs from the stove, setting it on the table.

'Yeah, get the applesauce and sour cream from the fridge.'

341

I pulled open the refrigerator. 'So what big plans do you have for me?' I felt like a little girl who was going to spend the day with a favorite auntie, one who always planned the most delightful adventures.

Elaine pinched off a piece of hot latke, popped it in her mouth, and said, 'A meemaw selffen ayday.'

'A what!?' I asked, setting the applesauce on the counter.

Elaine grinned, swallowing. 'A me, myself, and I day. You need to step out of your box, girlfriend. Then you'll see those curtains.'

'Mad City, here we come!' Elaine yelled out her open window as she roared her Volvo wagon down Johnson Street. 'First stop, Evan!'

'Close your window, you maniac!' I shouted gleefully. 'It's freezing! Who's Evan?' I asked, reaching back to give Heloise a pat. She was riding like a queen in the backseat. Elaine had some frames and other supplies in the way back, so we'd put Heloise on the bench seat behind us. I could tell from her expression that Heloise took it as a promotion. She shoved her head between our seats, suggesting another promotion.

'Evan is going to give you a beautiful new do,' she said, reaching over Heloise's head and gently tugging on my ponytail.

Panic rushed through me. All I'd had for decades was a trim. If I had a headache, I'd indulge in a shampoo. And I only ever went to the cheap clip joints. I didn't like the sound of going to 'Evan' for a haircut. Too pricey. And too risky.

'Uh, Elaine, I don't suppose this "Evan" works at a Quickie Clips, does he? And besides, I just got a trim not that long—'

'I'm not taking you for a trim, Deena. I'm taking you for a whole new do. You need to know you're still in there somewhere. And, no, Evan owns a fabulous salon, Deedee Sweet. But don't you worry what will soon be your bee-you-ti-ful little head; this whole day is on me. This is your birthday present and Christmas present. We are going to have some fun today!' She ended with an evil cackle, but reached over and patted my knee.

Deedee Sweet. What a name. My hated nick-name, no less. I didn't relish turning my locks, mousy and mundane though they were, over to someone who'd named his salon Deedee Sweet. But too soon, Elaine turned into the snowy parking lot of a small strip mall, and pulled into an empty spot, directly in front of the salon. Hanging above it, a truly sophisticated sign in what looked like copper lettering on brushed platinum: SALON DIX DIX-HUIT. I called up enough of my high school French to know that that was ten eighteen, pronounced *dee deeze-wheat*. It was the address of the place. I was still laughing at Elaine's pronunci-ation as she pulled on the parking brake, and switched off the ignition. 'Here we are, my friend. The new you awaits!'

I stopped laughing, my white fingers gripping my seat cushion.

Evan was very kind, soothing my panic and constantly reassuring me that I'd love it, that he was going to 'frame your lovely heart-shaped face' and 'lighten the load of your life by lightening your hair with kisses from the sun.' Okay. So it was pretentious and ridiculous; I felt like a princess, complete with a maidservant in the form of a young woman who brought me coffee in a lovely china cup, with saucer, as I sat with my hair in little pieces of foil. At one point I looked at myself in the wall of mirrors across the room; I looked like a Reynolds Wrap battlefield. Next to me, Elaine had had a 'get-the-gray-out' dye job, and now sat deep conditioning with her head wrapped in what looked like a giant baggie. I wondered how many lunches the supplies on the top of our heads would hold. You can take the mom out of the kitchen, I thought, a bit morosely.

But when it was all over, Evan was right. I did love my hair. Elaine had finished before me and had taken Heloise on a brief walk along the strip mall. As they stepped back into the salon, I looked up from my *People* magazine.

'*You* are gorgeous!' Elaine shouted. Heloise wagged her tail, just happy to see me. Any me. I twirled and grinned, then impulsively threw my arms around Evan, then Elaine. Then Heloise.

Elaine paid the bill (I didn't dare ask, or even

linger), and we headed out to the car. I couldn't stop myself from leaning over and gazing into the side-view mirror. I was almost unrecognizable. What had been fairly long, nondescript brownish hair was now a shoulder-length, layered style that, as Evan had swooned, 'moves like a spring breeze.' The highlights did indeed lighten my face, and load. I felt ten years younger and ready for our next adventure.

Heloise jumped into the backseat and lay down. 'It is sooo fun taking her into shops,' Elaine gushed as she started the car. 'You feel like you're with the Queen of England or something.'

'I know. It's sometimes intense, isn't it, how she draws attention to you.'

'Not intense! I love it!' she said, the color high in her cheeks as she looked over her shoulder, backing the car out.

'You look great, Elaine,' I said. 'And I feel great. Thank you again so much.' I couldn't help myself. I pulled down my visor mirror and admired my hair again. 'He really is good, isn't he?'

'Sometimes you really do get what you pay for, Deena,' she said, bringing the car to the parking lot exit.

I ignored her pointed statement to my legendary stinginess, especially with myself. 'Where to now?' I asked, changing the subject. But I was genuinely excited. I was so thrilled with the outcome of her first stop, I was ready to completely turn myself over to her.

345

She accelerated suddenly, bursting skillfully through a bank of snow left by a snowplow. *'Shopping!'* she yelled as the snow flew from either side of us.

We got to the mall right about lunchtime, and Elaine again took Heloise's leash. The day-after-Thanksgiving crowds in the food court were thick and cranky-looking, no doubt from mall fatigue and hunger. But Heloise made nearly all of them grin and poke and point. Elaine waved to everyone like the Corn Queen atop her float.

'Hungry?' she asked, stopping in the middle of the food court.

'Actually, I'm not yet. I'm still full from that great breakfast you made.'

'Me too. Let's do Vicky's first, and then Maddie's for lunch. Definitely have to do Vicky's before eating anyway.'

Vicky's. A nifty local boutique? A nice, but affordable (I hoped) jewelry store? I was elated just with guessing. We strode down the mall concourse arm in arm, with Heloise on Elaine's left.

But my heart nearly seized as Elaine stopped in front of the last shop in the world I'd expected. Vicky's, it turned out, was Elaine's special name for Victoria's Secret.

'Elaine,' I hissed, leaning toward her, my hand cupped near my mouth. 'I *hate* this place.'

Elaine stopped in her tracks, Heloise by her side, just inside the store. Elaine looked quizzically at me. Heloise was staring at the carpet, ears up, head cocked, her gaze fixed on a lone sequin. 'Leave it, Heloise,' I told her. Her body was quivering with desire. She could almost taste that sequin. It was there for the picking. But she didn't. I could tell she was using every bit of her willpower to not lick it up. '*Good* girl,' I told her. I took the leash from Elaine and turned to leave. 'We'll just wait outside.'

'Wait!' she said, pulling me back. 'Why do you hate Victoria's Secret?' She was not whispering. I felt flustered, embarrassed. I looked at Heloise. She was looking up at me, waiting for direction. She had resisted the sequin. I was so proud of her. She'd come so far.

I glanced around the store. There were two employees, both blonde, one in her twenties and the other I guessed in her late teens, each helping customers on the floor. But behind the cash register was a dark-haired woman, not too much younger than me. She wasn't rail thin, either. She wore a bright turquoise blouse and big tortoise-shell glasses, a large colorful beaded chain securing them around her neck. She was laughing and chatting animatedly with the customer at the counter. The customer! *She* had to be closer to my mother's age than my own.

'Okay, then,' I said. 'Heloise, let's go!' We strode into the store, and, as usual, everyone looked at Heloise, then me, smiling, admiring. Heloise was holding her head high now, not tempted by any more carpet treats. I followed suit, lifting my chin a bit, trying to be confident.

Elaine and I stopped to finger some elegant scented satin eye masks, a palette of soft earthy tones. I picked up a beautiful red-and-gold one. It immediately made me think of Amy's robe. It would be the perfect Christmas present, a little thank-you from me. I found one in a box, and left Elaine sorting through them, looking for a boxed green one for Wendy.

As Heloise and I strolled past the myriad stands and bins filled with a rainbow of tiny bras or panties, I suddenly had an image of decorating a Christmas tree with these. I shook my head, amused at the thought, my new hair swinging lightly around my shoulders. Chuckling, I looked back toward Elaine, to beckon her over. Elaine might actually *do* a Victoria's Secret Panty Tree. But my view of her was obscured by two other middle-aged women holding up a skimpy feather-trimmed teddy and laughing uncontrollably. They saw me looking and blanched.

'The feathers are for warmth,' I said. And we all burst out laughing again.

'I don't mean to be hyperbolic, but this is the best damn salad I've ever had!' I leaned in and put another forkful of chicken mandarin salad into my mouth.

'Well, now!' drawled Elaine. 'That's probably just them bra and panties talkin'!'

We'd finished – successfully – in Victoria's Secret, and had landed in a darling little restaurant called

Maddie's. Elaine had been waving periodically at an amazing number of people she knew. Several had stopped by our table, commenting excitedly about the opening.

'It's going to be mobbed there tomorrow, isn't it?' I asked her during a lull.

Elaine knew I wasn't a confident mingler. 'You'll be fine! It'll be a blast. You'll see. But first—' She sat up, clasping her hands under her chin, leaning toward me. 'I want to get you something *spectacular* to wear.' I started to protest, but she wagged her finger at me. 'You be quiet! Look, there are so few times you can really dress up anymore. So, until one of us gets invited to an inauguration or coronation and invites the other, my art opening is our chance to strut the poodle!'

I laughed at Elaine's version of 'puttin' on the dog.'

'I *have* something wonderful!' I said, lifting the pink-and-white-striped bag at my feet. The nude, slightly push-up satin bra and matching bikini panties would make even my turtleneck and corduroy jumper feel sexy. I had originally selected some floral cotton briefs in Victoria's Secret, but Elaine had ripped them from my hand and steered me toward a leopard-print camisole set. We'd compromised.

'Not to mention *this*,' I said, cupping my hands under my hair. 'Plus, I did bring a dress from home, you know. You've done enough. Really, Elaine.'

She held up her index finger. 'Just one dress. *Please?*'

'Look, the haircut was a really generous birthday present. And I love it! And the—' I lowered my voice, leaned forward, '—*underwear* is a unique and wonderful Christmas present. But enough is enough, E.'

'Let me just take you to this one store.' She took my hand. 'I don't want to get crude, but Deena, you know I can afford this. Wendy is doing *very* well, and my art is taking off. We have no kids, no tuition. We don't even have a dog to support.' She reached under the table for Heloise, who was, as per her usual splendid restaurant behavior, lying placidly, watching the world. 'Let me spoil you for one day. Please?'

'I just don't know how to accept all of this,' I said softly. She patted my hand.

'I know. That's the point, dear. You don't know how to let others give to *you*. It doesn't all have to come from you all the time, D. Besides, just wait till you see these dresses!'

The store was small, but amazing. Très chic boutique. There were about fifteen round racks, each holding nothing but jaw-dropping dresses of luxurious silk, chiffon, satin, and I didn't know what all the fabrics were. But if it was slinky, sexy, or sensuous, this store had it. Some dresses were long, some midcalf, a few scandalously short. Some were backless, some strappy, some high-necked with cutaway shoulders. Many were colorful, hand-dyed works of art. They were soft, flowing, elegant. I'd never even imagined myself in a dress like these.

I slowly pushed the hangers around one of the circular racks, thinking to find something that I would wear again. But they were all way out of the PTO annual dinner realm.

'How 'bout these?' Elaine held three dresses, one a beautiful green-and-blue swirly number that I was sure would make me feel like a mermaid wearing the ocean itself. Another had spaghetti straps and was solid black, save for three deep red-orange poppies cascading down the front. The last looked almost Grecian. It had two layers, a mocha-colored satin underneath, a soft, sheer buttery-yellow top layer. The overall effect was a smoky gold. It had a low but not indecent neck-line, a series of delicate folds of fabric falling sensuously over the bust, a fitted waist, a flowing knee-length hemline.

'That gold one looks too small,' I said, eyeing the waist.

'I don't think so, Deena-leh! I think you need to resize your eyes to your new bod, girlfriend. Try them all on!' She thrust them at me, squealing and shimmying. She couldn't have been having more fun if she was ten and dressing her Barbie in every gown she owned.

I went into a fitting room and stripped off my clothes. All of them. I held the gold dress in front of me on its hanger. Maybe. I put it back on the hook and reached into my Victoria's Secret bag. I put on my new bra and panties, then slid the smoky gold number over my head. The fabric was a caress on every inch of skin it touched, as if made for my body. I looked in the mirror.

Wow. The color perfectly brought out the highlights in my hair, or vice versa. I didn't know. I didn't care. This dress made me look *good*. I'd never looked like this in my life. I didn't have to try on the others. In this dress, I could hold my own. I felt whole in this dress. I felt commanding in this dress. I could take on the world in this dress.

But first, I would have to shave my legs.

CHAPTER 26

We spent the evening recuperating from our shopping adventure, once again ending up sipping drinks in the hot tub, but this time I'd opted for a grape Gatorade. I slept peacefully that night, waking only once, dropping my hand over the bed to touch Heloise, who was herself sleeping contentedly on a big quilt. I smiled, rolled over, and went back to a dreamless sleep.

Saturday morning I headed out with Heloise, walking the mile or so into town in the crisp morning sun, giving Elaine and Wendy some alone time. I bought champagne for the surprise Wendy had told me she had for Elaine that evening, before the opening, and a pot of wildly fragrant white narcissus for their house. The three of us then spent the afternoon resting, chatting over tea. At about three, we started getting ready. It took hours, but was such fun, taking turns in the shower, helping each other with zippers, hairpins, necklaces. Maybe the biggest surprise of my afternoon was when Wendy took my cheap (but new!) panty hose from me and gave me instead a beautifully boxed pair that actually felt like satin on my shaved legs. The hours flew by; the laughter, appraisal, reassurance and girliness was transcendent.

'You look fantastic, E,' I told her, holding her hands, admiring her clingy, knee-length sparkly red dress. She had a small glistening barrette on one side of her head, a circle of real diamonds and rubies. In a barrette! Not from Wendy. A gift to herself.

'Thanks! You too. See, I told you. Isn't this fun? I feel like I'm going to my first prom and I'm going to be crowned homecoming queen!' she gushed.

I laughed, nodding. I didn't see any reason to point out to her that prom and homecoming were two different events.

Wendy's surprise honked outside. As we threw on our coats, I grabbed the champagne from the fridge. Wendy patted the canvas bag on her shoulder. Her wink told me the glasses were inside. We stepped outside and Elaine clapped her hands like a little girl. The white stretch limo was the perfect touch to what promised to be a once-in-a-lifetime evening.

The driver had pulled under the dry carport, easing our entry, and soon we were all four settled around the horseshoe-shaped leather seat. Elaine was still pink with excitement and pride. I knew she'd worked hard for years for a show of this magnitude. This was another coming-out party – this one, however, was joyous, as a known and in-demand artist.

Wendy and Elaine sat on the end, facing the front. I was on the side, facing them. Wendy opened the champagne, careful to keep it off her silvery-gray satin pantsuit. Her long red hair was wound up into a twist, held with a long silver clip. She was the picture of elegance. Heloise lay on the floor in the middle of it all, also dressed up for the occasion with her K-9 Eyes jacket, plus a glittery silver bow that Elaine had attached to her collar.

'Whoa!' said Wendy, laughing. The champagne bubbled over the side of her glass as the limo bounced over the snowy road. Leaning forward, she sipped the overflow while Heloise made short work of the few drops that landed on the carpeted floor.

When we each held a full glass, Wendy raised hers in a toast.

'To the love of my life, whose passion for so many things keeps the passion in *our* lives.' We clinked glasses. All three of us were teary.

'No crying, dammit! Mascara!' barked Elaine, blinking upward, waving air at her eyes.

Fifteen minutes later we were hurriedly polishing off the bottle of champagne as the limo pulled to a stop in front of Gallery One, just off the square. The driver opened the door and Elaine stepped out first, to applause from her beaming friends, shivering under the awning. Two of them unrolled a red carpet, from awning to curb, for her to step onto. She threw her head back and laughed, looking like a Hollywood starlet. Wendy pointed to one then another, trying to get me started on some names, explaining that most were some of Elaine's many art friends, who'd volunteered to put the finishing touches on the show and organize the catering, so that Elaine could have the past two days off. Which, I was gratefully aware, she'd spent, in every sense, on me. I could see the adoration in their faces for my longtime friend. I was proud and honored to be among them.

Wendy gestured for me to climb out next, and I buttoned up the white wool coat she'd loaned me, grateful for this elegant finishing touch to my outfit for the evening. My puffy down jacket would have lowered the overall effect of my ensemble by several notches.

As I extended my legs and took the driver's offered hand, I was extremely grateful for his firm grasp, and also for the red carpet. I'd been wondering how I would trek through the snow in these strappy beige sandals, also Wendy's, which, although very sexy and perfect with this dress, were a little big for me. But it was either these or my brown loafers. I hadn't worn heels in a long time, and it was tricky enough for me to walk on a dry floor, let alone a snowy sidewalk. I lifted the long, slim strap of the evening purse Elaine had loaned me over my shoulder. The black satin purse didn't hold much more than my credit cards, the two hundreds from Neil, and a tube of lipstick, but it was classy. Between the haircut and shopping and borrowing, Elaine and Wendy had taken Eliza Doolittle and made, well, at least Eliza Do-a-little-more.

Once I'd climbed out of the limo, I gave Heloise the command to jump out. 'Okay, girl! Let's go,' I said enthusiastically. But Heloise didn't immediately see the logic in getting out of a nice, warm, well-lit limo to head into the dark and bitterly cold night. Wendy encouraged her from behind, and I pulled on the leash. Reluctantly, she jumped down onto the carpet.

Immediately the awning group broke into a chorus of 'awws' and 'ohs.' Elaine looked back at me, her smile a hundred watts. She reached for the leash, which I handed over with a laugh. I didn't know how much Elaine was in love with Heloise, and how much she loved the attention Heloise drew. Both equally, I was sure. As Wendy climbed out, the group again applauded, then we all made a dash for the warmth of the gallery.

Inside, the colors shouted like a jubilant riot. The paintings on the wall were various dimensions, from one that was bread-loaf size, to a few very large ones, over four feet by five feet, and many in between.

I was awestruck. Elaine was a master of color. Every painting was a vibrant explosion. Most were of local scenes around Madison. The terrace at the U. The farmer's market downtown. The carousel at Ella's Deli. Kids playing with buckets at the edge of Lake Monona. The skaters at Tenney Park. I returned to the one of Ella's Deli. Incredible. She'd really captured something here. Kids, joyous on their colorful carousel animals. Parents, leaning on a railing, watching, but with different expressions. Some chatting, some looking relieved to have a moment's respite from their energetic children. On a nearby bench, an old man, his hat on his lap, watching the children. How to describe the expression on his face? I shook my head in true awe. The color, the faces, the movement. Elaine was going to be big. I wandered on. In the next section the work was more fantasy-like. The smallest one, near the bar, caught my eye. I strolled over. It was about ten inches high and six inches wide. It had a deep blue background with a peach-colored woman, arms reaching up over her head, chin lifted, as though she was at the beginning of a back dive. She was smiling, headed upward toward a multi-colored sun, just the rays visible at the top. Looking closely I saw that the woman was being lifted by hundreds of tiny women angels under each arm. It was titled simply, *Woman.* The price was $100.00. I touched the frame with one finger, then rushed back toward Elaine, reaching into my purse.

It took me a minute to make my way through the growing crowd. As I approached from behind, Elaine didn't realize I was there, but Heloise did. She popped up from her seated position at Elaine's foot to turn and greet me, whapping several shins with her wagging tail in the process. I cupped her chin in my palm and kissed her forehead. Elaine turned around, grinned. 'Oh! Everybody! This is my friend! My wonderful friend Deena! From Colorado!' Elaine was speaking only in exclamation marks this evening. I smiled shyly at the large mass of people.

As the group resumed chitchat, I leaned in toward Elaine. 'E, you know your painting, *Woman*?' She nodded.

'It's sold,' I told her emphatically, pressing one of the folded hundreds Neil had given me into her hand.

Her eyes opened wide, then her arms did. 'Awesome!' I returned the hug. The crowds were pressing in on us again. I felt compelled to give Elaine up to the dozens waiting to congratulate her.

'I'll see you later, sweetie. It's all great, Elaine.' I gestured around the gallery. 'Just so great. Do you still want to keep Heloise with you?'

'Hell, yeah!'

I gave her hand a final squeeze and headed back to my painting. *My* painting!

I had another hundred burning a hole in my purse. Maybe I'd buy something else. I looked around; there was nothing else of a similar size, therefore, I surmised, nothing else at this price. I looked at *Woman* again, loving it more by the minute. It was enough. It was perfect. I sighed, then nervously surveyed the room. In the back of the gallery was a separate section where most of the furniture was displayed. It was all similar to Elaine's kitchen table.

Despite the buzz from the champagne, I wanted to hit the bar first, have a glass to hold on to, at least. I knew no one but Elaine and Wendy, and they were each mobbed with people already. I realized it would be a long evening, hopefully not as bad as the agonizing one I'd spent at Neil's thirtieth high school reunion several years ago. I don't know why I went to that. Another misplaced sense of duty, no doubt.

'What can I make for you?'

Wow. This bartender was nice-looking! Thick, wavy dark hair, ice blue eyes. Like a young Bill, I realized, though they didn't otherwise look much alike. This guy was even more handsome! I felt a warmth spread through me, and champagne brave.

'Well, I don't know,' I said, just the tiniest bit flirty. This guy was sexy, with a capital sex. He was wearing a soft, white, brushed-cotton shirt, sort of Romeo style. Probably gay. But I could make him whatever I wanted. I was liberated by geography and anonymity. Plus, I decided there was a certain safety in flirting with a man I'd never see again. 'What's the most sophisticated drink you know?'

He laughed, sexily flipping his bangs out of his eyes with a flick of his head. 'I guess that depends on your definition of "sophisticated." But there's a drink called a Sophisticate. It's rum, cranberry juice, melon liqueur, some lemon-lime soda. I add a squeeze of lime. Want one?' He raised his eyebrows invitingly above those blue eyes. How did this guy work with ice cubes? Didn't they melt at his very glance?

I nodded, struck dumb suddenly.

As he pulled out a cocktail glass and a silver shaker, I carefully constructed his story. He was straight. Looking for someone older, wiser, but with no big commitments. He was merely looking to bestow some youthful sex on an appreciative, experienced woman. His name would be . . . Trevor, I decided.

Whoa. What was up here? What bizarre dance were my hormones doing now?! I had gone from a nearly asexual being to a woman who felt like having sex again. Sometime. Like, maybe pretty soon.

So, Trevor. 'Are you an artist, too?' I asked, placing my right index finger on the table for no known reason. I must have seen it in a movie or something. My eyelashes involuntarily fluttered. I straightened up. Too many movies.

'No. My field is less lucrative,' Trevor said, smiling. Perfect white teeth. The temperature of the room was rising. Then his words sank in.

'Less lucrative than a starving artist? You know she's been at this for years and this is her first big show? She's just starting to make some money at her art.' Whoa. Just how defensive did that sound, I wondered.

Trevor smiled again, his eyes again lingering the sweetest of seconds on mine. Maybe he's looking at the crow's-feet. No, Trevor would be attracted to my eyes, finding them deep pools of experience and perception.

'Yeah, I know. But there's not even a market for my field, outside of teaching. I'm getting my Ph.D. in philosophy,' he said, pouring rum into the shaker with three long, smooth, up-and-down moves of his arm. 'Most towns aren't willing to pay great thinkers just to have them around anymore.' He added a good dose from a green bottle, a honeydew melon on the label.

'Did they used to?' I asked. In went the cranberry juice. The open neck of his shirt widened as he twisted to put the bottle back in the large cooler, exposing just the right amount of chest hair.

'Well, probably not, now that you mention it,' he said with a chuckle, twisting back. Now a splash of soda pop. He grinned directly at me as he shook the silver shaker.

'Hee, hee,' I laughed stupidly. But I felt grand.

He poured the drink into a glass, slipped a lime wedge on the edge, and handed it to me with a pink napkin. I took a sip. Wow. Strong. Tasty.

'Mmm, good!' I said, feeling like there was surely something more sophisticated one should say upon tasting a Sophisticate.

Trevor sat back on his stool, arms folded, still looking happy to look at me. Even doing so with a bit of intensity. I took another sip. If this wasn't a flirty look he was giving me, what was? Good question. How the hell did I know what that was anymore? I sipped again, thinking I should say something witty as he stared at me. But I could be totally off base here. This could be wishful thinking at its height. He was probably gunning for a tip. I looked for a tip jar. There was none. Just a little sign in a silver frame that said NO TIPPING, PLEASE.

Trevor jutted his chin at me. I'd seen that in movies, too. 'So, what do you do?' Before I could respond, he held up his palm. 'Wait, let me guess.' He sized me up. And down. 'You're a model; in fact, I think I recognize you. Were you just on the cover of the Lands' End Christmas catalog?'

Damn! He *was* flirting! *With me!* I laughed at his absurd but good-natured line. 'Oh, *right*!' I said, flipping my hair as I lifted my glass to my lips, never taking my eyes off Trevor's. *You're a married woman, Deena.* I took another sip of my drink.

'No, really. If it's not you, you're her twin! Did you see it? The one with the mom and dad and two kids on Christmas morning? I called it the family from Lake Wobegon.' He laughed. 'You know, where all the men are . . . Wait, the women are . . . .' He deftly grabbed and opened two bottles of beer and handed them to a young man at the end of the table. He shrugged, shook his head and said, 'Well, they're all above average and better-looking. Something like that.'

I laughed again, this time at his not-quite-correct recitation of Garrison Keillor's description of his fictional townspeople. I also found it amusing that the model he mistook me for was a mom. At least I knew he was sincere. I also loved that it wasn't just middle-aged women who couldn't remember things.

A nattily dressed older couple arrived and ordered sidecars. I had no idea what a sidecar was, but Trevor evidently did and went immediately to work concocting them. I turned to survey the gallery and was stunned at how it was filling. I could only barely glimpse the food table across the room. Loaded with fattening hors d'oeuvres, no doubt. The drink I had in my hand was enough of a dietary diversion for the evening. But I was a little hungry.

I sipped again from my glass, trying not to make too much eye contact with any one person, but trying to look like I'd be open to someone, anyone, introducing him- or herself to me. I didn't want to be one of those pathetic women who stands and talks to the bartender all night. I mean, I would. It's just that he had a job to do, and that part was always awkward, where you have to turn away and sip your drink as though you were just going to do that anyway and these people ordering drinks really weren't interrupting you. All of which was exactly what I was doing now.

I decided to leave Trevor. It just wasn't working out. He was too young. In time, he'd recover, find someone new. I looked around the crowd, spotted a lithe young woman with shiny, straight blonde hair, wearing a short leather skirt and a white angora sweater, the bell sleeves nearly covering her delicate hands. She was about Trevor's age. Very hip, nice-looking. Yes. There she is. Trevor's perfect match. Sylvia. A dancer.

No. It would never last, not with him being a philosopher. One of them had to be solvent. I thought a minute. A dental hygienist. *But!*, she's about to go on *American Idol* and win a recording deal. She'll go by just her first name. Like Cher. *Sylvia.*

Time to step away from the bar, Deena! I decided to go check out the furniture. I began to work my way through the crowd. I smiled, people smiled back. A young couple was worming their way toward me, no doubt to the bar. He was separated from her by a thickness of two or three people, still holding her hand, leading her, both their arms fully outstretched. She was stuck in the crowd, laughing. I turned sideways, letting her through.

'Thanks!' she said. I nodded and grinned. David and Dannica. Everyone's favorite couple at parties. Fantastic dancers. But behind on their . . . rent . . .

I stopped my little game as I realized I was just on the edge of the furniture gallery. But the crowds were at a standstill, admiring Elaine's work. I sipped my drink, scanning the masses. It was a hip and fun crowd. One man had blinking Christmas lights along the lapels of his white suit.

But my eyes stopped on a breathtakingly hand-some man across the room. He was staring at someone behind me. I turned, but saw no one returning his gaze. I turned back and saw him let out a small laugh, pointing at me. I turned away, my heart pounding, then snuck fleeting glances out of the corner of my eye. He was more my age, but he, like Trevor, was drop-dead handsome. Kind of a George Hamilton look, but with a little Omar Sharif thrown in. He saw me looking, so, what the hell, I stared back. He was tall, olive-skinned, had smoldering dark eyes, and a smile that seemed born of innocence but shaped by expe-rience. He wore a tan mock turtleneck. It looked like cashmere. His eyes trained on mine, he jutted his chin toward me, and I almost burst out laughing. Did all men learn this somewhere? The chances were very good that both Trevor and George-Omar were gay. Elaine had once told me that gay men are notorious flirts with women. Especially older women.

I looked at him, acknowledging him with just the slightest lift of my eyebrows, a slip of a smile. I looked down, sipped my drink, then turned away. I continued trying to make my way forward, my breaths quick, adrenaline-charged. I felt the hemline of my dress swing sensuously around my knees as I pushed my way through the crowd, thinned slightly here – it was now solidly packed around the bar. I looked back toward George-Omar. He had not dropped his gaze, and he too was making progress across the room. Toward me. I turned my back to him, slid my rings off. I must have lost weight in my hands now, too. They came off so easily.

I slipped the rings into my purse, stepping as quickly as I could into the furniture gallery, a flash of warmth rushing from my hips to my chest and up into my face. Not a hot flash. I hadn't had one in months. No, this was an inferno of guilt, excitement. Anticipation.

I felt . . . anything but invisible.

CHAPTER 27

He was behind me. Right behind me. I didn't have to look. The pulse of current throbbed into my back. I shook my head, trying to clear the feeling. What was this? He was attractive, but I mean, really! I wasn't even myself.

Or, maybe I was. Maybe this was a deep-down Deena. A Deena who felt and risked, and was free. And I liked it.

The crowd was thickening again here in the cordoned furniture gallery. People were pushed into one another like cows in a branding pen. Happy, inebriated cows.

We all seemed to be enjoying the forced intimacy. People nodded and smiled at one another as they squeezed past, chests brushing chests, hands on another's waist or hip to help insinuate themselves through the dense humanity. The soup of scents was intoxicating in and of itself. I took another sip of my drink.

Oh! His sweater brushed the back of my bare arm. It was definitely cashmere. My legs no longer contained bone and muscle. A watery gelatin at best. Oh, how I'd missed this feeling. This electric connection to myself.

I tried to look at the artful chair in front of me. *Concentrate on the chair, Deena!* Cats. This one had cats all over it. Cats chasing mice. Cats . . . climbing – *I can smell his cologne.* Cats. Cats hanging from a tree branch. Cats dancing . . . Cats . . . *breathing on my neck.*

A hand on my back, firm, determined.

'Excuse me . . .'

His voice was deep, like Omar's. I couldn't begin to remember what Omar Sharif's voice sounded like, but why not?

I turned my head. It was really the only portion of my body I *could* turn.

'You're from Colorado, right?' he asked pleasantly.

A stupid – I'm sure it was stupid – smile broke out on my face. It pleased me to think I physically looked like I was from Colorado. Slowly, a thread of sense penetrated my alcohol-saturated brain. *You don't look like you're from Colorado, idiot! He was probably there when Elaine announced it.*

'Georgia, actually,' I said in my best Southern accent. *Who* was *this person in my body, using my mouth?* It didn't matter. I could be anybody here. Anybody but Deena Munger, Mom. Deena Munger, Wife.

His smile fell away, replaced by confusion. I giggled. 'I'm just kidding!' As my elbows were pretty much pinned to my sides, I raised the fingers of my non-drink hand toward him. 'I'm

Deena—' I said, stopping myself. First names would be enough tonight.

He took my hand, smiling broadly. His perfect teeth were almost blindingly white, his deep brown eyes sexy orbs of intent. His tanned face was a mocha dot in a sea of Wisconsin winter white, save for two black women chatting in a large group around Elaine. He looked like he could be Italian. Or maybe a hot-blooded Spaniard.

He bowed his six-foot-plus frame slightly; really, there wasn't room for more than an exaggerated nod. 'Pleased to meet you, Deena from Colorado. I'm Kent, from Wisconsin. Kent Mills.' Didn't sound either Italian or Spanish. We shook hands and he smiled again, this time looking relieved to be talking to someone. Maybe he was some sort of fifth wheel here tonight, too.

I looked into his eyes, trying to keep my own from crossing. The room had become gauzy, was starting to spin. And someone had put on some loud jazz. There was a speaker just above us.

Kent almost had to shout. 'May I just say that that is a stunning dress. Really.' He blushed, and I felt my heart melt a little. 'Can I get you another drink?' He nodded toward my drink hand. I looked at my glass, held at an angle that could quite possibly suggest a certain level of intoxication. Taken aback, I realized I had indeed drained it already.

Even in my alcoholic stupor, I knew he was casting out with a sparkly little fly to catch a fish. Me. But I liked being a fish. Being a fish was thrilling. This man, a handsome man, called me attractive. Surely a little catch and release couldn't hurt.

'No, thank you. I've probably had enough to drink tonight anyway,' I said, nearly having to shout my confession over the noise. I just hoped my speech wasn't slurred. I put my cupped hand to my mouth and he bent forward to hear. 'How do you know Elaine?'

He shook his head. 'I don't. I'm a friend of a guy who came with his fiancée. Kind of an interloper, really.' He smiled shyly. 'I don't really know anyone else here. Well, besides you, that is.' That was sweet; he had a very amiable manner about him. He paused a moment, looking around the room. 'But I'm very impressed with her artwork.'

'Are you an artist?'

He laughed. 'God, no! Far from it. I'm in IT. But I'm a fairly avid consumer of art. I'm one of those uneducated art buyers who just' – he made quotation marks with his fingers – ' "knows what I like." And you? Are you an artist?'

I felt confusion cross my face. Was I an artist? No. 'Well, I used to think I'd do art, one day.' But what? But I got married, had kids? I changed the subject. 'I've never bought original art before, but I actually bought one tonight.' I was nearly shouting over the noise. Plus, I was oddly excited to tell him this. Remarkably, he seemed thrilled that I had. His face lit up.

'Really?! Which one?'

'The little one, by the bar.'

'The Goddess one? I *love* the color in that, not really my subject matter though.' He grinned. 'But I'm blown away by the one of Ella's Deli. The carousel?' I nodded. 'Great color there, too. And movement. The kids faces on the carousel? Brilliant. And the old man watching? So poignant. Like youth and color and life flying by him, but he's happy, seeing life go on or something, y'know?' Yes. Yes. Both grinning, we nodded at each other like a couple of bobble-head dolls.

I was getting a headache from the music and the shouting, but I was loving talking to Kent. He was . . . perfect.

'Would you like something to eat?' he shouted, looking across the packed room toward the equally crowded food table. 'I used to play football, about a million years ago. I could run a down-and-out pattern, maybe tackle a few people near the cake, intercept that old guy going for an egg roll, wing one over to you.'

I laughed again and he smiled, looking bashfully pleased that he'd made me laugh.

I looked at the array on the table, breaded this, fried that, chips surrounding heavy dips, desserts. Classic Elaine. 'Too bad they don't have a salad bar.' I laughed weakly, afraid I'd just sounded like the quintessential girl-date.

'No kidding? Me too! I'm kind of into health food.' We again looked at each other appreciatively. Now he cupped his hand and I leaned in. 'I've got my car here. Would it be terribly bad form if we ducked out for a bit? There's a place not too far from here with a nice little salad bar. Kind of a health food place.'

I was no longer drunk. No longer playing the role of the flirt in an old Doris Day movie. I was genuinely attracted to this man, this very nice man, and it scared the hell out of me. But in a bizarre way, I treasured the feelings. All of them. I was alive with feeling. On some level, I had to do this. I felt that hard shell cracking open again, fresh air rushing in.

I nodded. 'Let's do it.' Okay, then. I'm going to have an aff—

I couldn't even say the word in my thoughts. So this is how this happens. Surprisingly quick. Easy. But I also knew it was the lubricant of alcohol that would slide me over this line.

My heart was beating in an oddly pronounced way. *Thump-ump, thump-ump, thump-ump.* As if it wanted to make me aware of the work it was doing.

'I'm sure our friends would understand,' I said. 'I really need a healthy meal. Let me just go tell Elaine.' I was still surprised, stunned really, how easily my foot slid out of the domestic boot of my life. And into this glass slipper.

Kent offered me his hand, and I took it, large, square, almost meaty, but soft, gentle. He led the way through the crowd, toward the coatracks, with me in tow. He kept looking back over his shoulder to check on me, once even mouthing, *You okay?* Nodding, I followed him, just as Dannica had

373

followed her David. But I did not throw my head back and laugh, nor even smile. This wasn't something I wanted to do; this was something I had to do. Although I did admit to feeling the drug of attraction and anticipation. A drug I hadn't tasted in a long time. We retrieved our coats and started working our way back toward Elaine, my hand still in another man's hand.

Elaine had her back to us, sitting in one of her painted chairs on a kind of dais, entertaining her public like a jovial queen on her throne. It was only then that I thought about Heloise. She was lying under Elaine's legs, her back to me.

How could I have forgotten about Heloise? I could bring her to the restaurant. But what about after? What about after.

I told Kent to bring the car around, that I'd meet him outside. He nodded, and alone made surprisingly quick progress to the door, exiting before I'd even gotten to Elaine. I waited for access, then caught Elaine's eye and waved rather frantically.

The crowd parted to let me through. Heloise immediately jumped up, spun around, greeting me with ears up, tail wagging. How did she know? Had she smelled me? 'Hello, girl. Good girl. Now down.' She obediently lay back down, ears still up, awaiting my next command. She gave my shoe a little lick as I leaned in close to speak to Elaine. 'I'm going to get some dinner, maybe take a taxi and sightsee the old MadTown at night. I need a proper meal to soak up this alcohol.' *And I see a curtain.* Elaine laughed and patted my arm. I could tell she was feeling some buzz herself.

'Can Heloise stay with you?' I asked. Let's just break all the rules tonight. Heloise was only supposed to stay with an approved sitter. Well, I approved of Elaine. So did Heloise.

'*Can* she?! Absoposolutely!' She was shouting louder than necessary, even over the music. 'Have a good dinner!' She waved me off.

I laughed, suddenly feeling free, buoyant. As if I'd been given permission. 'I will. Thanks so much for looking after my girl. Has she been out?'

Elaine nodded. 'Just took her a few minutes ago.' I squeezed her hand and smiled, then rose to leave, but Elaine grabbed my shoulder, pulling me back toward her. She'd seen Kent after all. My heart skipped a beat. She pressed something sharp into my hand.

'Take my key, Wendy's got hers. Do you have money for both taxi and dinner?' I nodded, relieved, and patted my purse. 'Okay. Our address is nineteen-oh-one Lake Street,' she said. 'Got that? Nineteen-oh-one.' I nodded again, and smiled. As if I could forget, after all the cards and letters I'd addressed to her over the years.

As I turned again, Heloise jumped up, clearly expecting to go with me. I reached down, scratched her ear. She tried to lick my hand but I stopped her, for once certain that my actions were justified. I kissed her head and left.

The cold air outside was like a slap, immediately sobering. Kent was waiting behind the wheel in his small SUV in the valet area, his headlights illuminating a few straggling snowflakes. He was bent forward, head turned, scanning for me out the passenger window. As I stepped outside, his face broke into a broad, delighted smile. He waved energetically. How long had it been since my mere appearance made someone that excited? Well. Tonight. Heloise.

I climbed in and the already heating leather seats were warm and caressing. He had Andrea Bocelli playing on his CD. 'All set?' Kent asked.

'Yeah.' I smiled back at him. Our eyes locked for a brief moment, then he turned, shifted into first, and slowly pulled away. I leaned back, closed my eyes, breathed, letting the aria bathe me, Bocelli's voice serene and sacred. Despite the heat now fully on in both the car and the seats, I had goose bumps. I felt the car turning left, then a bit later right, then another quick right and we stopped. I heard Kent pull on the emergency brake.

'You still with me?'

I opened my eyes. We were already in the parking lot of the restaurant. The simple, unlit sign read THE HARVEST.

'Yeah. His singing. Better than any Christmas carol.'

Kent nodded. 'Couldn't agree more.'

I undid my seat belt. 'You weren't lying when you said "nearby"!'

'No. IT guys never lie,' he said with a joking seriousness. 'We sometimes speak a language no one else can understand, but we never lie.' It suddenly occurred to me that I'd just assumed IT meant information technologies. But here I'd left a party with a man I really didn't know at all. What if it meant International Terrorist?

'So, that's, uh, information technologies, right?'

He laughed and said, 'Well, we often refer to computers as Infernal Technology, but yeah, that's the technical name.' He really did have a lovely smile. 'Let me get your door for you.' He jumped out and scurried around, holding on to the car for security in the icy parking lot. I took my hand off the door handle and waited.

'Watch your step. It's slick out here.' He offered his arm and I took it. We inched our way across the parking lot, laughing in relief when we stepped into the warm, dimly lit restaurant.

The place was all rough-hewn wood, maybe six tables and three or four booths, each with small candles on plain white tablecloths, and quiet as a church. We were seated immediately in a small booth near a paned window of the same wood. I slid across the bench and looked outside as Kent slid in across from me. The window looked out on a little park of some sort, with a meandering path lit by short lamps with triangular tops. A hedge separating the restaurant from the park was draped in blinking Christmas lights, twinkling under a translucent blanket of snow.

The hostess handed us menus and pointed to a sign on the table. She read it aloud: 'We serve water on request only, as we feel it can interfere with the digestive process.' Kent looked at me sort of questioningly, and I looked at him. We smiled at the same moment and in unison said, 'I'd like some water, please.'

She nodded pleasantly and left.

'Do you come here often?' I asked, sliding out of my coat. Almost immediately I wanted to shove the clichéd line back in my mouth. But Kent took it as the sincere question I'd intended.

'Yeah, pretty regularly, enough to know that that hostess is new. But I haven't been here in probably over a month. I was at a conference in France for almost three weeks.'

'Wow! France. I've always dreamt about going there one day. But I don't like to fly.' He looked at me with a note of surprise, but at that moment our hostess returned with two smallish glasses of room-temperature water. I immediately took mine, grateful for the nonalcoholic hydration. I drained it. Kent laughed, and pushed his untouched glass toward me. 'Thirsty girl! Here, have mine. I'll ask for more.'

I reached for his glass and raised it toward him in a kind of toast. 'Thank you so much. I didn't realize how thirsty I was.' He used hand signals to tell the hostess we needed more water, and as he did I asked, 'Are we going to get admonished for completely destroying our digestive process?'

He laughed, shook his head. The hostess soon brought us a full pitcher, again room temperature. I filled both our glasses as Kent watched appreciatively.

'You've got beautiful hands, strong, but very feminine.' I set the pitcher down hard, and my eyes closed involuntarily, a pain in my heart.

'Thank you,' I said quietly, desperately wishing he hadn't made that particular comment. Nearly Neil's exact words, from so many years ago, on one of our early dates.

The waitress appeared and we both ordered the salad bar. As we were sliding out of the booth to go up to the little covered wagon that housed it, Kent gently touched my hand as he leaned over and whispered, 'Wait'll you see the sign up here.' His touch was electric, but it now felt like some harmful voltage, rather than a surge of energy.

As I approached the stack of plates, I saw another small sign, and it made me turn and smile again at Kent.

Our Salad Bar Is All You Should Eat.

We carried our laden plates back to our booth and got to work on them right away. After a few minutes of silent but enthusiastic eating, I leaned back, sighing. I felt awkward with the silence, but Kent smiled and continued eating. I chewed a cucumber slice and stared out the window. It was snowing harder now. The lights on the hedge were still shining from underneath, but if it kept up, they'd soon be obscured. The snow on the ground was soft, undulating, a smooth but crystalline surface from the new flakes. The row of short lamps along the path looked like little Chinese snowmen. I took another bite, remembering years of building snowmen with my kids. And one year, a huge, sinuous dragon. It had snowed over two feet, and no one could go anywhere, not even Neil. The five of us had worked on it all morning. Later that day I'd taken pictures of all three kids, and Nan and Sara, all sitting between the spikes on the dragon's back. And Sara had insisted on taking one of me and Neil, calling us 'the Dragon Masters.' I could see us, right out there, Neil's arm slung over my shoulders, me leaning into him, our cheeks red, both smiling.

'You okay?' Kent asked. I realized my fork was on my plate, both my hands flat on the table, as if I was about to rise up. I nodded, but didn't look at him. He gently reached over and touched my left hand, saying softly, 'Deena?' I suddenly pulled my hand away.

'Kent, I'm married. I'm married.' I looked down again, and barely whispered, 'I'm married. And I think I want to stay married.' I looked up, surprised and grateful that I wasn't crying. He leaned back against the wooden planks behind him, his eyes wide.

Finally, he spoke. 'I see.' He looked disappointed; I couldn't tell if it was in me or at the situation, or both.

'I'm so sorry. I – You are very attractive, and just the nicest man, but – I've been having trouble, at home, and – Well, I thought . . .' I shook my head. 'I don't know what I thought.'

'Deena?' I looked up at him. His eyes were tender. He offered me both his hands across the table. No longer guilty, but still tentative, I reached over with both of mine. 'You're doing the right thing. I didn't know. I wouldn't have – Well, not that anything would have, tonight, that is –' We both smiled; then he got serious again. 'But if I'd known you were married, I still would have asked you to dinner, but just very aboveboard and all.' I squeezed his hands, so grateful for his understanding, his kindness.

He squeezed back, but then let go, leaning back again. 'I was married. My wife had an affair. It's devastating. Completely devastating. That's why I said you're doing the right thing. Go home, fix what's wrong, or end it. But don't make what's wrong worse.' He rubbed his face, shaking his head and laughing slightly. 'God. I'm sorry,' he said, picking up then putting down the water sign from the table. 'You've gotten nothing but little lectures on what's good for you here tonight.' I laughed, wanting to hug him, but even more, needing to leave.

I stood, grabbing my coat and shouldering my purse. 'I have to go. I'll pay for dinner on my way out.'

Kent rose too, putting his hand up. 'No, Deena. Really, I'll get it.'

I looked him in the eye. 'Kent, you are a terrific guy. Some woman is going to get very lucky with you. But I need to pay.' He nodded, looking at me as if he wished the situation wasn't what it was. I returned the look.

'Can I . . . at least give you a ride back to the party? Or to Elaine's?' he asked, starting to rise.

I shook my head. 'No. I'll get a taxi. But thank you, Kent. Thank you so much.' I took a deep breath and looked at him as if I was looking at myself. 'I need to find my own way home, too.'

I didn't have to ask if he understood.

CHAPTER 28

On the flight to Denver the next day, I drank nothing but water as we soared along at some unthinkable altitude. Heloise was fast asleep, worn out by the eventful weekend. She relaxed much more quickly this time, nervous only with the noisy takeoff. Her calm now soothed my own nerves. If I had physical contact with her, I could even look out the window, so with my foot lightly massaging her stomach, I stared at the billowy clouds below. I imagined myself walking on them, swimming through them, piling them on my face and head, making a cloud beard and hat, throwing handfuls up into the air for Heloise to leap and grab at.

The plane banked slightly, bringing the afternoon sun in my little window. I briefly wondered what had caused the myriad scratches, on both the inside and outside of the two windowpanes. Don't even go there, I told myself. Instead, I glanced at the outside edge of the brilliant sun, realizing we were several miles closer to it here. I thought of Icarus, then quickly decided that that was not a good thought either, and stared again at the whipped-cream clouds. Amazing, really, that a bit of water vapor could look so gorgeous and solid. And not be real. Not solid-real anyway.

I stretched my legs out, slipped off my shoes, and rubbed my toe behind Heloise's ear. She lifted her front paw and placed it appreciatively on my shin, opening sleepy eyes, staring at me, then her heavy lids closing again.

I loved Neil, still, somewhere. But we'd let so much evaporate. Our marriage, our individual identities. We'd slowly relinquished ourselves to our roles. But for three days in Wisconsin I had felt like something other than water vapor. Maybe not the real Deena, whatever that was, but something solid. At thirty-one thousand feet, I wondered if there was some way to end my marriage. And then begin it again.

I looked outside, at the endless sky, the curve of the world. And how odd and marvelous it was that the sun shining through all those tiny scratches made the air outside seem sparkly.

Even though I only had my carry-on, Neil and I had agreed that the baggage claim would be the easiest place to meet. He was in the very back, leaning against the wall. He was watching a large group in front of him. A gaggle of about seven grinning grandparents, who all seemed to be attached to the same two little kids, were leaning forward or tilting their heads to the side to catch every word from a little girl wearing a pink plastic

384

backpack as she animatedly described her first flight. Neil looked up as Heloise and I came across the wide square. He took a double-take, squinting slightly, looking at Heloise then back at me again.

Long before we actually got to him he awkwardly extended a white conical package. Flowers. My heart twisted, both touched and pained. I couldn't say he was smiling exactly. But nor was I. Exactly.

Heloise finally spotted Neil, and her walk immediately changed to an eager, leash-pulling, whole-butt-wagging waddle. A heat-seeking missile. A love bomb on a locked trajectory. With me stumbling behind, my arm fully outstretched, she parted the willing, smiling crowd, pulling me behind her like a water-skier.

Reaching Neil finally, Heloise thrust her head between his knees. He broke into a full grin. He squatted beside her and let her lick his chin, her wagging body threatening to capsize both of them. Without warning she shoved her nose into the bouquet, and before Neil could stop her, emerged with the bright orange head of a gerbera daisy in her mouth. We both laughed as I fished the contraband from her. Gerbera daisies. They used to be my favorite, till I found out how quickly they fade. Had I never told Neil that? Had I told him my favorites were now carnations? They can last weeks, with the right care. I wondered, there in the airport, if *his* favorite flower was still the lilac.

'I was going to bring her a big dog biscuit, but then I thought I remembered that she's not allowed to have any treats.' At that moment, Neil's brown eyes looked remarkably like Heloise's. 'You look . . . good,' he said. 'Different.' He wound his hand around his head. 'Your hair.'

'Thanks, Neil,' I said, finally setting down my bag and taking the again-proffered flowers. I wasn't sure whether his comment about my hair was entirely a compliment or not, but I was touched by his remembering about Heloise and treats. I quickly kissed his cheek. His aftershave was mixed with Heloise's distinctive smell – not quite the sweet puppy breath it once was, but still intoxicating to me. The aftershave was the same new one I'd noticed when he'd dropped me off. I felt a tiny flutter. Wings in a far-off country.

'I'm all set,' I said, nodding to my carry-on. I tucked the flowers under my arm and picked up my suitcase again.

'Did you have a good time?' he asked, reaching for my small suitcase, which contained, among other things, my carefully wrapped painting. I reluctantly let go. Suddenly, I wished I'd bought a little something for him. Not to mention Matt and Lainey. Oh, shit! Matt and Lainey. Wasn't a parent *always* supposed to bring home a little something for their kids from any trip? I knew Neil always did.

'Uh, yeah,' I replied finally. 'It was great to see Elaine. Neil? Can we stop by a gift shop? I want to get something for Matt and Lainey.'

He tried but was too late masking his expression: You mean you didn't?

'Sure,' he said, pulling his face into neutral and resuming his stride. 'But you don't need to do that. I don't think they're expecting anything.' I looked at him from under my lashes in a 'since when do teenagers not expect things?' look. He shrugged and we veered toward the shops on the main concourse.

Neil held Heloise as I poked through the miniature Colorado license-plate name key fobs, and the myriad Broncos and Rockies paraphernalia. Why hadn't I gotten them each a UW hoodie? That's what they'd both have liked. I could have easily picked them up when Elaine and I were at the mall. If it had occurred to me. I felt selfish as hell.

And just a little victorious.

'Never mind, Neil,' I said, turning to leave. 'They don't want anything here.' We headed for the exit.

Our conversation was strained as we drove home. I told him we'd had chicken and dumplings for Thanksgiving dinner. He said there wasn't much turkey left for Amy to take home, so he'd invited them over for pizza the next night. We talked about the weather. It had been cold there, warm here. The sink had gotten stopped up. He'd plungered it open.

As we pulled into our driveway I was surprised to see the Christmas lights up. He'd helped me before, but never taken the initiative to put them up on his own. Especially this early. I saw in the living room window that they'd gotten a tree, too. And decorated it. Without me. I worried it'd be brown and dry by Christmas, but still smiled when I saw it. I'd have to raise the lowest ornaments.

Heloise was good, but her tail alone would make a clean sweep of the bottom tier of the tree.

Neil pressed the remote, opening the garage, but parked in the driveway. 'The tree looks nice,' I said.

'Yeah, Amy's real estate firm was giving them away. She nabbed one for us. Pretty nice one, considering it was free.' We both looked at it through the picture window. It was a fat, slightly squat fir. We usually got a pine. Easier to hang ornaments on. But this one looked softer. 'We saved the star for you.' We smiled at each other, briefly, awkwardly.

I took Heloise into the house as Neil carried my suitcase upstairs. I was running some fresh water into her bowl when Hairy strolled into the kitchen. Heloise bounded over but stopped abruptly, directly in front of Hairy. I set the bowl on the floor, warily watching them. Hairy stopped, stiffening. Heloise was vibrating. I could tell she was trying to decide between Cat Fun and Being Good. Finally she bowed slightly, *asking* him if he wanted to play.

'Good girl, Heloise,' I said. She looked at me, wagged her tail, relaxed a bit. Hairy stared at Heloise. I could see his thoughts: *Damn. She's back.*

Then I saw something else in his face. Right then, right there, he made his decision. His head raised, he continued across the kitchen floor. *Well, Doggie-Girl, while you've been away, I've reclaimed my house. Get used to it.* He strolled toward her water bowl, his furry paws each crossing in front of the other as he stepped. He bent and began to drink noisily, his white plume tail arcing gracefully back and

388

forth. Heloise and I stood motionless, watching. I think Hairy drank far more than he wanted, enjoying the audience and the fact that he'd 'taken over' her water bowl, despite having his own on the counter. Finally, the lapping stopped, and he sat, delicately licking a stray drop from the side of his mouth. He stared ahead, at neither of us. Heloise stepped carefully around him and began lapping from her bowl. The watering hole détente.

I bent down and scooped Hairy up, kissing his furry cheek. 'Hello, you old scalawag.' I gently set him on the desk and grabbed the can of Pounce from the top of the fridge. I shook out several onto the desk. As Hairy dove for one, I snapped another off the edge with my finger. 'Whoopsee!' I said, as Heloise lunged for it, gobbling it down so fast that I doubted she even tasted it.

'I saw that,' said Neil, coming around the corner.

I blushed. 'I had a little finger palsy.'

He smiled, pulling his keys from his pocket. 'I'm late to get Matt. He spent most of the weekend at Josh's. Lainey *did* spend the whole weekend at Nan's. She's not supposed to come home till six, give you some time to get settled before we bombard you with . . . us.' I raised my eyebrows and smiled. Neil did not. Heading toward the door, his back to me, he said, 'Why don't you unpack, relax. I'll pick up some pizza on the way home.' I had noticed a half dozen empty pizza cartons in the garage when we'd come in. Poor Neil had probably eaten a lot of pizza this weekend.

'Are you sure you're okay with pizza again?' I asked. Now Neil blushed slightly.

'Yeah, it's fine. Your bag's upstairs.' He walked out the door.

I watched his retreating back, said, 'Thanks,' and stood alone in the kitchen.

I poured myself a tumbler of orange juice, grateful for the carton in the fridge. It was practically the only thing keeping the mayonnaise company. I'd gotten hooked on OJ again at Elaine's. I'd get back to my diet tomorrow, I promised myself.

I sipped my juice at the dining room table, thumbing through the newspapers there, neatly stacked, looking unread. I looked at the front pages, then picked through the fat Sunday paper, starting with, just for fun, the glossy travel section with a cover story on cruises. Next I read 'Dear Abby,' then scanned the local section. A name jumped out at me from the funeral notices. *Wenzell.* My hands went cold, my heart in my throat as I read.

A PRIVATE SERVICE FOR
LAURA WENZELL WILL BE
HELD AT TWO O CLOCK
SATURDAY AT THE
COMMUNITY
CONGREGATIONAL CHURCH,
2122 MESA DRIVE.

I tore through the other days' local sections, looking for her obituary, found it in Thursday's paper. Laura had died the day I'd left. Wednesday. The day before Thanksgiving.

'Oh, Merle,' I said out loud. I clasped my hands together, touching my forehead to my knuckles, not breathing, tears sliding down my cheeks.

I found his number in the phone book, but there was no answer. Not even a machine. I dug through my drawer of greeting cards, selected a blank card, a photograph of Turret Peak, wrote him a quick note, addressed it from the phone book, and left it on the desk to go out in the morning's mail.

I decided to go directly upstairs, before Neil and the kids got back, unpack, and take a hot bath, even more grateful now for the half hour still remaining of the cushion of time that Neil had thoughtfully built into the evening's schedule.

I mounted the last step, both Hairy and Heloise trailing behind me like an uneven bridal train. I walked down the hall to our bedroom, stopping to straighten a family photo – all of us gathered in front of a Christmas tree, Lainey, a baby in my arms. I stepped back, looking up and down the hallway at the years of smiles. The pictures all seemed lower. It felt like I had been gone weeks, not days.

I stepped into our bedroom. My suitcase was not on the neatly made bed. I checked the other side of the bed. Then the closet. No suitcase. I sat on the edge of the bed, then nodded, remembering. A tight breath slipped out of me. I walked to the other end of the hallway to Sam's room. My suitcase and purse were on the bed.

I unpacked quickly, hanging my new dress in the guest bedroom storage closet, tucking it into the hanger bag with my wedding dress, briefly fingering its yellowed lace, then closing the closet. The new underwear I stuffed in the back of Sam's top dresser drawer, behind all of the bras and panties I'd transferred in there months ago.

Unpacked, I was left with a pile of laundry, which I gathered into my arms. But at the top of the stairs, I stopped. I walked instead into the kids' bathroom, dumping my armload into the laundry hamper. I couldn't yet face the basement full of laundry.

I took a magazine into the master bath and turned on both taps full blast, dribbling a purple concoction of Lainey's called Lavender Bliss into the stream. I sank into the warm water, the bubbles up to my neck. I sighed audibly. Heloise came into the bathroom, rested her chin on the edge of the tub.

'Hey, girl! Want a hat?'

I placed two fingerfuls of bubbles on the back of her head, a pointed little elf cap. Then I reached in with my cupped hands and placed a beard of bubbles on my chin. I turned to Heloise. 'It's good to be home, isn't it, girl?'

When I came down for dinner, clean and warm, wrapped in my plummy bathrobe, I held my arms out to Matt and Lainey. My head was still in a towel turban; for some reason I didn't want to do the whole new hair thing with my kids tonight. Greeting Matt was the same, like hugging an ironing board. Lainey hugged me, tightly, but wouldn't look at me, but then did, briefly, searingly, then quickly away again.

We sat immediately down to dinner. The only sound was the occasional clink of a fork in a salad bowl. I was touched, and a little amazed, that Neil had made a salad to go with the pizza. I pulled small pieces of pepperoni and cheese off the bread, ate them with my fingers, in between bites of salad.

'Did you have fun with Nan, Lainey?' I asked, breaking the silence. Lainey's eyes, never looking up, darted toward Neil, almost imperceptibly.

'Yeah,' she said, now staring at her plate. I waited, but nothing more.

'What'd you do?'

She shrugged. 'Talked, mostly.'

'Matt? What's new with you?'

He shrugged. 'Nothing much.' He wouldn't look at me either.

The awkwardness was inevitable, I supposed, no one knowing quite where anything stood. We'd all have to piece ourselves back together.

After dinner, Neil offered to clean up. 'You must be tired after your trip,' he said. 'Why don't you go to bed early, catch up?' He smiled, nervously touching the corner of his eye. He returned to filling the sink, squeezing in dish soap, the water making a high foam. Soon we would have to address the broken dishwasher. But not tonight.

I kissed his cheek, which stopped him, a plate in his hand.

'Thanks for dinner, Neil. For the pizza, and especially the salad.' He nodded, staring at the sink. 'And thanks for cleaning up. Sure I can't help?'

He shook his head, giving me a tight-lipped smile. 'I'm getting good at it.' I went up to bed.

Matt and Lainey were already in their rooms, doors closed. I stood in front of Lainey's door, raised my fist to knock, then dropped it to my side. Better to talk in the morning, when we weren't all so tired. I shuffled into Sam's room, closing that door, too.

I awoke in the darkness, blinking my eyes and running my hand along the headboard, trying to get a bearing on where I was. I dropped my hand over the bed, for Heloise, then heard her heavy breathing from her bed near the desk. I saw Sam's clock, stark red numbers announcing it was 2:13. I watched it blink to 2:14. Then 2:15. I stretched, awake and alert. Agitated, even. I stretched again, then slid my hand under my nightgown, running it along my pelvis, my stomach. I not only hadn't gained weight on my trip, it felt like I'd lost another pound or two. Must have been all that walking. I ran my hand again over my abdomen, then my hips.

My hand continued its inventory, cool against my warm breasts, thighs. I closed my eyes. A photo album in my mind flipped through pictures of me and Neil, all shots of us before the kids. College, dating, meeting his parents, him meeting mine. A road trip, driving from Wisconsin to Colorado, through Minnesota, South Dakota, Wyoming. We'd made love in all those places. Each time I'd found a new piece of myself to give to him, yet never feeling like I was giving myself away. Maybe because I'd gratefully accepted the pieces of him he'd tenderly given me.

I pushed back the covers, walked to the door. I turned to look at the sleeping Heloise, motionless and tranquil on her bed. I looked at her the way I used to look at the kids when they were little, stunned at a whirling dervish so utterly stilled, blanketed with innocence through the simple act of sleeping. I pulled the door quietly closed behind me and padded silently down the hall.

He'd left the west blinds open; a three-quarter moon hung outside the window, laying a rectangular quilt of light across the bed, spilling onto the floor. I pulled off my nightgown and slid under the covers next to him. His breathing was slow, almost silent. I inhaled, his true scents enveloping me like a warm wave. His smell, like him, was naked, body and breath without pretense of artificial odor. It was deep, sweet, and real.

I lightly kissed the freckles on his shoulder, then ran my finger over them. He moved his jaw slightly but didn't wake. I lay my head next to his on the pillow, my body soaking in his warmth. Remembering.

I raised myself on one elbow. Slowly, I moved

my hand along his arms, first one, then the other. I ran my fingers through his sparse chest hair, felt his pectorals, then his rib cage, abdomen. He too had lost some weight, I thought. He felt trimmer, firmer. I moved my hand down. Definitely firm there.

He groaned softly. I couldn't tell if it was *I don't really want to wake up*, or, *Keep going*. One way to find out. I moved on top of him and his hands moved to my hips, his eyes slowly opening. I watched as a labored consciousness slowly flowed into his pupils. A different flow surged beneath me.

He whispered, without inflection of any kind, 'Deena . . .' It was the only word spoken between us.

When we'd finished, the moon had sunk below the mountain ridge, and we lay in the dark, silent. Almost immediately his breathing became regular again. His jaw was slack, a half snore beginning. Suddenly cold, I pulled the covers up to my chin and rolled over, reaching to click on the electric blanket for warmth.

CHAPTER 29

S tanding at the trailhead, I inhaled the crisp, clean air. It was a glorious winter day, Colorado at its best. But even I felt Laura's absence from the world.

I'd tried to get there early, but the snow had slowed us down some. I wanted to give my condolences to Merle in person, before he got my card. I didn't want to go to his house, in case he still had company from the funeral.

Although Neil and I hadn't talked this morning – he had slipped out without waking me – I felt alive with possibility. My trip, and then reading of Laura's death, had opened something in me. Shaken something loose. I suddenly felt focused on the rest of my life, instead of what was left of my life. This first day of December felt more fresh and filled with possibility than any New Year's Day ever had.

Even the weather had cleansed the earth; the vast whiteness lay before us, offering yet another clean slate. It was cold out, but not the bitter temperatures it had been in Madison. It had snowed several inches, and the foothills were spectacular: white-crested mountain ridges, frosted evergreens, white rolling hills. Like most Colorado storms, this one had packed up every shred of itself and moved out quickly, leaving only that blue, blue sky. Forecasters were calling for more snow tonight, but today was crystalline sunshine.

I jogged in place to keep my blood moving, checked my watch again. It was now well after Merle's usual start time. Maybe it was too soon for him to resume his walks. But I was sure he would still get Teddy out, as he said, for his 'daily constitutional.' And I couldn't imagine him going anywhere but here. Especially now. I decided to head up. Maybe we had just missed him.

Heloise and I took off up the trail at a good clip. I wondered if I'd have to adjust to the altitude again, after just a few days away. But I felt like I could climb Everest today. The snow on the trail was already packed down by other feet, both canine and human. I urged Heloise into a trot. We made it to the bench in good time. But there was no sign of Merle and Teddy.

I sat on the bench, catching my breath. Heloise kept a steady watch downhill. I knew she knew who we were waiting for. She turned when an elderly man walking a black Scottie came ambling down from the upper trails. The Scottie was alternately wading through the deeper snow on the sides, and trotting along in the trodden path behind his owner. As they approached, I said good morning.

He nodded. 'What a day, eh?'

'Yes,' I replied. 'It's lovely. Excuse me, but do you by any chance know Merle Wenzell? He walks up here with his collie, Teddy?'

'Yes. So sad, isn't it?'

'Yes.' I nodded soberly. 'How's Merle doing?'

'Well, it was hard enough when his wife passed, but that was a blessing, in its own way. But then Teddy going too, so soon after.'

'What?' I jumped up from the bench. 'Teddy?'

His hand went to his chest. 'Oh, I'm sorry. I didn't realize – yes. Teddy died, let's see, I think it was Friday. Just a couple of days after Laura. Kind of like what you hear about with spouses. When one goes, the other goes.' The man pointed. 'He passed away right here, at this bench. That's why I thought you must have known. I guess the old dog just knew he wanted to go here, and he curled up and drifted off. I helped Merle carry him down.'

I didn't want to fall apart in front of this man, but I couldn't stop the tears streaming down my face. I held Heloise's leash against my heart. 'Oh, no. Poor Merle. Oh, not Teddy too.' I dropped back down to the bench. Heloise moved close to me, licking at my hand. The man sat next to me and tentatively patted my knee as I stroked Heloise's head.

'I know, dear. I dread the day when Blackie here passes, too,' said the man. 'But us old codgers who have old codger dogs, we have to be braced for it.

399

Now granted, the timing was hard, but I think Merle was ready. You know what he told me, when we were carrying him down?' I shook my head. ' "He just went to be with Laura. They're playing together, right now." '

It was all I could do not to sob like a baby. The man patted my knee again. 'But you've got a young pup there,' he said energetically, clearly uncomfortable with my emotion. 'He'll be with you plenty more years.'

I wiped my sleeve across my eyes. I looked at him, smiled weakly, then looked at Heloise. For the first time I let myself think about the phone call that was just three or four months away, telling me the date of the truck that would take her back to California, and out of my life.

I waited till the man excused himself, resuming his walk down the mountain, before I let myself break down completely.

I cleaned up at home, quickly made a coffee cake, then put it and Heloise in the car and drove over to Merle's house. I didn't care who was there. I had to see him. He answered the door, looking stooped and drawn. But he smiled when he saw us.

'Well, you girls are a sight for sore eyes.' He studied my face. 'Who told you?'

'I saw Laura's notice in the paper yesterday, after I got back from my trip. Then, up by the bench this morning, a gentleman with a black Scottie told me about Teddy.' I reached out and touched his arm, still holding the door. 'Heloise and I had been hoping to find you and Teddy there. Oh, Merle, I'm so sorry.'

'Please, come in.' His eyes were full. He turned away and led us toward the kitchen. I saw no sign of guests. Any who'd come for the funeral had evidently left. I looked into the living room, saw the afghan neatly folded over the back of Laura's empty orange chair. The hospital bed was gone, the TV silent and black but for a reflected rectangle of window light filled with naked tree branches across the dark screen. The rugs were still rolled up against the wall. The echo of her absence was palpable.

'The water's hot,' he said, as we stepped into the kitchen. I saw the white kettle on the stove. He touched three fingers to the wooden handle. 'Tea?' he asked, looking at the stove.

'That'd be lovely, Merle, thank you. I brought a coffee cake. Can I cut you a piece?'

He was rummaging through a cabinet, his back still to me. 'Won't ever say no to a treat. Like a dog, that way.' There was silence between us for a moment, then only our respective clinking of china cups and plates. Finally he turned, his familiar grin back in place, but his eyes still glossy.

As I cut the cake, I watched Heloise sniff around the kitchen, looking up at me at regular intervals. I sent her the thought, not wanting to say it out loud: *He's gone, baby. Teddy's gone.* She finally turned twice and curled up in his corner, her paws tucked under her, head on the floor at a twisted angle, everything about her bereft. I reached down and stroked her back.

That night at home Neil called from work saying he'd be very late, not to wait up, and that he'd catch a bite somewhere. I sighed as I put the rest of the lasagna in a Tupperware.

I slept in our bed that night, but I might as well have been alone. He'd evidently slipped in noiselessly, out the same way early in the morning. I wouldn't have known he was even there but for yesterday's work shirt and underwear in the hamper and the tea bag in the sink. I made a small pot of coffee, drank a cup, ate a hard-boiled egg and headed out in the car with Heloise.

As I pulled into a parking spot, I could see Merle waiting for us. I'd driven to the trailhead, deciding it would take us too long to walk there in the deepening snow. We'd had another four or five inches overnight; it was still lightly snowing. Gone were the blue skies, but the temperature was more moderate, though still right around freezing. Merle wore a dark blue down parka with the hood up, puckered tight around his thin face, the cord in a bow under his chin. There was something absolutely right about his thick tweed pants and maroon gaiters hooked to his boots. I had on Lainey's snow pants, Matt's snowboarding jacket, and my own hiking boots. I was going to have to get myself some good winter outerwear of my own.

We looked at each other, then simultaneously opened our arms and hugged before the three of us headed up the trail.

CHAPTER 30

It took us almost twice as long as usual to get to the bench through the snow. My quadriceps and glutes were burning, and I longed to sit down. I cleared the bench seat with my straightened arm, scraping all the snow off to one side. Merle and I both gratefully dropped down, the pile of cleared snow on the ground on Merle's side, Heloise on mine.

Our breath puffing out in front of us, we each surveyed the transformation of a world gone white, listening to the silence imposed by this frozen blanket. Several small birds flitted noiselessly around the tree in front of us. The only tracks other than ours – a rabbit perhaps? – went from the tree, past the bench, and then disappeared into the trample of footprints on the main path. But it was something near the bench that caught my eye.

'Look at that, Merle!' I said quietly, leaning forward and pointing to his right.

'What?' He glanced around, clearly expecting to see an animal or bird.

'That pile of snow. Does it look like anything to you?'

He tilted his head to one side, studying the mound.

He looked at me blankly. I rose, handed him Heloise's leash, and stepped over to the leaning pile. I studied it for a moment, then with my gloved hands, packed it. I carved out a notch below the top mound. I packed the base some more, shaping it as I went, the body, the head. It was perfect packing snow. My skin pricked with pleasure and excitement, like a swarm of happy bees dancing just under my skin. I pulled off my gloves, dropped to my knees. I used my fingers to shape the front legs, ears, eyes, and finally, tail. I dug down through the snow and found three small rocks. I placed them on either side of the head and at the end of the snout. I stood, stepped back, and admired my work. If I did say so myself, a recognizable dog, sitting attentively by Merle's side.

'A tribute to Teddy!' I said, flushed with pleasure and cold. I clasped my hands near my mouth and blew into them, hiding my smile.

'That's really quite remarkable, Deena,' said Merle softly, gazing at the snow dog. He looked at me, first tenderly, then that twinkle came into his eye. 'Remarkable how it doesn't look a lick like Teddy.' A pause. A smile. 'It's the spitting image of Heloise!' He stood and stepped to my side and put his arm around my shoulders. 'You have a talent here, my girl. A real talent. It's a fine tribute. Teddy and I thank you.'

★ ★ ★

After our walk, I'd invited Merle out to lunch. He'd politely declined, wanting to rest. Impulsively, I'd decided to go anyway.

As I lifted a forkful of mushroom and Swiss cheese omelet toward my mouth, I marveled at how something that I used to hate, eating alone at a restaurant, had become comfortable, a treat, even. A faint snore came from under the table, making me smile.

I glanced at the newspaper, then pushed it aside. I didn't want to hide from this solitude. My foot found Heloise, and I felt utterly content. I wondered if I'd enjoy, or even be bold enough to try, meals out alone when Heloise was gone. I thought I would.

Time suddenly felt like velvet – soft, inviting. I sat in my booth, savoring the texture and tastes of the omelet, listening to the occasional restaurant clatter of silverware and dishes, the floating pieces of conversations, the smells of grease and yeast and coffee. I felt grateful for every tiny detail of being alive in this moment.

I looked out the window, watching the cars creep by on the snow-packed road. An employee was shoveling the walk in front of the restaurant. A mom, an orange-snowsuited toddler, and their beagle were out for a walk together, stopped for the moment next to a huge blue spruce. With my fork held just above my plate, my gaze lingered on the three. The dog sniffed, lifted his leg on the trunk of the tree, his snow-covered muzzle pointed toward me. The child, too small and bundled for me to tell if it was a boy or girl, stared up at a branch, as if daring the snow balanced there to fall. The mom, her child's hand in one hand, the leash in the other, stared sightlessly ahead. The child pulled her toward the tree, a snowsuit waddle, pointing up excitedly at something in the branches. The dog, spying the approach of another dog and walker, pulled in that direction. Mom's arms were stretched out nearly horizontal on either side. She closed her eyes, tilted her face skyward.

I motioned to the waitress, asked for the bill and a box for the rest of the omelet.

It was less than a mile away. Parking might be an issue, but maybe the snow was in my favor. I was lucky and found a spot just up the street from the store. The Art Department. I hadn't been there in years. I walked past the aisle of paintbrushes, past the tubes of acrylics and watercolors, trying not to think about the numbers of each lying fallow and petrified in my basement. Heloise and I wandered through the aisles till I found it. I surveyed my options, then grabbed two blocks of Marblex and strode toward the checkout counter, Heloise trotting to keep up with me.

At home, I unpacked the dresser first, carrying armfuls of underwear back into our bedroom and stuffing them in my top dresser drawer. I pulled the Victoria's Secret bra and panties toward the front. Who knows, I thought, I might even wear them tonight. Get Neil's attention while he's awake this time.

After I moved all of my things back to the master bedroom, I set to work on Sam's furniture. One by one I carried down to the basement his bedside table, a beanbag chair, and from his closet a large orange construction cone I'd never even noticed. I briefly wondered where he'd gotten it, then decided I didn't want to know and tucked it in amongst the camping equipment. I rested my hand on the nylon bag holding the tent, smiling, wondering what it would be like to go camping with just Neil. We'd never done that.

Back in Sam's room, I pushed his dresser into his closet, stripped his bed, and threw an old sheet over it. In the garage I found some plastic sheeting that I'd saved from painting the dining room two years ago. With the blocks of Marblex warming under each of my armpits, I brought it up to Sam's room.

Heloise had been following me except to the basement, but now stared at me from the doorway, not sure what to make of my frenzy. I put the clay on the plastic-covered dresser, and sat in the chair, grinning uncontrollably, fear and excitement holding hands in my stomach. But I wasn't quite ready to begin.

I surveyed the room. A single shelf held Sam's

old CD player; we'd gotten him a smaller one to take to college. I looked at the walls. They could use painting. Should I paint? Something different. Bright. Teal? *No. You're avoiding this! Just get started. Unwrap them!*

Okay, I bargained with myself, I wouldn't repaint the walls, but I did need one more thing. I jumped up and ran downstairs. Heloise, tired of following me up and down, waited at the top, then lay down with a *humph,* her front paws dripping over the edge. I looked at her and laughed, then jogged to the living room. I was a four-year-old setting up a tea party. I rummaged through the CDs, found it, and ran upstairs, leaping over Heloise. I popped in the disc, but didn't hit PLAY yet. I trotted into the bedroom. Our bedroom. I found the painting and carefully pulled off the bubble wrap as I walked down the hall, back into Sam's room—

No. Not Sam's room. I made myself say it out loud as I stood in the middle of the room, hugging the picture. 'My studio.'

I lifted a baseball plaque off the wall and hung *Woman* on the exposed nail. I took a deep breath. Finally, I pushed the PLAY button on the CD player. I lowered myself almost reverently into the chair, aware of my strong quadriceps easing me down. I unwrapped the clay, breathing in its smell of wet basements, spring rains, and possibility. Carole King began singing as I wrapped my fingers around the cool hardness, sunk them in, again and again, till finally the clay began to warm and yield to me.

Almost two hours and two dogs – one sitting, one lying down – later, I looked at the clock, aghast at the time. I decided I really should have *some* domestic task done before everyone got home. I admired my dogs, each about the size of a hot dog bun. I'd had a little trouble with the faces, but I just kept looking at Heloise and, bit by bit, was able to mold them into shape. I even got a different expression on each dog's face, one alert, the other placid. I washed my hands in the kids' bathroom, an exhilarated face staring back at me from the mirror.

I was energized enough now to deal with even the mountain of laundry I knew waited for me in the basement. I grabbed both bags from each hamper and carried them, Santa Claus style, down the two flights of stairs.

The laundry nearly covered the floor. But someone had made an effort. Instead of just one pile, there were three: whites, darks, and colors. Never mind that there were hand-wash and dry-clean-only items in every pile. And someone had more than just sorted; on the drying rack was one of Lainey's favorite sweaters, now sized perfectly for a smallish poodle. If Lainey had shrunk her sweater like that, she would have had a fit of hysterical crying and thrown it away, not spread it neatly on the drying rack. Matt almost certainly wouldn't attempt laundry, and if he did, I doubted he would do Lainey's laundry. It had to have been Neil.

Neil. I smiled, dropping my armload, then sorting it into the existing piles.

Humming, I picked up a wool sweater of Matt's off the darks, and a silk blouse of Lainey's off the whites. Several of Neil's white shirts were in there, too, and one by one I pulled them out, holding it all in my arms. It *was* sort of an art, doing laundry.

I put the sweater and blouse into an empty laundry basket, and dumped the armload of Neil's shirts into another. I always washed his shirts separately, so I could iron and starch them right from the washer. As they tumbled into the basket I noticed a spot of red amidst the white. I grabbed the stain treatment from the cabinet and reached for the shirt. My arm extended, I froze, bent over like an old washerwoman. I stared at the shirt.

The earth went quiet, ground to a halt on its axis.

Lipstick. The unmistakable waxy mark of lipstick, smeared on one shoulder of a shirt.

Slow motion. My arm reaching out. Fingers touching fabric. Lifting, holding it before me. The basement floor began to give way, slowly at first, like an elevator, then plummeting.

My left hand grabbed on to the folding table. The lipstick was bright red. A color I'd never worn, except years ago one Halloween when I'd dressed up as Cruella De Ville for Sam's first-grade party.

I brought the shirt to my nose and inhaled, wanting to stop myself but unable. No perfume, at least. Just remnants of his deodorant and aftershave.

That *new* aftershave.

He'd worn Old Spice forever, and suddenly he was wearing – I didn't know what. I ran from the basement. I took the first flight two stairs at a time, my heart pounding, the shirtsleeve in my hand, clenched to my chest. Heloise was standing at the top, once again overjoyed to see me return from the basement. 'Move! *Move!*' I pushed her aside with my knee. I raced down the hall, flew up the second flight, Heloise bounding behind me, grabbing at the shirttails, loving this new game.

'Heloise! No! *No!*' I yelled, stopping in the hallway, grabbing her collar and jerking upward. '*No!*' She immediately sat, ears flat, apologetic for her glee. I ran into the bathroom, my heart shattering for too many reasons.

I yanked open the medicine cabinet. There. A small cobalt-blue bottle. My arm felt separate from my body as it rose, my fingers reaching out. I touched it, then rotated the bottle.

Aramis.

I tried to breathe through shrunken lungs. My hand shaking, I picked it up. I'd read the magazine articles, seen a dozen Oprah shows on cheating husbands. I knew the signs and now easily found them, scattered over the past month or so. Trying new things. *Like aftershave.* Sleeping in separate rooms. *He'd put my suitcase in Sam's room, unbidden.*

Distant, uncommunicative. *He'd been so distant at the airport, at dinner, even making love.* Losing weight, working out. *He'd felt trimmer, more muscular.* For her. I looked again at the shirt. Here in my hand was the signal flare to beat all, the most clichéd sign a wife could ever get, a crimson scream of infidelity emblazoned on the shoulder of his shirt.

I sat on the edge of the tub sucking in short ragged breaths, concrete setting up in my chest, arms, and legs. Heloise stepped tentatively into the bedroom, stopping in front of the bathroom, looking everywhere but at me. Her head, ears, and tail drooped. She looked like she was melting. Maybe everything was.

I stood, leaned over the sink, thinking I might be sick. I turned on the tap and splashed cold water on my face, forcing my breathing to deepen, slow down. I pulled the hand towel off its ring, patted my cheeks, eyes, mouth. I looked in the mirror. The pale yellow towel, sunflower they called it, dropped limply into the sink. I stared at my new hair around the same old face.

How arrogant I'd been! Assuming my husband was there for me to leave. When had he left *me?* Had it been weeks? Months? *Years?* Heloise lay down in the bedroom, waiting, unsure. I sat again, this time on the closed toilet. I looked at the shirt on the edge of the tub. The life force dripped out of me, as guilt and shame flowed in.

I'd been distant.

I'd moved into the other room.

I'd left town.

I'd pulled my wedding rings off.

I'd gone out with Kent.

Was Neil's affair any different from what I'd been thinking about for months? Had, for a brief couple of hours in Madison, planned to do?

Yes. I hadn't done it.

CHAPTER 31

But who? When would he have—
Oh my God. Amy.

Thanksgiving. Turkey. Pizza on Friday. My husband was having an affair with our divorced neighbor. How tawdry and clichéd could it get?

I ran downstairs, a booming sound in my ears. I flung open the front door and ran down the driveway, barefoot. I stopped, standing at the bottom of the driveway, dirty, icy tire tracks ribboning the concrete. I looked across the street at Amy's house. A small snowman stood outside. Nan's work, I was sure. The snowman's stick arms had fallen to the ground, its three round segments now merging into one another, giving him a squat, fun-house-mirror look. I turned, and on numb feet I walked back into my house.

I drifted from room to room, my steps leaden, my feet burning as they warmed. It seemed like every room knew.

She was here, whispered the sun room. *When you weren't.* The walls had heard her words. Had the dining room listened to her Thanksgiving prayer? Which chair had she sat in? My chair? My glossy dining room table had held her turkey. 'Her' turkey that she didn't even cook, didn't open the oven door every half hour, turning her head at the blast of heat. Didn't dip the baster into the pan, squeezing the juices back over the top, over and over, like liquid love, while the kids and Neil played Monopoly in the next room. No, she'd played Monopoly with them.

I stood at the sink, my hands holding the edge of the counter. After dinner, had her arms been in my sink, next to Neil's, her laughter spilling over as they did dishes together? As mine once had, years ago. Neil used to offer to help me every night. In fact, for a while, when each baby was just home from the hospital, he'd insisted on doing the dishes. Then, too soon maybe, I'd insisted. Taken over. Your workday's over, shoo, I'd say to him.

I hung my head. Elaine was right. I was the one who'd refused to punch my own time card.

As I roamed through the downstairs, Heloise followed at a distance, ears flat, head low. I trudged upstairs, my hand gripping the banister, pulling my weight up. I walked the length of the hall, touching a picture here, there. T-ball and baseball teams. The goofy basketball ones of the boys, one knee down, one boyish hand holding a basketball on the upraised knee, hands and balls and smiles precisely placed. A similar one of Lainey, just a year old, with a soccer ball. I'd insisted on getting these formal shots, despite the exorbitant fee charged for a single eight-by-ten.

But now I much preferred the small four-by-six snapshot of eight-year-old Sam at the end of the driveway, arms raised, face skyward, having just thrown the basketball backward over his head toward the basket above the garage; and the one of Matt, maybe four or five, in his swim trunks, sitting on a beach ball under the sprinkler, eyes closed, grinning ear to ear. And this one. I ran my finger over the pink double frame, the left picture Lainey at three in her pink tutu, arms overhead, her chubby fingers not quite touching, the companion picture about a year older, naked in the garden, covered in mud, tiny mud cakes on a leaf serving platter on her thigh. I scanned the celluloid history of life as a family. Like multicolored beads on a string. A necklace of memories. Now broken. The beads clattering to the floor.

I walked into the bedroom. Sitting on the edge of the bed I picked up the phone, dialed.

'Hi, Phyllis, it's Deena. I need to speak to Neil, please. It's urgent.'

I heard Phyllis's breathing quicken. 'Is – Are . . . ? Yes. Of course. I'll get him, Deena.'

I tried to steady my own breathing as I waited. I pulled a pillow from under the bedspread, held it tight to my chest.

'Deena?' Neil's alarmed voice.

My heart. I couldn't speak with it there in my throat. I swallowed. 'Neil, the kids are fine, but I need you to come home, right away. Please.'

417

'What's wrong?! Deena?' There was real panic in his voice.

'The kids are fine.'

'You said that. Deena, I've got patients this afternoon. What's going on? Are you ill?' A pause, then, softly, 'Is something wrong with Heloise?'

'No. Neil, I've never asked you to leave your work like this, for me. Never. Please do it now. Just this once.'

A painfully long silence. Then, slightly muffled – I imagined his hand lightly over the phone – 'Phyllis, call Mrs Ye and—' He would be running his finger across the schedule book now. 'And the McKenzie twins' mom, she has a different last name, Johnson, I think, and – whoever this is. Reschedule them all, please.' Now he spoke directly into the phone. 'I'm on my way, Deena.'

It wasn't twenty minutes later I heard the front door push open. I was still sitting on the bed. Heloise left my side in a single movement, bolting down the hall, her toenails on the oak stairs sounding like she was sledding down, not running.

'Hello, girl,' said Neil. I could hear the affectionate thumps he gave her. 'Deena?'

'Up here,' I called back. 'In the bedroom. In *our* bedroom.' I heard his long legs taking the stairs two at a time, Heloise's toenails right behind him.

Neil joined me on the edge of the bed, Heloise wedging herself between our legs. 'Deena? Sweetheart?' His hand tentatively touched my hand. 'What is it?' His face was both frightened and steeled.

I turned toward him, not with the fierce and defiant expression I'd thought I'd have, but with an openness and conviction that surprised me. I suddenly knew that either way, I was going to be okay. If it ended here, I could start anew. I knew what I wanted, but either way, my life lay before me, not behind.

'Neil, I want us to be together. I want us to work on this. I want to be *us* again. But I want to be *me*, too. I want us both to be whole. I want to do art, get a job. I want you to work less, do things, fun things, just for yourself, too. I want to be alone sometimes, but be together forever. I want to grow old with you, Neil.' It all came out in a clump. All my truths.

His eyes closed, he let out a huge breath, then looked at me, his brown eyes soft. 'Sweetheart, you don't know how relieved I am to hear you say that. I want that, too.' He leaned in again, to kiss me, but I stopped him, my hand on his shoulder. Heloise lay down, her chin resting on my foot.

'So, will you stop seeing her?' I looked him in the eye. 'Is the affair over, Neil?'

His face twisted, his eyebrows questioning, then hurt and incredulity washed over him.

'Deena—' he began, shaking his head. '*I'm* not seeing anyone. What are you talking about? I thought *you* might be having an affair. *I'm* not. What in the world made you think that?'

My eyes locked on his. 'Neil, I found one of your shirts. Downstairs. It had lipstick on it. Red lipstick. You changed aftershave. You've been working out. You put my suitcase in Sam's room. You—' I looked at him. 'Neil, I know I've been kind of lost for a while. We both have. But Neil—' I looked straight ahead. 'It's Amy, isn't it?'

'Oh, *sweetheart!*' He tried to put his arms around me but I pushed them off. 'Oh my God, Deena. No. No! I'm not having an affair. I'm so sorry you went there with that.' I opened my mouth, but now he stopped me, holding up his hand. 'I can see how you did. I completely see. I'm sorry. But let me explain. Oh, God! *Amy?* You thought I was having an affair with *Amy?*' He shook his head, laughed lightly. My back straightened, the defiance and anger there after all, surging up my spine. He quickly continued. 'The lipstick is from – a patient. Sort of.' I could feel my eyes burn with suspicion. 'Wait, Deena.' He grabbed my hand firmly, but tenderly. 'I've got patient confidentiality here.' That was true. I knew that some doctors played a little fast and loose with telling stories about their patients, thinking if they didn't use any names it was okay to talk about them. But Neil had always been extremely circumspect about his patients and their visits, sharing very few specifics over the years. I'd always respected him for keeping their privacy sacrosanct. But this was different. I needed to know.

'Can you at least tell me how the lipstick got there?'

He sighed. 'I'm going to do more than that, because I think you need to know. And she's not technically my patient, I guess. Besides, Lainey knows. Nan told her. And Lainey told Matt.'

Lainey? Nan? Matt? Now I felt the confusion contorting my own face.

Neil took my hand again. 'Sara's pregnant.' It took several long seconds to sink in, then my posture slumped, my eyes squeezed shut, a maternal concern nudging aside all other emotions. I looked at Neil, and he explained how it had unfolded. 'She seemed upset over Thanksgiving, then again Friday night when they came over for pizza, but, you know, I figured it was because Amy'd made her come over here, not hang out with her boyfriend, that kind of thing. Well, Lainey spent the night with Nan on Saturday, and I guess Sara broke down and told both girls, then they persuaded her to come talk to me. She came over around eleven, her eyes solid red from crying, but she'd put all this makeup on and everything.' Neil shook his head. 'She tried so hard to act grown-up, tough it out. Poor thing. I didn't examine her, of course, but we talked, she showed me the pregnancy kits she'd used. Two of them, both clear positives. I told her I'd help her get right in to the clinic, and until then I couldn't absolutely confirm it, but that, yes, it looked like she was pregnant. She just collapsed on me. I'm sure that's where the lipstick is from. Poor kid has been through the ringer this past year with Amy and Marty splitting up. Now this.' He paused, and

421

gently, briefly, touched my hand. 'Lisa Radelet, the ob-gyn at the clinic, confirmed the pregnancy. I guess Sara wants to keep it.'

I exhaled a breath the size of the world. Relief at the lipstick's source. Crushing concern for Sara. Amy. Even Nan. 'Oh, Neil. Has she told Amy yet?'

'I don't think she has, no. Lisa referred her to a counselor at the clinic, to help her with that, and everything.'

'Oh, Lord. They have only just gotten on their feet! What are they going to do?'

'Muddle through, I guess. Same as we all do.' He sighed, then smiled. 'Probably be ringing our doorbell a lot.'

I was a torrent of mixed emotions, but I couldn't help but laugh. Neil reached for me, then stopped, arms open, asking. I leaned in, took him into my arms. We kissed. In a way we'd not kissed in a long time. We didn't even hear the door open, but Heloise tore out of the room and again tobogganed down the stairs.

'Hullo, Wheezy! Who's a good girl?!'

'Hey, puppy! Hey, girl!'

Matt and Lainey, home from school. Neil and I pulled apart, still grasping hands.

'Oh, great. A moment of intimacy interrupted by our kids. How many times has *that* happened?' said Neil. I laughed, embraced and kissed him again quickly, then we both stood. We walked down the hall together, holding hands. We still needed to talk, but now was not the time. Tonight. In bed.

At the top of the stairs we greeted the kids. They could not have looked more surprised to see us both, no less holding hands at the top of the stairs. They elbowed each other, grinning. They probably thought we'd been having sex. Let them think.

'Hey!' I said, turning to Neil, then to the kids. 'Let's go bowling tonight!' A chorus of moans from Matt and Lainey. 'Come on!' I implored. Then in a temptress singsong, 'I'll make bowling dinner.'

'And Wayfarer cake?' asked Lainey.

'Yep,' I said, grinning.

'Ex-cell-ent,' said Matt, nodding deeply with each syllable.

CHAPTER 32

Heloise and I found Neil and the kids in lane eight, just finishing a game. We'd taken separate cars, since I wanted to put the roast in the Crock-Pot and get the cake in the freezer. Not because I had to, or because it was expected, but because I really wanted to. Neil and the kids had gone on ahead to get a lane before the after-five crowds rolled in. Fairview didn't have a bowling alley, so we'd driven the twenty miles to Clifton, where bowling had never gone out of style.

Neil handed me my shoes, a sedate tan and red. I looked at his. Fluorescent pink. 'Nice shoes, dear.'

'He *asked* for them, Mom! Can you believe that?' shrieked Lainey, delighted. 'The guy gave him a pair like yours, but he saw those hideous things in his size and *asked* for them.'

Matt looked at his father, and with a great deadpan said, 'Yeah. It's confirmed now. Dad's definitely gone over the edge.'

Laughing, I laced up my shoes while they typed my name into the computer. When I looked up, it wasn't my name at all up on the screen above our heads. It was Heloise.

'How 'bout I take this turn for you, girl?' I asked Heloise. She wagged her consent. I selected a ball from the nearby rack and flung it down the alley. It looked good at first, but it was spinning wildly and tipped into the gutter just before it reached the pins.

'Gutter ball for Heloise!' Matt shouted. I had my hands on my knees, laughing.

At first Heloise was a little fearful of the loud crashes of balls hitting pins. But she was completely mesmerized by the ball return machine, and sat for nearly fifteen minutes watching as balls rose magically from the dark netherworld then slid out onto the channel. When no balls came, she sat with her head tilting to one side then the other, wondering where they were. Then she'd hear the *shunk shunk* of a ball being sent back up, and she'd stand and greet each one, ears cocked and tail wagging as it came rolling out. Matt nearly fell out of his chair laughing at her.

'She's so cute, Mom!' said Lainey. 'And she has really grown up. She's so good now. Who knew my mom could train a dog so well?' she said, poking me in the arm.

'I knew,' said Matt, without turning toward us. He was at the line, ready to take his turn, ball under chin, eyes focused on pins. 'Look how good I turned out.' He looked back over his shoulder, giving us raising and lowering Groucho Marx eyebrows, to our collective delight.

Neil and I sat on the bench watching the kids

take their turns. Neil put his arm around behind me, tentative, sliding it first against the bench, then around my shoulders. My skin tingled. I felt every inch of where his arm was touching my back, how his fingers gently gripped my arm. I tipped into him. We looked into each other's eyes, silent, yet so many things being said. Matt had to snap his fingers in front of us to let us know it was our turn.

It was dark and cold and snowing hard when Heloise and I came out of the bowling alley. Neil and the kids had already turned in all the shoes and headed for home to set the table. Neil had offered to make a salad, his 'specialty,' he'd said, grinning. I got stuck in a conversation about Heloise with the family waiting for our lane. They were interested in raising a service puppy.

'It's a lot of work,' I told them, Heloise sitting perfectly by my side, 'but very rewarding.'

'Has your whole family been involved?' asked the mom, her three kids, maybe five years younger than mine, looking on.

I smiled. 'Well, they've been sort of drawn into it.' My hand went to Heloise's head by my knee. 'I think it's safe to say that we've all fallen in love with her, and that's a big part of the training.' I told them about the Web site where they could get more information and finally excused myself.

The snow that had been melting in the after-noon had now turned to ice, covered with a coating of fresh dry snow. Heloise and I took tiny, careful

426

steps as we navigated the icy sidewalk and parking lot. When we reached my car I couldn't help but smile. Someone, maybe all three, had cleared the snow and ice from the hood, roof, and all the windows. I had to help Heloise into the back, all sixty-four pounds; her back paws had no traction on the ice.

As I maneuvered the car out of its parking place, I was grateful for the expensive studded snow tires Neil had insisted we get for my old wagon several years ago. I'd argued at the time that it was like putting diamond earrings on a corpse. Several snowstorms had convinced me that Neil had been absolutely right.

I eased my foot onto the accelerator and slowly made my way through the parking lot and onto the street. Triangles of snow fell from each streetlight; the roads of Clifton were nearly deserted at a little before seven p.m. Only one or two cars crawled by as I exited the parking lot. It was like a frozen ghost town, but beautiful, and I felt the sanctity of the season.

I decided to head south and east, take the interstate home, thinking it'd be clearer than the smaller roads. I inched up to the stop line at a red light. I'd have to make a left turn, then quickly merge right, to the on-ramp to I-25 just a short distance ahead.

I looked in my rearview mirror. Good. No cars behind me. I'd be able to turn and merge, taking my time. I saw Heloise's silhouette. She was sitting, her large body leaning sideways against the back of the backseat, her nose nearly touching the side window, gazing outside. She made me smile, for about the millionth time. I clicked on the radio, pushed a couple of buttons, Christmas carols on nearly all the stations. I stopped on 'O Little Town of Bethlehem.' One of my favorites.

How still we see thee lie . . .

The windshield wipers seemed to keep time. I sang along and Heloise pricked up her ears. 'Above thy deep and dreamless sleep . . .'

The arrow finally turned green, and I touched my foot to the accelerator, the back of the wagon fishtailing slightly, but then the tires gripping, gaining traction, and I inched forward. Barely over the stop line, I glanced ahead to where the on-ramp was, then above me to make sure the arrow wasn't one of those ridiculous short ones; it wasn't, thank God; it was still green. I glanced in the rearview mirror to check behind me again. Still no cars. Good. *You're fine, Deena. Relax.* Other people were smart not to be out driving on these treacherous roads.

Heloise groaned softly, and in the mirror I watched her slump noisily to the floor, ready to sleep through the drive home. 'The everlasting light . . . ,' I sang lustily.

Neither of us even saw the other car coming.

My first thought was that a bomb had gone off. There was a tremendous bang, crunching of metal, glass shattering. The air bag exploded into me,

428

striking my right cheek, as I felt thrown one way, then the other as the car spun. My head slammed into the side window as the car filled with the chalky, smokelike residue from the air bag. Finally, the car came to a rest, pointing one hundred eighty degrees from where we'd been. The radio played on; I realized the car was still running. I reached for the key and immediately felt like a knife had plunged into my chest, my seat belt pulling tight over the pain. I couldn't reach the key.

While mortals sleep, the angels keep.

The air in the car was getting harder to breathe. Coughing and choking, I screamed for Heloise. I couldn't see her in the rearview mirror. I couldn't find the release button for the seat belt. My chest hurt. I clawed with my right hand around my side, trying to feel for it. Felt the back of the hand brake, couldn't remember if it was up or down from that. *It's square, on the side. Find it!* There. I moved my thumb to the top. I pushed down, heard the click, pulled the straps away from me, pushing the limp air bag out of the way. I reached for the key, and again, the pain in my chest. I couldn't turn the key. I was dizzy, my eyes were stinging. I couldn't see through the smoke. There was a metallic taste in my mouth.

'Heloise!' I tried to turn around, to look for her, but cried out again with the stab between my breasts, down my side. I quickly felt for the door handle, pawing frantically at the whole panel. I tried to remember the layout of the armrest, the buttons,

429

the release handle. Dammit! I'd been driving this car forever! Where was it?

'Heloise?' I called, softer now, crying, one hand still feeling for the door release. 'Heloise, baby. Please be okay. I'm coming, girl.'

How silently, how silently.

I wiped my face with my other hand. I couldn't tell if the wet was tears or blood. Finally I found the little recessed handle. I pulled, but nothing happened. I felt for the unlock button. Everything was taking too long! It was just behind the handle, I reminded myself. *Calm down. Breathe.* Another sharp pain between my breasts. Finally, I unlocked the door and pulled again on the handle. It felt like magic when the door opened.

I sucked the cold night air into my lungs, coughing, pain searing my chest with each breath, but the clean air was a welcome relief from the thick, ashy air inside the car.

Heloise probably couldn't breathe either!

I put my foot down on the ground and stood, but with my first step I slipped and fell on the ice, hitting my elbow and chin. Sobbing, I called out again, 'Heloise!'

Someone was picking me up. 'Let me help you, ma'am. Here, come away from the car. There's smoke.' I heard a siren in the distance.

I screamed again, 'Heloise! She's in the back.' Someone was wrapping a blanket around me. The wet on my face was now dripping off my chin. 'My dog! My dog!'

'Someone's checking on her, ma'am. They're getting her out now.' It sounded like a horn was blowing. Was that in my head? I couldn't focus my eyes. The man wrapped an arm tightly around my shoulder, essentially dragging me away from the car. Another man appeared under my other arm, and together they lifted me, my body limp, my feet barely skimming the ice. The pain in my chest and side was excruciating.

'This way. Over here, ma'am.'

I tried to pull away, pushing his shoulder from me. 'Heloise,' I cried. 'I'm so sorry!'

'Waddn't your fault, ma'am,' the man said. 'Jerk ran a red light, never even braked. I was behind him.' Through my tears I saw that my good Samaritan was wearing a tan suede coat. The last thing I remember seeing was a red streak of blood smeared across one shoulder of that nice suede coat.

I woke up in a darkened room, but a stream of ghostly yellow light was coming in the window from the streetlight outside. A monitor beeped a hushed rhythm. A green light glowed from a box to my right. Neil was sitting in an upholstered chair, pulled close to my bed. He was holding my hand. His chin was down, his eyes closed.

Hospital.

Heloise!

I hadn't felt any pain till then.

'Neil,' I whispered, squeezing his hand. His eyes jerked open and almost immediately began filling.

431

'Oh, Deena! Oh, my dear, beloved Deena,' he whispered. He brought his head to my hand and ever so gently kissed my knuckles.

I squeezed his hand. 'Neil? Is Heloise . . . ?' I could barely get the words out.

'She's okay, sweetheart. She's okay.' Relief surged through me, leaking out my eyes. 'She was scared, of course,' continued Neil, patting my hand, 'but the paramedics checked her out, brought her with you to the hospital. There didn't seem to be any serious injury, but I called Bill. He came right away, took her to an all-night vet, because she was limping. He said she has a bruised shoulder, so she may limp for a bit, but she's okay. He offered to keep her for us, but I said no, that we wanted her with us.' Neil smiled. 'She's with Matt and Lainey in the waiting room. Last I saw they were taking her out to do her business, and she was leading them with the leash in her mouth.'

My tears flowed freely now. 'Oh, thank God,' I cried.

'Deena?'

I looked at him.

'I love you.' His eyes were spilling over now. Still holding my hand with his, he pushed the back of his other hand over each eye, wiping the tears away. 'Oh, God, Deena. I was afraid I'd lost my chance to tell you. I thought I'd lost you, when, when you went to Madison. Then, when the police came tonight, I thought I'd *really* lost you, you know?' He cried audibly, hard squeezing sobs.

My tears were sliding down my temples. Neil shook his head, getting control, and grabbed a tissue from the side table and gently dabbed at the sides of my eyes, my pillow, then his own eyes. He leaned over, and as gently as lips can be set upon lips, he kissed me.

'Neil?'

'Yes, darling?'

'I love you, too.' We squeezed hands again, just breathing.

Finally Neil sat up, took a deep breath, forced a smile, recovering his composure. 'Okay. Whew. You ready for your visitors now? The kids wanted me to get them as soon as you woke up.' I nodded again, not even trying to speak, still just trying to breathe. Neil gave each of my hands, still in his, a kiss, then rose. 'I'll go give them a shout.'

He held the door open as Matt, Lainey, and Heloise came in, all bumping into each other and the door frame, each trying to be the first through, including Heloise. No threshold manners here. Both kids had a hand on Heloise's leash, obviously a compromise as to who would bring her into my room. It hurt to do so, but I couldn't help laughing. They all three seemed to be wagging their tails as they saw me.

Though my cracked sternum and ribs were painful with almost any movement, the day I was to leave the hospital I was feeling much better, but looking worse. Purplish circles had appeared under each of my eyes. My cheek had a long scratch running diagonally across it. My chin and elbow were both swollen and bruised, ironically from my fall getting out of the car, not the accident itself. Despite my injuries and appearance, my heart was light. The day before I'd had some of the best medicine of all: Sam had called. On my fiftieth birthday. Neil and the kids had brought me a cake, Wayfarer, of course, the one I'd made. They promised a better celebration later, when I was more up to it. But my main gift had been hearing from Sam.

Neil had left him several messages the night I was admitted to the hospital, and the next day. When he didn't call back, Neil had called the dean. It turned out that Sam had been staying with 'a friend' and had lost his cell phone. But the school had tracked him down in class, taking a biology final. He'd immediately borrowed a class-mate's cell phone, run outside, and called me.

It was short but sweet. In a five-minute conver-sation he'd asked about five times if I was really okay. I'd finally assured him that I'd be fine, told him to go back to his final. Abruptly, he said, 'Mom, I got invited to a friend's house on Catalina for Christmas, but I could come home.'

'That's sweet, honey. But that's okay. Catalina sounds like a wonderful opportunity,' I said, and meant it.

'Well, if you're sure. But I definitely want to come home over spring break, Mom. Spend some time with you, and meet Heloise.' Quietly, he added, 'And maybe do some skiing, if you're up to it.' I smiled again, my eyes speaking volumes to Neil, who was sitting in the chair next to my bed, where he'd been for the past two days.

'Sure, hon. We'll meet you at the airport with bells on.'

'I was thinking a road trip, actually. A friend has a car, a safe one, Mom, and wants to see Colorado. Would that be okay? To bring . . . a friend?'

A friend. I looked down at Heloise. She was lying contentedly on the floor on a folded dark green hospital blanket Neil had put down for her. Her blonde hairs were already all over it.

'That'd be great, honey. Is this a *special* friend?' I asked teasingly, immediately worried I shouldn't have.

But he laughed and said simply, 'Yeah.'

It was like a lone sequin on the floor, but I left it alone. 'Great. Now go finish your exam.'

He said he would call again after his last final.

Now Neil and I were waiting for my hospital forms, and for the doctor to come do my final checkout. It was taking forever.

'Can't you just check me out?' I asked Neil.

'I'd love to!' he said, lustily.

I swatted his knee, then sighed. 'I guess that's out of the question for a while.'

'Yeah,' he said. 'Again.' He smiled. 'But as long as I can hold your hand . . .' He did.

'Neil?'

'What?'

'I'm still, well, a little confused, I guess. You know, I don't mean to beat a dead horse, maybe I've seen too many Oprah shows, but on the top-ten list of how to tell if your spouse is having an affair, you gave me about eight things to worry about. Not just the lipstick, but there's the new aftershave, and you put my suitcase in Sam's room, not our room, and then when I went in that night, and we –? Well, you didn't exactly respond enthusiastically. You were pretty distant.'

'Deena, I've been trying to respect *your* distance! Your self-imposed distance.' He softened his voice. 'I've been having my own crisis, you know, wondering if you were going to leave me. And the kids.'

I was quiet, humbled. 'I'm so sorry, Neil. I didn't do things very well. I just needed some separation, some identity. I didn't know how to get it.' I felt truly contrite, but still confused. 'But, why the new cologne? And you must be working out because– ' I cursed the schoolgirl blush heating my face. 'Well, I can tell, could tell the other night.' He smiled, sat up straighter, pulling in his stomach.

I laughed, but quickly added, 'Neil, every women's magazine I've ever read about how to tell if your husband is having an affair, well – it's all the things you've been doing.'

'Deena.' Now there was just a hint of irritation there. '*So have you*. You may not know this, but I read those magazines, too. Sometimes. I've got them in my waiting room. I've seen the articles, the lists.

In fact, your behavior made me seek them out.' He began itemizing on his fingers. ' "Does your spouse suddenly want to take trips alone?" "Is he or she getting involved with projects or groups that you're not involved with?" "Has communication broken down?" ' He paused, looked at me, then the floor. ' "Is your sex life suffering?" '

My God, I could see it now. I had been trying to tease myself out from the knot of my family, trying to see if I could be separate, but I had also been myopic and self-absorbed. I looked at Neil, took his hand again. 'I am so sorry, Neil.' I took as deep a breath as my chest would allow.

'So, when I came in the other night? Should I not have? You were hardly there.'

'I just didn't know what the hell was going on, Deena. I mean, we've hardly spoken, then you go away, and, you have to agree, it wasn't exactly comfortable at the airport. Lainey and Matt and I all knew about Sara, but it wasn't like I could just sit you down and tell you all about it. I didn't know where you were, where we were, you know? And then, wham! You sneak into my bed. I was a little confused, Deena. And yes, I was a little out of it. I'd taken a sleeping pill. I haven't been sleeping very well in there. By myself.'

'And the cologne . . . and, *doing laundry*, and working out?'

He gave me a crooked smile. 'It's those women's magazines. Did you read the one called "The Top Ten Secrets of Happy Couples"?' He made quotation marks in the air. "Spice things up! Change your scent! Pursue your own interests! Keep yourself fit and healthy!" He cocked his head, looked away a minute, smiling, then looked at me. 'God! It's the same damn list they use in both the "How to Keep Your Marriage Healthy" and "How to Tell If It's Not" articles, isn't it?' I could hardly believe it, but when he said it, I had to agree. We smiled at each other, then Neil's face became suddenly serious. 'I missed you, Deena. I missed us. I didn't know what to do. It was like it became completely impossible for us to talk to each other. When you moved out of our bedroom, I sort of shut down, buried myself in work. Then when you told me you were going on a trip, alone, I realized everything was at stake. I tried . . . changing. I read a bunch of those articles. I just knew we had to change *something.*'

Heloise adjusted her position on the floor, groaning softly, but it sounded like a commentary on our foolishness.

'So do you like the new cologne?' he asked shyly.

I brought his hand to my cheek. 'It's okay.' I gave him a sympathetic smile. 'I miss the Old Spice.'

He laughed. 'That's a relief. Me too.'

I was overcome with love for how much he'd gone through, how much I'd put him through. But also glad that we'd both arrived where we had. Still cradling his hand by my cheek, I was

438

unable to speak. He slowly leaned over, again softly touching his lips to mine. Maybe our millionth kiss. We gazed into each other's eyes. I had to look away briefly.

'Deena?'

'Neil, I thought about it. About having an affair.' His face fell. 'But I didn't! I didn't. I'm so sorry. I'm sorry, Neil. I don't know what I wanted exactly. I just felt like all you saw in me was Wife, all the kids saw was Mom. I was desperate to have someone see Deena. For me to feel like Deena. I didn't even know what that was, much less how to do it. I was lost.'

Neither of us spoke for a minute, then Neil looked at me, his face wan. 'Are you found? Are we?'

I knew he wanted me to say, right away, an emphatic yes. But I couldn't. 'I'm finding myself. I'm emerging. I feel kind of like a teenager finding out who I am all over again. It's kind of exciting, but it also kind of sucks.' We both laughed.

'I know. I feel the same way sometimes.'

'I think we can find our way back to us, too. As long as we both want to. As long as we both try. Maybe go talk to someone, professionally.'

He nodded, his eyes welling again, his unshaven chin quivering slightly. 'Please let's try, Deena.' I nodded back, relief, exhaustion, and hope surging through me. But I seemed to finally be out of tears. Finally.

Neil let out a small laugh, brushing his own

tears away. 'I want to hold you so much it hurts!' He touched my cheek and whispered, 'I love you, Deena.'

I kissed his hand again, unable to speak. Apparently I was not out of tears. I probably never would be.

CHAPTER 33

My cracked ribs and sternum were healing, albeit slowly. The chinook winds of February ate up any snow that fell, so I was given the okay to go for walks as soon as I felt up to it and as long as the trails remained clear. But I was strictly forbidden from holding Heloise's leash, even though she was so well trained now she rarely pulled anymore. I was, in fact, under doctor's orders (both from the hospital and the one I was married to) not to lift anything 'heavier than a bag of marshmallows.' I'd dutifully followed instructions, although I really didn't have any choice. My family made me sit like a queen while they took over, mostly, but not entirely, co-operatively.

'Spaghetti and meatballs *again*?' complained Matt at dinner one night.

'Fine, you cook dinner then, Mr Feathers,' chided Lainey. She'd been doing a lot of the cooking, and her repertoire was quite limited. Matt, on the other hand, had been doing most of the laundry and had earned that nickname when a down comforter had burst a seam in the dryer.

It wasn't entirely his fault; I'd told him to put a clean shoe in with it to fluff it up, and he figured if one shoe would fluff, four would super-fluff. Neil was orchestrating everything, assigning the kids chores they'd never done, and even cooked dinner himself my first night back. He'd gotten a recipe for meat loaf from a nurse at work.

We'd just finished eating it when the doorbell rang.

Neil led Amy into the living room as Matt was settling me on the couch with my requisite propping pillows. Heloise was in the kitchen; I could hear Lainey playing with her with a tug toy. Their favorite new game was for Lainey to sit in the rolling desk chair and get Heloise to tug her round the kitchen. Almost certainly not sanctioned, but they both loved it.

Amy was carrying a ridiculously large bouquet of white daisies, and my Tupperware container with something rattling around inside. She handed it to me while Neil took the flowers and went to find a vase. I took the lid off and smiled at Amy. Inside were two large cans of chicken soup.

'I thought about just mixing them up and bringing the soup over all hot in the container and saying I'd made it, but I knew you'd know the difference.' She smiled and scratched her elbow in a shy and charming way.

Neil and the kids kept themselves scarce while Amy and I talked in front of the fire. I asked about her job. 'It turns out I'm really good at selling houses!' she said, fingers on her chest in a 'who knew?' fashion. 'Plus, I can kind of set my own schedule, which is really good. Especially now.' She then told me that she and Sara and Nan were all in counseling, both separately and together, that they all liked the counselor, that it was slow, but good.

And Sam had called three or four times in the weeks since I'd gotten home. I'd learned that the way to get him to talk was to listen. It sounds simple, even stupid, but I found it incredibly hard. I sometimes had to bite my tongue through long, awkward silences. But by not asking, Sam had offered that her name was Bree. That she was from California. She was premed, too. Her mother was a pediatrician, her father a fourth-grade teacher.

On January 19, Neil and the kids had given us a joint birthday celebration, when Heloise turned one, and a little more than a month after my fiftieth. I got four blocks of Marblex from Lainey, a one-hundred-dollar gift card to the Art Department from Neil, and from Matt, a small wood door plaque he'd made that said simply: MOM'S ART STUDIO. Heloise got four new chew toys, all of them K-9 Eyes- and Heloise-approved.

Throughout my recovery, Neil had taken responsibility for feeding Heloise her meals, and he and the kids shared responsibility for taking her out to the yard each morning and night. They even gave her a bath when she got into some mud on one of my weekday walks in the foothills. But it was Merle who held Heloise's leash on those walks.

The day after I'd come home from the hospital, Merle too had brought me flowers. I introduced him to my family, so proud, as Merle took one hand at a time in both of his, first Lainey, then Matt, then Neil. The following week, Merle and I resumed our walks. By mid-February we'd worked up to walking all the way to our bench.

It was after one of these walks, as Merle and I were just sitting down to a cup of tea at my little kitchen table, when the phone rang.

'I'll just let the voice mail get it,' I told Merle.

'It might be one of your kids,' he said. He knew me too well.

I was grinning when I picked up the phone. 'Hello?'

'Calling to check on the patient!' said Elaine. She'd called half a dozen times since the accident.

'Hey, Elaine!' I said, nodding gratefully to Merle, who was waving me on to have a conversation while he sipped his tea and played with Heloise.

'How's it feeling?'

'Coming along. I'm not allowed to do very much still. But Merle and I are taking Heloise on lots of walks, at least.'

'Good!'

'How are things there?' I asked.

'Well, I happen to have some exciting news, girl-friend! Really exciting!'

I thought I should offer to call her back, after

Merle left, but I was too curious. 'Tell me quick! Merle is here. We're having tea.' I watched Merle's mouth move unconsciously with Heloise as he held one end of her rope tug and she pulled the other.

'Okay, I was going to give you a hint, but I'll just tell you: Wendy and I got a baby!'

I'd been about to sip my tea but stopped, the cup at my lip. *A baby? At their age? When their careers were in the stratosphere?!* 'A *what*?!'

'Okay, maybe I better give you that hint: Meow.' Another pause, then Elaine jumped in again. 'Oh, for crying out loud, Deena! We got a cat! From the shelter.'

A rush of relief swept over me. 'You had me scared there for a minute, E! A cat. That's great.' I shook my head, amused at both Elaine and Merle. He was trying to take a sip of his tea while still playing tug with Heloise, and tea sloshed over the side of the cup as she gave a big pull.

'And I have to tell you how we picked her, from all the others.'

I looked at Merle again. He'd gotten Heloise to release the tug rope, had set it on the table, and was now standing at my pantry. He pulled out a package of Oreos and looked at me. He pointed to them and then to his mouth in an exaggerated mime, a question mark on his face. I nodded deeply, grinning.

'Okay, how'd you pick her out?'

'Well, for one, she's older. We didn't want to do

the whole kitten thing. But mostly, her name. Guess what it is?'

I had to force myself not to laugh. Too painful. 'I have no idea.' I waited. Nothing. 'Elaine! What?!'

'It's *Dina*! But with an *i*! Can you stand it?!' She laughed and snorted. 'But mostly we call her Meshugana, after you, of course.' Now I couldn't help but laugh at the term – Yiddish for 'crazy one' – and had to again hold my ribs. Merle was the picture of delight as he untwisted an Oreo.

Elaine paused briefly, then in her singsong added, 'Call me tonight and I'll tell you all about her!'

I hung up, shaking my head. 'My friend Elaine,' I explained to Merle. 'She's the artist I went to visit in November?' Merle nodded. 'She got a cat.' I left it at that. Merle had just lifted the teapot to warm my cup when the phone rang again.

'I'm sorry, Merle. I'll just let the voice mail get it.'

'No, please, go ahead. Kids?'

I picked up the phone, certain it was Elaine again, with one little cat story she would blurt out, then hang up.

'Hello?' I said, half laughing already. Merle and Heloise were back to the rope, giving happy little grunts as they tugged.

'Deena? Hi, Bill here.' I shook my head slightly, clearing the debris of fractured expectation.

'Oh – Hi, Bill! Sorry, I was expecting someone else. Hi. How are you?' I asked cheerily, wondering why Bill would be calling me.

I froze, my heart pounding. No. It was too soon.

'I'm fine, Deena, but I'm making the hard call to you now, my dear.' Neither of us said anything. I sat at my kitchen table feeling gravity increasing again.

'Deena?'

'Yes. I'm here.'

'You know what this is about, then?'

I could only squeeze out the one word. 'Recall?'

'Yes. I know it's a tad early, but, well, because of the car accident, national wants Heloise to have "Pre-Eval" – it's a special health and temperament evaluation for dogs who might be traumatized in any way. Then, assuming she passes, they'll start her in guide school with her group.' He paused. I said nothing. 'Josie's flying out with a BSD. She wants to fly back with Heloise.' He paused again. And again, I said nothing. 'I'm sorry we didn't have more notice. I suspected this might happen, but I just got word last night.'

'So this is it?' I asked softly, staring at my knees. I couldn't bear to look at Heloise.

'This is it,' Bill said, equally softly.

I couldn't argue. I couldn't debate. I couldn't even beg. It was the deal from the beginning. I just hadn't expected it to be this soon. 'When?' I asked, holding the phone with both hands. Merle reached over, aware of the drama, maybe even aware of what it was about. He placed his hand on my shoulder, his aged grip holding me together. I looked at Heloise now, standing with the rope

447

tug hanging from her mouth, wanting her play-mate back. My sternum ached. Or maybe this time it wasn't my sternum.

'Friday. Day after tomorrow. You can take Heloise to the airport and meet Josie there. Or I can take her for you.' I could hear him breathing. 'If you want me to.'

I couldn't speak. Two days! Two days was all I had left with her? This was too fast, too sudden.

'Deena?'

My lungs felt useless, but finally I whispered, 'I'm here.'

'I'm so sorry to do this, while you're still recovering and all. The timing is terrible for you, but it works out much better this way for national. And for Heloise. She doesn't have to go back on the truck. She gets to fly, and she's already an experienced flyer, thanks to you.' Now there was silence between us. Finally Bill spoke. 'Why don't we let this soak in and I'll call you tonight. Okay?' Again, no words would come. 'Deena? Are you alone now? Do you want me to come over?'

I looked at Merle, felt his strong old hand on my shoulder. I sat up straighter, cleared my throat. 'No, I'm not alone. I'm okay.'

'Okay. I'll call you later then.'

I hung up without saying good-bye.

CHAPTER 34

Thursday night, well past midnight, Neil and I lay awake in bed holding hands, alternately talking and being silent together. I knew I wouldn't sleep tonight, our last night with dear Heloise. She was asleep, on her red plaid bed, in the corner of our bedroom.

Neil had already arranged for the day off tomorrow. He'd told his nurse to inform his patients that he was seeing his adopted daughter off to college.

'Deena?'

I turned my head. The room was aglow from several large scented candles we'd lit. We'd fed Heloise a steak dinner as a good-bye treat, and now were paying the price in the form of her gaseous emissions, but the candles helped. Neil was up on one elbow, looking down at me, his eyes soft, caressing.

'Yeah?'

'I think we should start dating again,' he said, 'truly courting each other. You know? We need to get to know the people we've become, or are becoming.' He smiled. 'Or will become, sans kids.'

He rolled away from me. 'I'm going to click on the light. Watch your eyes.' His voice was excited, childlike. I covered my eyes and heard the light snap on. Slowly, I moved my hands away, blinking to adjust. Neil rolled back toward me, holding something. 'I stopped by a travel agent.' He handed me a dozen or so brochures. Some were for cruises, one for various tours through Europe, another a B & B two hours away in Breckenridge, another a romantic getaway near Estes Park. There was even one in there for an artist's retreat in Door County, Wisconsin.

'I thought maybe we should each take one trip a year on our own, and then one or two together, just the two of us. I think we need both now, time alone and time together.'

'We can't afford all those trips!' I said, elbowing him, but thrilled to my core.

'Yes, we can. We can't afford not to. We're okay, Deena. More than okay. We've been saving like pack rats our whole lives.'

'But *three* college tuitions?' I asked.

'You and I worked in college. Sam's working, got a scholarship. But even without that, we'll be fine. But between you and me, they don't need to know that. I think it means more when they have to contribute.' I knew exactly what he was talking about. He exhaled deeply. 'Life's too short, Deena.' He looked into my eyes. 'We need to spend a little time, and money, on ourselves.' He took the brochures from me and clicked off the light.

I waited for my eyes to again adjust to candle-light.

We held hands under the covers, watching the lights flicker on the bumpy ceiling.

'Neil?'

'Yeah.'

'It's scary.'

'What is?'

'This. This next phase that's almost here. Well, it's begun, I guess.'

I thought he'd give me another confidence-building speech, but he didn't.

'Yeah, it is.' There was another silence.

'I've given notice at the clinic,' he said softly. 'They're up and running now, they don't need me. And I'm going to cut back on my practice a bit, at least keep it as close to forty hours as I can.' He popped up on one elbow again. 'I want to learn to fly-fish!'

I laughed, holding my rib cage for support. I patted his shoulder. 'I'll teach you everything I know,' I said. 'It'll take about a minute.' He leaned over and kissed my cheek.

An hour later, we were both still awake, still holding hands under the covers. Heloise was fast asleep but was making flapping noises with her big lips and letting out high-pitched little woofs. We could hear the toenails of one foot scraping against the wall as her feet twitched. I squeezed Neil's hand and we both chuckled.

451

I wished I could see her dreams. I was sure she was running. Leashless. Free. I let myself imagine that she was running, slow motion, across a flower-filled meadow. I let myself imagine that I was there, too. I let myself imagine that she was running toward me.

Neil let go of my hand and gently stroked his knuckles against my arm. I couldn't help but smile. But this wasn't 'sex knocking.' We both knew my ribs still couldn't handle that particular activity, which, confoundingly, seemed to have had the effect of making me hornier than I'd been in years. Or maybe it was hormones. Or maybe it was just seeing Neil again, with new eyes.

No, this was an 'I'm here' touch, 'just so you know.'

I turned my head and looked into his eyes, his face sideways on the pillow, looking into mine. How many times I had stared at that face over the years, seeing the creases around his eyes deepen, the age spots rise to the surface like a soft image on a darkroom photograph, rising to the surface to show something true, and real. I touched the gray around his ear. My hand dropped to his shoulder. Now his fingers touched my cheek. I reached toward him, ignoring my ribs pinching in pain. I put my lips on his shoulder, kissing him softly, ran my finger over the constellation of freckles there. I knew that pattern better than any in the sky.

I suddenly knew exactly how a lost sailor must

feel, when finally he sees a night sky that is achingly familiar to him. *There! There are the stars I played under, loved under, grew up under. The ones that were always there, even in daylight when I couldn't see them.* When he first sees those stars again after his long voyage, he knows he's on his way home.

CHAPTER 35

I'd offered to excuse Matt and Lainey from school, but neither wanted to face the airport good-bye, especially in front of a stranger. Last night we'd let them feed her that steak dinner, dropping little tidbits into her bowl. And just as Neil and I had suffered through it last night, Josie would probably have to deal with Heloise's flatulence on the airplane. But we'd all three needed to love this dog in every way we could on her last night with us, and for Heloise, food was love. But then again, walks were love. Chewing was love. Us coming home, through the front door or from just the other room, was love. It was all love.

Their school backpacks by their sides, both kids knelt and placed their arms around Heloise's neck, one on each side. Heloise tried to lick the tears from both their cheeks, one then the other. Hairy sat on the stairs near the door watching us, his plumy tail slowly swishing back and forth across the oak. Matt stood first, heaving his backpack onto his shoulders. He headed out the door, silent. Lainey whispered something in Heloise's ear. I couldn't hear. I didn't ask. It was between them. Lainey stood, looked at me, then wrapped her arms around me, gently, remembering my ribs, but shaking with quiet sobs. I cried, too, holding her tightly, ribs and everything else aching.

Choking back sobs, she lurched out the front door to Nan, who was waiting with Matt in the driveway. She sandwiched in between them, the three encircling each other with gangly arms, Lainey's head resting on Nan's shoulder, then all three headed down the driveway. I squatted next to Heloise, staring out the glass door, my arm over her shoulders, and we watched them walk down the street toward school, Heloise's ears up, her tail motionless behind her.

Josie was standing to the side of the check-in counter. We wouldn't be able to go down the concourse with her because of security. We had to say good-bye here, in front of businessmen going to Toledo, families going to Florida, and others who would undoubtedly be on Heloise's flight to California.

Neil squatted next to Heloise first, facing her, cradling her head in his large hands. Heloise sat patiently, her green jacket freshly laundered and pressed. By Matt. Neil kissed the top of her head.

455

'Do us proud out there, girl. Be a good student. Study for your tests,' he said, trying to muster a little laugh. 'You'll . . .' He stopped, his voice caught in his throat. Eyes closed, he touched his forehead to her head and she licked his ear. He took a deep breath and whispered, 'You'll always be our girl.' He stood abruptly, taking several steps backward, pressing his thumb and middle finger to his closed eyes.

I knelt next to Heloise, wrapped my arms around her shoulders, lay my head against her neck, my silent tears flowing into her fur. How many times had I cried into her? How many times had she consoled me? How many times had she forgiven me for my crimes of ignorance or stupidity? Countless ways, countless times.

She chewed at my hair. I didn't want to increase her anxiety. I pulled away and looked at her, kissed her cheek, inhaled her still-sweet breath once more as she licked my hand, telling me it would all be okay.

'You go, girlfriend,' I whispered, trying so hard to conjure the ebullience of Elaine in those words, but failing miserably through my weeping. 'I'll miss you, my dear Heloise. I love you. I love you.' I kissed her soft ear one last time, then rose, pulling in ragged breaths. I handed the loop of the leather lead to Josie, who took my hand very briefly in both of hers, then took the leash from me, turned, and headed briskly away. Neil and I clutched each other, sobs making us shake as we watched Heloise go, her ears up, tail waving in her wholehearted, hip-wiggling walk, eagerly anticipating whatever great adventure might be around the next corner.

EPILOGUE

The sun was blazing. It was probably close to ninety degrees, even at the picnic table in the shade of the cottonwood. It was even hotter in the parking lot.

It had been unusually hot all summer, and September hadn't offered much relief yet. In late June, Neil had insisted we put in air conditioning so I wouldn't swelter in my studio. Also, I think, because I'd started staying many more than the part-time hours I was paid for at the Fairview Artists' Co-op, simply for the air conditioning there. Our marriage wasn't perfect, but we were in a second honeymoon, to be sure. And like Merle and Laura's cantaloupes, any sweeter and it might have been too perfect.

Neil and I had escaped the heat for a few days in July, at the little B & B in Breckenridge, just the two of us. Both Matt and Lainey had had summer jobs, both were driving now, and they shared an old Volvo we'd bought them; they paid the insurance. Both were saving money. Matt decided to take a year off to work before heading to college – he'd received a deferred acceptance to the Rhode

Island School of Design. I'd have a son on each coast next year. Lainey was saving for college, and a senior trip to France with her French class.

In August, Neil and I had flown to California. We'd spent two days visiting Sam and Bree (although we stayed in a comfortable motel). We'd had a lovely few days hosting them in March, and when we visited them in Palo Alto, we were again charmed by her, as well as their tiny apartment, their commitment to each other and to saving the world. We hugged them both good-bye, then Neil and I drove our rental car across the bay. For Heloise's graduation.

It was bittersweet, seeing her again. I wasn't sure she'd remember us, but she did. Neil and I both cried at the ceremony, where the puppy raisers, many of whom, like us, had flown in from out of state, handed the leash over for the last time, to the blind man or woman who'd been working with their assigned dog for the past month. It was graduation for everyone.

I walked across the stage with Heloise, toward Margarita, who stood waiting for us, her eyes covered with sunglasses, her head swaying back and forth, listening for us. She was a beautiful petite woman from Spain. She had been on the waiting list for a guide dog for four years. She had flown to the United States by herself, taking leave from her job and family for a full month, so she could be trained with one of the dogs that had already completed the months of guide training at the center. She was assigned to our Heloise. I could tell they had bonded deeply already.

I liked Margarita very much, and we had several nice chats that day, despite her lack of fluency. She called Heloise Hay-loh-eese. But she'd learned all the commands in near-perfect English. Margarita and I had been e-mailing several times a week since graduation. The first one I received from her had me weeping at my computer.

> Dear Deena and family:
> How do I tell yous how I grateful to be here with the onederfull Heloise? You have give of your harts and this dog so much love that she now . me. Forgive me my English and I will not take so much time it will take for to use my dickshunary. Heloise is opening the world with me. So many peoples now talks to me, on bus, on train, on street, because I with Heloise. Heloise make me one of the world now. How do a person like me say thank you, muchos gracias, for this? It is not enuf so I tell you I love you with Heloise.
> Sinseerley,
> Margarita

Now we were sitting at the same picnic table in the shade of the same cottonwood where I'd watched the young boy spend a last few minutes with his black Lab, a year and a half and a lifetime ago.

All five of us sipped Icees we'd bought from the 7-Eleven across the street. The rest of the crowd sat under other trees, or nervously milled around the hot parking lot. Bill was standing with two new raisers under the awning of the building. I waved to him. He was waving back when we heard it. The entire crowd turned at the sound.

The now-familiar green-and-white motor home eased into the parking lot, maneuvering its way around to the side of the building where there was shade, the crowd there parting as if Moses himself was driving. There was a short delay, then finally the door opened and Josie jumped down.

'Hey, y'all! It's hotter'n H-E-double toothpicks here, so make sure you keep all the dogs off the asphalt as much as possible. Same as usual, we're gonna deliver the pups and then we'll load the recalls. As soon as we call your name, step right up, get your pup, then scoot on out. I don't want to keep this thing running at idle with the AC on in this heat too long, so we're going to have to really move along today.'

She disappeared into the truck, then quickly reappeared with a sleepy little black Lab curled in her elbow. Her assistant stood next to her with the paperwork. 'Franks! The Franks family,' she called out. A dark-haired girl of about seventeen jogged up and took the pup into her arms.

'Hey, Mom!' said Matt, tapping excitedly on my arm. 'That's Zoey! From the art center!' I smiled and nodded as I recognized her. Matt worked with her as a volunteer at the Head Start building, the same building where he and Josh had done the mural. He and Zoey both taught art classes to kids after school. They weren't dating, just friends, but both were interested in the Rhode Island School of Design. She'd learned about raising a K-9 Eyes dog from Matt.

'Meet Hildegard,' Josie shouted, for all to hear as she handed the puppy to Zoey.

'Hildegard!' Zoey said, her face crinkling in amusement. She grabbed the paperwork, then jogged back to her mother, the puppy's head bouncing in her arms. Matt and Lainey were repeating the puppy's name, laughing out loud.

Josie called out several more names, then finally 'Munger!' I let Matt and Lainey go collect our little blond pup. A neutered male this time. We knew his name would begin with L.

Matt held out his arms, and Josie delivered the roly pup into them. Lainey immediately stroked a finger under its chin. 'Meet Louis!' said Josie. Matt elbowed Lainey, grinning knowingly. Lainey had gone out a couple of times this summer with a boy she'd met swimming at the rec center, one Jake Lewis. The kids immediately turned and walked back toward us, both beaming. Louis was bigger and much darker than Heloise had been, a lot of red in his coat. His jaw was more square than Heloise's and his tail thicker. It stuck out from under Matt's elbow, wagging wildly. Matt, still cradling him, held him up to meet us. Louis happily licked everyone, anointing us one at a time with his little tongue. When Matt held him out to me, I carefully grabbed him under his front armpits, breathing in his wonderful puppy breath. I held him in front of me. Dripping position.

'Nice to meet you, Louis,' I said, staring into the little dog's dark brown eyes.

'Louis, this is Mom,' said Lainey, holding one of his chunky paws, big for his age. 'Do what she says and you'll be fine.' We all laughed, then stopped abruptly as we heard Josie shouting out another name. She'd been calling them out the whole time, but this one we recognized.

'*Wenzell!*' Josie repeated, louder. I handed Louis to Neil, who held him like a baby, paws flopping over in relaxed right angles. Neil bent down, kissing Louis's round belly. I hooked my arm through Merle's.

'We're coming!' I shouted, as we jogged across the parking lot. We knew his puppy's name would begin with E; we had discussed many possibilities over countless BBQ dinners in both our backyard and Merle's, but all of us hoping beyond hope it would be Elaine.

I unhooked my arm and reached for the paper packet as Josie handed Merle the fuzziest little German shepherd puppy I'd ever seen.

'Meet Electra!' she said.

I tried hard not to laugh as Merle took the bright-eyed pup into his arms. She squirmed a little; he deftly repositioned her.

'There you go, little, uh, Electra,' he said.

I glanced at my family. Neil was still holding Louis, his eyes shining. Matt and Lainey were falling all over each other, laughing at this fuzzy pup and her gum-popping name.

They collected themselves as we approached. Merle was glowing, his expression eager, and just a little apprehensive. He clutched Electra close to his chest till we reached my family. I took Louis from Neil, and Merle and I set our two pups on the grass so they could get to know each other.